The Tannhauser Contingency

Chris Egghart

To Jonas
Happy Birthday
Hope you like it

Riverdale Books
Riverdale, Georgia

The Tannhauser Contingency

Riverdale Books
is an imprint of
Riverdale Electronic Books
PO Box 962085
Riverdale, Georgia 30296

This book is a work of fiction. Names, characters, places and incidents are either the product of the author's imagination or are used fictitiously. Any resemblance to actual events, locales, or persons, living or dead, is purely coincidental.

ISBN: 1-932606-12-2

Library of Congress Control Number: 2006902909

Printed in the United States of America

The
Tannhauser
Contingency

Tannhauser Code name. From the Wagner opera Tannhauser. Story of a mythical German knight, his fall to sin and quest for redemption.

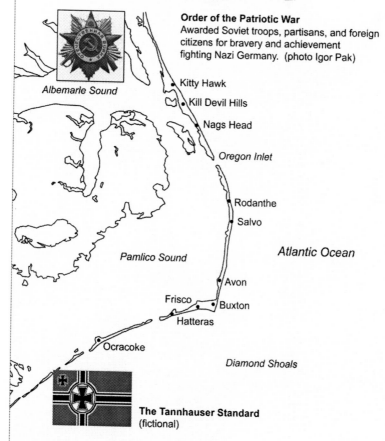

Order of the Patriotic War
Awarded Soviet troops, partisans, and foreign citizens for bravery and achievement fighting Nazi Germany. (photo Igor Pak)

Albemarle Sound

Kitty Hawk

Kill Devil Hills

Nags Head

Oregon Inlet

Rodanthe

Salvo

Pamlico Sound

Atlantic Ocean

Avon

Frisco

Buxton

Hatteras

Ocracoke

Diamond Shoals

The Tannhauser Standard
(fictional)

Cover Art: Minh Nguyen
Design: Chris Egghart

Foreword

IN THE HISTORY OF THE UNITED STATES' INVOLVEMENT IN WORLD WAR II, it is a little known fact that the first major action involving Hitler's forces took place along our Eastern Seaboard. Early in 1942, Nazi U-boats appeared off the coast of an America totally unprepared for war. Over the next few months, hundreds of ships fell victim to U-boat torpedoes. These losses were kept secret by the wartime government. Even more inexplicably, countermeasures to the German threat were slow to be taken. The waters off the Outer Banks of North Carolina, long known as the Graveyard of the Atlantic, found particular favor among the U-boat captains and more than 70 ships were lost in this area alone.

The Tannhauser Contingency is set primarily on Hatteras Island, North Carolina, and begins with the secret mission of the *U-491* during the final weeks of the Third Reich. While the story is pure fiction, much of what unfolds in the following pages does so within the context of actual historical situations and events. Also true to fact is that among the many dozens of ships sent to the bottom along the Outer Banks, lie the hulks of at least five U-boats—sunk as the tide of war turned against the German raiders. Recently, the wreck of a U-boat presumed to have been lost off West Africa was found along the New Jersey coast. What other mysteries might lie

undiscovered amid shifting sands in the Graveyard of the Atlantic?
No one knows.

Author's Note

WHILE THE TANNHAUSER CONTINGENCY IS FICTION, MOST OF THE places described therein are real. The Outer Banks of North Carolina, with their raw natural beauty, wind scoured beaches, and ever changing weather, provides both the backdrop and the inspiration for this novel. Also adding color is the rich history of the barrier island chain and its people. Although much of the setting is real, any resemblance of characters in the story to actual persons, living or dead, is largely coincidental.

Further, the real *U-491* was never commissioned into the German Kriegsmarine. On the other hand, the remarkable voyage of *U-977* from Norway to Argentina at the end of the war as described in the novel, is factual. No fully satisfactory explanation was ever provided as to why the *U-977* embarked on its marathon voyage. At the time, bona fide suspicions were held by Allied intelligence that the boat was to transport money or high value individuals to South America, perhaps even Hitler himself. Nothing was ever substantiated.

Construction of the boat that was to have been the *U-491* began in the North German port of Kiel during July 1943. Work was halted as the vessel was nearing completion, probably to favor more advanced U-boat types that the High Command hoped would reverse their desperately declining fortunes in the Battle of the Atlantic. The best available records indicate that the *U-491* was broken up for scrap in late 1944.

Or was it?

Chapter 1

April 23, 1945
South of Diamond Shoals, Cape Hatteras, North Carolina

SLOWLY, SILENTLY, EXCEPT FOR A THROATY HISS from the ballast tanks, the *U-491* broke surface. For several minutes the German submarine hung motionless, decks awash with only the conning tower protruding from the ink-black water into a moonless Carolina night.

The portal hatch opened with a dull clank and Kapitänleutnant Hans-Jurgen Heidenreich heaved himself up the ladder onto the narrow bridge. The stifling confines of the U-boat gave way to a rich ocean air. A stiff southeast breeze whipped thick droplets that pelted the captain's face. After having crossed the North Atlantic through several freezing gales, KptLt. Heidenreich paused and savored the warm breath of the nearby Gulf Stream waters before tightly buttoning his oilskin against the driving rain.

The *U-491* had arrived off the coast almost a week before. Days were spent lying on the bottom, amid the currents and shifting sands of Diamond Shoals. Each night, after the moon was down, the U-boat would briefly emerge from its underwater lair to fully charge its batteries, then descend beneath the waves to await the appointed time.

The exact purpose of the mission was secret, unknown to even the captain. The dispatch, drafted and sealed by Admiral Dönitz himself, was not to be opened until position was established off the American coast. Otherwise, orders were explicit: Avoid contact with the enemy at all costs. No vessel was to be attacked regardless of opportunity.

✠   ✠   ✠

Final outfitting and provisioning were made in Danzig during late March. Prior to that, the U-boat was held in port for most of the winter. The layover followed a torturous five-week run from the Mediterranean to the Baltic. Allied ships and planes were everywhere. More than once the *U-491* was chased down and depth charged relentlessly. Heidenreich used every trick, drew on every ounce of skill, courage and intuition he possessed to elude their unseen tormentors. Sheer fortune undoubtedly helped.

During one of the engagements, two enlisted men, despite being hardened by a half-dozen North Atlantic patrols, cracked and ran amok. Two pistol shots momentarily betrayed the U-boat's position to the pursuing ships' hydrophones. The German captain's reaction was purely reflexive. Total discipline had to be maintained if they were to have any chance of surviving their steel-encased hell under water.

✠   ✠   ✠

"Permission to come on the bridge," the second watch officer called from below.

"*Ja,*" Heidenreich snorted, and the man scampered up the ladder and through the hatch.

The officer leaned over the railing and cast an eye toward the darkened shore. "Perfect night, don't you think, Sir? Quite dark, actually."

The captain didn't reply. The officer was new to the boat, assigned just for this mission. Several other men also came aboard in Danzig. These new men, however, did not fully replace the seamen drafted to another vessel while they were in port. Consequently, the U-boat sailed with barely half the normal crew.

Heidenreich suspected a political officer was among the new faces. He did not trust the man standing beside him and detested the notion that anyone aboard might consider themselves above his command.

✠　　　✠　　　✠

The wind had risen to a steady 30 knots. Whitecaps broke across the deck plates and swirled around the conning tower. Through the misty darkness, the German captain could barely make out low clouds racing across the water. The rains came in fast moving bursts. Between the downpours, thin patches of starry sky appeared, only to be swallowed by the next squall. Heidenreich winced at a distant flash of lightning hazily illuminating the horizon.

The first officer joined the two men on the bridge.

"What is the status of the cargo?" Heidenreich shouted above the rush of the wind and rain.

"All is in order. The boxes are being positioned by the forward hatch. Another twenty minutes, I should think."

"Good. See it is finished."

The first officer and second watch officer disappeared down the ladder, to be replaced by a lanky ensign armed with large binoculars and a signaling lamp. Two more men emerged lugging heavy ammunition drums. The gunners shouted gruffly at each other while bringing to firing order the quadruple 20MM anti-aircraft cannons mounted on the half deck behind the conning tower.

Below was a beehive of activity. After days of tense boredom, the crew sprang into action, moving the heavy metal boxes forward through the narrow gangway. The waterproof containers were roughly the size of small steamer trunks. Constructed of welded aluminum, they looked like oversized biscuit tins.

This is genius or sheer madness, Heidenreich thought, inside the shipping lanes like this, a few kilometers off the American coast.

At first he doubted the orders when he unsealed them:

RENDEZVOUS ELEVEN KILOMETERS DUE SOUTH
OF CAPE HATTERAS. NIGHT OF APRIL 23.
NEUTRAL FREIGHTER RIO TINTO. URUGUAYAN
REGISTRY. 2000 TONS, BRIDGE AMIDSHIPS,
SINGLE STACK AFT. AWAIT SIGNAL VESUVIUS.
RESPOND RIO-RIO-RIO. TRANSFER CARGO.
WITHDRAW FROM COAST.
     FINAL DISPOSITION OF VESSEL AND CREW
IS YOUR DISCRETION. GOOD LUCK.
     GROSSADMIRAL KARL DÖNITZ

Heidenreich knew there would be no returning home. Fuel was nearly exhausted, with less than a thousand liters of diesel left—certainly not enough to reach any neutral port. He wondered what "your discretion" meant.

Even if he had the fuel to again cross the Atlantic, there would be no port to return to. The German submarine had slipped out of Danzig just hours ahead of the advancing Soviet Army. Final days in port were nerve-wracking as delay followed delay while the mysterious cargo was assembled. For half a week one heard the rumble of artillery to the east.

Danzig was a major embarkation point for refugees, mostly ethnic German civilians fleeing the Red Army's vengeful surge westwards. By the time the U-boat was ready to sail, the Wehrmacht was in full retreat from the city and the port clogged with civilians who now had nowhere to go. Nonetheless, a peculiar calm pervaded the city; a sort of melancholic, slow motion panic. People milled about the streets or sat sullenly on their luggage, seemingly resigned to their fate as all sense of place, order and hope faded away. Not the most fearful of the lot could fully imagine the horrors about to befall them.

The dull thump of mortars and the crackle of small arms fire drifted across the harbor from the city outskirts as the *U-491* finally slipped its moorings. The German submarine glided past the crowded docks, nosed its way out of the harbor and disappeared into a frozen haze which hung over a glass-smooth, gunmetal gray Baltic Sea.

✠ ✠ ✠

Perhaps this is the best way, Heidenreich thought. The more audacious the plan, the more implausible the location, the better the chances. The last few days had given him plenty of time to mull over his mission. It was normal operational procedure for orders to remain sealed until the U-boat was at sea. Sensing the gravity of the responsibility with which he had been charged, Heidenreich took the extra step of not sharing the orders with anyone aboard, including his first officer, whom he trusted more than any man alive. Needless to say, there was considerable speculation amongst the crew as to their destination.

More than once Heidenreich pondered the possibility the mission was a set up—perhaps there was to be no rendezvous and the cargo was meant to fall into American hands. Standing on the darkened bridge, Heidenreich wondered if they were about to be pounced upon by half the American coastal defenses, his men and vessel to be sacrificed in some desperate ploy by the High Command.

But to what end?

With each spell of doubt, Heidenreich chastised himself for overly scrutinizing his orders. I am an officer of the German Navy, he told himself. Orders were to be followed without question.

He could not keep from wondering, however, exactly what was in those unusual looking boxes.

✠ ✠ ✠

Heidenreich knew these waters well. His first command took him off the coast of North Carolina during early 1942. That spring Hitler's *Unterseeboote* turned the coastal waters from Hatteras to Moorehead City into a killing zone. The area had long been known as the "Graveyard of the Atlantic" for its treacherous shoals, swift currents and violent storms. These same elements gave ideal cover to the marauding U-boats. The United States was woefully unprepared to meet the German threat. Merchant ships traveled alone without protection. At night they were easily spotted, silhouetted against the glowing lights of the coastal communities. Some German commanders became so bold they conducted surface attacks by daylight, virtually within sight of the U.S. coastline. Deliberate official inaction and secrecy only made matters worse for the terrorized merchant fleet.

The war on America's doorstep was no secret to the inhabitants of the Outer Banks of North Carolina, however. Smoke from doomed vessels was a regular sight on the horizon and lifesaving stations were kept busy pulling survivors from the water. The bloated or burned bodies of seamen washed up on the beaches were a grim reminder of the tragic cost of human life in war.

✠   ✠   ✠

It was so easy then, Heidenreich thought, peering out into the blackness. The "American Turkey Shoot" Dönitz had called the U.S. campaign. We thought we were invincible, the captain mused. Now there is no "We." Of the dozens of officers in his graduating class, Heidenreich was the only one left alive. Each received their commission and was given command of a new vessel in December of 1941. Most did not make it through the end of '43.

I'm still not dead and I'm right back where this terrible business first began. Life is very strange indeed, he thought.

Dönitz could not have chosen a better man for the mission, for KptLt. Heidenreich was as skilled and disciplined as any commander in the U-boat fleet. Though not a tall man, he carried himself with a bearing which made him seem larger than life. His facial features were equally imposing, in particular his deeply set, icy blue eyes. While at sea, his prominent jaw lay hidden behind a bushy beard. Thick shocks of light brown hair, streaked with gray, hung from underneath a soiled captain's cap. A deeply lined face belied his 37 years of age.

Heidenreich's first sinking had been in these same waters. Upon being hit, the tanker, carrying aviation gasoline, exploded and burned, setting the surrounding seas aflame. After watching the carnage from the bridge, Heidenreich developed a certain distaste for the gruesome nature of his profession. After that night, there was little thrill in a victory for him and a sinking elicited only a fact-filled entry into the ship's log. On the other hand, he never questioned the morality of the war and all its killing.

KptLt. Heidenreich thought of himself as apolitical and eschewed, at least when out of port, the speech-making and indoctrination sessions expected of a U-boat captain. His own sense of duty, however, bordered on the fanatical. Despite the staggering losses he'd seen inflicted on the U-boat fleet, not for an instant, not even in his darkest and most perilous hour, did he waver in his commitment to the German cause.

His crew was intensely loyal and looked upon their commander with a respect bordering on awe. No one would question the man who had, on so many occasions, brought the ship to safety when all were certain they were lost. At no time, however, did Heidenreich allow anyone to sense the fear that never left his body.

Normally calculating and composed while in action, only once had Heidenreich given himself over to emotion. Only one time did he allow hatred to cloud his judgment—only to emerge victorious and exult in the destruction of his foe. They had been trailing a North Atlantic convoy steaming south of Greenland. The U-boat cruised on the surface, following the tell-tale smudges on the horizon while keeping a watchful eye for Allied escort ships or a long-range Liberator aircraft.

Under cover of darkness, the German submarine circled ahead and worked its way into the midst of the convoy for a surface attack. Heidenreich fired four of his last five torpedoes. All either missed their mark or failed to detonate. Attempting to withdraw, the U-boat was spotted by a destroyer and forced down. The next seven hours were spent in an agonizing cat and mouse game with half a dozen escorts. As if in a lethal stakes chess match, the German submarine crept through dark frigid waters, continually altering course and depth to outmaneuver the pursuing surface ships. Often the escorts would drop their depth charges well off target. Still the detonations resonated loudly throughout the U-boat, rattling everything onboard.

At other times, Allied sonar would lock on. As sound travels many times better through water than air, virtual silence had to be maintained aboard lest the ships pinpoint the U-boat's position. At irregular intervals, the unnerving metallic chirp of sonar signals echoed through the hull. Heidenreich hissed course changes to the helmsman while the rest of the crew waited for whispered commands to be relayed from the control room. Mostly, they just waited.

All aboard could hear the screws repeatedly churn the waters overhead. Against all logic, men stared anxiously upward as if they might actually catch sight of the TNT-laden barrels drifting down from above. The unbearable silent wait would be broken by the unmistakable detonator click instantaneously followed by a thunderous shock. Again and again the U-boat shook as if struck by a giant sledge while men clung to what they could to keep from being thrown about. Lights flickered and blinked, momentarily plunging everything into total darkness. Paint chips drizzled from overhead as cork insulation dust filled the intolerably depleted air, rife with the pungent scent of fear.

After each depth charge pattern, damage reports were quietly relayed to the control room. Then the waiting would begin anew. All the crew could do was hope and pray the pressure hull could withstand the pounding.

Finally, the squadron withdrew to rejoin the convoy. Heidenreich had found a pronounced thermocline, which offered some cover from the enemy's sonar. This, together with steadily deteriorating weather on the surface, had caused the ships to lose contact. A single corvette, however, one of the new fast destroyer escorts, stayed behind, convinced the U-boat hadn't been destroyed.

The small ship crisscrossed the U-boat's position, continually probing with sonar. The repeated, methodical sweeps failed to identify the motionless U-boat, but allowed the corvette's supposed quarry to plot the unvarying search pattern.

Under normal circumstances, Heidenreich would have waited it out, thankful to have survived to fight one more time. But with his frayed nerves at an end, he began to vehemently curse the small vessel.

Heidenreich had locked wits with many Allied captains, coldly trying to anticipate their tactical moves. For some reason, this encounter fast became personal. In his mind he could picture the opposing captain on the bridge. He wondered who this man was and what drove him not to give up. Heidenreich felt incredible anger well forth. Anger gave way to rage until the German captain could barely contain himself.

On the next sweep, Heidenreich inched the boat into an intercept position. Taking advantage of the blind spot in sonar occurring in a short radius directly below the transmitting ship, he ordered the U-boat to periscope depth. The corvette passed virtually overhead, nearly clipping the conning tower.

Heidenreich raised the periscope, rotated it 180 degrees and locked it down. Like a cat ready to pounce, every muscle in his body was taut. He ordered the stern tube fired. To Heidenreich, the sound of his one-word command seemed to emanate from outside his own body, echoing within the confines of the control room. His fingers curled around the periscope bars so tightly the blood was squeezed from his hands. The corvette heeled hard to port. Seconds later the torpedo exploded squarely amidships, lifting the vessel clear out of the water. The force of the detonation struck the U-boat so hard some aboard were violently thrown to the floor. Heidenreich managed to steady himself on the periscope bars to watch the corvette break in two and disappear as debris splashed about the churning waters.

What followed was a five-minute tirade. Heidenreich screamed and swore, cursing the destroyed ship and its dead captain as the repressed emotions from months of undersea combat spewed forth in one cathartic spasm.

The fury passed as quickly as it came. Heidenreich ordered the tanks blown and the *U-491* broached the surface. After receiving reports of only minimal damage sustained, the captain grumbled out a course heading and retired to his quarters. From that moment, no one on board ever spoke of the episode, not even in passing.

✠   ✠   ✠

Standing on the darkened bridge, Heidenreich felt the wind drop as the rain subsided to a misting drizzle. Patches of starry sky appeared. With the wind down, the men on the conning tower were free to communicate without shouting. Yet, no one spoke. Though alone in their thoughts, each man felt a common bond. It was a camaraderie only combat submariners could know—a bond which transcended rank, disparate backgrounds and personal animosities. It was a bond that arose from working, eating and sleeping in an unbelievably cramped, clammy, foul-smelling space—a duty bound, windowless world where night or day have no meaning and existence was regimented by rotating shifts, all under the unyielding yellow glow of incandescent lights. Most of all, theirs was a bond, forged in the cauldron of their collective terror, consummated by a shared, unspoken, wretched homesickness felt in the face of death.

As the most ruthless of warships swayed gently beneath their feet, each man on the bridge was awed by the sublime beauty of the night.

The first officer emerged through the hatch. "Everything is ready, Herr Kapitän."

"Very well," the captain replied. "Now we wait."

Chapter 2

April 24, 02:00 hours
Naval Air Station, Norfolk, Virginia

THE FLIGHT CREW WALKED ACROSS THE WET TARMAC TO THE WAIT-ing PBY-5 Catalina. Wearing bulky suits strapped with Mae West life vests and oxygen masks, each man climbed the narrow ladder and squeezed through the small hatchway just aft of the cockpit.

The Catalina flying boat was not a pretty aircraft. With amphibious fuselage slung under oversized wings, it could be considered downright ugly. On land the PBY looked even more awkward. Two large observation blisters protruding from the aircraft's midsection did little to enhance its looks. Yet to the hundreds of aviators and sailors rescued at sea throughout the war, the approach of a "P-boat" was the prettiest sight in the world. Practically obsolete when the war began, the Catalina was not very fast, nor particularly maneuverable. Its reliability and extreme operating range, however, made it the workhorse of U.S. Naval Aviation. The PBY Catalina was equally adapted to patrol missions, search and rescue, and to the role of long range bomber.

"Number one ignition," the young pilot said briskly, trying to cover his obvious apprehension. "Number two ignition."

In short succession, the two 1,200 horsepower Pratt & Whitney radial engines sputtered, coughed, then roared to life.

"Oil pressure number one, check; number two, check."

Lieutenant Emory Walker sat calmly behind the controls while the student crew rehearsed the pre-takeoff routine. The cadets were barely out of their teens. Although they had nearly completed their required hours, this was to be only their second bombing run using live ordnance.

Final preparations were made, including a last check of the 250 pound bombs slung under each wing. The ground crew cut wire straps securing the fuses, pulled ladders away and waved to the pilots in the cockpit. Seated on the pilot side, Eddie "the Kid" Fischer pushed open the throttles and the aircraft lumbered down the taxiway. The plane turned and came to a stop at the end of the runway to await final clearance.

"You're on Kid," Walker quipped, as the tower crackled in over the headset.

Fischer throttled the engines to near full power before releasing the brakes. The Catalina lurched forward and gathered speed down the darkened runway. After what seemed like an eternity, the young pilot pulled back on the yoke and the aircraft eased off the tarmac and began a shallow climb.

"Not bad Kid, not bad," Walker said, sliding closed the cockpit side window. "What's the matter? Cat got your tongue? You're not saying much."

"It's nothing, Sir. Except… well, it's… I just got a feeling about tonight."

"If you can't talk just level her off at 7,000," Walker moaned, wishing he were anywhere but flying around in the middle of the night with a plane full of high school kids.

Behind the pilots, the navigator/bombardier was busily plotting their course heading under the dull red glow of the small chart lamp. The flight was to take them south over the Carolina Sounds, down along the Outer Banks and then out over the ocean for a navigation exercise. The training mission was to finish at dawn with a bombing run over the range at Duck, near the northern end of the barrier island chain.

"Got a couple of live ones on board tonight," Walker said. "Been a good while since I've blown the shit out of something. Kind of miss it actually."

"Do you really, Sir? I mean it must have been tough... losing all those guys and all, I mean."

The instructor didn't respond. Outwardly Walker acted as if he truly did not care about anything. He was a gruff man who continually taunted his students. Over the last year and a half, the endless training flights had, on several occasions, nearly cost him his life. He brushed off each incident with apparent indifference, except to heap verbal abuse on the terrified cadet who nearly brought them to disaster. Bluster and bravado aside, Walker was an exceptional pilot and a very competent instructor. It was, however, the very last thing he wanted to be doing.

Lieutenant Walker spent the first half of 1943 in Alaska, flying long range bombing missions against the Japanese-held islands at the end of the Aleutian chain. Any day the skies permitted, Walker and the other men in the squadrons flew the lumbering Catalinas on marathon missions out of Cold Bay, relentlessly taking the war to the remote Japanese toehold on American soil. These aviators received little recognition for their valor. Walker saw many a crew fall victim to mechanical failure, anti-aircraft fire or to the cruel variances of Aleutian weather. After the decimated squadrons were withdrawn, Walker was transferred and reassigned to a desk job in Virginia.

A short while later he was called up as a flight instructor. His advancing age of 34, as well as public displays of an intensely mercurial personality convinced a Navy doctor he was no longer fit to fly combat missions. Walker hated his job and burned to rejoin the fight and avenge his lost friends and comrades.

"I'm unfit to kill Japs, but good enough to putt around with punks who couldn't fly a kite," he often ranted at the officers club to anyone who would listen.

Now, by a twist of fate, after battling Japanese invaders on the continent's western tip, Lieutenant Emory Walker was about to meet America's other adversary, just off the beaches of its eastern coast.

✠   ✠   ✠

As the Catalina droned across the darkened waters of Pamlico Sound, the blue, ghost-like haze of exhaust flames was all that betrayed its presence in the pitch black sky. Fischer cut a wide turn over the northern end of the Outer Banks and began to follow the thin ribbon of land south toward Cape Hatteras. Far below, the surf glowed faintly in the starlight. The student pilot kept the plane orientated to the dim line. Just after passing over the tiny villages of Kill Devil Hills and Nags Head, a large thunderhead heaved into view directly ahead. Lightning flashed almost continually, illuminating the billowy tower from within.

"Let's go around it," Walker said tersely. "Navigator, plot us a new heading. Make the course corrections for the leg south of Hatteras."

A quick acknowledgment came over the intercom.

Walker turned to the student pilot, lowering the mike from his chin. "Take her down to 3,500."

A broken line of thunderheads boiled and flashed off the starboard side as the plane banked away from land and toward Diamond Shoals.

"Get on the horn and inform Norfolk about the change in flight plan," Walker ordered. "And tell them we're going to scrub if this weather gets any worse."

A few minutes later the radio operator came back over the intercom. "Sir, I can't raise anyone at Norfolk. We seem to be transmitting all right, I think; maybe they've gone to sleep."

"Oh, great!" Walker said out loud. "We're up here in this shit with the radio out."

The instructor briefly contemplated calling off the flight and returning to base, then thought otherwise. "I'm not about to do this again tomorrow night," he mumbled. Walker turned to

Fischer at the controls. "Hold her steady, Kid. We're gonna to ride it out."

The plane made its way south over the open ocean. Walker partially slid back the cockpit window and breathed of the cool night air rushing through the opening. He recognized the faint glow of the false dawn as Venus neared the eastern horizon. Walker continued to gaze out over the vastness of the Atlantic. Occasional bolts of lightning flashed across the western sky. Suddenly the intercom crackled to life. It was one of the gunners from his post along the observation blister.

"Lieutenant Walker, Sir, I saw something on the water about a mile off the port side. Sir... it looked like a sub!"

Walker felt his stomach tighten, for he had seen the same dark shape, illuminated by a distant flash of lightning. He felt a familiar surge of adrenaline run through his body.

A U-boat... this close? he thought. Not this late in the game! Couldn't be!

"Hold your course, son," he said in a steady voice, not daring to believe what he thought he just saw. "Double back after five miles... not too close, now."

The Catalina banked around, dropped another 1,000 feet and came in low over the area in which the two men spotted the dark shape. The gunners rolled open the observation canopies and leaned into the slipstream for a better look. All eyes strained into the darkness, yet nothing was seen. Walker took over the controls, throttled back and began flying a lazy figure-eight pattern. About 10 minutes passed but nothing was spotted.

"Sir! Sir! I think I have something at about four o'clock!" an excited voice came in over the intercom.

"Maybe it's one of ours," Fischer offered, not really believing there had been anything there in the first place.

"Well, we're gonna find out then, aren't we," Walker responded with a grimace. "Get some torches ready," he called to the gunners.

The instructor executed a wide turn and throttled back even further, easing the already low flying plane into a shallow, powered glide. Their altitude dropped steadily. The rush of air over the wings was audible over the popping and wheezing of the nearly idling engines. Fischer bit his lip and breathed a prayer while Walker counted seconds.

"Now!" Walker yelled, and first one then a second magnesium flare tumbled from the aircraft's midsection.

The Germans on the bridge froze like deer in a spotlight.

"*Gott im Himmel!*" Heidenreich cried out.

For a split second the German captain stared in shock at the twin engine flying boat bearing down through a blinding glare. Walker peered through the open cockpit window in equal disbelief. The Catalina passed so close he could make out the figures standing on the conning tower. He recognized the unmistakable, sinister outline of a U-boat just as the flares hit the water. Jagged yellow flames leapt from the exhaust ports as the aircraft's engines screamed to full power.

"*Flieger! Flieger!*"

The call sent every man on the U-boat scurrying, as the cry of a plane spotted was synonymous with the order for an emergency dive. To be caught on the surface by aircraft was every submariner's nightmare as it often meant swift death.

Heidenreich's mind raced to weigh his limited options. Did they have radar?! Patrol boats from Ocracoke could be here within minutes. More planes at daybreak. Destroyers from Norfolk. Surrender was out of the question. Perhaps playing dead could buy time?!

His hand was forced by the deafening muzzle blasts of the 20MM cannons directly behind his head as the gunners opened fire.

"Did you see that?!" Fischer shrieked. "Oh, Jesus Christ! They're shooting at us!"

The aircraft shuddered and yawed as a burst of cannon fire raked the starboard wing.

"Arm 'em!" Walker yelled into the intercom over the roar of the wide open engines.

The bombardier squeezed into the cockpit. Panting incredulously, he clutched at the pilots' headrests before shimmying himself forward into the nose of the aircraft.

"I can't believe this shit!" Walker growled.

Glowing tracer shells streaked past the canopy to drift lazily off into the night.

"Dive! Dive!" Heidenreich screamed, scrambling down the conning tower ladder. He was followed by the two gunners and panicked ensign.

Walker pulled the Catalina into a high, banking turn, mentally calculating their relative position. He leveled off, then pushed the plane into a powered descent toward the target's anticipated location. At a range of less than a mile, the bombardier yelled he'd spotted a phosphorescent wake directly ahead. Silhouetted in the watery reflection of the morning star, the U-boat lunged forward, desperately flooding its ballast tanks to find the tenuous safety of the darkened shoals.

"I see it," Walker responded, his voice thick but calm. He made the course adjustment. "Steady... Steady."

The plane came in just over the surface. One bomb hit the water and skipped clear over the U-boat while the other struck broadside, sending up a huge geyser just behind the low-flying aircraft. The force of the direct hit heeled the German submarine partially on one side. It rolled upright and disappeared into the roiling waters.

Walker made several passes over the site with the landing lights on. A sheen of oil and bits of floating debris were all that marked the spot where the U-boat went down; otherwise nothing was to be seen.

✠   ✠   ✠

A feeling of utter unreality pervaded the aircraft as Walker set course for Norfolk. The intercom stayed silent. Everything happened so fast no one could fully comprehend what transpired. Soon thereafter, the first gray light of dawn revealed the damage to the starboard side.

"Lieutenant, you'd better come look at this," one of the gunners called over the intercom.

Walker turned the controls over to Fischer and made his way back to the observation blisters. A line of cannon shell holes dotted the underside of the wing and the entire area was streaked with hydraulic oil. The sight of the damage drove home the reality of their situation. Back in the cockpit, Walker cursed out loud as the starboard engine began missing badly and the aircraft became increasingly unresponsive and difficult to control.

The crippled plane flew across Currituck Sound and directly into a squall line moving along the North Carolina-Virginia border. It was then the cantankerous instructor went stone quiet and the rest of the crew knew for sure they were in serious trouble.

The ceiling lifted slightly and the horizon brightened on the final approach to the Norfolk Naval Air Station. Finally, the runway came into view, the tarmac glistening under an aluminum-colored sky. Suddenly, a massive wind burst buffeted the aircraft. The deck seemed to fall from underneath the cabin. Within seconds, the flying boat slammed into a cornfield, bounced across a country lane, skidded into a tree line and disintegrated in a massive ball of fire.

Chapter 3

South Beach, Hatteras Island, North Carolina

THE STORMS OF THE PREVIOUS NIGHT HAD GIVEN WAY TO A WARM and brilliantly clear afternoon. Sandpipers scurried along the beach, oblivious to the half-naked form sprawled along the water's edge. Too weak to pull himself further onto the beach, the man lay face down a few feet from the surf. Wracked with pain and nearly unconscious from exhaustion and loss of blood, he tried to recall what had happened.

He was at his duty station in the engine room when the U-boat was hit. Knocked momentarily unconscious by the force of the blasts, he was pushed through a gash in the shattered hull by an escaping pocket of air.

All he could remember was breaking the surface and grasping at some debris. While clinging to the flotsam, a strong southeast wind pushed him steadily toward the beach. By mid-morning he could make out the dunes on shore. A relentless chop washed over his head every few seconds. His eyes burned and he was sick from swallowing seawater. He kicked with his legs until his strength gave out, then just hung on, fighting the temptation to give up and let go. Finally, he felt a curling wave lift him. He tumbled forward to feel soft sand. The wash receded, leaving him kneeling on all fours. He crawled a few feet and collapsed. After some time he came to, noting his shadow lengthened, before again losing consciousness.

✠   ✠   ✠

A horse and armed rider came plodding up the beach. A Coast Guard Auxiliary, no more than seventeen, dismounted. The rider cautiously approached the prone figure, which he took to be a corpse washed up on the beach. The boy froze in his tracks when the oil-stained form slowly turned its head to reveal an unblinking, blood-shot stare.

"*Hilfe... Hilf mir, Mensch.*"

The guardsman stepped backward, unslung his weapon and fumbled to work the bolt of the ancient but well-oiled Springfield.

The guardsman backed toward his horse, remounted and galloped off. He returned a short time later accompanied by a flat bed truck full of well-armed civilians from Hatteras village. A host of weather-beaten faces collected to stare down at the man lying in the sand as he deliriously babbled in German. Together the men lifted him onto a stretcher, covering him with a wool blanket. The stretcher went onto the truck. One of the villagers reached across and offered a drink of water. The man on the stretcher nodded weakly and allowed the bottle to be pressed against his lips. He drank in short gulps before rolling on his side and vomiting.

By the time the entourage reached Hatteras village, word spread and a small crowd formed. A Naval officer appeared. The crowd parted slightly to let him pass.

"So what exactly is going on here?" the officer demanded.

The guardsman saluted crisply. "Found him on the beach, Sir!"

"And?"

"He speaks in Kraut, Sir. Could be an infiltrator," the young man beamed.

The officer leaned over the stretcher for a look and immediately said, "Get this man a doctor."

✠ ✠ ✠

The stretcher was carried to Dr. Clark's house and laid out in the parlor. After some searching, the doctor was located and summoned.

Dr. Clark was a fixture on the island and had attended the births of most of the men standing around his parlor. With wavy, snow white hair, ruddy complexion and a soft, paternal manner, he looked the very embodiment of the country physician.

"So what have we here?" Dr. Clark asked with interest.

"We foon 'im washed on the beach," one of the men volunteered. "He's cut on his chest an's been throwin' oop."

The doctor directed the men standing about to lift the stretcher and set the ends on two chairs turned toward each other. He rigged an IV bottle and hung it from the coat stand. Inserting the needle, he took note of a small scripted tattoo on his patient's right arm.

"This man may be German," the officer stated. " I consider him my prisoner."

Dr. Clark cut away what was left of the man's shirt. "Well, we can hardly consider him a threat to anyone at the moment," he said inspecting the wound. The doctor glanced over at the other men in the room, most of who were still armed. "Now, if you gentlemen will remove yourselves and your weapons, I can get to work."

The men drifted out the door. A few returned to their homes, while others lingered in front of the house, smoking cigarettes and idly speculating as to how the man might have ended up on the beach.

After about half an hour the officer stepped back into the parlor. "How's he doing?"

"The man is severely dehydrated. He's also lost a fair amount of blood from a deep laceration across his chest. I've cleaned the wound and I'm about to stitch him. It's a clean cut, all muscle tissue. Should heal just fine."

"There's a detachment of Marines on their way from Ocracoke," the officer began. "The boat may already be in the harbor."

Dr. Clark drew a breath. "I would strongly advise against moving the patient, at least tonight. He is in severe shock and must remain still."

"Then he should stay, providing you have no objections to quartering him. We'll need to post a guard, of course."

"Sounds fine to me. Now if you would excuse me, please, I need to finish here."

The old doctor began stitching while his patient watched him work though expressionless eyes. As soon as the doctor finished, the man lay his head back and drifted into a shallow sleep.

After leaving the room to wash up, the doctor returned and pulled a chair up to the stretcher. There was something very different about the man's looks, he thought. Doctor Clark sat and studied his patient. The man had dark brown, almost black hair. His skin was light but had a noticeable olive tint. His flesh tone, together with striking blue-green eyes and a prominent nose, seemed to betray a Mediterranean origin. His broad face and stocky build, however, reminded the doctor of what he thought of as Slavic traits. High cheekbones and slightly almond-shaped eyes added to the man's unusual, almost exotic appearance.

The doctor gathered the cut-up remains of the man's shirt, noting KESSEL printed above the breast pocket. The Marine guard arrived a short time later. Dr. Clark handed the guards the shirt fragment and offered them a pitcher of ice tea and a deck of cards before going upstairs and retiring for the night.

Early the next morning the Marines carried their prisoner to the waiting PT boat. The fast craft made quick work of the ride across Hatteras Inlet and down the island to the small base at Ocracoke harbor. There the prisoner was taken to sick bay behind the main crew barracks. Windows in the room were barred and a guard posted outside.

As soon as the guards closed the door, the prisoner began to take stock of his surroundings. He had noted prominent landmarks on the journey, and the number and type of vessels and berths when the boat docked. Based on what little he saw, he tried to envision the size and layout of the facility. Though escape was not an option at the moment, he mentally prepared for any future circumstance.

Later in the morning, the door opened and an elderly black cook entered, carrying a bowl of pea soup on a tray. The prisoner intently watched the man's approach, trying to recall if this was the first African he'd ever seen up close and in person. He judged the man's age to be 60 years or more.

"Yo' sho' is makin' fo' a fuss 'round here," the cook laughed, shaking his head. "Gots ever'body all riled. Where's you from, anyways? Washed up like a log. Talkin' 'at German. And now you ain't sayin' nothin'. Lordy, Lordy."

The cook stood grinning, his teeth and white hair in marked contrast to his coal-black skin. He set the tray down on a small table alongside the bed. "My name be George," he went on cheerfully, "but mos' folk call me Rooster. That 'cause I be up so early. Here, 'av dis. Yo' needs yo' strength."

While watching his approach, the prisoner was struck by the Black man's open demeanor and simple mannerisms. But behind the cheery face he saw a razor-edge sadness in the old man—a melancholy which spoke of the knowledge and experiences of a lifetime, masked by a wall of contrived patter.

The grin faded as his eyes met the prisoner's piercing gaze. "Lordy! Yo' 'nough to give a body da creeps!" the cook spat while slowly backing toward the door. He gave the prisoner a long, cautious look before knocking three times for the guard to let him out.

✠   ✠   ✠

"Where did you come from? Washed up like a log." The cook's words kept running through his mind. So perhaps there were no others, he thought. What about the aircraft? They had to know!

He could recall the chaos that broke out when the emergency dive order was shouted. Beyond that, things just went blank.

Realizing he was hungry, he cradled the bowl in his left hand and drank in shallow sips. Having finished, he again tried to reconstruct the events of the last two days.

A short time later, a medic came to change his bandages. Having dressed the wound, the medic prepared to administer a morphine injection. Despite his pain, the prisoner steadfastly refused the shot. The medic finally just shrugged and left.

Lying on the cot, he listened intently to the comings and goings outside the window. Sometimes he caught brief fragments of conversation, though nothing of any interest. At about three in the afternoon the guard at the door changed.

"So any word on where the Kraut came from?" the new man asked.

He could just barely make out the voices through the thick pine door.

"Nobody knows," the other soldier replied. "They say they're gonna take him to Norfolk tomorrow, though. Least we won't have to stand here no more."

✠   ✠   ✠

The cook returned about the time the light outside the barred window began to fade. Carefully avoiding eye contact, he placed a plate of biscuits and another bowl of pea soup on the table by the bed, and quickly left the room.

✠   ✠   ✠

The prisoner awoke to see two Marines standing over him. Behind the silhouetted figures, the first light of day filtered through the window.

He tried to collect his wits. They must have given him a sedative, he thought. Or maybe he just passed out. He couldn't be sure.

"All right, you. Time to go," one of the Marines said gruffly.

Supporting him by either arm, the Marines walked their charge across the compound. Small groups of uniformed men watched the mysterious prisoner being led down the dock to where the moored PT boat lay shrouded in a thin veil of exhaust, its engines idling restlessly.

The amber shades of dawn had given over to a bright, clear morning by the time the boat reached the mouth of Ocracoke Inlet. After clearing the shoals, the helmsman throttled up and the sleek wooden vessel was quickly on plane. Behind the small bridge, the prisoner squatted uncomfortably between his escorts. The captain ordered his vessel steered directly for Hatteras Cape Point. They rounded the narrow spit a mere hundred yards from the surf and turned northeast for the run up the coastline. The black and white striped Hatteras lighthouse grew larger on the port side, then receded astern.

After an hour and a half, the throttles were dropped back to navigate the narrow channel and tricky currents of Oregon Inlet. The PT boat docked at the ferry landing along the north side of the main channel. There a somewhat worn looking three-quarter-ton truck stood at the ready and the small entourage climbed aboard to continue the journey north.

Along this uninhabited stretch of coast, the road consisted of a sand track which constantly threatened to swallow the struggling vehicle. Sometimes the driver would find a break in the dunes and steer them directly onto the beach where the sand was left packed down by the receding tide.

The ride on the back of the truck was bumpy and the prisoner's wound ached terribly. One of the Marines reached over to offer a cigarette. He had not smoked since Danzig, and these were American cigarettes of the best sort. He graciously accepted and raised his cuffed hands to shield the lighter. Drawing deeply, he leaned back, surrendering to the pleasure of tobacco.

✠   ✠   ✠

They passed through Nags Head and Kill Devil Hills, and by early afternoon arrived at the Albermarle Sound ferry. Unknown to anyone, they were almost precisely retracing the last flight of the downed Catalina, the chance encounter with which resulted in the destruction of the U-491 and the loss of all but one of those aboard.

Chapter 4

Norfolk Naval Base, Norfolk, Virginia

CAPTAIN ROMAN EDWARDS OPENED THE FOLDER TO REVIEW THE dispatch from Ocracoke for the third time. Edwards meticulously prepared for every case and this one promised to be interesting. The facts were simple but intriguing. An individual is found washed up on the Outer Banks near Cape Hatteras. The persons who find him note he has "Kessel" printed on his shirt over the breast pocket. In delirium, the subject rants in German. A local doctor treats him for shock and dehydration and stitches a laceration across the pectoral area.

Edwards closed the folder, picked up the phone and rang Lieutenant Commander Sutherland. "Sutherland, what's the status on the Hatteras case?" he demanded. "Well then, I want the man brought directly up here when the examination is finished."

Edwards leaned back in his chair. Outwardly, his appearance was more of a Marine Drill Sergeant than a Naval Intelligence officer. A rigid manner and bearing added to the impression.

Edwards was well known within the Department as a bit of a loose cannon, and for being difficult to work with. A dedicated career man, Edwards wished he could be anywhere but Virginia. Several incidents, however, mostly involving superior officers, had sidelined his career.

Lieutenant Commander Sutherland entered the room, accompanied by a second officer who introduced himself as an interpreter. Edwards and his adjutant were as different as night and day. Sutherland was an attorney before the war. He came from a prominent New England family and attended Harvard Law School. Tall and slender with slightly effeminate ways, he looked younger than his years. Sutherland joined the Navy in a fit of patriotism the day after Pearl Harbor, only to rely on family connections to avoid combat ship duty. Inwardly, Edwards despised the man for his elitist attitudes and endless references to his privileged upbringing.

"Bring him in and let's get on with it," Edwards said curtly.

"Guards! Bring in the prisoner," Sutherland shouted through the door.

It opened and two Marines strode in with the prisoner between them. They saluted stiffly and left.

"Please sit down," Edwards said while motioning with his right arm to a chair in the center of the room. "I think you have some explaining to do," he went on. "Would you mind sharing with us who you are and how you found your way to North Carolina?"

The interpreter mechanically presented the question in German while Edwards retained eye contact with the prisoner.

The prisoner deliberately did not respond. He had been preparing himself for interrogation ever since he'd been taken off the beach, and was determined not to give anything away before he could fully size up his adversary.

"Let's get the pleasantries over with," Edwards said lightly. "I trust your stay in Ocracoke went well. How was the ride on the truck?" The sarcasm was but thinly veiled.

"*Ja, alles ist gut abgelaufen.*"

Edwards paced the room with his hands clasped behind him. He stopped to face the interpreter, who was waiting impassively. Standing off to the side, Sutherland shifted his feet, feeling like he was back in the courtroom. Sutherland never lost a case until just before the war. The one case he lost, he lost in a big way. In fact, he'd been made a fool of. He remembered how his opponent repeatedly built up, then eased the tension level on the stand before systematically breaking down witnesses during cross-examination. Sutherland glanced at his superior officer, clearly recognizing the same tactic.

"You having been out of uniform releases me from all articles of the Geneva Convention. Understand I can have you shot as a spy this very day," Edwards stated calmly. "Now again, what is your name and how did you find yourself on a North Carolina beach?"

The prisoner drew a breath with which to speak.

"No, no. How rude," Edwards interrupted. "Allow me to introduce myself. I am Captain Edwards." He motioned to the other officer. "And this is my associate, Lieutenant Commander Sutherland."

Sutherland waited for Edwards to begin in earnest. He knew the good cop–bad cop routine and could expect things to get ugly fairly soon. Edwards continued to pace, occasionally stopping to ask his prisoner a few seemingly irrelevant questions.

"That will be all for today," Edwards said abruptly. "It's late. We shall continue tomorrow."

The Marines returned and took the prisoner to a tiny holding cell in the basement of the building. A steel toilet took up one corner and a green canvas cot stood against the far wall, leaving little additional space.

The prisoner eased himself flat onto the cot, resting one forearm up against the cinder block wall. His interrogator had given him nothing. He sensed the man planned to cut the interrogation short—maybe he only wanted to feel him out, perhaps take advantage of his tired and disorientated state. What did they know? Laying and staring at the ceiling, he mulled the same questions over and over. What was this Edwards holding back? What about the aircraft? What happened to the aircraft?! Maybe the flak got it, he suddenly thought. Two long bursts were all he could remember reverberating through the hull. What were the chances? He had to know.

After straining to recall what happened after hearing the cannon fire, he realized further speculation was pointless and his wits were best saved for the following day. He closed his eyes and rested.

✠   ✠   ✠

The morning session began with the same questions.

"I am Konrad Kessel," he responded in German to the interpreter's inquiry, figuring someone must have taken note of the name on the shirt when he'd been found.

"And where are you from, Herr Kessel?"

"I am an Uruguayan national."

"How is it you speak German?"

"My family emigrated from Germany. In the early thirties. It was hard times you know."

"How did you find your way from Uruguay to... say, North Carolina?"

"I fell off my ship. Was it two nights ago, or...?"

Edwards rolled his eyes even before the interpreter finished. "What was the name of your ship?" he asked, feigning patience.

Kessel hesitated for just a fraction of a second. "The *Rio Tinto*."

Edwards nodded. "Go on."

"I was on watch and had a little to drink. More than a little, actually, but no one could tell. I leaned over the rail to relieve myself. I must have fallen."

Edwards paced the room. He turned to the prisoner. "An interesting story. I guess everything is explained. Tell me then, what was your mother's maiden name?"

"My mother never married."

"What was her name then?"

"Brenner. She died when I was a child."

"And what was your father's name?"

"I wish I knew," the prisoner replied, the corners of his mouth turning up into the faintest of smiles.

"Have you any brothers or sisters?"

Edwards continued the line of questioning, with each inquiry more mundane than the last.

"What was your home address, in, where was it? Montevideo?"

"Actually…"

"What was your ship's cargo and what was your last port of call?" Edwards interrupted, his voice taking an edge.

Kessel hesitated for a second or two. "Baltimore," he then said flatly. "We were sailing in ballast."

Edwards placed his hands on the table, leaned toward his prisoner and said, "You'd best be speaking the truth."

✠   ✠   ✠

The prisoner was taken back to his cell. Two floors above, Edwards continued to pace, carefully recounting the session. He felt something was amiss—the man must be something other than he claimed to be. There was something unusual, something very wrong about him, and his story. The more Edwards walked the room, the more determined he became to find out just who this man was.

Lieutenant Commander Sutherland strode in and handed Edwards a manila folder. "Here are the reports you asked for," he said crisply. "As to any unusual activity in the operations area, there isn't much to report. You know of the Catalina that went down just short of the Air Station?"

"Yes, I do." Edwards said, looking up from the papers.

"They were supposed to make a bombing run over Duck. I checked down there—seems the plane never made it to the range. They just finished clearing the wreckage. No trace of the ordnance, nor of any detonations."

"Was there any communication?" Edwards quickly asked.

"None. I checked the tower logs. Last contact was when take-off clearance was given."

Edwards ran his hand across the back of his neck.

"They might have been in trouble," Sutherland offered. "Dropped their load over the water on the way back."

Edwards said nothing.

✠   ✠   ✠

While Edwards resumed pacing his office, Kessel lay in his cell recounting the session with equal care. Bit by bit Kessel came to the realization that they did not—could not—know of the U-boat. The aircraft must have gone down, he decided. There was no other way. With the conclusion came the realization he must be the only one left alive. The thought relieved him.

✠   ✠   ✠

The afternoon session began much like the morning one. Edwards kept prying into every corner of the man's life, searching for any inconsistencies in his responses, seeking any clue which might give something away. Try as he would, he could not crack into his prisoner. Edwards saw the facade, but did not know what lay behind. The man seemed to have a vague, yet satisfactory response to every question. Instead of wearing down, he sensed the prisoner's confidence had grown. The man had become less guarded with his answers. Cocky even. Sometimes it seemed as if he were mocking him. Edwards felt himself losing control of the contest and struggled to conceal his rising emotions. Attempting to maintain an even tone, his questions became clipped, his manner short.

"Tell me about your wound. How did you sustain the injury?"

Kessel turned to the interpreter. "*Es war...* "

Edwards whirled around striking his fist on the desk. "*Speak English!*"

Edwards motioned for the interpreter to leave. "Talk to me!" he demanded, returning his attention to the prisoner.

The two men glared at each other.

"I must have caught on something when I fell off the ship," Kessel finally stated, with only a hint of an accent.

"From now on the interview will be conducted in English," Edwards ordered. "Guards!"

The Marines burst into the room and escorted Kessel out the door.

✠   ✠   ✠

Sitting behind his desk, Edwards felt a certain satisfaction from the exchange—a minor victory of sorts. Perhaps this will slow him down, he thought.

Sutherland had been waiting in the hall for Edwards to finish. "Checks out, Sir," he said walking in. "*Rio Tinto*. Tramp steamer out of Montevideo, 1,800 tons. Mostly does the Caribbean–Central America circuit. Uruguayan registry. Unloaded hardwood and tinned beef in Baltimore last week. Cleared port on the morning of the 22nd." Sutherland looked up from his notes. His eyes met Edwards'. "Sir, that would put her off the Outer Banks about the time the guy was found."

"Son of a bitch," Edwards hissed.

Sutherland laid the papers on the desk saying, "The guy could be legit."

"He's a fucking liar!" Edwards snarled. "Everything about him absolutely reeks of bullshit!"

"Take it easy will you. You're going to give yourself an ulcer."

"Already have one."

"Lets go over what we have," Sutherland began smoothly, trying to keep Edwards from pitching a tantrum. "So the guy washes up on the beach, half dead, no identification. In delirium he speaks in German, apparently his native tongue. Claims his name is Kessel, and to have fallen off a neutral flag ship."

"I know the story!"

"He seems to check out."

"Something about him just isn't right," Edwards sighed, collapsing into his chair. "I can't help but feel everything he says is a lie."

"Have you thought about some amobarbital?" Sutherland offered.

"Don't really believe in the stuff," Edwards replied. "It's not all that effective. Besides, I don't think it would do any good with this guy. He's a tough nut. Anyone can see that."

"By the way, how did you know he spoke English?"

"It was his little smirk. It wasn't hard to figure."

Sutherland again tried to focus on the man's story. "Anyway, he gets drunk, takes a piss and falls overboard..."

"Now this *Rio Tinto* is nowhere to be found and won't respond to any calls!" Edwards burst out.

"This is still war time. Radio silence is the norm."

Edwards took a moment to collect himself, then asked, "So what else did you find out?"

"One thing is kind of strange," Sutherland began, his voice taking on a vague air of concern, "I got copies of the departure papers. They stated Jacksonville as the next port of call. So I phoned down there and the harbormaster's never heard of a *Rio Tinto*."

"Why am I not surprised?" Edwards growled.

"We could contact the Naval Attaché in Montevideo and get him to look into the matter."

"That could take weeks," Edwards sighed. "What do we do in the meantime?"

✠   ✠   ✠

At nine o'clock sharp, the guards brought Kessel in to begin a third day of interrogation.

"Good Morning, Captain Edwards."

"You will speak only when you are spoken to," Edwards stated, trying to suppress the anger building in him all morning. "Now, tell me, what was to be your vessel's destination after Jacksonville?"

"I am an ordinary seaman, I know not..."

"Liar!" Edwards yelled, ripping open his desk drawer. He pulled out a locked and loaded .45 and at point blank range, leveled it to the man's head. "*You lyin' bastard! You're a fuckin' plant!*" he roared. "*Talk to me or I'll blow your fucking head off!*"

The man's mouth went dry as dust, yet his face failed to register even a hint of fear.

Sutherland burst through the door directly behind the seated prisoner. The Lieutenant Commander froze in his steps as he found himself staring past a pistol-clenching fist, directly into the wildly blazing eyes of his superior officer. Sutherland inched sideways, desperately trying to purge the mental image of the prisoner's brains splattered across his dress whites.

Edwards pressed the weapon flush to the man's forehead and curled his finger ever tighter around the trigger. Small beads of perspiration quivered above Edwards' upper lip. Purple veins seemed ready to pop open all across his glistening brow. The prisoner did not so much as blink.

Sutherland reached for the window and threw open the latch. Distant cheers and cries of celebration drifted into the room. Car horns beeped crazily. One by one, booming ship horns and the shrill steam whistles on the dockside cranes joined in the pandemonium.

"Sir, Sir," Sutherland stammered.

"*Shut up, college boy!!*" Edwards screamed, his eyes locked into the prisoner's icy stare.

"Sir! The Germans, they've agreed to surrender! The war in Europe is over!"

"I know it's over, you imbecile," Edwards growled, lowering the weapon and dropping his voice about 30 decibels. "I'm the ranking intelligence officer on this base. *Remember?!*" Edwards waved with the sidearm toward the door. "Now get him the fuck outta here!"

Chapter 5

"THE ADMIRAL WILL SEE YOU NOW, CAPTAIN," THE SECRETARY SAID dryly. Her eyes followed the officer across the room.

Edwards strode into the office and came to attention before the admiral's desk. "Good Morning, Sir."

"Good Morning, Captain," the base commander said sharply. He remained seated while Edwards stood stiffly before him. "You know I'm not a man to beat around the bush, so let's get right to it. Captain Edwards, I have come to greatly appreciate your service," the Admiral went on, trying to force a conciliatory note. "As you may well know, some people do not fully share this sentiment. I've gone to bat for you several times; I didn't expect you to disappoint me."

The Admiral rose and walked around his large oak desk to where Edwards was standing. "Frankly, you've pissed a lot of people off around here!" he half yelled in Edwards' face. "Including myself!" He turned away to look out the window in the direction of the harbor. Both hands were clasped tightly behind him. "I think if you can get a handle on your problem, you could be a truly outstanding officer, truly outstanding." The Admiral turned back around. "Captain Edwards, you are authorized to take medical leave, effective immediately. It's a three week stop over."

Edwards swallowed. " Sir, I am in the middle of an investigation and…"

The Admiral cut him short. "Lieutenant Commander Sutherland has briefed me on the case. He will be handling the details."

"What details?! …Sir!"

"Lieutenant Commander Sutherland seems to think the man's story may be legitimate. Mind you, the whole thing sounds mighty strange to me, but I'm not at all sure it makes any difference at this point."

"What has Sutherland recommended?"

"The man will be repatriated at the earliest possible date."

"You mean give him fifty bucks and pack him on the next boat to South America?" Edwards asked incredulously.

The Admiral nodded. "In the interim, he will be detained at a local POW facility."

"But Sir! The man…"

Edwards was again cut off in mid sentence. "The war with Germany is over, Captain!" the Admiral said sharply. "Now before long this base will be asshole to elbow with personnel returning from Europe. Preparations are already underway. We'll need all our resources to deal with the crush."

Edwards glared sullenly at his commanding officer.

"That will be all."

Edwards nodded grimly and turned to leave.

"Captain Edwards."

Edwards stopped and turned to face the Admiral. "Yes?"

"Just relax and you'll feel better when you get back."

✠   ✠   ✠

The next day Kessel found himself on a buoy tender chugging across the mouth of the Chesapeake Bay. Kessel convinced his escorts to allow him on deck, where he sat and basked in the fresh sunshine. After spending the better part of a week in the darkened basement cell, the sun and salt air were nothing short of intoxicating. Off the stern, a hazy sky melded with the bay waters along a dull blue horizon.

All too soon the tender pulled into Cape Charles harbor on Virginia's Eastern Shore. An Army staff car was waiting on the dock for the lone prisoner. Riding in the back seat, Kessel took in the fertile bounty of the surrounding land. He gazed out the window at the ripening fields of winter wheat that panned into the distance. Between the cultivated expanses, dense tracts of woods shaded marshy streams.

Every few miles, the road passed a cluster of tar paper shacks. A riot of colors hung from clotheslines stretched between the dilapidated structures. Withered old black men lingered on ramshackle porches while half-naked children played in the dusty streets. Nestled amid the vast fields, the hamlets were surrounded by tidy garden plots. Some had a diminutive, whitewashed church set in the village center. Beyond the farm labor settlements, newly planted corn stretched to the horizon, broken only by strips of forest. Occasional farmsteads punctuated the wide-open spaces. To Kessel, this landscape bore a distinctively feudal aspect. Though the farmhouses were relatively modest, two-and-a-half-story frame dwellings, with their steeply pitched roofs they rose like small castles over a manicured, dead-level countryside.

A short time later the car pulled up to the camp. The facility looked like any other and Kessel briefly wondered if they were built to some common design the world over. Wooden posts held a tall, steel-mesh fence topped with barbed wire. A double-door gate swung open and the car scooted past the spindly guard tower complete with searchlights and a machine gun mount. As the car motored through the gate, row after row of wood-frame barracks came into view.

The car came to a stop and two soldiers opened the door. They escorted the prisoner across the compound to the infirmary where the camp doctor gave him a cursory examination.

"Come back sometime and I'll take out those stitches," was all the doctor said before signing the papers and handing the clipboard to the attendant.

After being issued standard cotton blues, the newest, and undoubtedly the last prisoner to be processed into camp was led to his bunk in Barracks Number 42.

✠   ✠   ✠

While taking in his new surroundings, Kessel was struck by the relaxed atmosphere pervading the camp. It also seemed nearly empty. Then, at about five o'clock, buses and trucks began to roll through the front gate. Most of the men who shuffled from the vehicles were from the remnants of Rommel's once vaunted Afrika Korps while others had been captured in Italy. Many were well into their third year of internment. Etched into their drawn and dour faces was the weariness brought by the endless toil in the surrounding farms and fields.

✠   ✠   ✠

The new prisoner kept to himself and the other men showed little interest in who he was or where he came from. A few casual questions were posed and he steadfastly retold a deliberately vague story about his service as a merchant seaman.

Mostly, Kessel rested and tried to regain his strength. Within a relatively short time span, his wound healed remarkably well. The sutures were removed and the doctor declared him fit for work.

The first week out, Kessel and the other men of Barracks 42 were assigned to pack cucumber crates. The work was backbreaking and the heat nearly unbearable. When he'd first arrived in camp, Kessel was pallid and weak. The physical labor toned his body and his skin tanned quickly under the blazing early summer sun. Before long he turned such a dark shade of bronze, the other POWs took to calling him "The Moor."

Although the labor was hard, Kessel much preferred the fields to sweltering in the barracks. The repetitive nature of the work gave it a ritualistic quality. In its own way, the daily tedium made the weeks pass. Numb with exhaustion at the end of the day, his mind was spared the searing memories that had long shadowed his soul. Only rarely did the nightmares come.

✠   ✠   ✠

"Inspection!" The barracks door flew open. "Inspection! Let's go, all of you!" the *Feldwebel* yelled.

A ruddy-faced Austrian, all of 19, rolled off the bunk above Kessel's. "Leitnitz, the bastard!" he growled. "Doesn't he know the war is over?"

"Even in defeat, order and discipline must be maintained," Kessel said wearily, mimicking the German ranking officer. "Spoken like a true Prussian."

"It's Saturday. Can't he just leave us alone?" the Austrian grumbled.

All around, men streamed out of the barracks into the compound and pretended to stand at attention. *Oberst* Axel Leitnitz, the ranking German officer in camp, walked down the long rows of men, occasionally stopping to berate a soldier or two. Kessel and his bunkmate stood near the center of the front row. Leitnitz' blather became audible as he moved down the ranks. The officer swaggered past the two men. He stopped to squint back at Kessel. A flash of recognition crossed his face.

"You!" Leitnitz bellowed. "I know you!"

Kessel did not reply.

"General Giesel's staff I should think. Yes, I remember you."

"You must be mistaken, *Herr Oberst*," Kessel said evenly.

"Come now, 1943, Odessa, then Sebastobol. The Crimea is so lovely in the summer," Leitnitz said, his eyes narrowing to mere slits. "What brings you here?"

"I am a citizen of a neutral country," Kessel sighed. "I am being held under special administrative detention pending repatriation."

Leitnitz moved closer still, carefully scrutinizing him from different angles.

"I never forget a face, especially one as ugly as yours," he sneered. "Whatever happened to you? Obviously you're not dead. Talk was you deserted. How the devil did you end up here?"

"Check my dossier at the commandant's office. You will see I am not the man you are speaking of."

Leitnitz breathed directly into Kessel's face." I think I just might do that," he said, then turned and continued down the line.

"What was that all about?" the adjacent man asked, as soon as the officer was out of earshot.

"I don't know," Kessel said out of the side of his mouth. " Just look at him though, he's not right."

"This is true."

✠   ✠   ✠

With the inspection finished, the men had the rest of the day off from work. Skies became overcast and a refreshing sea breeze blew across the dusty compound. The break in the heat lifted everyone's mood. Some of the men engaged in spirited games of volleyball. Others just lounged around, savoring the break in the weather. Kessel propped a chair up against the barracks' doorway and sat lipping a toothpick. He casually took stock of the volleyball matches while perusing year-old issues of "Life" magazine.

Later, there was roast chicken in the mess and it felt, just a little, like Sunday at home.

✠   ✠   ✠

The early morning air was thick with dew as the second ranking German in camp made his way across the compound toward the officers' latrine. Cloaked in semi-darkness, the camp seemed deserted. Far in the distance, a dog barked. Otherwise not the slightest sound challenged the stillness of dawn. The man lay awake for hours. Unable to get back to sleep, he figured he might as well go to the latrine and begin his day. He pulled open the stall door and recoiled in horror.

" Arhhhg! *Auch du Lieber Gott!*" he cried out.

The sudden shock made the sight seem worse than anything he'd witnessed on the battlefield—Leitnitz sat slumped on the toilet beneath the single light bulb, his formerly white nightshirt saturated with blood. Dried rivulets crisscrossed his bare legs. Crimson puddles, rust red and crusty along the edges, lay on the concrete floor around the dead man's feet. Leitnitz' arms dangled to either side, palms facing outwards. One side of his neck was neatly sliced, the carotid artery severed. With his head cocked aside, the wound

gaped open. Dozens of flies swarmed along the gash, eagerly sow-
ing the seeds of their larval young.

"*Guards! Guards!*"

The dogs along the perimeter barked incessantly as doors
slammed open all around.

A burly sergeant was first on the scene. "What the fuck is
going... Oh, Jesus Christ!" The man turned away with his hand
over his mouth.

After a moment, the sergeant regained his composure and
turned to look at the dead officer. The camp commandant came
storming across the compound, cursing whatever it was ruining
his Sunday morning sleep.

"It had to be an officer," was all he said after the initial start
passed. "Do you know how much paperwork this is going to take?
And on my day off, no less."

The three men began to study the scene.

"How long do you think he's been dead?" the commandant
asked.

"About an hour or two, at least," the other two men agreed.

The sergeant noted the window to the latrine was broken and
pointed the fact out to the camp commandant. A thin, approximately five inch long section of glass pane lay on the floor under
the limp fingers of the dead man's right hand.

"Looks like he did himself in," the commandant observed.

"You don't really think he did this to himself?" the sergeant
asked skeptically.

"Do you see anything to the contrary? I mean, look around.
With this much blood, do you see any smears, any signs of a struggle? No. It looks every bit a suicide."

Both the German officer and the sergeant had their doubts.
Neither figured Leitnitz to be one to take his own life, nor did the
corpse look the part. In death, Leitnitz' face seemed frozen in the
look of mortal fear.

The commandant turned to the German officer, asking, "Any
idea why anyone would want to do the guy in?"

"He was not the most popular man here," he replied in his heavily accented English. "But to do such a thing as this... I don't know."

"What about taking his own life? Did you ever get the impression he might be suicidal?"

"One never knows of such things. Maybe the stress from the front..." he paused as if in thought. "The East was pretty rough going."

"Yeah, yeah, war is hell," the commandant sighed, quickly losing interest in the matter.

"Paybacks are worse," the German officer said under his breath.

The sergeant turned to address the camp commander. "Colonel, Sir, I really don't see how this man could have done this. The way I..."

"This was a suicide, plain and simple!" the commandant stated, cutting his sergeant off in mid sentence. "Now get some people and clean this mess up. I want a full report on my desk by this afternoon."

"Yes Sir!"

Chapter 6

THE LEITNITZ AFFAIR WAS FODDER FOR CONVERSATION AROUND the camp for a day or two but interest soon faded and the daily work routine continued unabated.

One afternoon, while the men of Barracks 42 were packing vegetable crates, the tractor pulling the loaded wagons began to stall. The farmer, after tinkering with the engine, took to cursing and beating the recalcitrant machine with his canvas cap.

"It's the carburetor," Kessel called out to the farmer once his outburst was over.

"Oh, yeah? How do you know?"

"I can smell the gas. Here, let me see the screwdriver," he said, walking over and taking the tool from the man's hand.

Within a few minutes, the adjustment was complete and the engine ran flawlessly.

"You know much about engines?" the grateful farmer asked.

"I was a shipboard mechanic in the Merchant Marine," he lied. "I was studying to be a engineer when the war started."

"You speak English very well."

"Thank you. I have studied many years."

A small boy, barefoot and dressed only in denim overalls, stood behind his father's leg, blinking wide-eyed at the German soldier.

"Name's Schifflett, Earl Schifflett," the farmer said. Then, almost as an afterthought, he extended his hand to the POW.

Schifflett spoke in the clipped southern accent peculiar to the isolated Virginia peninsula. Kessel thought he detected a hint of British in the farmer's American speech.

"Tell you what, I got an irrigation pump motor over on the other side of the farm giving me fits. Maybe you could take a look at it," Schifflett said, shooting a glance at the guard who wandered over to see what was going on.

The bored soldier nodded, saying, "Just don't be too long. And bring him back when you're done."

Kessel climbed onto the tractor and rode with Schifflett to the well house.

"So what's the matter with it?" Kessel asked, while surveying the assembly.

"Dunno. Runs for about five minutes and cuts off. Does it every time."

"I think I might be able to take care of that."

Kessel unbolted the electric motor from the pump assembly while Schifflett watched. Both men heaved the motor onto the tractor wagon. The farmer drove them to the work shed where he left the German to begin his work.

Kessel had the motor broken down with the major components spread out on the workbench when a small stone came flying through the open shed doors. The missile crashed into the wall a few feet from his head before falling harmlessly to the floor. He spun around to see the little Schifflett boy dashing away, flailing his arms in feigned terror.

"Little prick!" Kessel muttered, turning back around.

By late afternoon, the motor was back together and running like new.

Before long Kessel developed a reputation among the local farmers for being able to fix just about anything. With the wartime labor shortage, mechanics were few and far between and Kessel found his talents much in demand. As often as not, he would spend the day tinkering with equipment or machinery rather than working the fields.

✠   ✠   ✠

Almost daily, rumors circulated about the camp that the first prisoners were about to be sent home. Finally, after weeks of speculation, 300 men were sent packing for Norfolk. Units interned the longest were moved out first, while the remainder were chosen by lottery. Each evening, the men anxiously awaited any word as to which barracks might be the next to leave.

Even as the camp began to clear out, the daily work routine continued for those who remained. The men toiled through the heat and stifling humidity, bolstered by the thought they would soon be going home.

The day at the Schifflett farm was particularly long and hard, and all were relieved to see it end. Thoughts were on the mess and the evening's rest as the men boarded their bus. Kessel watched the bus depart through the small grime-caked window of the utility building in which he had been working. The guards, as was now often the case, neglected to take a proper head count. As the bus rolled out of sight, he stood into the open and waited until the raised dust had drifted away. Kessel then began walking east, in the opposite direction, down a weed-choked farm road.

The blazing afternoon sun mellowed and a faint ocean breeze blew in across the fields. With it came the scent of salt air. Kessel kept walking. After a half mile or so, fields gave way to dense woods. Towering pine trees formed a fragrant canopy over a narrow, shell-strewn path. The woods ended along a sandy terrace, where Kessel found himself staring across the open vista of a huge salt marsh.

Seemingly endless expanses of marsh grass stretched before him, shimmering iridescent green in the late afternoon sun. A web of muddy creek channels lay exposed by the ebbing tide. Far in the distance, the dull haze of ocean spray hung low over the Atlantic barrier islands. Carried on the gentle wind, the sound of surf was audible amid the rustling pines. To his right, a decrepit dock extended out into the creek. The pilings were covered with growth and some nearly eaten away at the water line. At the end of the dock, a small wooden scow rested forlornly in the mud. Still tethered to a piling, the derelict vessel filled with water on every flood tide.

Kessel ambled onto the dock and took in the breeze wafting across the open marsh. The brine tinged air filling his senses was faintly foul, yet strangely alluring. In a curious way, the scent was provocative. Ancient. Elemental. For a fleeting moment, it seemed to tug at some diffuse, unfathomably distant memory—almost as if the warm, turbid waters were exuding the primordial essence of genesis itself.

The late afternoon light had given over to the lingering glow of evening. Kessel watched the pale form of the nearly full moon appear over the vast marshlands. To his amazement, thousands of fiddler crabs emerged from their muddy lairs and scurried across the exposed creek bottom. The creatures were so numerous the entire flats seemed to quiver as a single living mass. He stood on the dock, transfixed by the scene. Just then, a Great Blue Heron swooped in for a landing, its magnificent wings splayed wide. In a single instant, every crab was gone. After a few moments, each of the creatures cautiously reemerged.

Suddenly, Kessel felt a pair of eyes on his back. Trapped on the dock by the impassable morass all around, he cursed himself for having lingered in such an exposed location. He wheeled around to face the tawny figure of a woman, a mere stone's throw away.

"I've startled you," the woman said calmly.

"What do you want?" he demanded of her.

"I was gonna ask you the same thing-—seein' you're standin' on my dock."

Kessel stared at the woman. She had a graceful build, making her seem taller than she actually was. In the warm glow of the waning sun, her skin radiated the color of polished mahogany. Bare-footed, she wore only a faded blue, sleeveless dress. Her long black hair was tied in a ponytail that fell casually across one shoulder.

"I followed you from the farm," she said, breaking the momentary silence.

He had seen no one.

"I'm Carmen. Who you be?"

"My name is Konrad Kessel."

"You talk funny. You one of them Germans, ain't you?"

"I am originally from Germany, yes."

"You from the camp, but you didn't leave with the others," she stated. "Guess 'at makes you a 'scaped prisoner."

"Yes, I suppose one could consider me an escaped prisoner."

"Don't worry, I won't tell nobody," she said coyly, while stepping onto the dock. "You're the mechanic, ain't you? The one who fixes stuff."

"How do you know this?" Kessel asked, thoroughly intrigued but still wary, and perhaps a little perturbed by her forward manner.

"I been workin' on the Schifflett farm too," she said, moving closer still.

The two stood facing each other. Kessel took the woman to be in her mid-thirties or so. Maybe more. She was quite dark, yet her features had an eastern appearance. Strong cheekbones framed pearly, coffee-colored eyes. Her threadbare dress covered breasts that heaved slightly as she breathed. In one instant, Kessel grasped just how strikingly attractive this woman was, making her sudden, unexpected appearance seem all the more unreal.

"Why you run away?" she asked, turning toward the water.

Kessel watched her saunter down the dock, his eyes tracing her backside. She moved with an ease that was mesmerizing. Every inch of her radiated a subtle, unself-conscious sensuality.

"I am not sure," he called out to her. "I just felt like getting away."

"Will they be lookin' for you?" she asked, glancing back over her shoulder.

"I doubt they even know I am gone. At least not yet."

She reached for a rope and pulled a burlap sack from the shallow water beneath the dock.

"You hungry? Got some oysters. It's too hot to keep 'em out of the water. They're plenty good now though."

Kessel nodded, his eyes not moving from hers.

"Come with me, then," she smiled.

Saying nothing, the two made their way through the darkening pine woods until they met with a fork in the narrow path. Holding to the left, they came upon a tiny frame house, set back in a clearing. A large, well-tended vegetable plot flanked the diminutive structure. The house and garden were enclosed by a fence constructed of driftwood and weathered planks. Next to the makeshift fence gate, a scruffy rooster attentively watched their approach while a half dozen hens strutted about, methodically pecking in search of the day's final tidbit.

The door to the house opened with a slight creak. Inside, the air smelled of horsehair mattress, wood smoke and kerosene. Carmen struck a match and lit a small lantern.

Kessel looked around. Roughly hewn pine boards comprised the floor. A small hearth with a clay daub mantle was built into the gable end of the single room. The firebox and chimney were made of crumbling brick, salvaged from a derelict house whose long-dead owners had been of far less modest means. Herbs and dried bean pods were strung over the mantle. A large iron bed frame with a mattress covered by a patchwork quilt stood against the far wall.

"Sit yourself down," she said, reaching for the handle of a large knife, the blade of which had been snapped short and ground to a blunt end.

"This is your home?" Kessel asked.

"It surely is. I own it. The house and the land up to the creek. It was mine and my man's."

"Your man's?"

"He's dead," Carmen said, sitting down at the small table across from him. She reached in the bag and pulled out a clump of oysters, each shell as large as the palm of her hand.

"I am sorry."

"That's okay. It's been near ten years now."

An awkward silence ensued.

"He was a good man," Carmen finally said in a measured tone.

She wedged the short blade between two gnarled and muddied shells.

"This place was our dream—a place that was all ours. You know, get a job o' work when we could, but live mos'ly off what the land and water give us."

Kessel said nothing.

"In the winter he was gonna guide for the rich folk. Duck hunting," she said, sounding wistful. "He knew these backwaters better than any man alive. Grew up in 'em."

"What happened?" Kessel asked, not wishing to pry but seemingly unable to divert the conversation.

"Nat… Nat was a hustler, a professional gambler. Plied his trade 'long the docks and shipyard bars 'cross the bay. He was good. We'd saved enough to buy this place, so he was gonna give it up. Retire, you know." She paused and drew a shallow breath. "Was stabbed to death over craps in Portsmouth."

Kessel sat and watched her pry open the oysters in silence. One by one the stubborn mollusks yielded to a quick turn of the dull blade. Carmen laid the half shells on the table, rose and walked toward the hearth. She opened a trap door in the floor, reached into the small brick-lined cellar hole and pulled out a pot of cooked greens. She put the greens on the table and fetched some corn bread and a mason jar of pepper sauce from the cupboard.

"Please eat," she said, sitting back down.

Kessel reached with his fork and tried to impale one of the gray, gelatinous masses. Following her lead, he finally lifted the shell up to his mouth and slurped up the quivering contents. She watched him chew gingerly before swallowing.

"You like oysters?" she asked.

"I have never had oysters. They are quite good. Salty, kind of like the ocean smells."

The two sat and finished the simple but satisfying meal.

Kessel put the last shell down and reached for a piece of corn bread. "Are you African?" he asked.

Carmen lowered her eyes and smiled. "No one ever asked me that before, at least not like that. No. My family is Mattaponi. I grew up on the reservation."

Kessel's eyes widened and his hand dropped from his mouth. "Reservation?" he asked. "You are American Indian?"

"Yes."

"I have always dreamed of the American West!" he said excitedly. "As a boy I read all the Karl May books."

Carmen again smiled. "The Mattaponi, we live in Virginia. The reservation's on the other side of the Chesapeake Bay. Richmond's as far west as I ever been."

"There are Indians here in Virginia?!" Kessel exclaimed, ignoring the corn bread he still held in one hand.

"There're two tribes, the Mattaponi and Pamunkey. We each have a reservation along the rivers that bear our names."

"Your people, on the reservation, do they live in teepees?" he asked in all seriousness.

Carmen burst out laughing. "No!" she said, still laughing and shaking her head. "Our people been on the reservation a great many years. The old ways are so long gone my grandfather's grandfather wouldn't 'a' remembered 'em."

Unfazed, Kessel continued to question her about her people and life on the reservation. He sat enthralled by her descriptions of the tangled swamps and forested riverbanks of southeast Virginia.

"Oh yeah, some of us still fish and trap 'long the river," she went on. "Spring's 'specially good. That's when the shad and herrin' come up to spawn. Some years the fish be so thick their tails would churn up the water. With a dip net everybody could get all they needed. Most of it we salted down in barrels. I like 'em smoked better, though. Families with a boat and nets did real good with shad. The roe always fetched a good price in town."

"Why did you leave the reservation?"

"Momma sent me to live with my auntie in Norfolk so I could go to a school for colored folk."

Kessel cocked his head quizzically.

"Learned me to read and write," she said with obvious pride.

"Colored?" he asked, studying her.

Carmen again smiled. "African, like you says. You see, they was always Negroes 'mongst us. In the olden times, slaves would run from their masters and live with my people in the forest. Later, free Negroes lived near our lands and some took them to be husband or wife."

She paused a moment. Her brow furled slightly.

"To the white man though," she said slowly, "we was all colored."

A short silence followed.

"And your family, did they stay on the reservation?"

"My daddy died of drink when I was little. Momma stayed on, but she wanted me to leave; wanted me to have a better life."

"Your people on the reservation, they were poor?"

"Not ever'body lived on the reservation. Some folk owned land and made a livin' farmin'. Others went to the city to find work. On the reservation though, yeah, mostly we was poor."

Kessel sensed she no longer wished to speak of her earlier years. "So what do you do now?" he asked.

"I work for the Schiffletts. You know, clean some and take care of the little boy." She paused contemplatively. "Some Saturday nights I still dance at the Roadhouse. Do whatever it take to get 'em farm boys to give up some of their hard-earned dough."

Kessel kept looking directly in her eyes.

"What about your family?" she asked, trying to shift the subject from herself. "Was your daddy also a fightin' man?"

Kessel's eyes took on a sudden sparkle. "I am but one in a long line of proud warriors from the lands across the great eastern waters," he said holding back a smile.

Carmen laughed and moved to playfully slap him across the chest. He caught her hand in mid-air and clasped it down against the table. Their gaze met. Neither moved. Holding on, he stood and swung himself around the small table, seating himself on the bench beside her. He relaxed his hold and ran his fingers across the top of her hand, up the length of her arm and across one shoulder. Carmen momentarily lowered her eyes. He paused on the back of her neck before running his hand through her long black hair. Saying nothing, he continued to stoke her hair, then traced a finger along the contour of her face.

The two sat beholding each other in the sanguine glow of the lantern's light. The mutual attraction was as raw as it was powerful. Something had happened between them on the dock. She knew he felt it too.

For days, Carmen secretly watched him work around the farm. Now, she seemed wholly unprepared to live out what had only been an impossible fantasy. A vague fear tempered her desire. She felt so open—so vulnerable to this man who seemed to peer into her very soul with eyes that betrayed nothing. She turned and straddled the bench to face him, tentatively lowering her hands into his. The essence of arousal coursed through her like bolts of electricity.

"How were you captured?" she whispered hoarsely, trying to postpone what they both knew was inevitable.

"I don't remember."

She looked into his eyes and saw he spoke the truth.

"In fact, I am not even sure why I am still alive," he let out, then quickly steeled himself so as to reveal nothing more.

"And before you was captured, you see much fightin'?" she asked, clinging tightly to his broad, muscular hands.

He hesitated before answering. " I remember only too well…" his voice trailed off.

A long silence followed.

She searched his face for the slightest clue to his thoughts, but saw none.

Kessel leaned forward and kissed her, his hands lingering on her shoulders. With one even motion, he peeled down the straps of her dress. Her body tensed and shuddered as his hands, then mouth found her breasts. He placed his hands on her slender waist and lifted her onto his lap. Straddling him, she locked her arms around his neck. She reached down, unbuttoned his shirt and pressed her chest to his. Clutched in each other's arms, they began to gently rock to and fro. Flesh moving against flesh, their skin became fiery to the touch. Over and over their hands and lips eagerly sought of each other what they could.

Clenched together, two near strangers—both outsiders amongst their own—found mutual refuge in their passionate delirium.

He stood up with her in his arms and lay her on the quilt. Again and again, one, then the other, cried out to the rhythmic pulse of their lovemaking.

✠   ✠   ✠

Carmen slept perfectly still, hands cupping his shoulders, her long black hair splayed across him. Her soft breath curled across his chest. He gently stroked her forehead, still damp from the passion passed. Kessel watched a silvery patch of moonlight creep across the floor and move up the wall. Finally, when the first rooster crow signaled the coming of dawn, he closed his eyes and allowed himself an hour of shallow sleep.

✠   ✠   ✠

Kessel slipped out of the bed and began to dress. Carmen lay watching his every move. Words failed them both. He looked at her, and turned away. Neither could hope to express what they seemed to be feeling. Again he turned and looked at her as if to speak, then simply ducked through the door.

She listened to the crunching of his foot steps recede up the oyster-shell path.

She'd been with more than a few men since her husband died. Some nights alone she anguished in fear she might be slipping into prostitution.

But never here! Never in this place!

In a very real way, the house was sacred. Sacred, for it remained the sole physical construct of her dashed dreams; the hopes and dreams for a future she knew was never to be. Year after year, she clung to the memories of what once was, while the shanty slowly fell apart around her.

Only after the last footfall faded did she begin to weep.

✠   ✠   ✠

Kessel's bunkmate burst into the work shed. "Konrad!" he panted, having just run from the bus. "Where have you been?!"

"You wouldn't believe me if I told you," Kessel replied, continuing to rewind copper wire around the starter motor armature, the casing of which lay disassembled on the workbench.

"You haven't heard! Everyone is talking!"

"What, do they think I've escaped?"

"Not about you. Besides, the Amis didn't even notice. We covered for you. Good thing we came back today, though. No, we're going home!"

Kessel whirled around. "When?!"

"Tomorrow! We're knocking off at noon today. You're going, too! There's a ship leaving for Buenos Aires. From a place called Newport News."

Kessel said nothing.

"I thought you'd be happy," his bunkmate said, looking confused.

Kessel just glared at him and then, without speaking, returned his attention to his work.

"Never could figure him," the man muttered, shaking his head as he walked back toward his comrades.

✠   ✠   ✠

Kessel finished putting the starter together and carried it to the tractor. Later, when the job was complete, he made his way to where the rest of the men gathered for the buses to pick them up. Their excitement was palpable and many talked eagerly of all the things they planned to do when they finally got home. Off to the side, one man sat alone under a tree, his chin resting on one knee. Kessel made his approach.

"What's your name, soldier?" he asked, effortlessly slipping into a North German dialect.

"Udo Cizinski," the man said without looking up.

"You don't look so happy. What's the matter, don't you want to go home?"

"No, it's not that," he replied after a long pause. It's just, well… I certainly don't like it here, but… I hate Germany."

"Why?"

"For one thing, it's full of Germans. And there's too damn many of them."

"This is true," Kessel agreed. "No family or anything?" he asked, sensing an opportunity.

Again, the man took time to answer. "There was only my mother. But she's gone. Killed in the bombing. I'm not even sure exactly when. I think when we were on the ship coming over." His voice held more bitterness than pain.

"Where was home?" Kessel asked, emphasizing the past tense.

"In the Ruhr. I hear it's a real mess over there."

"Yeah, that corner got it real bad. There's not much left standing, from what I understand."

Cizinski looked up at Kessel. "You're the fellow from South America, aren't you?"

"Konrad Kessel," he said, extending his hand. "From Uruguay, Montevideo, to be exact."

"How'd you land over here? In this place?"

"Believe me, it's a long story."

"What's Montevideo like?" Cizinski asked. "I've never heard much about Uruguay."

"That's because nothing much ever happens there."

"I kind of like that."

"It's warm most of the year, and sunny," Kessel added.

"I like that too."

"It's the restaurants I like the most though. The best Italian kitchens outside Italy, maybe better. And cheap, too."

"I grew up in Italy," Cizinski said, turning to seat himself facing Kessel. "I really don't know why father took us back to Germany—to the Ruhr, of all places. *Gott*, between the rain and the pollution, you don't see the sun for weeks."

"Not much of a place to live," Kessel acknowledged, sensing the man was taking the bait.

After some more small talk he made his play. "If you hate Germany so much, why don't you go somewhere else?"

Cizinski sighed. "Like where?"

"You could go to Uruguay," Kessel said smoothly.

"Yeah, how?"

"Easy. We switch places. You become me and I you. They are going to put me on a freighter bound for Buenos Aires the day after tomorrow. You could go as me."

"Will it work?"

"It can be done," Kessel declared confidently. "I assume they will be issuing identity papers for transit."

"Yeah, that's why we're going back early today."

"Then we just switch. You go up when my name is called, and I do the same when yours comes up."

"It can't be so easy."

"Why not?"

"If you're from Uruguay, then why do you want to go to Germany?" Cizinski suddenly asked, his eyes narrowing slightly.

"Believe me, it's a long story."

"Tell me," he demanded.

"Well, a while back I got into a spot of trouble. Actually there was this woman."

"Naturally."

"Anyway, there was this woman, a girl really. That's sort of what the problem was. It was this honor thing with her brothers, all four of them. You know how it is with these Spaniards—hot tempers, sharp knives and all."

Cizinski smiled. "So I've heard."

"I signed on with a departing merchant ship to give things time to cool down. That's how I ended up here... well, sort of."

"Hasn't it been long enough?"

Kessel pretended to contemplate the question. "I've had plenty of time to think things over during the last few months," he began, sounding pensive. "I ran from home when I was fifteen. Sailed the world over. Landed in South America. You see, I've got family I haven't seen in ten years. My parents run a dairy farm in Schleswig-Holstein. They're getting older and need help, particularly now, after the war and all."

"What if they find out I'm not you?" Cizinski asked, realizing this man was truly serious.

"Just tell them the truth. Tell them I put you up to it. What are they going to do, shoot you? This is America! Believe me, they want to be rid of you just as much as any of us want to leave. The worst thing that can happen is they put you on another ship with the next batch of blokes."

"You're right. I have nothing to lose by trying."

"That's right," Kessel agreed. "Then it's settled?"

"Yeah, I'll do it. I mean, why not?"

"Good."

✠   ✠   ✠

Early the next morning, long before first light, the men of Barracks 42 boarded buses for the ferry terminal at Cape Charles. A festive mood held sway as the government chartered extra plowed across the Chesapeake Bay for Norfolk. At mid-morning, the POWs boarded a troop ship which, just days before, had disgorged a full load of homecoming GIs. By nightfall the ship cleared the Virginia Capes and was steaming northeast across the open Atlantic.

Amongst the many hundreds aboard was the new incarnation of Udo Cizinski.

✠   ✠   ✠

Later that night, deep in the bowels of the ship, few of the soon-to-be ex-POWs slept. Most lay awake in their bunks, wondering how they would begin anew, and what might be left for them amid the smoldering ruins of their shattered land.

Chapter 7

July 20, 1993
Oden's Dock, Hatteras village, North Carolina

CAPTAIN ERIC GREGORY MADE HIS WAY ACROSS THE DESERTED parking lot toward the marina docks. It was just after 5:30 am. He strolled past the row of moored sportfishing boats, palely illuminated by a single mercury vapor lamp. Coffee in hand, he stood at the end of the walkway and gazed beyond the breakwater jetty. Captain Gregory breathed deeply. Not a puff of wind stirred. The waters of Pamlico Sound lay glass calm amidst the velvety shades of the rapidly fading night.

For the past five days, the Outer Banks were buffeted by a rare summertime nor'easter. It was almost a week since any boats were able to go out. The third day was the worst. During the morning, restaurants and gift shops in the village were crowded with sullen-faced tourists seeking refuge from their motel room walls. By afternoon, few even tried to venture outside and brave the relentless winds. The surf crashed on the beaches with a fury normally seen only during the worst late winter storms. On the fourth day, the weather had still not let up. Tempers were running short and there was plenty of ill humor to go around. All Gregory and the other captains could do was wait it out and try not to think of the money they were losing.

Gregory sipped his coffee. Behind him, the marina had come to life. Voices called to each other across the small harbor. Engines burst to life and the sweet scent and guttural hum of idling diesels filled the air. The first of the clients appeared, milling about the parking lot while chattering excitedly in anticipation of the day's fishing.

Gregory walked back toward the *Hawkeye*. He had taken delivery earlier in the year. After half a lifetime of working someone else's boat, Gregory had not fully gotten used to the idea of owning his own. As he did almost every morning, he paused a moment and took in her tapered lines—all forty-seven feet of hand-laid fiberglass. The hull was lovingly sculpted, yet stout to take any wave. Twin 600-horsepower Cummins could make her fly. Short of his only child, Jessica, who was off at college, the *Hawkeye* was everything he loved. Every love has its cost, and this one came with a $200,000 note at eight percent.

Gregory climbed onto the flying bridge and waited impatiently for his mate to show. A few minutes later, Billy Page shuffled down the dock, late as usual. The captain gave the mate his daily lambasting. Billy Page ignored the tirade, busily bringing out rods and icing the fish boxes.

"Gonna get 'em today?" the mate asked, as soon as the captain was through berating him.

"I hope so," Gregory replied gruffly.

The captain and mate were nearly twenty years apart. However, more than age differentiated the two, for their backgrounds and personalities were like night and day. Nonetheless, despite their obvious differences, and outwardly antagonistic relations, the two-man *Hawkeye* crew were best of friends.

Gregory was a relative newcomer on the island. He had drifted onto the Outer Banks as a young man in the early 1960s, finding work on a shrimp boat, then as a mate with the charter fleet before deciding to settle down and make the island home.

The Pages, on the other hand, had lived on Hatteras for gen-
erations. Billy Page's grandmother claimed her ancestors were
among the remnant band of green-eyed Indians reportedly
encountered by the first English settlers to the island chain. Billy
Page didn't really believe he stemmed from a wretched lot of ship-
wrecked sailors cast ashore on an unexplored island to take up
with the local savages—though it did make for a good story.

Billy Page was an easy-going type with an appreciation of life's
simple pleasures. While many young people left for the mainland,
Billy Page was content to stay. In fact, at 27 years of age, he had
only been off the Outer Banks a half dozen or so times, mostly for
court dates.

Billy Page had unkempt, blondish hair and a light, almost wiry
build. Always in need of a shave, he never seemed to be without a
several-day growth of facial hair. No more, no less. The ever-pres-
ent stubble showed yellow highlights that stood in contrast to his
deeply tanned face.

Despite Billy Page's relatively small size and apparent mild
demeanor, he was not a person anyone on the island would want
to cross.

While the mate was as modest as any man, the captain was a
gregarious sort. At six foot, three inches and 240 pounds, with
wavy, bright orange hair, he made an imposing impression on anyone he met. Gregory's fair complexion, however, was hardly suited
for a life under the sun. Nonetheless, his trademark floral hat and
wrap-around sunglasses seemed to complement his perpetually
sunburned face.

Gregory could spin sea stories with the best. His outrageous
tales and infectious humor could make the hours pass, even on
the slowest of fishing days. Truly one of a kind, women loved him
and men sought his company. Captain Eric Gregory was loud,
irreverent and perhaps more than a little vain. He also was, hands
down, the best charter boat captain on Hatteras Island.

✠   ✠   ✠

Fishing was good before the storm. Business could have been
better. The *Hawkeye* was anything but fully booked and Gregory

had fallen behind on his loan payments. But if the captain was worried, he hardly showed it. Gregory waved his clients aboard with a broad grin and a round of handshakes. The party consisted of construction company executives from Washington, DC. They were regulars at the marina, to whom the *Hawkeye* had come highly recommended. Gregory knew he had to build his client base, and steady customers were hard to come by. He had to have good day.

Expectations ran high as the *Hawkeye* roared through Hatteras Inlet headed for the Gulf Stream. Within an hour, the lines were overboard. Gregory trolled in a zigzag course along the edge of the underwater canyons, confident they'd soon find the action.

An hour passed. Then another. Gregory ordered the lines in and headed north, ever watchful for a color change, a variance in water temperature—any clue to help them find fish.

The sun climbed higher into the July sky. As the day got brighter, the Gulf Stream waters turned an even darker shade of blue. It was a hue like none other on earth. Ever changing from day to day, this morning the warm waters radiated a dark cobalt, which at times seemed almost black. Even after more than a thousand trips offshore, Gregory could still marvel at the abrupt color change marking the west wall of the Gulf Stream. To this day, he'd never forgotten the first time he'd beheld the crystalline river of tropical water flowing freely across the open seas.

A school of flying fish broke surface just off the port side. The creatures scooted overtop the swells, their winglike fins glinting in the bright sunlight. Gregory wheeled the boat across their path, sure that some hungry predator lurked just below the breaking fish. Nothing. He kept a straight course, then circled around. Finally, the outrigger clip gave way with an abrupt twang.

"Fish on!" the mate yelled.

All five clients eagerly vied for the rod. A minute later, the small dolphin fish lay flapping in the box—hardly a prize after two hours of trolling, especially considering the heavy tackle they were using.

Gregory made another pass over the same area. "Must have been a solitary fish," he called down from the bridge. "Loners are usually a lot bigger. Got some really nice ones before the blow."

Two of the clients mumbled something to each other. Gregory scanned the horizon. Everything looked so good when they'd first gotten out. Some days are just like this, he thought.

He tried a different spot. Still nothing. The air back in the cockpit was hot, and the mood decidedly unfriendly. Grumbling about the lack of fish, the clients sat shirtless amid the coolers swilling beers, their flaccid bodies glistening pink in the mid-day sun.

"You fellas want to try inshore?" Gregory finally asked, knowing they had but an hour left. "Looks pretty beat out here."

At first no one said anything. Then two of the men nodded in agreement. The others began to debate the merits of paying for a Gulf Stream trip, only to fish inshore.

"Okay, let's do it," one of them, whom Gregory figured to be the trip leader, shouted up to the bridge.

"Billy, you heard the gentleman, bring in the lines," Gregory called down to the mate.

As soon as Billy Page was done, Gregory put the boat under full throttle. Twelve hundred horses of power dug in and the big sportfisherman took off at a clean 35 knots. This ought to wake them up, he thought.

Gregory knew most every captain on the island and was tight with the commercials. He'd heard a surprising number of large king mackerel had been taken fairly close in just before the storm hit. Whether or not they were still there was anyone's guess. He knew it was a gamble, but he had a hunch it might just pay off.

Before long, the thin line of Hatteras Island appeared on the horizon. Gregory eased back on the throttles and switched on the depthfinder. In short order Billy Page had the lures in the water.

Gregory stood on the bridge, surveying the surrounding water. He curled his fingers around the bridge railing. Gregory had the gift truly good fishermen seem to have—that being the sense of knowing just when something was about to happen. Clues were subtle. A nervous splash of a single small bait fish or the briefest, hovering hesitation of a seabird in flight. Perhaps it was a faint, slow-moving shadow caught out of the corner of the eye. Or a barely perceptible gloss on the water—oil given off by the savaged bodies of bait fish being fed upon far below the surface.

"Heads up, Billy boy," Gregory cautioned the mate. "I think we're on them."

Suddenly the bottom alarm on the depth-finder let out its shrill electronic whine.

"What the hell?"

In nearly the same instant, two of the trolled lures disappeared in a frothing spray.

"Fish on! Two fish!" the mate cried.

Chaos broke out in the cockpit. Two clients struggled with the rods that were nearly doubled over the side of the boat while the other men enthusiastically offered instruction and encouragement. After a spirited fight, two amberjack, each almost 60 pounds, were brought to the gaff. Gregory motored back to the same spot and cut the engines. This time the clients broke out lighter tackle with which to throw surface plugs. The first cast resulted in an instant hook-up. The explosive strike was met with howls of delight. Ninety minutes later, two more big jacks were in the cooler, and they fought and released a dozen or so more. Gregory did his best to control the pandemonium, maneuvering the boat while shouting incessantly at both his mate and clients. Finally, all were too exhausted to even try and take another fish.

"Well folks," the captain bellowed from the bridge. "I think we've had a good day."

A round of applause came up from the cockpit. Billy Page quickly put away the gear. Gregory smiled at the scene below. Everyone settled back to a round of cold beers. Each battle was already being relived, complete with hand gestures and appropriate sound effects. Gregory punched in the GPS coordinates before making for the inlet.

Over the next few weeks, Gregory made a point to stop over the same location if he needed to round out an offshore day. He also made good on several half-day inshore trips and it was not long before other captains got wind something was up. Gregory, however, remained characteristically vague as to how he'd been finding the action. In the close-knit but highly competitive world of the Hatteras charter boat fleet, the coordinates of some uncharted bottom structure, particularly one that consistently held fish, might as well be the recipe for the Manhattan Project.

✠   ✠   ✠

Jessica chose the first two weeks of August to come and visit from Chapel Hill. Born of his tempestuous, short-lived first and only marriage, Gregory's daughter had grown up with her mother in Ohio. Gregory lost touch for a number of years after his ex-wife moved out of state. It was only recently he and Jessica had become close again, and her annual visits were fast becoming a cherished summertime tradition for them both.

In the time they had not seen each other, Jessica had remained a child in her father's mind. During those years, she had blossomed into a woman and Gregory was at a loss for words when she appeared unannounced at his door one afternoon.

His daughter had her mother's delicate features and ashen-blonde hair, cut at shoulder length. Little of his Scottish blood seemed to show for her skin was always tanned. She carried the same bouncy, free-spirited personality he once loved in her mother. All in all, Jessica so reminded him of his ex-wife it took him a good while to feel comfortable around her.

Unfortunately, this visit coincided with the onset of a heat wave. By Jessica's second day, a stifling calm settled over the island. The Gulf Stream moved close to shore and the air felt downright tropical. What little breeze each afternoon could muster pushed the gulf waters in even further until they were nearly on the beach. Day after day, the Atlantic lay down, shimmering turquoise like a Caribbean flat. Mornings began clear and bright with puffy white clouds dotting the horizon. By midday, temperatures soared into the nineties and most everyone sought shelter indoors or under shade. An eerie stillness filled the blistering afternoons; a silence broken only by the occasional drone of high flying aircraft or the passing buzz of a stray dragonfly.

✠   ✠   ✠

With not much to do during the latter part of the day, Jessica took to waiting for her father to come home from the marina, then fixing him a sandwich.

"So when we going fishing, Daddy?" Jessica asked as soon as he walked through the door.

He had been looking forward to taking her out on the new boat ever since she'd arrived, and his party for the next day canceled. "How about tomorrow?" he suggested while easing himself into his sofa chair. "Maybe when the sun gets a little lower. We could make an evening of it."

"That's cool," Jessica replied.

"Cool," Gregory echoed, before taking a bite of the sandwich and reaching for the television remote.

✠   ✠   ✠

Billy Page met them in the parking lot. After a short ride out through the inlet, Gregory slowed the boat to trolling speed.

"This is the spot, Jessie," he called out, continually shifting his attention between the GPS unit and the depth-finder. "Billy, get the rods ready."

Standing on the bridge, Gregory looked down into the slick water along the shaded, lee side of the hull and was mildly shocked to see bottom. Ripples of sand were clearly visible some seventy feet down. Gregory again referenced his electronics, thinking he may have erred in positioning the boat. He cast a reaffirming glance toward shore.

Gregory looked back into the water to have a huge dark shape fill his vision. For a moment he thought a whale passed under the boat. He cupped his hands around his temples. Squinting, he could make out the narrow deck of a steel-hulled vessel, lying slightly to one side.

"I'll be damned," Gregory said softly. "So that's what we've been…," his words stopped short.

As the *Hawkeye* drifted, the blue-green form of a U-boat moved through his view like an image scrolled across a TV monitor. The tapered stern was clearly discernible. Then came the conning tower, followed by the outline of a cannon barrel silhouetted against light-colored sand covering that portion of the deck. Most of the bow appeared to be buried. Gregory made out the very prow just before losing sight of the wreck under the hull of his own boat. He bolted upright, wincing from the sudden glare.

"Jesus, Eric!" Billy Page called out from the cockpit. "You okay? You look like you just seen a ghost or somethin'."

Gregory rubbed his eyes.

"Daddy! What's the matter?"

"It's nothing, Jessie," he stammered. "I just think we should try somewhere else."

Chapter 8

GREGORY STOPPED OFF AT THE MIDGETTE MART AND PICKED UP frozen pizza to have for dinner. Once back in the truck, he sat absently behind the wheel with the key in the ignition. Earlier, he had dropped Jessica off at some friends'. Although she promised not to be late, he doubted he would see her until the next evening. He pushed thoughts of his daughter from his mind and tried to focus on the events of the afternoon.

I've fished these waters for twenty-some years and never knew the thing was out there, he thought. The image of the sunken submarine kept flashing through his mind. The view of the wreck was so vividly clear he began to think it might have been a hallucination. For an instant, Gregory feared he might be slipping. He quickly recounted finding the wreck, then fishing it a half dozen or more times. "No, I'm not going crazy," he said aloud. "Oh, great, now I'm talking to myself!"

Gregory fired the engine, wheeled the truck around and headed for the house.

Captain Eric Gregory was not a man easily bothered. Yet driving home, he felt strangely apprehensive. Somehow, he wished he hadn't seen what he had. Some things should be left as they are, he repeatedly thought. Driving on, he wished the mark on the depth-finder had remained just that—an anonymous blip on a liquid crystal display screen—the electronic echo of some long forgotten vessel, one of hundreds scattered across the Graveyard of the Atlantic. Just a place to fish.

✠   ✠   ✠

Gregory told no one what he had seen. His mate, however, knew something was up. Billy Page could not recall ever seeing his captain act as strangely as he had the afternoon when they'd pulled off the wreck. He'd been waiting for an explanation, but none was forthcoming.

"Eric, what got into you the day we took your kid out?" Billy Page casually asked one afternoon, while scrubbing and hosing down the boat.

"I didn't like the spot."

Billy Page had a habit of prying into one's most personal matters, while pretending not to be the least bit interested. "I dunno," he pressed on, "I was just wondering why we moved, that's all."

"It's nothing."

"Come on," Billy Page said, his voice taking an edge. "What's up, Bubba?"

Gregory put down the wrench he was working with and ran his fingers through his orange mane. "Well," he began slowly, "you know the wreck we've been fishing, the one we first hit all the amberjack at."

"With the fat guys?"

"That's right. Well I got a good look at it the other day when the water was so clear."

"And?"

"It's a submarine."

"What kind of submarine?" Billy Page asked, seemingly unimpressed.

"A German submarine, a U-boat!" Gregory exclaimed. "What else could it be?"

"And this has got you all bent outta shape?"

"It's just weird. I've been fishing these waters for twenty-some years. Never known it to be out there. It's like it just popped up out of nowhere or something."

"That is pretty weird," the mate agreed. "You don't suppose it's been buried in the sand do you?"

"I've thought about that."

Both men continued with their work. Billy Page scrubbed the cockpit area while the captain resumed tinkering with the throttle controls. The mate stopped scrubbing, leaned on the brush handle and said, "You know what that could mean, don't you?"

"What?"

"It means the thing may never have been dived on. There could be some really good shit in there."

"Don't think I haven't thought about it."

The mate raised the hose and began to spray down the cockpit.

What do you think we could get from it?" Gregory asked, after a minute or so passed.

Billy Page coiled the hose. "I've always wanted a Luger," he said wistfully, not unlike a kid wishing for a candy bar.

"I didn't ask you what you wanted!" Gregory snapped. "How can we make some money?!"

Billy Page ignored the minor outburst. "Hardware, plates and dishes. Anything with eagles and swastikas. People will pay good money for that kind of stuff. Maybe we could even get the periscope off."

Gregory took in the thought. "The thing to do is get a close look at it," he said.

"You know who you need to talk to then. Your buddy Preston. He'll want a piece of the action, but he could tell us exactly what we could do. Preston's the pro. Talk to the man, Eric. "

"I'd rather not," Gregory said plainly.

✠   ✠   ✠

Gregory spread the chart out on the kitchen table and carefully plotted the coordinates of the submarine wreck. He stared at the pencil mark before rolling out a second chart showing most of the wrecks, as well as major bottom features all along the continental shelf. Just as he suspected, nothing was indicated anywhere in the vicinity of where he'd seen the sub.

Hunched over the charts, Gregory felt a sudden tingle of excitement. He leaned back in the chair, relishing the sense of discovery that came over him. It was a heady, privileged feeling, quite unlike anything he'd ever known.

Gregory reached for a small stack of books he'd picked up at the Burrus Red and White Supermarket on the way home. They were glossy paperback publications meant primarily for the tourist trade. He opened *The Atlantic Turkey Shoot: German U-boats Off the Outer Banks* and found himself engrossed by the accounts the fateful spring of 1942 when ship after ship fell victim to German torpedoes. Gregory had heard old-timers talk about the war years, but never really paid much attention. Photographs of familiar places, as well as the faces of those who fought, suddenly made it all very real. Gregory hardly noticed it was after eleven. He leafed through both volumes of Shipwrecks of North Carolina, pausing on the service photos of the lost vessels. Gregory studied the lines of the *U-85*, sunk off Nags Head in 1943. He lingered on an aerial view of the tanker *Dixie Arrow*, adrift and burning fiercely under calm, sunny skies. The caption stated much of the crew was lost to the oily inferno.

It was well after midnight. Gregory rolled up the charts and stacked the books. He went back to the bedroom, lay down and tried to sleep.

✠   ✠   ✠

Preston Sinclair was a man whose given name hardly fit his rough-edged persona. Forty-something with a stout frame, an oversized graying mustache and short, greasy ponytail, he looked every bit like a biker.

Gregory found him behind the house working on an outboard motor. Preston Sinclair's property was essentially a salvage lot, with various pieces of equipment, cast-off machinery and miscellaneous junk items strewn about. A derelict-looking military surplus ambulance stood in the back corner of the cluttered yard. In the other corner, a dented aircraft drop tank lay amid a mass of tent poles and lawn chair frames. Beside that was a chicken-wire fence enclosing a mound of crushed beverage cans the size of a

Volkswagen Beetle. "My rainy day fund," Sinclair would say to anyone who asked why he never cashed in his aluminum hoard.

Gregory and Sinclair were once close friends. Years ago, they'd had a falling out that came to blows. Some folks said it was over a woman. Truth of the matter be known, Hatteras Island simply was not big enough for both their egos. Though things supposedly were patched up, they never really had much to say to each other since.

Gregory watched him work, fully aware that Sinclair knew he was standing behind him.

"Eric!" Sinclair exclaimed, still hunched over the outdoor workbench. He dropped the socket drive he had in his hand and reached for a rag. "What a pleasant surprise."

Sinclair finished wiping his hands before turning to face his visitor. Gregory saw he wore a torn, faded T-shirt with "Surf Naked" printed on the front. It was too small and did not quite cover his bulging midsection. A pale crescent of belly peeked out from above the waistline.

"What's up?" Sinclair grinned.

"I thought maybe I could talk to you about something," Gregory replied somewhat hesitantly.

"Any time old buddy. Whaddya say we go inside?"

The two made their way around the side of the weathered clapboard dwelling. Sinclair's house stood on the edge of Buxton Woods, north of Frisco. Tucked in from the main road and surrounded by dense stands of vine-covered trees, the lot gave the impression of a jungle clearing. The haphazard growth perforating the yard added to the effect.

While Sinclair claimed to be a salvage operator, underwater demolition was his true specialty. If the Coast Guard needed a navigation hazard removed, they knew who to call. Preston Sinclair was an artist with high explosives, with C-4 far and away his favorite medium. It was a skill acquired during an eight-year stint as a Navy SEAL.

Other than a small hand-painted sign by the main road that read SINCLAIR'S MARINE SALVAGE AND SMALL ENGINE REPAIR, Sinclair did not advertise. Work came to him. He managed to pull himself together to do a job about every eighteen months or so. That would usually hold him over for about a year. The rest of the time he would tinker about, pretending to run a repair business.

✠   ✠   ✠

With the windows curtained, it took a moment for Gregory's eyes to adjust to the dim interior light. He saw the inside was as cluttered as the yard. The living room was furnished in a mixture of nineteenth century heirlooms, a 1960s lime green vinyl sofa and Wal•Mart ready-to-assemble cabinets and shelves. An assortment of junk items filled most available floor space. Looking around, Gregory felt like he was standing in a thrift store.

They made their way to the kitchen.

"Long time, no see, Eric," Sinclair said, reaching into the refrigerator for a couple of fresh Coors. "How ya been?"

"Pretty good," Gregory replied, palming the ice-cold beer that came sliding across the counter.

Sinclair seated himself at the small Formica covered kitchen table, carefully maneuvering his considerable mass between the legs of the folding metal frame. He looked up at Gregory from underneath a greasy, turquoise-brimmed Miami Dolphins cap. His pale eyes were bracketed by deep crow's feet. Grayish stubble covered the lower half of his leathery face.

Gregory joined him at the table.

"So what's this you want to talk about?" Sinclair asked. His teeth showed a yellow cast.

Gregory cleared his throat. "Well, lemme start from the beginning. This summer, I've been fishing a wreck. Didn't think much of it, really, but it's kind of strange 'cause I'd never known it to be there. And it's not on any chart I've seen."

Sinclair listened with obvious interest.

"Back when it was so calm, I got a look at the thing from the surface."

"How deep?" Sinclair cut in.

"About seventy feet, maybe a little less. But listen, I looked down from the bridge and saw it was a submarine. Just lying there on the bottom like a toy or something. It seemed in perfect shape."

Sinclair shifted in the chair and ran his fingers across his stubbly chin.

"So I've been doing a little research trying to get a handle on it but haven't come up with anything. Now I know about the *U-85* off Nags Head..."

Sinclair cut him off in mid sentence. "Where is it?"

"Just off Diamond Shoals."

"What's it look like?"

"I think I saw a deck gun. It had to be a U-boat. This close, I just don't know why it's not charted." Gregory paused. "You don't suppose it could have been buried in the sand all this time, do you?"

Sinclair leaned across the table. "You're sure of what you saw?"

"Yes, I'm sure!"

"It's not only possible, it's probably exactly what's going on. The shoals change all the time. You know that. We just don't know what all's out there."

The two men sat quietly for a moment. Each knew the other's thoughts, but neither wanted to be the first to speak.

"So why are you telling me this?" Sinclair finally said, knowing full well why his old friend was sitting at his table. He relished the fact Gregory came to him for assistance, and he wanted to hear him ask for it.

"Cut the crap Preston!" Gregory snapped. "I'm talking business here. This thing could make us money."

Sinclair nodded approvingly.

"Look," Gregory sighed, giving in. "I got a kid in college. With the new boat and all, things have been pretty damn tight. I got the coordinates. You got the know-how. I thought maybe we could work somethin' out."

Sinclair leaned back in his chair. His face broke into a wide grin. "First we'll have to get a closer look, you know, just to make sure you haven't been getting too much sun again."

Gregory ignored the crack.

Sinclair tilted back his beer, downing the remaining contents in one long gulp. "When can we go out?" he asked, exhaling deliberately and wiping his chin.

"How about Monday? I ain't booked and Billy can dive with you."

"You got yourself a deal."

✠   ✠   ✠

Billy Page was first at the dock. He carefully placed his air tank on the weathered creosote planks and tossed the bundled wet suit onto the deck of the *Hawkeye*. Billy Page did most of the minor prop and hull work around the marina. It had been a long time, however, since he'd done an open water dive. He'd been looking forward to today and couldn't wait to see this mystery wreck for himself. Gregory and Sinclair pulled up almost simultaneously and the mate helped get the gear on board.

Preston Sinclair was all business. Gone was the boorishness and smart attitude of the week before. There was a crispness to his every move.

In a matter of minutes everything was stowed. Billy Page freed the mooring ropes and Gregory backed the *Hawkeye* out of her berth.

"You say this thing is about 70 feet down?" Sinclair half-shouted over the burbling diesels.

Gregory began to fiddle with the GPS. "More or less. The bottom is uneven."

"What's the water been like?"

"Been kinda dirty," Gregory replied, guiding the boat through the narrow breakwater jetty. "I don't think the current's gonna be bad today, though. I'm gonna try to put us right over top. You and Billy can follow the anchor line down."

Sinclair grunted an acknowledgment.

The morning was cloudy and nearly wind-still. With the seas down, the *Hawkeye* made short work of the eight mile run. Gregory throttled back and began to circle the site, probing with the depth-finder.

The anchor splashed overboard and line raced from the drum. It hit bottom and they swung to face the current. Gregory cut the engines.

"This is it, boys," he exclaimed. "She's right under us. I couldn't 'a got y'ail any closer."

Billy Page and Sinclair began to suit up. For Sinclair, it was no easy task. Gregory thought the straining wet suit would burst apart before Sinclair finally managed to zip in his bulging midriff. The divers helped each other with the air tanks. Sinclair talked incessantly as he worked, belting out instructions and verbally checking off equipment. He strapped on a flashlight before wetting and adjusting his mask. Billy Page and Gregory watched him go over the side of the boat and disappear beneath the surface. The mate sat down on the gunwale, flashed a grin, bit down on the regulator mouthpiece and rolled backwards.

With the divers overboard, Gregory found himself alone in the cockpit and was struck by how quiet it suddenly was. With a bit of a start, he realized it was only the second time he'd been on the *Hawkeye* by himself. He distinctly liked the feeling. Gregory flopped into the fighting chair and put his feet up. A light breeze slapped the waves against the side of the hull. His boat heaved slowly in the gentle seas.

✠   ✠   ✠

Sinclair and Page worked their way down the anchor line. A recent storm had stirred the water and visibility was limited, perhaps 30 feet at best.

As they descended, a huge cloud of bait fish passed overhead, momentarily darkening the surrounding waters. Several toothy predators lingered along the edge of the school. Both men eyed a small hammerhead shark as it lazily finned by, seemingly oblivious to the intruders in its domain.

A dark shape materialized below. As the divers worked their way down the line, the hulking form grew larger until it took up their entire field of vision. Gregory was right, Sinclair thought. He couldn't have gotten them any closer. The anchor lay dug into the bottom mere yards from the wreck.

The two divers hovered along the down-current side of the hull. Both stared at the conning tower looming before them, then exchanged wide-eyed nods. Billy Page was keenly aware of his breathing. It was quite rapid and clouds of bubbles rushed up past his mask. Sinclair, too, was flabbergasted. Somehow he'd had his doubts about the whole thing and was not prepared for the sight that lay before them.

The upper portion of the conning tower was encrusted with sponges, barnacles and a variety of marine growth. Behind the bridge, the railings that once enclosed the half-deck and anti-air-craft mount were splayed out at crazy angles. The twisted steel rods were covered in long, hair-like strands that fluttered slowly in the current. A clear break in the growth was visible near the base of the conning tower. Below that line, the exposed portions of the wreck appeared virtually clean, and in remarkably good condi-tion. These areas were just beginning to be colonized. Patches of bottom paint were visible on the lower reaches of the hull.

The vessel lay partially on one side, leaning away from the div-ers. Sinclair noted the deck pitched downward at an angle, which would leave the bow buried. The aft section rose slightly, disap-pearing into a blue-green twilight.

The whole area teemed with marine life. Along a featureless, sandy bottom, any structure is a magnet for most everything that swims. Small fish are the first to arrive, seeking shelter and feed-ing on growth the wreck supports. Larger fish are soon drawn in and within a short time, the newly lost vessel is transformed into a minor reef community.

Billy Page looked around. Hordes of bait fish congregated on the lee side of the hull. Pods of bluefish attentively patrolled the edges of the wreck while a large cobia lingered overhead, ever watchful for a chance at an easy meal.

Sinclair motioned Billy Page to follow him aft. The underside of the hull tapered toward the stern, leaving the bronze screws hanging just off the bottom. Amazingly, both looked as if they had just been fitted. Each was devoid of growth and bore a dull luster where shifting sand scoured the metal. Sinclair circled the twin rudders while Billy Page peered into a stern torpedo tube.

Sinclair motioned to the front of the wreck. The conning tower again loomed into view, then receded behind them. Sinclair realized he had lost his dive partner. He doubled back to find Billy Page hunkered down behind the deck gun. Billy Page gripped the breech lock with both hands and brought his fins up under the recoil dampers. Again, Sinclair waved him forward. Billy Page let go with one hand, raised it over his head and began moving it in circles like a rodeo rider. Sinclair just shook his head.

As Sinclair had surmised, most of the bow lay buried, with only the very prow protruding from the sand. They turned back, following the narrow deck plates to the conning tower.

Something caught Sinclair's eye as the two men worked their way past the shattered bridge. Just below the line demarcating the old and new growth, a patch of light gray paint was visible. He unsheathed his knife and began to scrape away at the fine film covering that portion of the conning tower. Sinclair recognized a faint image of the number four, standing approximately two feet tall. More a stain on the heavily oxidized steel than anything else, the hazy form was enhanced by but a few flecks of paint. Part of a second digit was also visible. Sinclair moved back a few feet, pointing to the number. Billy Page reached for his knife and both men began to carefully clean the surrounding areas.

Sinclair motioned his partner back. He slouched down and moved his head aside so the dull light filtering from overhead lay obliquely across the conning tower. The vestigial image of the entire number was then discernible. It read: *U-491.*

✠   ✠   ✠

Billy Page burst through the surface just off the bow of the *Hawkeye.*

"That was intense, man!" he yelled, taking in a mouthful of water. He coughed loudly and struggled to clear his regulator.

Gregory bolted from the fighting chair in a momentary panic. He had been fast asleep. The sun had come out and his body was wet with perspiration.

Sinclair came to the surface directly behind the mate. They made their way around to the stern. Gregory tossed a small rope ladder over the transom and helped the two men with the air tanks. Billy Page was the first back into the boat.

"Eric, you should see this thing! It's all there, baby!" he burst out as soon as he caught his breath.

Gregory shot Sinclair a probing look.

"This is good," Sinclair said. "This is very good."

✠   ✠   ✠

The three men sat around Sinclair's kitchen table. Gregory heard all about the dive on the way in, yet insisted they again describe in detail everything they saw on the bottom.

"So you're sure it's a German sub?" Gregory insisted. "Could it be something else? You said it looked almost new."

"Of course I'm sure, damn it!" Sinclair blurted. "Sure as I'm sitting here. I dived on the *U-85* again and again during the '70s—picked it over pretty good, too. I know a U-boat when I see one. And we got an ID! I'm telling you, we saw the number on the conning tower—*U-491*, clear as day... well, almost."

Gregory turned to his mate who nodded enthusiastically.

"So what we do next?" Gregory asked. "Preston, how can we make some money offa this?"

"The first thing we do is not tell anyone what we saw today," Sinclair stated firmly. He looked over at Gregory. "Eric, how many people know about this?"

"They're sitting here. Me, you and Billy."

"Good. Let's keep it that way."

Chapter 9

A SMALL CRAFT ADVISORY HAD BEEN POSTED THE NIGHT BEFORE.
By 6:00 am, Marine Warnings were out for the offshore waters. A
strong cold front pushed across the coast and, coupled with low
pressure over the Canadian Maritimes, the system was produc-
ing northerly winds of near gale force. Skies remained clear and
sunny, however. Gregory met his party at the dock and informed
them they had to scrub for the day. It was never an easy thing to
do. Some of the group had driven hundreds of miles for a day offshore, or planned their summer vacation around the trip. Gregory
assured them that they could reschedule at the earliest open date
and the fishing would only be better later in the fall.

With the fleet in, most of the marina had the day off. It was
also Jessica's last day on the island, for the semester was about to
start. Back at the house, Gregory helped her to the car with her
luggage.

Their time together passed so quickly, he thought. Summer
was his busiest season. Except for the one afternoon on the water,
it seemed they hardly saw each other. Gregory felt a twinge of
regret as he placed the suitcases in the trunk. Next year, he vowed,
I'll make more time.

"Thanks, Daddy," she said, throwing her arms around his hefty waist.

"Study hard, Darling, and be careful. You know what it's like these days."

She pushed herself away saying, "Daddy, I wasn't born yesterday."

"No, not yesterday, not quite."

"Not to worry," Jessica said, closing the car door.

She rolled down the window to flash her mother's smile. Gregory watched his daughter back out of the driveway, waving to him all the while. He raised his hand and waved back. The car turned, stopped and sped away.

Feeling more than a little wistful, Gregory lingered in front of the house. The modest saltbox was clad in graying cedar shakes with windows and trim neatly painted white. Also freshly painted was the large screened porch that wrapped three sides of the building. An overgrown bayberry hedge bordered the small yard, the front of which was lined by sun-bleached whalebones.

Gregory climbed the porch steps and was about to go inside when he spotted Sinclair's truck turning in off the main road. "Oh shit!" he sighed.

The miserably rusted out International Harvester pickup came careening up the sand drive. Most of the back of the truck had long since fallen away and the bed consisted of salvaged, salt-treated boards bolted directly to the frame rails. Tires were nearly bald and every window cracked or dinged. As best as Gregory could tell, the cab may once have been blue, but he couldn't be sure. Billy Page was riding shotgun. Even from a distance, Gregory could tell they'd been drinking.

The two spilled from the cab. Billy Page wore only flip-flops, shorts and wayfarer sunglasses. Sinclair had on the same shirt as the week before.

"Eric! " Billy Page called out, making his way toward him. "Preston's got a plan. Wait'll you hear 'bout this!"

Sinclair stumbled up the steps and eased himself onto the glider that sat on one end of the porch. Billy Page remained standing.

Gregory folded his arms across his chest. "Okay, what's this you've come up with?"

Sinclair rocked back and forth. "The first thing we need to do is try to get inside," he said, grinning. "I was hoping we could go back out again soon. We really need to know what kind of shape the inside is in."

"I'll have to check my schedule. I'm booked through next week for sure."

"Sometime soon anyway. If we could get inside, we might can get some stuff out right away. Stash it at my place. I'll make the calls and we'll split everything three ways."

"We'll figure the details later," Gregory sighed. "What's this plan of yours?"

Sinclair's expression turned serious. "I've dived on two U-boats," he said evenly. "The *U-85* was okay. Didn't do so well on the *701*. If this thing is virgin, there's bound to be some stuff on board. I'm just not sure it would be worth our while, though."

"What do you mean?" Gregory snapped, obviously irritated and not at all sure what Sinclair was getting at.

"I mean it's not gonna make us rich."

"I never said anything about getting rich! What the hell are you talking about?!"

Gregory shot a glance at his mate, who just grinned back at him.

"Feature this," Sinclair said, bringing both hands up over his head and splaying his fingers. "We go out there and raise the fucker! The whole thing—all at once. Sell it to the highest bidder. A complete Nazi sub! I'm looking at seven figures here. Big, big numbers. Whaddya think?"

Gregory blinked at Sinclair in complete disbelief. "I think you're drunk, that's what I think!" he bellowed. "Raise it?! You? Just like that?!"

"Why not?"

"Why not? What's the biggest thing you ever brought off the bottom? What?!"

"A fifty-four-foot trawler," Sinclair replied, sounding defensive.

"And how deep?"

"About 15 feet but that's beside the point."

"In the harbor! And you think you're gonna go out there and just pull up a thousand-and-some-ton submarine?"

"It's been done before," Billy Page interjected.

"A lot of things have been done before," Gregory half yelled. "Jesus! I finally have a day to myself and you guys have to come over here and waste my time!"

"Eric, he's got a plan!" the mate protested.

Gregory scowled at Sinclair.

"A submarine should be easy," Sinclair began, unfazed by Gregory's tirade. "Surface ships are watertight only on the underside."

"Uh-huh," Gregory said sarcastically.

"Once they fill up and go down, what can you do? Submarines are different. They're supposed to be underwater. All we have to do is make the thing tight, force the water out, and she comes up like a cork. Then we tow her to, say, Moorehead."

"You're a flake!" Gregory snapped. "A flake and a drunk! I can't believe I'm even listening to this horseshit."

Sinclair rose to his feet. "You know what your problem is, Eric?" he growled, his voice steadily gaining strength. "You don't think big! No vision! Things are always just fine and dandy the way they are."

"Listen," Gregory shot back, trying to keep his anger in check. "I got my dick sticking out a quarter million bucks and you're telling me I ain't got no balls! I got a business to take care of, that's what I got! I don't sit on my ass drinkin' beer all day. You got some nerve gettin' on my case."

Gregory turned to face the driveway, sliding both hands into his back pockets. "I came to you because I thought we might make a little money, that's all," he said, still looking away. "And now you're going off half-cocked on some fuckin' fantasy. I shoulda known."

Sinclair kept talking at Gregory's back. "It's no fantasy, Eric, just listen to me. I didn't say it was gonna be easy. But I'm sure we can do it. Here's the plan. It'll take two barges and a tug, two cranes and some heavy-duty compressors."

"And where are you gonna get a tug and some barges?"

"We need some backing, I'll get to that. First step is we seal her up—weld the hatches if they ain't tight, custom form some drop plate to cover any failures in the hull. Then we cut into the steel and bolt in couplers for air hoses. Once everything is secure, we crank up the compressors and force out as much water as we can."

Gregory wheeled around and eyed Sinclair, who continued with his pitch.

"If she doesn't float up, we rig the cranes bow and stern and give her a boost."

"And when she's up?" Gregory asked. The anger seemed to have dissipated.

"There're two 10,000 gallon steel tanks sitting behind the Texaco. Just been replaced. I know where I can get at least two more. We rig 'em with seacocks and couplers, flood 'em to neutral buoyancy, maneuver 'em to either side so they're wedged against the pressure hull and the raised deck. Chain 'em down with come-alongs and heavy-duty turn buckles, then clear 'em. That'll give us all the flotation we need, along with extra stability. Just for good measure, we run a hose or two along the tow lines and keep the compressors going."

"And then?"

"We pull her to where we can get her out of the water. Either in dry dock or on a railway. If not in Moorehead, then Newport News."

Gregory folded his hands together. Somehow the concept no longer seemed quite so ridiculous. As outrageous as the plan was, it almost seemed plausible.

"It just might work," Billy Page added.

"It might work," Gregory said carefully. "But would it pay?"

Sinclair reached into his shirt pocket and pulled out a folded sheet of paper saying, "I'm looking at about a hundred thousand dollars to do this."

"And you really think someone would pay that kind of money for a rusty old German submarine?"

"Eric," Sinclair said earnestly, "I wouldn't even try to pull something like this off if I didn't have a buyer already lined up. Trust me on this one."

Gregory could not believe he was actually beginning to take Preston Sinclair even half seriously.

"What do ya think?" Billy Page asked.

Gregory glanced at his mate, winking twice. "I don't know. Maybe we could make enough money to buy Preston here a new truck."

"Ain't nothing wrong with my truck!" Sinclair snapped.

Gregory turned earnest. "There's one major problem I could foresee," he said guardedly. "What if the hull's full of sand?"

"Then all bets are off. We'll know when we get inside. When can we go back out?"

✠   ✠   ✠

The mood on the Outer Banks, though not yet tense, was one of expectant caution. Hurricane Emily, already a major storm packing winds over a hundred miles an hour, was churning through the eastern Caribbean. The latest forecast models had it tracking straight for Bermuda. Emily was also gaining strength with every passing day. Over the last few years, the Carolina coast had seen a number of close calls. It had been quite some time, however, since the last direct hit.

Gregory had a bad feeling about this one. He was not alone. Talk of the storm track was the main topic of conversation all about the island.

Even though the hurricane was still many hundreds of miles away, the first effects were already making themselves known. Rolling swells greeted the *Hawkeye* as it passed through Hatteras Inlet. Once out in open water, though, seas were less noticeable. The boat raced along, cresting each lazy swell before easing into the following trough. From the bridge, Gregory could see the horizon take on a rippled contour.

Sinclair and Billy Page sat in the fighting chairs, resting. As soon as Gregory slowed the boat, the two men got up and began to prepare for the dive. Sinclair opened a hard plastic case and handed Billy Page a small underwater video camera.

"I had to call in a big favor to borrow this thing," he said. "Don't lose it. It costs a bloody fortune. Hold it steady on me once we get down there. And keep it rolling."

"What are you gonna do?"

"I'm just gonna be poking around. Hopefully the water is clearer today."

Sinclair stripped off some duct tape and affixed an extra regulator to the back of his tank. Next came two heavy-duty flashlights and a spool onto which a nylon cord with knots tied at one yard intervals was coiled.

Billy Page was visibly apprehensive. "Do you really think we can get inside?" he asked nervously. "Never done a penetration."

"Just follow me and do exactly as I do. If we get in, I only go far enough to get a good look. The main thing is, I want to get some footage. Believe me, I don't want to take any chances."

"Be careful," Gregory hollered, as the two heavily laden divers went over the side.

Sinclair and Billy Page worked their way along the starboard side of the wreck. The water had cleared considerably since their last dive. The improved visibility in no way detracted from the mystique of the wreck. If anything, it made for an even more intense visual experience.

Billy Page followed about 20 feet to the side of Sinclair, recording his movements against the backdrop of the sunken submarine. At regular intervals, Sinclair stopped and posed in front of features such as the conning tower or the deck gun, gesturing with one hand while looking straight into the camera. Billy Page got the feeling he was filming a promotional video. In a very real way, he was.

Significantly more growth showed on the hull than when they made the first dive. The bottom was also changed. Low ridge-like mounds punctuated the sea floor down current from the wreck. Portions of the hull previously not exposed were now visible.

Billy Page saw it first. He tugged at his partner's arm and pointed toward a darkened area on the hull just above the sand line. They moved closer to investigate. A small section of steel plate curled inward. Most of the apparent break in the outer hull seemed to extend below the sea floor, leaving only an arch-like gap visible. The sandy bottom funneled down to the opening, giving the appearance of an oversized groundhog burrow.

Sinclair motioned to the opening. Billy Page vigorously shook his head. Sinclair could not hold back. He maneuvered himself into position and stuck his head into the break. The flashlight beam faded into a murky darkness. Sinclair backed out and reached for the metal rod behind his knife sheath. Driving the rod into the sand, he gestured for his partner to stay put with a hand on the line. Three sharp pulls would be the signal for assistance. Sinclair checked his air and nodded. Billy Page handed Sinclair the video camera and watched him slide head first into the narrow opening. Halfway in, he briefly hesitated, fins protruding near vertically. Two short kicks and he was gone.

Sinclair found himself suspended in one of the main ballast tanks. From inside the narrow space, he could see the break in the outer hull was much larger than it first appeared. Minor cascades of sand drizzled in from above.

A layer of fine silt coated everything and each movement stirred up billowing clouds. Visibility was soon near zero. A web of pipes partially blocked his way. Working forward, Sinclair slowly peeled line from the spool, counting the knots as they passed through his fingers. Behind him, the light coming through the break in the hull manifested itself as a nebulous haze.

Sinclair's hand struck solid steel. He groped until he felt his arm slip into a crevice-like fissure. The crack in the pressure hull was just wide enough for him to partly squeeze through. Inside, the water was still and gin clear. The flashlight probed the inky darkness. At first, Sinclair recognized only a maze of rusted pipes and valves. Only after he saw the small prop at one end did he realize the flashlight beam was tracing a torpedo. A narrow metal framework rested on the cylindrical form. Glancing up, he noted an unbroken light bulb screwed into a ceiling fixture.

Sinclair craned his head to follow the illuminated patch across the far wall. He burped a short stream of bubbles as the light suddenly framed a human skull that stared directly back at him. Minus its mandible, the skull rested on its upper dentition. A single gold tooth gleamed in the dim artificial light.

Sinclair maneuvered the video recorder through the fissure and began to pan the interior, methodically moving the flashlight in unison with the camera. He paused for a full ten seconds with the skull centered in the view finder. A more surrealistic image would be hard to imagine, he reflected. Fine silt lay collected on top of the cranium and around the eye orbits. Propped on the metal framework, the skull reminded Sinclair of a morbid find he'd once seen gathering dust on a relic hunter friend's mantle.

He managed to turn himself around and follow the knotted cord toward the smoky light filtering in from overhead.

Billy Page could not have been happier to see him re-emerge from the hull. Sinclair had been inside for perhaps four or five minutes; to Billy Page, it seemed like an hour. Hovering on the bottom, he had become thoroughly chilled inside his wet suit.

✠   ✠   ✠

Gregory was equally relieved to have them back on the boat.

"I can't believe you went in," Billy Page exclaimed, spitting out his regulator mouthpiece.

"Believe it," Sinclair replied calmly.

Billy Page began to peel off his wet suit. "Whadidya see?" he asked anxiously.

"A lot of stuff. I got to look all the way inside."

"No shit! What's in there?!"

"Dead men for one. There's a skull on a shelf. It looked like somebody just set it there."

"Really? Wow, that's wild!"

"What did you expect ?!" Gregory yelled down from behind the wheel. "Come on. Let's get out of here!" he ordered.

Billy Page joined Gregory on the bridge. The radio remained tuned to the NOAA weather band.

"What's the latest on the storm?" the mate asked as soon as they were underway.

"It doesn't look good," the captain replied stoically.

✠   ✠   ✠

The word back at the dock was that evacuation orders were likely to go out the next day.

Chapter 10

A BRILLIANTLY BLUE LATE AUGUST SKY GAVE NO HINT OF THE COMing storm. Throughout the day Park Rangers and Sheriff's Deputies made the rounds, knocking on doors and cruising the streets with loudspeakers blaring. The evacuation order was mandatory. All non-residents were to be off the Outer Banks by 6:00 pm.

All afternoon a steady stream of cars snaked north toward the mainland bridges. By evening, the surf built to the point where Highway 12, the only road off the island chain, was in danger of flooding at high tide. The road would soon be impassable if the storm moved any closer.

Gregory and Billy Page spent the afternoon battening down the *Hawkeye*. Inflatable bumpers were strung and the boat securely tied down, leaving enough slack for the inevitable storm surge. Most everything of value was taken off board.

"What do you think it's gonna do?" Billy Page asked, carrying an armful of rods and reels to the truck.

Gregory replied, "I think it's gonna get real ugly."

Further speculation seemed pointless. After finishing at the marina, they went home and did what they could to prepare for the storm.

Although some residents chose to leave for inland shelters, others were determined to hang on and the supermarket was jammed with people stocking up on supplies for the coming days. Across the island, preparations went on at a steady, methodical pace. Windows were boarded and vehicles moved to higher ground. Water, ice and food were set aside. Soon there would be nothing left to do but wait.

Everyone was hoping the hurricane would veer away and spare the coast. With every passing hour, the hope faded and the probability of a direct hit became all but certain. Emily slowed to a crawl, yet showed no sign of weakening. If anything, she began to tap the warm waters of the Gulf Stream and was steadily gaining strength. By nightfall, tropical storm force winds were being recorded at the Diamond Shoals light tower, while the full fury of the hurricane raged just one hundred miles from shore.

Dawn broke warm and muggy. Gregory decided to have a look over the dunes before the storm hit. Peering out to sea, he watched the blood red sunrise be swallowed by a wall of pitch black clouds. Wispy vapor-like strands streaked across the sky ahead of the gathering gloom. The wind built rapidly, turning the already violent surf into a churning frenzy. It was nowhere near high tide, yet the breakers were already gnawing at the dunes. Telephone wires whistled and moaned as Gregory wheeled his truck back into the driveway and scurried for the house.

Gregory walked through each room making sure everything was in order. He remembered to fill the bathtub so he would have water to flush the toilet. His sinuses ached as the air pressure continued to drop. He clicked the television on just as the house lost power. With the windows boarded, Gregory sat in the near pitch darkness and listened to the wind begin to howl.

Slowly at first, then with ever-increasing intensity, the house began to shake. Just as Gregory thought the wind could blow no harder, the first tree snapped. The 18 inch pine in the backyard gave way with what sounded like a rifle shot. Still the wind kept building. Rain and debris pelted the side of the house until the constant drumming became one massive roar.

Gregory had been through a good many storms, but it had never been like this. At mid-morning, the weather station in Buxton recorded sustained winds of 135 miles per hour just before the instrument was blown off the tower. Near horizontal sheets of rain, laced with flying debris, lashed across the darkened island. The worst was yet to come. Early afternoon felt like the end of the world was at hand. The raging winds came in from the northeast, nearly pushing the Sound completely over the island. Water ran three feet deep in the streets.

Gregory dived to the floor as a section of plywood was violently torn from the living room window and the wind burst through in a spray of glass and rain. He retreated to the hall amid a swirl of household papers. To Gregory, crouched low in the hallway, time seemed suspended. He felt his flesh tingle and hair stand on end just before a thunderous lighting flash discharged mere yards from the house. For a span of two or three seconds, he could anticipate the peak gusts by the approaching sound of splintering trees. A cramping knot of fear repeatedly tightened his midsection. When the peaks hit, the house shook violently on its foundation.

As fast as it came on, the wind and rain began to subside, then stopped all together. The sky brightened and a few rays of sun peeked through the cloud cover.

The storm had turned and the eye wall was moving away from land. It was over.

Outside, the silence was deafening. Thinking at first the eye must be over the island, Gregory hesitated before venturing far beyond the threshold. In the eerie calm, thick dewy drops hung from the tangled debris. The afternoon air was warm, wet and magnificently clean. It was as if the tempest, in all its violence, purged the atmosphere of every impurity.

Gregory looked around. The house had done better than he feared. Other than the one broken window, damage seemed confined to the cedar shakes missing from two sides of the building. The yard, however, was a mess. Branches, splintered wood and whole trees lay helter-skelter. Out on the main road, the power line was down with sections spitting blue and yellow sparks.

Gregory finished surveying the damage. After half an hour with the chain saw, he managed to get his truck out of the driveway. Emergency crews were already clearing Route 12 and he drove straight to the marina. After passing a 20 foot center console boat lying upside down on the side of the road, Gregory braced himself for the worst.

He turned into Oden's Dock to see the *Hawkeye* resting snugly in her berth. She looked to be unscathed. Several commercial boats had not fared so well. Their pilothouse roofs and radio masts were all that showed above the surface of the muddied harbor.

Billy Page sat at the end of the dock, casually smoking a cigarette.

"Man, that was something else," he grinned as Gregory walked up. "Did you hear the wind?"

"What's she look like?"

"Took on some water, but that's about it. Been running the extra bilge for 'bout 30 minutes now."

"How'd you make out?" Gregory asked, still looking over his boat.

"Good, I think. Everything's still standing. My brother lost his truck, though. Washed right into the Sound. Damnest thing I ever saw."

"I think we both came through lucky," Gregory said. "From the looks of it, some folks didn't do so good."

Billy Page nodded.

✠   ✠   ✠

The hurricane was front page news across the nation. Not surprisingly, Dan Rather was one of the first media personalities on the scene, surveying the island in a helicopter and reporting directly from the door of the low flying aircraft. Most of the reports described Hurricane Emily as having delivered a "glancing blow" to the East Coast before turning back out to sea. To the residents of the Outer Banks, from Avon to Ocracoke, the glancing blow was more like three full rounds with Mike Tyson.

Living on an Atlantic barrier island comes with its share of adversities most residents just take in stride, and by early the next morning the clean-up was well underway. Highway crews with loaders and motor graders pushed errant sand off the streets. Bit by bit, power was restored. Folks banded together to help less fortunate neighbors. Windows were replaced, roofs patched and endless piles of debris collected to be hauled away or burned. Within a week or so, life on the island pretty much returned to normal.

Once the cleanup was finished, the most visible and lasting effect of the storm remained the destruction wrought on Buxton Woods. Widely recognized as the most pristine temperate maritime forest on the East Coast, this unique natural resource lay ravaged by the terrible winds. Ancient live oaks littered the ground, with many of the surviving trees all but stripped of their leaves. Entire stands of pines were uprooted, their barren trunks leaning in a single direction like sea oats before a stiff breeze.

⚔   ⚔   ⚔

Preston Sinclair popped the tape into the VCR and clicked the play button. It had been well over a week since the dive. Things were so hectic after the storm he hadn't had time to even think about the U-boat. He began to study the video footage, trying to assess the integrity of the vessel. Sinclair recognized the damage to the outer hull was far greater than it seemed when he had been in the water.

"This may be a problem," he said to himself upon viewing the gaping break in the steel.

The screen went black before the flashlight lit up an interior view of the submarine. Sinclair noted the skull recorded in the picture was resting on a bunk, not a shelf.

He let the tape play again. By the second time around, he had a better feel for the interior layout of the submarine. Just when Sinclair was about to stop the tape, a dull metallic gleam caught his attention. Well forward of the break, near the dimly lit periphery of the flashlight's reach, the camera panned across what looked like a large metal box. Sinclair hit the pause button and squinted at the frozen frame. He couldn't be sure, but there looked to be several similar items laying about.

Wonder what those are? he mused, before rewinding the tape and turning his attention to other matters.

✠　　　✠　　　✠

"All right, let's give it a try," Gregory shouted down from the bridge. "This spot's been real good lately."

The clients eagerly reached for the rods while Billy Page began to dollop spoonfuls of chum overboard.

"What's that?" one of the men waiting along the gunwales asked.

"Ground menhaden," the mate replied. "Greasiest fish in the ocean. Really turns 'em on. Just don't get it on your skin, though. The oil can pass right into your blood—even your farts will smell like fish."

"You're lying!" the man exclaimed.

"Here, you wanna try?" Billy Page grinned, holding out a ladle full of the brown, soupy mixture. "Rub your hands in it. Your wife will love you for it."

The whole back of the boat burst out laughing.

Gregory bumped the *Hawkeye* in and out of gear, keeping them positioned just up-current from the wreck. Billy Page threaded a small treble hook through the nose of a live menhaden and tossed the squirming bait overboard. It swam away from the boat, nervously splashing the surface.

"Swim little fishy," the mate called out. "Mister King's got a bead on you."

He handed the rod to the client, who grinned approvingly.

"What wreck we on?" the man asked.

"*British Splendour*—tanker. Took a German torpedo early in World War Two."

"Isn't that one a little closer in?" a second client, who was standing behind them, asked.

"Oh, there're a dozen or more around," Billy Page said vaguely while reaching back into the bait well. "Can't keep 'em straight. Cap'n knows 'em all. Don't worry, he's gonna put us on fish."

Once the lines were out, Gregory flipped on the depth-finder. It was almost an afterthought, so much had he come to rely on the

GPS. Originally developed for military use, the system was keyed to overhead satellites to instantly compute one's exact location, to within yards, anywhere on earth. When GPS first came out, most captains scoffed at it as just another rich man's toy. Soon prices dropped to within reach and everyone bought one.

Gregory squinted at the depth-finder screen. The display showed the bottom flat as a pancake. He switched to side scan mode. Still nothing. A quick check of the GPS unit indicated it was reading properly. "That's weird," he muttered.

He turned on the Loran to double check his position. The two seemed to agree. Gregory took the boat out of gear and began a slow drift toward the exact spot were the U-boat had lain. Nothing.

Twenty minutes passed without a strike, after which the captain ordered the lines in. Gregory made a series of zigzag passes across the area before putting the *Hawkeye* under full throttle and roaring east toward the shipping lanes.

"Where's he going?" one of the clients yelled.

"I don't know," Billy Page shouted back. "Maybe he's heard something on the radio. We'll find out when we get there."

✠   ✠   ✠

Gregory eased the *Hawkeye* stern-first into her berth. The boat came to a standstill without as much as kissing a piling. Billy Page secured the mooring ropes and the murmuring diesels fell silent. Much to the delight of some of tourist onlookers, a half dozen large king mackerel and a hefty cobia were heaved onto the dock. Other captains, who had already moored, watched the display with more than passing interest. The Cape Hatteras King Mackerel Tournament was still a month away. Gregory took top prize last year and had every intention of repeating. Even though it was only September, the *Hawkeye* was already bringing in what were likely to be some of the biggest kings of the year.

"Nice fish!" someone called out from an adjoining boat. A few low whistles rose up as the largest king mackerel, easily topping 40 pounds, came off the boat.

The clients milled about the dock, savoring the attention. After a round of photographs, the catch was hauled off to the cleaning tables.

It had been a good day on the water. The clients were good company, which unfortunately, was not an everyday occurrence. They were thankful for each fish and thoroughly enjoyed every aspect of the trip. Before departing, they let the crew know they would be back, and would surely recommend the *Hawkeye* to their friends.

Even though the party did not appear to have been mon-eyed, they tipped extremely well. Billy Page whistled briskly while cleaning the boat. As soon as everything was stowed, he hurried off—intent on spending most of the wad of fresh bills bunched in the front pocket of his cut-off shorts.

"Six o'clock, Bubba!" Gregory called out after him.

When most everyone left, Gregory re-boarded the *Hawkeye*, certain he'd forgotten to switch off the electronics. He scaled the ladder to the bridge. Everything was in order. From his perch on the bridge, Gregory looked out over the breakwater. September was his favorite time of year. The early autumn sun had noticeably mellowed from just a few weeks before and the soft, late afternoon light cast golden ripples across Pamlico Sound.

Just then Preston Sinclair's truck turned off the main road and into the marina. It crunched to a stop at the dockside edge of the gravel lot.

"Oh, no. Wonder what he wants," Gregory sighed aloud.

"Eric!" Sinclair yelled from out of the cab. "I want you to come over and see something."

"Can't it wait?"

"Come on. I think you'll like it."

Gregory climbed off the boat and reluctantly agreed to follow Sinclair home. Hopefully this won't take too long, he thought.

✠   ✠   ✠

The image of the conning tower filled the television screen. Although the picture was somewhat dim and grainy, the view had much the same effect on Gregory as it had on the divers who witnessed the scene firsthand. Gregory intently studied the details of the vessel he'd only glimpsed an outline of from the surface. He sat on the very edge of the sofa for the whole five minute long clip.

"What do you think?" Sinclair asked. "Pretty incredible, huh?"

Gregory didn't respond.

"Nice camera work on the inside," Sinclair added, complimenting himself. "The hull took quite a whack. Looks like it might have been rammed. Betcha that's exactly what happened! Collided with a freighter and went down. Ka-bam. Yeah, must be why no one ever knew it was there. This is incredible! I mean people dream about stuff like this—Eric? Eric! Are you listening?"

Gregory grumbled an acknowledgment. Sinclair was fast getting on his nerves.

"Just wish the hull was in better shape. As for our plan, this is going to…"

Gregory cut him off in mid sentence. "We got a bigger problem."

"What do you mean? What kind of problem?"

"It's gone."

"What's gone?"

"The wreck. The U-boat. It's gone," Gregory declared. "I was on the spot today."

"It can't just be gone!"

"It's gone."

"Are you sure you were in the right place? Is there a problem with your stuff?"

"It's gone. I double and triple-checked the GPS against another wreck."

Sinclair's face went blank, then darkened. His brow furled as the corners of his mouth turned downwards. "Then it's back under the sand—after Emily."

Gregory nodded. "The sea gives and the sea takes away."

"*Goddammit!*" Sinclair burst out, ripping off his cap and flinging it across the room. "Why can't… why can't just for once… *Fuck!*"

Sinclair momentarily sulked, facing the wall, then began to pace the room. "We need a plan B," he blurted while walking in ever-tighter circles.

"No. You need a plan B," Gregory said. "I don't want anything to do with this."

"Why?! What's the matter with you?!"

"The video's pretty morbid," Gregory let out. His voice sounded tired. "How many more men you think are down there?"

"I'll edit it."

"That's not the point."

"What is the point?" Sinclair demanded. "You afraid of ghosts or somethin'?"

"They're dead," Gregory sighed. "Leave 'em be. Besides, I don't know why we're even talking about this. The sub is gone—buried under only God knows how much sand. You'll never get at it. Just forget about the whole damn thing."

Sinclair collapsed into the sofa. Gregory got up to leave.

Sinclair's expression perked. "If you want out, gimme the coordinates."

"No."

"What do you mean, 'no'? " Sinclair whined, standing back up.

"Just like I said. No! I came to you because I thought maybe we could make a little something—not to get involved in some big scheme. Listen, things are looking up with the boat. I'm booked through Thanksgiving. I really don't have time for this kind of shit. Okay?"

"I know where it is," Sinclair said, as if rising to a challenge.

"To within a mile—or five," Gregory countered. "There's a lot of sand out there."

Sinclair leaned toward him. "A magnetometer sweep would turn it up in no time," he said defiantly.

"Then go get yourself a mag-o-meter—or whatever. But you ain't draggin' it behind my boat."

Gregory stood and stretched. "Man, I'm tired," he yawned. "Do whatever, Preston," he said, opening the door. "Just leave me out of it. I'll see you later."

Chapter 11

SUMMERS LINGER ON THE OUTER BANKS OF NORTH CAROLINA. Although the weather remained warm, ever-shortening days heralded the coming change of season. Autumn on the barrier islands brings a spectacular display of sunsets, and this evening was to be no exception. As the October sun sank lower, brilliant streaks of red and yellow filled the western sky. Off to the east, the faint scarlet hue tinting the horizon all afternoon flared into a rich, lavender colored glow.

Sinclair made his way from the lighthouse parking lot across the low dunes. Sinclair didn't fish much. Calm autumn evenings such as this, however, sometimes found him on the beach casting for speckled trout. He desperately needed a few moments to relax and wetting a line never failed to help clear his mind. Everything moved so fast he could scarcely believe it. There had been meetings to attend, presentations to make. Now it seemed as if it were all about to pay off. Nothing like being in the right place at the right time, he thought.

The green water was clear and still. Sinclair removed his shoes and rolled his pant legs up. He made his way along the water's edge, tossing the small lure over the gently lapping waves.

In short order, his effort was rewarded by a stringer of nice sized specks. After making a final cast, he stood and watched the afterglow fade across the darkening waters. Night was falling fast as he walked back up the beach, the sand under his bare feet still warm from the afternoon sun. Up ahead, the beam of Cape Hatteras Lighthouse methodically sliced the evening air.

On the way home, Sinclair picked up a bag of ice. He dropped the catch into a cooler on the porch and poured the ice over top, reminding himself to clean them first thing in the morning.

The evening's excursion had its desired effect. For the first time in many weeks, Sinclair felt relaxed and at ease. A welcome drowsiness crept over him. He shuffled to the bedroom, undressed and slipped under the covers.

Just as he closed his eyelids, the image of the sunken U-boat crept into his semi-consciousness. Laying in bed he tried to clear any thoughts of the wreck from his mind. For the last month and a half, he had thought of little else. Now all he wished for was some much needed rest. Sinclair rolled over and buried his face in the pillow.

They're metal boxes! What's in the boxes?!

Sinclair bolted upright, wide awake. Sweat seeped from his pores. "Submariners don't carry luggage!" he panted. There's hardly enough room to turn around! What's the matter with me?! he thought. God, I've been stupid!

So engrossed had he been in the technical challenges and logistical details of the project, he'd not given the slightest thought to the metal boxes on the video. His mind raced. Nazi mystery sub! No one knows it's there. Cargo on board. Oh, God! This could be big, he thought. Really big!

Sinclair struggled to free the bedding from around his legs. Wearing only ratty boxers, he barged into the living room and switched on the VCR. The tape stopped at the frame where he thought he'd seen the boxes. There was no doubt. They were metal canisters — two, maybe three. He squinted at the screen. The image was grainy and the canisters lay jumbled along the dimly lit periphery of the flashlight's reach. He thought he saw others, but couldn't be sure. After viewing the clip a dozen or more times, he clicked the television off, went to the refrigerator and fumbled for a beer to calm himself.

Sinclair spent years in the company of professional treasure divers—mostly in South Florida. Theories about Nazi treasure hoards had often been a late-night conversation topic. He'd heard all the stories. Unimaginable riches were said to have been sunken into an alpine lake in Austria. Other theories had millions in gold bars shipped to South America.

Tales of stashed German plunder filled the popular imagination for decades. Many people placed considerable credence in the stories and quite a bit of serious research had been conducted on the matter. One noted historian claimed Himmler and Goering had each personally amassed a fortune in gold, jewels and art works, worth hundreds of millions in the current market. Nonetheless, not a dime's worth of the supposed secret loot was ever recovered.

Sinclair frantically paced the room. That's it! he thought. It's got to be! God only knows how much it's worth! The more he thought about the metal boxes, the more convinced he became of their contents. Before long, he was in a complete frenzy.

During those years as a hired diver, Sinclair worked for wages or the promise of a modest cut, sometimes risking his life for very little reward. All the while he dreamed of the one big payoff that would set him up—put him on easy street. It was right here, he anguished. And now I've pissed it away!

Sinclair flopped onto the couch and tried to concentrate. Options seemed limited. There was one person he knew he could turn to. He thought about making the call, but was loath to do it. On the other hand, something had to be done. He was in way over his head. I can't let this one slip away, he thought.

He reached for the telephone on the end table, then thought otherwise. After sitting and downing a couple more beers, he picked up the receiver and dialed the number, beginning with the South Florida area code.

Chapter 12

MAGGIE TINSLEY WATCHED FROM BEHIND THE MIDGETTE MART register as the blue and white Ford pulled up to the gas pumps. Gregory got out of the pickup and waved through the window for a fill-up. Stopping at the store was an after work ritual of sorts and Gregory normally stopped in whether he needed anything or not.

For her, Gregory's short visits ranked as one of the highlights of the day. A divorcée of about fifty, the woman had an exuberant personality and a seemingly inexhaustible zest. Her graying hair was cut short and she was rarely seen out of high-top sneakers. She was also fond of flannel shirts, at least two sizes too large. Her eyes took on an extra sparkle every time Gregory walked through the door. The long standing infatuation was a secret to no one.

To say Maggie Tinsley had the gift of gab would be quite the understatement. In addition, little of what went on along the south end of Hatteras Island escaped her attention, and during her working hours, the store functioned as nothing short of a clearing house for local gossip and all manner of inane information.

"Eric!" she exclaimed with a devilish smile as Gregory came through the door.

Gregory recognized the look on her face. It could only mean she knew something he didn't.

"I heard you got a billfish," she said, making change for the twenty.

"Yup. We had a really good day. Kind of surprised 'cause it's getting on in the year."

"That's not all I heard! Did you see today's paper?" She dropped a copy of The Virginia Pilot onto the counter.

MYSTERY WRECK: U-BOAT FOUND OFF OUTER BANKS, the headline screamed in large, bold letters.

Gregory's stomach churned.

"Look Hon," she said, holding up a second paper. "It's in The Washington Post, too."

WORLD WAR TWO GERMAN SUBMARINE
DISCOVERED OFF NORTH CAROLINA COAST
Shallow Water Find Confounds Naval Historians

Maggie reached for the Virginia paper while putting on her glasses. "It gets better," she said gleefully. "Look, it's a picture of Preston! And listen to this! 'Noted salvage diver and underwater researcher Preston Sinclair...'"

"What!?"

"It says, 'noted salvage diver and underwater researcher Preston Sinclair discovered the U-boat while on a fishing outing last summer.'" Maggie looked up over her glasses. "Underwater researcher? Can you imagine? Preston? Really!" she exclaimed in her Carolina drawl. She raised the paper and resumed reading aloud. "Although unsure of the exact date the U-boat went down, Sinclair has determined the wreck to be in excellent condition. 'What we have here is an exceptional find,' Sinclair says. 'The submarine represents a true time capsule. Further research...'"

"I've heard enough," Gregory growled, storming for the door.

"Eric! Where are you going?" she called after him. "I heard you found the wreck. Eric! What's going on?"

"Some other time. Gotta go."

The truck screeched out of the parking lot, leaving behind some rubber marks and a lingering patch of blue smoke.

☩   ☩   ☩

Gregory roared down the sandy drive leading to Sinclair's house. The old International rust bucket was gone. In its place stood a brand new four-wheel-drive Dodge Ram pickup—candy apple red with chrome trim. The glare off the polished metal was blinding. Gregory jumped out of the cab and made for the porch. He repeatedly pounded the doorframe as flakes of peeling paint collected at his feet.

Sinclair appeared behind the screen door. "What's up, Eric?"

"You tell me!"

"Guess you saw the paper today," Sinclair said sheepishly.

"You're damn right I did! I thought we had an agreement. I've never heard so much bullshit in my entire life! What the hell is going on with you?!"

"Agreement?" Sinclair shot back, his voice suddenly firm. "We ain't got no agreement! You said do what you want. So I did. All you said was 'leave me out of it.'"

The two stood glaring at each other through the dilapidated screen door.

"Okay," Sinclair finally said. "Reckon I got some explainin' to do. Come on in."

Gregory stepped through the threshold.

"You wanna beer?"

"No. Just tell me what's going on."

"Okay, okay," Sinclair said, raising his hands. "It wasn't me, honest. It was the company's doing—a publicity thing. I just went along with it. I had to. They even told me what to say."

"What company?!"

"The company that's going to raise the sub," Sinclair replied in a casual, matter-of-fact way.

"What?!"

"Are you sure you don't wanna beer?"

"Yeah, I'll take a beer. I think I'm gonna need one."

Sinclair disappeared into the kitchen, reemerging with two frosty cans of Coors. "Why don't you sit down?" he motioned, easing himself into the sofa. "This may take a while."

"Now what's this about a company?" Gregory demanded, remaining standing.

"Well, you see, it's all kinda hush-hush. I approached these people with a proposition, for the hell of it really. I didn't think they'd go for it. But instead of asking me to leave, they wanted to know more. So I gave them the whole spiel."

"Let me guess. You asked for money to try and float the wreck."

"Not exactly. They're going to use their own contractors. This company, they're a top outfit who can really get things done. Believe me, money is no object." Sinclair leaned toward Gregory. "The budget for the first phase of the project is just over one and a half million," he said breaking into a wide grin.

"So who are these people?"

Sinclair leaned even closer and in a facetious whisper said, "I'm with Atlantis World."

At first, Gregory drew a blank. Then he remembered the newspaper stories. A shadowy investment group had taken out options on some properties inland from Myrtle Beach, South Carolina. Once a large parcel was consolidated, plans were announced for the construction of a massive, nautical theme park. The secretive and heavy-handed manner in which the project was put forth rankled the ire of many local residents. Environmentalists and preservation groups were in an uproar. The proposed park fronted some of the most pristine wetlands in all of South Carolina, and at least two major historic sites fell within the property boundaries.

"Atlantis World? The amusement park in South Carolina? The one that's got everyone so pissed off?"

"That's it," Sinclair said. "I really can't blame folks for being mad. It *is* pretty down there. Not a lot of people want to see the place taken over by motels and burger joints."

"Who's behind this Atlantis World anyway? They must have a shit load of money."

A mischievous smile crept across Sinclair's face. "I'm not at liberty to disclose such information," he said in a lawyer-like tone. "But I can assure you, it's no Mickey Mouse operation."

"Whaddaya mean?"

"Let's just say we may be talking about a family entertainment consortium with very, very deep pockets."

Gregory sat for a moment, trying to digest everything Sinclair just told him. "So Preston, what's your gig?" he suddenly asked.

"I got hired as a consultant." He flipped Gregory his business card. It read: Preston G. Sinclair/Associate Director of Historic Resource Acquisitions.

"What the hell is this?!" Gregory exploded.

"You like it?" Sinclair grinned. "I came up with the title myself. At first I thought they were humoring me 'cause I could put them on the wreck. But now I'm getting to do some neat stuff. And they really like my ideas."

"Wait a minute here," Gregory interjected. "How'd you convince these people you were qualified for the job?"

"They liked my background. And when I told them about my degrees, they really warmed up."

"Degrees?! Where did you get degrees?!"

"From the back of a magazine. I sent away for them."

"Oh, for chrissakes! I don't believe this!"

Preston Sinclair rose to his feet. "Look," he said sounding indignant, "I just thought I'd try doing something different for a change. I'm too old to be mucking about in freezing cold water." He sat back down, placing his hand on his calf. "Man, my Nam wound's been *killing* me. Some mornings, I'm so stiff I can hardly move my leg."

Gregory grunted and rolled his eyes.

Sinclair got up and went for another beer. "Besides, I needed the cash," he called out from the kitchen. "Haven't done a job in over a year."

"You can't just send away for a new career through the mail," Gregory insisted.

Sinclair came back in the room. "Already have," he shrugged.

"What if they find out you're a fake?"

"It don't matter. The job's only for a year, and the money is guaranteed. So I went out and bought a new truck. You like it?"

Gregory shook his head and sighed.

Sinclair broke into another grin. "You wanna see what I've come up with?" he asked with boyish enthusiasm.

"Sure, why not."

Sinclair strode down the cluttered hall, returning with a large carrying case and a wooden easel. The case held a set of spiral-bound, poster sized prints. He placed the prints on the easel in the center of the room.

"Wolfpack: Hunter-Killers of the Atlantic," he said proudly, pulling back the cover sheet. "That's gonna be the name of the exhibit."

The first print was a color, CAD drawing depicting the *U-491* as it lay on the bottom. Sinclair flipped the page to reveal a mock-up of the proposed exhibit. Next came an engineering plan for the site. The final page was another computer-generated illustration showing what the museum facility would look like, complete with miniature visitors and landscaping details.

"What do ya think?" Sinclair beamed.

"Where'd you get this?!" Gregory asked, totally incredulous.

"The drawing of the thing on the bottom, they made it from the video I shot. The company flew me out to California. These people have everything—whole rooms of artists and computer guys. It's amazing what they can do." Sinclair packed away the prints and folded up the easel. "The plan is to totally gut the thing and stabilize the metal. They were going to display it on land. I told them it would be just as easy to have it in the water. And much more realistic. See, all you do is excavate a basin, pour a large concrete pad, and anchor in a steel cradle to keep the vessel upright. The thing will be sitting on the cradle, not floating of course."

Gregory listened in near disbelief.

"You line the basin and connect it to one of the near-by canals. The water is tannic and dark. You won't be able to see much past the water line. The company had me meet with the consulting engineers and they really liked my suggestions." Sinclair paused momentarily, then continued with his spirited monologue. "The museum building is going to have an interactive display and a separate room for artifacts. One wall is going to be a reconstructed cutaway of a U-boat, showing what it's like inside one. Then there's the photo gallery, complete with video displays—Battle of the Atlantic."

Gregory was speechless.

"Anyway, that's what this is all about," Sinclair stated smugly.

"Sorry I asked."

"Who'da thought it would come to this, huh, Eric?"

"It's late. I gotta get going," Gregory said, totally exasperated. He turned for the door, then stopped and looked back at Sinclair. "Just one thing. How'd you find the wreck?"

"We did a fly-over. On the third pass, the needle 'bout jumped the scale. Made another dive, too. The conning tower's back out of the sand."

"I got to hand it to you Preston," Gregory said shaking his head. "I don't know how you come up with this shit. I'll see you later."

✠   ✠   ✠

Even for a Saturday night, the Mad Shrimper Bar and Grill was packed. The jukebox belted out a mixture of county-western tunes and rock numbers. Between the music and the incessant clash of billiard balls, the patrons nearly had to shout to be heard. A group of watermen clustered around the pool table, arguing loudly with one another. A haze of tobacco smoke filled the room.

Sinclair walked through the door and made straight for the bar. The men at the pool table stopped their bantering to focus attention on the newcomer.

"Well, if it isn't Preston Sinclair, the world renowned underwater researcher," one of them called out. Boisterous laughter followed.

"Hey, Preston!" another shouted. "I saw you on television. You're famous, man!"

Sinclair acknowledged them with a short grin and a tip of his cap as he walked past. Underneath one arm was a manila folder. He slid a barstool up next to Billy Page, who did his best to ignore him. Sinclair responded with a playful jab to the ribs.

"What's up, Preston?" Billy Page sighed, looking straight ahead.

"Got something right here I thought you might want to see." Sinclair pulled a large glossy black and white print out of the folder and laid it on the counter. "Commander of the *U-491*."

The photograph was of KptLt. Hans-Jurgen Heidenreich—a formal portrait taken after a successful patrol hunting North Atlantic convoys. In the picture he was clean shaven, revealing a robust jaw which stood in contrast to his otherwise rakish features. The German commander's head was cocked slightly to one side, the white captain's cap immaculate. A Knight's Cross hung on the collar of his heavily starched tunic.

Outwardly, Heidenreich carried the look of supreme confidence. His unmistakably blue eyes bored straight out of the monochrome print. It was the hardened stare of a determined killer. Yet, the same eyes betrayed a recognizable weariness. With a closer look, one corner of his mouth curled into a faint, sardonic smile. The curious expression conveyed a certain melancholy—resignation perhaps. As a U-boat commander, he must have known his days were likely numbered.

A small crowd gathered at their backs. Someone whistled as Sinclair held up the print over his shoulder for all to see.

"Man!" a voice behind them exclaimed. "Look at the fucker! Just think how many Joes the guy musta waxed."

"A lot, that's for sure," Sinclair shot back, pivoting around. "Twenty-one confirmed sinkings. Sent seven ships to the bottom on his first patrol—most of them right out there!" he said, motioning dramatically toward the front door.

He set the print back down on the counter.

"Were did you get this?!" Billy Page asked, transfixed by the image before him.

"I got this pinhead graduate college student doing research for me over at the German Naval Archives right now. This came express mail today."

The focus of attention quickly returned to the pool game, leaving the two men seated alone at the bar. Sinclair slid the photograph back into the folder. "You still pissed off at me, Billy?" he asked.

At first Billy Page did not respond. "You didn't find the thing," he finally said. "Eric did!"

"So?"

"I seen your new truck. You know what I'm driving." Billy Page swiveled in his seat to face Sinclair. "I thought we was gonna make some money, man!"

Sinclair cast a quick glance over both shoulders. "Look," he half-whispered. "I'm gonna swing another deal on this. I'm talking a real, real big deal. If it goes through, I'll make it up to you. Promise."

"Preston, your ship's been comin' in for as long as I've known you. Since when do you not have a deal going?"

Sinclair lowered his voice even further. "I mean it. This is big. Big! Trust me on this one."

"What are you gonna do? Buy me a new truck?" Billy Page asked sarcastically.

"A new truck won't be nothin'."

Billy Page lifted his beer and took a swig. "I'll believe it when I see it."

✠   ✠   ✠

Preston Sinclair flipped on the light in the living room, seated himself on the sofa and dumped the full contents of the manila envelope onto the coffee table before him. He shuffled through the pile of loose Xerox pages and photostats. The blizzard of papers detailed every technical aspect of the *U-491*. Each page had a short, translated synopsis written in red ink along the margin: *U-491*. Type VIIc. Commissioned in Kiel, December 1942. Performance specifications. Sea trails throughout January. Based in Lorient, France, balance of 1943, early 1944. North Atlantic sorties on three-month rotation. Intermediate-grade diesel rebuilds in April. More technical data on acoustic tests.

"How'd he get this stuff?!" Sinclair said aloud. Man, these Krauts are anal! he thought. They must have saved records of everything. Who needs to know this shit anyway?

An unstamped envelope lay at the bottom of the pile. He tore it open and unfolded a handwritten note. It read:

```
Dear Dr. Sinclair,
     I hope you will find this information useful in
your research. Things are going really well over
here and I am having quite the time. My friends are
so jealous. The stipend is holding up OK--I think.
One more thing might be of interest. By chance, I
met this Brit at the archives who is doing research
for a comprehensive book on the German Navy dur-
ing World War Two. He's a very eccentric fellow to
say the least. But he's big on U-boats and owns a
Kriegsmarine document listing dispositions of all
German submarines at the cessation of hostilities.
He claims the U-491 to have been tied up in Danzig
(Gdansk) from very late 1944, through the end of
the war. Will pick up a photocopy when I stop in
London on my way back to the States. See you soon.
                              Jason S.
```

Danzig! Sinclair thought. Well it didn't stay in Danzig, now did it? It's sitting half-buried on Diamond Shoals! Where the hell is Danzig anyway?

He stormed into the bedroom and began to tear away at an impossibly overfilled closet. All manner of junk spewed in every direction. After five minutes of frantic searching, he found what he was looking for—a roll of rubberized cloth sheets with historical maps printed on one side, the kind that used to hang in every classroom with the various countries shaded in gaudy colors. Years ago, he plucked them from the dumpster behind the High School, thinking they might be useful some day.

He rolled open the sheet titled Europe Between the World Wars and lay it across the floor. Close enough. His index finger traced the various coastlines until he found it.

"Danzig—on the Baltic… the Eastern Front," he whispered to himself. A second map caught his attention—The War in the East 1943–1945. He quickly rolled it open. Bold red arrows representing the Soviet Army's offensives jutted across the landscape. One hooking turn was shown encircling East Prussia. Underneath, the date read March–April 1945.

"Beat the Red Army out of town, did you," he hissed. "Why didya come all the way to North-fuckin'-Carolina?" Preston Sinclair rose off his knees and collapsed onto the couch. He was sweating profusely.

✠   ✠   ✠

The twin-engine Beechcraft came in low from the southeast. It banked steeply and settled in for the final approach to the General Billy Mitchell Airstrip. Spinning propellers caught the late afternoon sun as the aircraft glided past Frisco campground, touching down just the other side of the high, grassy dunes. A red Dodge Ram pickup stood waiting at the taxiway.

Chapter 13

Jessica stood smiling in the doorway. "Hi Daddy!" she giggled, throwing her arms around him.

"What are you doing here?!" Gregory exclaimed, thoroughly surprised at the unexpected appearance. "I thought you were at school."

"You know I have to go to Ohio for Thanksgiving, so I thought I'd leave a few days early and come see you."

"That's awfully sweet of you," he said, grabbing her bag. "Come on in."

A slightly awkward silence followed them into the living room.

"How are your classes?"

"Good."

"How's your fella' Jimmy?"

"I don't care. I hate him."

"Sorry to hear that," Gregory said, hiding his delight.

It took about half an hour to catch up on everything new. She wanted to know everything about the hurricane and who lost what. Gregory already figured there was more to the visit when she announced she was off to see her friend Jamie.

"I hate to do this, Daddy," Jessica said, "But can I borrow ten bucks? I'm running on fumes."

"Keep it," he said handing her a twenty. "I'm glad you came."

Jessica drove off to see her old friend. Gregory made a small pot of coffee and flipped on the computer to do some bookkeeping he'd been putting off. After about an hour, he finished up.

The afternoon had been cold and rainy and Gregory was feeling more than a little closed in. Certain his daughter would not be back until later that evening, he grabbed his jacket and headed out.

Driving down the road, Gregory got the feeling he was being followed. He glanced in the rearview mirror to see a charcoal colored sedan with heavily tinted windows so close on his tail the image of the grill nearly took up the entire mirror. It kept driving on after he turned into the Midgette Mart.

As always, Maggie Tinsley lit up as he walked through the door. "Eric, how are you? Haven't seen you in days!"

"Okay, I guess. Jessica's home from school. She came to see me."

"Such a nice girl. So pretty. You wouldn't believe the creeps who came in here the other day."

Gregory couldn't care less who came into the store. "What about them?" he asked out of politeness.

She probably related the story a dozen times this afternoon alone, but nonetheless began to detail the encounter with customary zeal.

"They were kinda dressed funny. And talked real funny-like. Well, one of them did. The other didn't do any talking at all. They come in here and the one guy starts asking all these stupid questions, like where was this and where was that, I mean, the island is only so big. And then they didn't buy nothin'."

"What did these guys look like?" Gregory asked, taking a sudden interest.

"I don't rightly know. They were wearing these dark sunglasses. One was pretty big though, and the other kinda weasely-like." She leaned against the counter. "Tell you what I do know though, one of them sure did smell bad." She raised her hand to her mouth and began to cackle. "I was thinking of asking them if they wanted to buy some soap and deodorant."

"You didn't happen to see what these guys were driving, did you?"

"All I saw outside was this dark car with dark windows."

Gregory didn't like the gut feeling he carried with him out of the store—a sense something was about to happen. Indeed, there were times when Gregory wondered if he were not clairvoyant. In reality, it was nothing more than the compulsive workings of a keen mind. Whether gift or curse, he couldn't be sure. On the other hand, the very blend of intuition and intellect is what made him such a successful fisherman and charter boat captain.

Before heading home, Gregory thought he'd check on the boat. Once at the marina, everything seemed to be in order. He glanced around the cockpit and ducked into the spartan cabin. Nothing was amiss. He climbed the bridge.

"*Shit!*" he burst out at the top of his lungs. "*Goddammit!*"

Two clipped wires hung limply from the bracket on which the GPS unit had been mounted. All his cursing did nothing to salve his anger. Several people came running down the dock, alarmed at the racket. Just as the tirade began to wane, Gregory realized the unit itself was perhaps not what the thieves were after. The thought was hardly comforting.

"What are you looking at?!" he snapped at the people standing on the dock. He stormed off the boat and the small crowd parted to let him pass. Gregory jumped into his truck and roared off.

Passing by the Mad Shrimper, Gregory saw a shiny red Dodge truck parked in the near empty lot. "Preston!" Gregory blurted, turning the wheel. He veered off the road and into the lot, braking to a hard stop next to the new pickup.

Sinclair sat alone at the bar. Judging from the glazed-over look in his eyes, Gregory figured he'd been there for quite some time. Gregory walked over and took a seat next to him.

"Wuzup, Cap'n," Sinclair slobbered. "Some weather, huh? Couldn't get a lick o' work done today."

"Preston," Gregory said calmly, "are you holding out on me? Is there something you haven't told me? Because if there is, you'd better get straight with me right now."

"Whoa, whoa, I sense a lot of hostility here."

"Cut the crap, Preston!" Gregory snapped. "Now I'll tell you what's up! First some assholes've been following me and now my GPS's been stolen. I might not be a rocket scientist, but why do I got the feeling this has something to do with the submarine — and that you know something I don't? Now what haven't you told me?!"

Sinclair blinked sluggishly against Gregory's hard, determined stare. A slow smile crept across his besotted face. Sinclair raised one hand and opened his mouth to speak. "There's one thing I can tell you," he began.

"What?!"

"You're gonna be sorry you wanted out, 'at's what." Sinclair knew he should stop right there, but better sense had left him about four beers ago. "There's more on the sub than rusty pipes and dead Germans."

"Oh, yeah? Like what?"

The words came out slurred. "Like gold bull-yon. Jewels, maybe. Plundered treasure of the Russian Czars. Fabree-shay Eggs, perhaps, oh yeah, yeah, yeah."

"You're drunk, Preston."

"I might be drunk," he grinned. "But soon I'm gonna be rich." Sinclair's expression went as serious as his intoxicated state would allow. "You see, there're these boxes on board. Ain't supposed to be there. It's cargo, don't you see! Cargo! Cargo on a U-boat nobody knows is there! Just think about it!"

"You're always so full of shit, I don't know what to think! Listen, I don't know what you have going, and I don't want to know. But whatever it is, just leave me out of it." Gregory broke into a yell, "*Out!* Do you understand?! *Out!*"

Sinclair held up both palms. "Okay, okay, as far as I'm concerned I don't know you."

"Good. That's the way I want it."

Gregory stormed out the door, leaving Sinclair staring blankly past his beer.

✠   ✠   ✠

Gregory saw the car just as he slowed to turn into the driveway. The same charcoal sedan which followed him earlier in the afternoon was sitting in the gravel lot, approximately 100 feet past the turn-off. He skidded the truck to a hard stop in the middle of the road. The sedan pulled out and accelerated north on Route 12.

Jessica! he thought. Gregory put the pedal to the floor and swung the truck into the driveway, slinging sand in all directions. His daughter's car was parked in front of the house. Heart pounding, he leapt out of the vehicle and barreled through the front door.

"Daddy!" she exclaimed. "I'm glad I caught you. I was just going back out."

"You're not going anywhere!"

"Why not? Daddy, what's the matter?"

"Listen, Jessie, you're staying right here with me. Tomorrow I want you to leave—first thing."

Jessica looked perplexed. "Is something wrong?"

"Just do what I say! Okay?!"

Gregory walked stiffly to the bedroom. He pulled his 12-gauge and a box of 00 buck out of the closet.

"I don't know who you *are*—but don't *fuck with me!*" he snarled, repeating the threat as each shell went into the magazine.

Jessica stood ashen-faced in the bedroom doorway. "Daddy, are you in some kind of trouble?"

"I hope not."

"Daddy, you're creeping me out." Her voice trembled. "Daddy, tell me what's going on."

Gregory put the gun back in the closet and walked over to his daughter. "I'm sorry. Didn't mean to frighten you," he said. "Maybe I'm over-reacting," he went on, sounding contrite. Gregory gently placed his large hands on her shoulders. "Listen, it's just there have been some very weird things going on around here.

I'm sure everything is going to be okay. I just think it best if you weren't around."

Jessica looked confused.

"Jessie, I want you to go to Ocracoke tomorrow and take the Swans Quarter ferry back. I'll call ahead and get you priority loading. I know it's longer that way, but just do it for me, okay?"

She nodded once.

"Everything is gonna be all right," he said with forced reassurance.

Chapter 14

CLIFTON ECHO MADE A FINAL INSPECTION OF THE SITE. Trash had been picked up and the assortment of tools that usually lay strewn about, neatly organized along the edge of the excavation area. The school group, fourth, fifth and sixth graders, were due to arrive any minute. He warned his small crew to watch their language as long as the children were around.

Echo was actually a little nervous. Conscious of any impression he might make on the youngsters, he pulled his cigarettes out of his shirt pocket and stashed them in his battered leather briefcase. He suddenly wished he'd shaven sometime over the last few days.

As soon as the school bus came bumping down the rutted drive, Echo and his two helpers pulled back a huge sheet of black plastic to reveal the partially excavated remains of a fifteenth century Coastal Algonquian Indian village. To an untrained eye, the site appeared to consist of random concentrations of oyster and clam shells, scattered between patches of soil stained gray-brown. The excavation was comprised of a series of ten foot squares set in a checkerboard configuration. A pattern of taut nylon twine formed a grid over the exposed areas. Each square was uniformly excavated to a depth of fourteen inches with plumb walls and impeccably leveled floors.

The students streamed out of the buses, shepherded along by their Civics teacher.

Echo liked to work in private, away from the public eye. However, when the woman came to him and asked if she could to bring her classes to see the site, he felt like he couldn't refuse.

The children gathered around the edge of the excavation, staring blandly at the empty squares.

The teacher said loudly, "Now class, this is Mr. Echo and he has been nice enough to show us his dig. I want you to listen very carefully to everything he has to say."

Echo stepped into the middle of the excavation area. He faced the students. "Okay, everyone, what do you see?"

Stony silence.

"Dirt," a boy in the back row said meekly.

"That's right. Dirt. Lots and lots of dirt. But it's different kinds of dirt, and that's very important."

Echo paused trying to gauge his audience. He seemed to have their full attention. Not used to speaking to children, he wondered if he could hold it.

"What were you expecting to see today?" he asked.

Again there was no response.

"What would one see in an Indian village?"

A girl up front tentatively raised her hand. "Indian houses."

"Yes, very good, houses," Echo replied. "So where are the houses? These people didn't sleep outside in the rain. Well, I'll tell you. I'm standing in what's left of one right now." He pointed to a line of dark circular stains by his feet, each approximately three inches in diameter. "See these funny looking round things here. These are post molds—stains left by small posts that rotted away centuries ago."

Echo pulled a roll of fluorescent orange flagging tape from his pocket. He began to mark each of the faint stains with a short section of tape, anchoring the bright tags in the sandy ground with a roofing nail.

"Some of these are kind of faded, so I'm going to mark them for you," he said, working his way around in an elongated circle.

"That's why we keep the site covered with plastic—to keep the sun from drying it out."

When he finished, the fluorescent tags formed an oval outline measuring approximately fifteen by twenty-five feet. Echo stretched his arms to either side and faced the children. "This," he said, "is an Indian house. What they did was cut green saplings and drive them into the ground, then bend them over and tie them off two by two. Other saplings were tied down horizontally around the outside to form a domed frame. They covered it with bark mats and grass thatch."

Echo looked up to see fifty pairs of eyes staring back at him. He wondered what the kids were thinking, or if they were even listening.

"It's called a wig-wam," he said, adding, "So I'll bet you're wondering where all the arrowheads and tomahawks are?"

A multitude of heads bobbed up and down.

"Artifacts!" Echo said in a purposefully loud voice. "Artifacts are important but they may not necessarily be the most important thing. What's important is what the artifacts can tell us. Now there's a saying in archaeology—it's not what you find but what you find out." He motioned across the excavation area with the sweep of an arm. "All this you see in front of you is part of a big puzzle, and we're here to figure it out. We look for clues. We look for clues to tell us who was here; what they did; what they ate." He pointed to the ground in front of him. "What their houses looked like; anything we can learn about how these people lived."

With the children's eyes following his every move, Echo walked over to a folding table set up to display some of the more interesting items unearthed at the site.

"Now, we've only found a few projectile points. These people didn't have a lot of stone to work with on the island, so much of what they used was made of bone or antler. Often we don't find those because they have disintegrated—but we do have their pottery."

He held up a few large earthenware shards with cord impressions on the outside, then showed them a small gigging point fashioned from a stingray barb. The children craned their heads to get a better look.

A hand went up. "What's that?" the child asked, pointing to the ground at Echo's feet.

Echo was delighted with the question. "Another clue. It's a pit—a hole the Indians dug in the ground. With time it filled in, leaving this darker stain. Sometimes the Indians put their trash in pits. That's good for us because we get to find what they threw away. This one's been half-excavated by the workers. You can see its original shape once the darker fill is taken out. All of the soil is carefully screened and every little thing kept. I think this pit was used for cooking, maybe for roasting a deer."

Echo scanned the crowd of young faces. "Anyone have any ideas what else pits might have been used for?" he asked of them.

"To go to the bafroom," one of the younger students in the front stated earnestly.

A few snickers arose from the back rows.

"I've never thought about that one," Echo replied with a smile. "On some sites though, you do find preserved... um... poop, if you will."

A volley of high-pitched giggles rang out.

"Tell you the truth, I wouldn't mind finding some preserved poop here. It can be an important clue—tell us what people were eating, or if they were sick."

The admission was met with a few shrill expressions of disgust. Most of the children, however, seemed to find the concept quite reasonable.

Echo appeared to be enjoying himself. Interacting with his young audience, his movements became relaxed and animated. The teacher stood watching him walk back and forth across the excavation area, gesturing with one hand and calling on pupils with the other.

Clifton Echo was in his late thirties. He was of medium height with a slim but sturdy build. Apart from intelligent, brown eyes, Echo possessed what could best be described as ordinary looking features. His face was tanned and somewhat weathered for his age.

Longish, dark brown hair fell from beneath a dusty baseball cap while a tattered blue bandanna hung around his neck. From his sand-colored sweater to his faded jeans and scuffed work boots, Echo seemed every bit what the children's teacher thought an archaeologist should be. She remained standing inconspicuously near the back of the throng, eyes carefully following his every move.

"So what do you think the Indians here ate?" Echo asked the children.

In an instant, a dozen hands shot into the air.

"Clams," one child stated proudly.

"That's right. Those are clam shells scattered in all those pits." He pointed to another pupil.

"Fishes and ducks."

"You bet."

By this time most every child had his or her hand in the air, pleading to be called upon.

"Deer!"

"You bet. Deer were just about their favorite food. Deer also provided them with many of the raw materials they needed—antler and bone for tools and weapons, hide for clothes. They used the brains for tanning the hides. Nothing was wasted. The guts were fed to their dogs."

"Nuts and berries! They ate nuts and berries!" one child blurted, unable to contain himself.

"Probably," Echo said smiling. "Those foods were certainly very important to the mainland tribes. Maybe not so much out here."

He again began to pace the excavation area.

"I'll tell you what else they ate. Corn. Squash. Beans. They grew a little of each. But mostly they ate whatever they could find. Turtles, bird eggs, green shoots in the spring, even grub worms."

A collective "*Yuck!*" rang out.

Echo saw the opportunity to instill a lesson of sorts.

"You know what else?" Not waiting for a reply he said, "Just because these folks didn't have metal tools, or big sailing ships like the Europeans did, doesn't mean they were primitive, or stupid.

Quite the opposite. Sure, they didn't have to go to school like you all do, but they had just as much to learn, maybe more. Everything they needed to live, they had to make themselves. Every father taught his sons how to make the tools he needed to survive. Every mother taught her daughters to make everything they needed. And they couldn't be lazy—you know why?"

There was no response from the crowd of children, only enraptured stares.

"Because if they were lazy, they died—starved to death! They couldn't go to Conner's Supermarket or the Burrus Red and White for their groceries. They had to go out and find, grow, or hunt down everything they ate. And there weren't any refrigerators around either. Any extra food had to be preserved for leaner times. Every child your age had to learn about hundreds of different plants; had to learn the ways of all the animals that flew through the air, swam in the water or scurried about the woods."

Echo looked over the crowd of intent young faces. He seemed to have made his point.

The teacher's strong voice cut in. "Okay, class, it's almost time for us to head back. Does anyone have any more questions for Mr. Echo before we go?"

The next ten minutes were spent answering a host of eager questions, many of them quite thoughtful. Aside from having been enjoyable, playing schoolteacher for half an hour offered Echo a number of insights he had not anticipated. Never having spent much time around children, he was taken by the stark clarity with which their little minds worked.

"Okay, that will be all, class. We have to go now," the teacher called out. "I want you to thank Mr. Echo for showing us his dig."

A single chorus of "Thank you, Mr. Echo!" rose up.

The children marched back to the buses, laughing and giggling all the way. Echo briefly held the teacher's smiling glance before she herself turned and boarded.

✠   ✠   ✠

It was only after the bus pulled out that Echo noticed the blue and white Sheriff's Department cruiser. Sheriff Winston, a tall sinewy man with black, well-lubricated hair, stood leaning against the side of the car, his arms folded tightly across his chest. A deputy sat in the front seat. They had been waiting for the children to leave.

The sheriff straightened and ambled toward Echo with one thumb tucked under his gun belt. He peeled off his dark glasses and hung them on his breast pocket. "Mr. Echo," he said in a relaxed, disarming voice.

"Yes?"

"It's been a while... Tom Winston," the sheriff said, extending his hand. He spoke with a silky smooth drawl.

Echo clasped the officer's hand. "Yes, it has been," he said mildly. "What can I do for you?"

"A lot, actually. I hope this isn't too much to ask, but I'm kind of in a bind."

"Anything. What's the problem?"

"There's been a murder," the sheriff said grimly.

Echo blinked hard.

Sheriff Winston ran one finger across his cheek. "I was just thinking maybe you could take that instrument of yours and help make a map of the scene."

"You mean the digital transit?"

The sheriff nodded. "Like you can imagine, we don't get a lot of killings 'round here. In the rare case it does happen, it's usually because someone is drunk and gets to fightin'. But I never seen anything like this."

"What do you mean?"

It looks to have been more like... an execution. I figured with your background and all, you could be of help."

Echo gave a weak nod.

"I want to find the bastards who did this and get a conviction," Winston said, his voice taking on a certain urgency. "And the last thing I want is some high dollar, silver tongued defense counselor calling my investigation into question."

"Did you call the state?"

"I most surely did. I wanted to get a forensics team down here from Raleigh right away. But being the day before Thanksgiving, they basically told me to get real."

"I don't know how much help I can be, but I'll do everything I can."

"Good," the sheriff replied. "We need to get going." He curled his nose. "Been there a while."

"Right, then."

They walked to the waiting patrol car.

"Do you know who the victim is?" Echo asked.

"I surely do. We made the identification on the scene. Had his wallet on him, along with thirty-eight dollars. That's why we figured it was no robbery."

"What's the name?"

"Preston G. Sinclair."

Chapter 15

THE BODY LAY FACE DOWN, ARMS EXTENDED TO EITHER SIDE. Outwardly, the cause of death seemed clear. At least three small caliber bullet wounds were visible on the exposed portion of the neck. The back of the head was caked in dried blood and Echo suspected several more entrance wounds were present underneath the thickly matted hair. Echo saw the throat was cut from ear to ear, nearly causing decapitation. An ugly black crust covered the sandy ground around the head and upper torso. Even though it was the end of November and the weather had been seasonably cool, the odor of early-stage decomposition was amply evident.

Echo and Sheriff Winston stood and surveyed the grisly scene. Two deputies crouched behind them, attempting to lift a latex cast from around a watery tire mark.

"I figured they must have brought him by car," the sheriff started. "I suppose they killed him here and left the body. We've been trying to get a cast of the tread but with no luck. The ground's just too damn soft."

"Assume nothing," Echo said somewhat absently as he examined the corpse. He had already noticed the gummy white residue clinging to the puffy and strongly discolored wrists.

"What are you looking at?" the sheriff asked.

"Assume nothing and just go with what the evidence tells you. For one, you see this white stuff here. It's probably from duct tape. You'd best take a sample of it."

"What does it tell you?"

Echo straightened and backed away. "I'm not sure. Let's take some pictures before anything gets stepped on."

"I already took pictures."

"I'll take a few more," Echo responded diplomatically.

He walked back to his own vehicle, returning with a 4X5 Speed Graphic, a heavy duty tripod and an assortment of film packs. He set the camera on the tripod and snapped in the holder containing black and white Pan-X. Sheriff Winston and the deputies watched him work.

"Let me get some overall shots before we do anything else," Echo said while taking a light meter reading. "If there's anything being missed, at least we'll have it on film. This stuff enlarges like you wouldn't believe."

The sheriff nodded. "Whatever you think best."

"Then I want to shoot some color. This won't take too long."

When Echo finished, a deputy helped him put away the gear. Within a minute or two, he had the transit up and ready to go. One of the deputies held the rod while Echo entered the data into the small microprocessor integrated with the instrument's optics. After the overall scene was charted, a plan-view of the body area was made, with the locations of the six .22 caliber shell casings scattered about, plotted on a one-centimeter grid.

Echo packed away the transit. He staidly watched Sheriff Winston begin to collect evidence.

"Twenty-two short," Winston said, carefully picking up the small shells with the end of a pencil and dropping them into a zip-lock bag. "Can get these anywhere."

"Pretty generic round," Echo agreed. "If I had to guess, I'd say they were fired from an automatic—small, deadly, easy to silence. I think you're right about this being a professional job. It would be unusual for them not to capture the shells, though."

Sheriff Winston continued to work. He snipped a lock of hair and cut away a patch of clothing for a fiber sample. Using a wooden Popsicle stick, he scraped off some of the white residue from around the wrists. Fingernails were cut and the grit underneath collected. Each of the samples were sealed in a plastic bag and labeled.

Even though Echo knew he had helped, he still wondered exactly why the sheriff called on him, and what was meant by "his background." He couldn't be sure whether Winston was referring to his training as a physical anthropologist, or if he knew of his years spent in the employment of the Central Intelligence Agency. Echo generally tried to keep the latter aspect of his past unknown to all but a few close friends.

Echo had completed his graduate work at the University of Tennessee when a CIA recruiter visited the campus. Deep in debt with school loans and with no steady job prospects, Echo was intrigued by the offer he was made. Once within the Agency, he caught the eye of at least one Langley heavyweight with his organizational skills and his ability to tackle encompassing assignments while keeping up with the finest of details. A meteoric career had him posted as deputy station chief in Tegucigalpa, Honduras. It was the mid-1980s and Echo liked being close to where the action was. At the same time, he felt certain most of his friends and colleagues back in the academic world would have shunned him if they knew what he was doing for a living.

His career with the CIA ended abruptly, by his own choosing. Once on the outside, Echo indulged himself in what was his true love. In the best tradition of the pioneering archaeologists, he funded his own excavations, allowing him to work whatever sites he wished. With no visible means of support, he maintained an unexpected inheritance had made him wealthy.

When Sheriff Winston was finished, the body was lifted onto a stretcher and carried to a waiting ambulance. An autopsy would be performed in Elizabeth City on Friday.

Echo and Winston watched the ambulance pull away.

"Did you know him?" the sheriff asked.

Echo hesitated a moment before answering. "Yeah, I knew him. Not very well, but I knew him. Hell, everybody knew Preston Sinclair. He was kind of hard to miss."

"This is true," Winston said sadly.

✠ ✠ ✠

Gregory sat stone-faced at the kitchen table while Billy Page continued to pound on the front door. Usually, Billy Page just walked in unannounced. Today he figured it would be best to knock first. The murder put everyone on the island on edge.

"It's me, Eric," he called through the screen door.

"Come in," Gregory said dully.

Billy Page shuffled into the kitchen. "Guess you heard about Preston."

"Yeah," Gregory said, staring straight ahead.

"What a freak out! Man, I don't know what to think."

"You don't understand."

Billy Page looked at his friend and captain and said, "No, I sure don't."

"You don't understand!" Gregory again said, his voice gaining strength.

"What don't I understand?"

Gregory faced the mate. "Someone took *Preston* out!" he shouted. "*Out!* Just like that!"

Billy Page was genuinely startled by the outburst.

"I'm gonna tell you something," Gregory ranted on. "Preston Sinclair might have looked like a goof, but the man was a motherfucker!" Gregory's voice kept rising in both volume and pitch. "I heard back in Nam he'd sneak out of camp at dark—show up the next morning at the perimeter with a whole string of ears tied around his belt! And lemme tell you I don't doubt a word of it!"

"He did what he had to do," Billy Page said glumly.

"He did it for *fun!*" Gregory wailed, rising from the chair. "When he was *bored!* God only knows what the government put him up to."

Billy Page didn't know what to say.

"And somebody took him out! Just like that!" Gregory stated, slumping back down. "Just—like—that!" he repeated, pronouncing every word as an individual sentence.

It never occurred to Billy Page that Gregory figured one or both of them could well be next.

"You sure seem shaken up by this," the mate said. "By all accounts you never much liked the guy."

"Listen—Preston and I go back to when your ass was in diapers!"

"Take it easy, will you. Don't get mad at me!"

Gregory resumed staring across the room at nothing in particular.

"Look, maybe you shouldn't be alone today," Billy Page offered. "Mom's cooking a 25-pound bird. Why don't you come over. There'll be plenty for everybody. We'll watch the game. It's Washington and Dallas—should be a good one."

Gregory declined the invitation and sat back down. Billy Page left, pushing closed the screen door behind him.

Gregory remained slumped at the table, his chin resting on tightly folded hands. He was certain the murder was in some way linked to the U-boat. Moreover, having put Sinclair on the wreck, he could not help but feel a sense of responsibility. Sitting alone, Gregory resolved to do whatever he could to find out what happened.

✠   ✠   ✠

The gray Crown Victoria carrying US Government tags eased down the narrow lane. Both sides of the drive were bordered by water-filled swales studded with cattails. Low overhanging pine branches created a tunnel-like effect. The dense forest opened to where an aluminum trailer, its formerly painted exterior oxidized a dull gray, rested on cinder blocks. A ramshackle, screened-in porch enclosed most of the front. Beyond the trailer, one of the ditches widened to meet a large freshwater pond. A gnarled but stout live oak, peppered with yellowish-green lichen, stood aside of the dilapidated complex. The pale, fragmented rays of the late autumn sun cast flickering highlights across the scene.

The porch screen door banged open and Clifton Echo emerged to receive his unexpected visitor.

"Clifton, long time, no see," a man wearing dark glasses, a starched white shirt and a brown blazer called out while stepping from the sedan.

It was Frank Bruford, an officer with whom he briefly worked at Langley. The years had not been kind and the man was carrying about forty more pounds than when Echo had seen him last. His hair had turned mostly white.

"Frank, Frank Bruford. Good to see you," Echo said, negotiating the rickety steps and extending a hand.

"Good to see you, Clifton."

"This is certainly a surprise. Won't you come in."

For a moment there did not seem to be much more to add.

"I can't believe you found me."

"It's my job to find people," Bruford said plainly. "Besides, we usually know where you are."

Echo did not like Bruford's tone. Though the remark didn't seem an implicit threat, he nonetheless wished it hadn't been made. He motioned to a set of lawn chairs on the porch. The two sat down.

"So how have you been?" Echo asked.

"Good."

"How are things at the Company, they still treating you okay?"

"I've stepped up a couple of grades, and after the last shakeup, I got promoted again. So yeah, I'm doing okay."

Echo smiled politely, lowering his eyes.

"Oh, you noticed. Desk job." Bruford laughed, patting his belly. "Too many hours in the Situation Room with the donuts. I got to start working out."

"So what brings you down here?"

"Business. I've come to ask a favor of sorts."

"I see."

Bruford got up and looked through the screen mesh at the swampy pond. He clasped his hands behind his back. "Now I know this is going to sound a little strange, but hear me out."

"Okay," Echo agreed.

"There's someone on Hatteras Island I'd like you to get to know," Bruford stated, suddenly looking uncomfortable. He loosened his collar. "Two folks actually. One's Russian—former KGB. The other is ours. They're here on an investigation. I'm asking you to introduce yourself and offer to help them in any way you can—and to keep an eye on them both."

"You want me to help a KGB agent operate, here, on Hatteras?!" Echo asked, amazed and perplexed at the request.

"Former KGB," Bruford emphasized. "It's a new world out there, Clifton. I know, it's strange for me, too. Old ways die hard. Things change though, and we have to move with the times."

"Who's the other person and what's his role in this?"

"Her role," Bruford corrected. "A Ms. Sandra Claremont. She's here to assist in any way she can—and keep an eye on Stanizlow."

"Then what the hell did you come to me for?!" Echo exclaimed, more than a little exasperated. By now he was certain he didn't want any part in whatever Bruford had in mind.

"She's not with the Agency," Bruford said, sounding almost pained. "We've been bypassed on this one. I don't know any more than what I've already told you. Except whatever is going on is big. It goes all the way to the top. This Claremont broad, she reports directly to the National Security Adviser. I heard, she has direct access to the president."

Echo was intrigued. "What's in it for me?"

"Nothing," Bruford shrugged. "I said it was a favor, not a business proposition."

The hint was taken.

"So you want me to spy on a couple of spies, so I can tell you spies what's going on, 'cause you all don't know nothin'!" Echo said, trying to keep a straight face.

"Clifton," Bruford let out patiently, "it ain't the old days anymore. Times are different." He stopped to search for the right words. "The Agency, well, to be honest, we've taken some hits lately—there've been some real slip-ups."

Echo smacked his lips, nodding once.

"I'm not making any excuses, mind you, but our stock is way down these days, especially on the Hill." Bruford struggled to keep his voice steady. "Shit, there're even some liberal congressmen calling to do away with us altogether. They want to abolish the Agency—farm everything out to other departments. We might all be out of a job."

Echo couldn't have cared less about Bruford's job security. "Tell me more about this Claremont character," he said.

"Never met her. All this was set up through the State Department. That's all I know, honest. But that's just it—we need to know what's going on. That's why I'm here talking to you."

Echo knew there was more to it than he was being told.

Bruford pressed on. "All you have to do is hang around, keep your ears open, and get back to me with what you find out. What do you say?"

Echo thought it over, wondering exactly what his former colleague might not be telling him.

"Sure, I'll do it," Echo then said gingerly. "Sounds like it might be interesting."

"Great!" Bruford reached into his jacket. "Here's a secure number where you can reach me."

Echo slipped the card in his pocket, asking, "How much longer are you going to be around?"

"A couple of days. I'm going to check into a motel and relax. Maybe do a little beach combing. I love it down here in the fall."

✠   ✠   ✠

Gregory stopped off at the store for a soda. Maggie looked back at him from behind the cash register, her normally cheery face somber and drawn.

"I'm so sorry about Preston," she said to Gregory.

"Me, too."

"Such a nice man, a little strange, but nice. I'll bet you Preston never hurt a fly."

Gregory paid for the drink.

She pressed a hand across her chest. "Murdered, he was! How perfectly awful. Who would do something like this?"

"I don't know," Gregory said, taking the change. "But believe me, I intend to find out."

Gregory turned and left the store without another word.

✠   ✠   ✠

The library parking lot was empty when Gregory pulled in. It was Saturday, shortly before noon. Just as he got to the double doors, one of them opened and an old man stepped through, squinting into the bright sunshine. The man wore tan cotton work clothes and a red plaid woolen hunting cap and vest. He peered at Gregory through thick, plastic-framed glasses. A deeply creased face and weathered hands told of a lifetime of labor amidst the salt and sun.

"Well, hello there, young fella," the old man crackled. He seemed surprised to see Gregory standing there. "I was just about to close."

"I'll come back some other time."

"Can I help you with something? It's no bother. I can open back up."

"I was just wanting to get a look at some old newspapers you might have."

"Come on then, let's go and see what we got."

"Are you sure? It's 'bout noon."

The old man let out a spry laugh. "Got all day my boy. Retired. I'm just subbing for my daughter-in-law. She's a little under the weather today."

"I'm sorry to hear that," Gregory said politely.

Their footsteps echoed through the short corridor. Air inside the small library was warm and slightly stale. The low angle midday sun shone through the dusty windows to lay in bright patches across the green tile floor. Gregory suddenly felt himself get sleepy.

"So what can I help you with today?"

"I'd like to take a look at some old newspapers from World War Two."

"I don't think we have many of those. Some of what we got's on microfilm. Some of it ain't. What exactly you interested in?"

Gregory began to think he might have come to the wrong place. In fact, he wasn't even exactly sure himself what he was looking for. "Accounts of ships being sunk, or any unusual happenings around Hatteras," he said, sounding tentative. "Particularly near the end of the war."

"You're looking into that U-boat, aren't you," the old man said with obvious self-satisfaction.

"I might be," Gregory replied. "But only if it can help me find out what I need to know."

"What might that be?"

"To tell you the truth, it's kind of personal."

The old man gave a shallow snort. "Don't mean to be mindin' nobody's business. Anyhow, you wouldn't find that kind of information in no newspaper. Was censored, you see. Couldn't let the enemy know what was happening, now could we?"

Gregory felt a little foolish. "Of course. I guess I wasn't really thinking. Sorry to take your time," he said, turning to leave.

"No, it's no problem at all," the old man countered. "Say, if you're interested in the war, then you should talk to my friend Norman. He knows just about everything that went on around here—starting from about 1930 or so. Norman, he fancies himself a historian of sorts. He's been writing a little history of Hatteras—you know, just something to keep him busy. He's long retired just like me."

"Where does this Norman live?"

"Tell you what. If you like, we can go visit him right now. Norman always likes people to drop by. Watch out though," he chuckled. "Norman's liable to talk your ears off if you give him half a chance. Once you get the old boy started, there's n-o-o-o stoppin' 'im."

"I think I'd like to talk to your friend."

"No problem at all. I could ride over there with you right now, if you don't mind giving me a lift."

"Sure."

The old man straightened and held out his hand. "Lester Brodie is the name."

Gregory clasped his hand. "Eric Gregory," he said warmly.

     ✠   ✠   ✠

True to his billing, Lester's friend Norman was a venerable storehouse of information, and wanted nothing more than to share as much of it as possible. Every other sentence began with either "Let me tell you" or "I remember when." Gregory continually prodded him about wartime events on the island. Responses to specific questions, however, quickly digressed into summations of who lived where, who got married to whom and who died of what and when.

"What about near the end of the war, any U-boat sightings, unusual happenings, rumors of anything going on?" Gregory asked. He already posed the same basic question twice and by now had the feeling the interview was going nowhere.

Lester interrupted his friend's rambling response to Gregory's inquiry. "The war Norman! He wants to know what it was like during the war!"

"The war! Rumors!? Oh, yeah, there were rumors a plenty," Norman exclaimed in a crusty voice. "German infiltration teams coming ashore was always a good one. Saboteurs were everywhere back then," he added, winking.

Lester leaned forward in his chair. "Some folks actually believed a Japanese midget sub was working the Pamlico Sound!"

Both old men let out raspy laughs.

"Did anyone actually know of any Germans coming ashore?" Gregory asked.

Lester cut his friend off before he could answer. "All that was a bunch of horse hockey! What would they of wanted out here anyway? There weren't nothin' of no import' 'round these parts."

"That reminds me, though," the other old man cut in. "There was this German-speaking fellow washed up one day. No one ever knew where he came from. Let me see," he said rubbing his chin. "Would have been in '45. Spring, if I'm not mistaken."

"Really?"

"Yup. Was the Wilson boy who found him, doing Beach Patrol. He's passed on now, though. Heart attack. Fell down dead just like that," Norman said, snapping his wiry fingers above his head.

"This man, what did he look like?"

"Didn't ever see him. A lot of other folks did though. Everybody was talking 'bout him. Kind of funny looking for a German—least that's what folks said. Half dead he was when they pulled him off the beach. Still, they said he had these eyes that would just stare right through you."

"What else do you remember?"

"I heard he had a small tattoo on his arm. Had a pretty bad cut, too. They took him over to Doc Clark who fixed him right up. Don't know what ever happened after that. The next day, the Marines came and took him away. That's 'bout all I can tell you."

"What about the tattoo?"

"It was just a mark of sorts. No one rightly knew what it was."

"Well, thanks. No one ever knew his name I suppose," Gregory said, hardly expecting an answer.

"Oh yeah! They did know his name. He had it printed on his shirt. I just can't rightly remember what it was. Tell you what though, I know someone who ought to be able to tell you."

"That would be great." Gregory handed him his *Hawkeye* business card. "Here, if you can come up with anything, please call me."

"Kessel," Norman said suddenly. "The man's name was Kessel. I'm sure of it. Everyone was talking about it. K-E-S-S-E-L."

Gregory thanked them both for their time.

"If there's anything else I can do, Captain, come on by. Hope we've been of some help."

"You just might have been," Gregory replied carefully. "You just might have been."

Chapter 16

CAPTAIN GREGORY WAS A MAN ON A MISSION. Most of his off days were spent combing the island talking to just about everyone who'd had anything to do with Preston Sinclair. After dozens of interviews, he managed to reconstruct much of the man's final days. Other than the bartender at the Mad Shrimper, it appeared Gregory himself was the last person to see Sinclair alive.

At least once a day, Gregory would pay a visit to Sheriff Winston. During times when the sheriff was out, he would pester the dispatcher or one of the deputies to fill him in on any new developments. Everyone on the small force had long since had enough of him.

"Hello, Mr. Gregory," Winston sighed as Gregory barged into the small office.

"Got something for you I just remembered."

"Later. I don't have time."

"I'm telling you, there've been these two guys hanging around driving a gray late model sedan. They followed me just before Preston was killed. Same time the GPS was stolen. I think they had New Jersey tags. I can't tell what they're up to but it's like they don't belong. I just know it!"

"This is *my* investigation, Mr. Gregory!" Winston said forcibly, while rising to his feet. "Allow me to do my job as I see fit!"

"I'm telling you," Gregory blurted back, undaunted by the sheriff's exasperated demand. "This goes way beyond Hatteras Island. This goes way beyond North Carolina. I think it's time we call in the FBI."

"They're already here!" Winston exclaimed, turning aside and throwing his hands in the air.

"Where?"

"At the Pines Motel in Buxton."

"You called them?"

"I didn't call anybody! Last week this woman agent, she comes into my office and…"

"A woman?"

"Yeah. She comes in with a letter of introduction from Washington, DC—all printed on fancy paper with the presidential seal—asking me to cooperate fully with her investigation. I told her I'd do anything I could. They—she and her partner—they seem to spend a lot of time snooping around the south end of the island."

Sheriff Winston's worn expression lifted. "Gregory, I'll make you a deal. I'll take you over there to meet them—but only if you promise to stop bugging me. You can bend their ears all you want with your theories on who killed your friend."

"I'll go over there myself, thank you. This FBI agent, what's she look like?"

"Good," the sheriff said smiling. "Just go to the motel and ask for Agent Claremont."

Gregory stormed out of the room without another word. Sheriff Winston glanced at his watch. It was almost four and he was ready to call it a day. He grabbed his uniform jacket off the coat hook.

"I don't believe this," the sheriff muttered, pulling closed the zipper and reaching for his cap. Just what the hell is going on around here? he thought as he locked the door behind him.

✠   ✠   ✠

The woman sat by the swimming pool in the motel courtyard. She noticed Gregory as he pulled up to the office but quickly returned her attention to the crossword puzzle she was working. A cellular phone stood propped upright on a small table next to where she was sitting.

Having made his inquiry, Gregory emerged from the motel office and walked straight toward her. She lowered the paper in her hand and cautiously watched his approach from over the top of green-tinted tortoise shell sunglasses.

"Agent Claremont?"

The woman rose from her chair, peeling away the shades. Gregory saw she stood almost as tall as he.

"Yes?"

Wearing jeans and a cardigan, with sandy blonde hair falling loosely about her shoulders, she was nothing like what Gregory imagined an FBI agent would be. But what struck him most was the inquisitive gleam in her eyes—and her smile—quick, friendly, unmistakably self-assured.

"I'm Eric Gregory," he said, hoping he hadn't been obviously staring. "I thought maybe I could to talk to you about the case you're on." Gregory was sure he stumbled over a word or two. "Sheriff Winston told me where to find you," he explained.

She extended her hand saying, "Special Agent Claremont, FBI."

"Pleased to meet you," Gregory replied. What an understatement, he thought.

"Won't you sit?" she said, easing herself back down.

Gregory pulled up a second chair.

"What can I do for you?"

"I have a special interest in this case," Gregory began. "You see, Preston Sinclair was an old friend."

"I'm sorry."

"Yeah, me too. I want to see whoever did it get nailed."

Agent Claremont nodded a polite acknowledgment.

Gregory commenced to explain about having found a previously unknown German U-boat wreck and how his mate and Preston Sinclair dived on it. He told her of his GPS unit, with the sub's coordinates, having been stolen, noting further he'd spotted two strangers following him. Claremont listened intently while rolling the eraser end of the pencil along her lower lip. Shifting in his chair, Gregory tried not to notice.

A man appeared behind them.

Claremont stood up. "Mr. Gregory, I'd like you to meet my associate here."

Gregory stood to shake the man's hand.

"Hello, I am Viktor Stanizlow," the man said in a thick Russian accent.

"We just call him Stan," Claremont said, laughing lightly.

"Does anyone call you Vic?" Gregory joked, sitting back down.

"No."

Viktor Stanizlow was a robust man with a broad, angular face. He had a ruddy complexion and dark, bushy eyebrows. By contrast, his tightly cropped hair was completely white. Though he was undoubtedly close to retirement age, his skin was taut and nearly free of spots or folds. Gregory noted the individual standing before him seemed to carry himself with a vibrant intensity more akin a younger man.

"Stan here used to be a colonel in the KGB," Claremont said. "Now he's over here as an observer of sorts—part of an exchange program we've set up to help our new friends learn to better fight crime in their own country."

"Times sure have changed," Gregory said back at Claremont, noticing for the first time the remarkable shade of her eyes. He made himself look away.

"They certainly have," Claremont agreed.

The sun had gone down and the streetlights in front of the motel flickered on.

"I'd like to talk to you some more," Claremont said somewhat abruptly. "Both of us would, I'm sure. Perhaps we could meet for dinner? Stan and I have been eating at the Tides. I love their seafood."

"I could do that."

"Let's say 6:30," she said, getting up.

"I'll be there."

Gregory watched her follow the Russian toward the rooms. Gregory's stomach did a slight flip as she turned at her door and cast him a short wave.

✠   ✠   ✠

Viktor Stanizlow listened intently as Gregory reiterated everything he told Claremont earlier. Stanizlow appeared to be particularly interested in the two men who went into the Midgette Mart. He barely touched his tuna steak while Gregory was speaking. Claremont happily consumed her broiled scallops.

"Tell you what," Gregory offered. "You should talk to Maggie Tinsley at the Midgette Mart. She saw 'em up close. She'll be working again tomorrow. I'm sure she'd love to talk to you." He let out a laugh. "She loves to talk to just about everyone."

Stanizlow looked over at Claremont and in his plodding speech said, "Let's do that in morning."

If Gregory had been paying closer attention, he might have noticed it was the Russian who appeared to be doing the investigating, with Claremont playing the role of observer. The man sitting across from him, however, was the last thing on his mind.

Gregory turned to Claremont. "How were your scallops?"

"Very good. Yesterday I had the flounder. I liked it, too."

Sensing an opening Gregory asked, "Have you ever been fishing?"

"Not in a very long time. Back when I was a little girl, in the summers, my uncle would take me out on Long Island Sound—flounder fishing actually. Flatfish he called them."

"I'm going offshore for tuna on Saturday, weather permitting. Would you care to come along?"

Claremont turned her head and gave him a quizzical look. Stanizlow appeared to be ignoring the conversation. Leaning back in his chair, he looked lost in thought.

"Oh, I guess I didn't tell you," Gregory added. "I'm a charter captain. I own the boat. I could take you out on it."

"I'd love to go, but being on the ocean usually makes me seasick."

"We could go out on the Sound," Gregory offered. "Do some flounder fishing. We grow 'em big down here in Carolina," he said grinning.

"Sure, I'll go," Claremont said after a moment's hesitation. "I'm sure Stan would want to go, too. Sounds like a good break. What do you think, Stan?"

Stanizlow just shrugged his broad shoulders.

Gregory gave her his card. "The boat's at Oden's Dock, right in the middle of Hatteras village. If anything comes up, just give me a call. Otherwise, say 9:00 o'clock Saturday?"

"Great."

✠ ✠ ✠

"Flounder fishing! Are you nuts?!" Billy Page hollered. He nearly dropped the heavy electric-driven reel he was spooling with fresh line.

"I'm taking Agent Claremont out. She wants to catch some flatties."

Billy Page looked at his captain in complete disbelief. "I thought we was gonna take some tuna! Christmas is comin'. I need the money!"

"We'll go some other time."

"Like hell!" Billy Page yelled. "It's supposed to lay down again today. They're slaying 'em out there! When was the last time we had weather like this?"

"I'm gonna want you along. I'll be teaching Ms. Claremont how to fish."

"I know what's going on here," Billy Page said, pointing a finger at his captain. "The secret agent babe's got you bent in loops."

"F-B-I! She's not a secret agent for chrissakes," Gregory shot back. "Now shut up, here they come!"

"Can't say I blame you, though," the mate said wryly. "I got a good look at her standing in front of the motel just the other day. Man, is she ever fine!"

"Shut up!" Gregory snarled out the corner of his mouth.

✠   ✠   ✠

It was one of those all too rare December days where the wind lay down to almost nothing. The *Hawkeye* chugged beyond the breakwater. From low over the horizon, the sun cast its soft light across the placid sound. All around, sky, land and water melded in a mosaic of pastel hues.

Claremont stood next to Gregory, almost giddy at the feel of morning air rushing past the bridge. She grabbed Gregory's arm. "Look at those birds!"

A flock of pelicans rested on an exposed sandbar that flanked the channel. The ungainly-looking birds stood on oversized webbed feet, their outrageously long beaks nearly touching the sand. Several turned their droopy heads and eyed the boat gliding by.

"Pelicans," Gregory said leaning closer. "Used to not see many of those. DDT 'bout wiped them out. They're coming back strong, though."

"We don't have them up north," she said, still looking back.

Gregory began to point out landmarks visible on the shore. He placed a hand on her shoulder and pointed to the old Coast Guard tower. "That's Hatteras Inlet," he said, motioning to the wide break in the shore. "It separates Hatteras and Ocracoke Islands. The inlet can be the hardest part of the run offshore. Out on those shoals, I've seen waves stand twenty feet high."

Back in the cockpit, Stanizlow leaned on the gunwales, watching the water rush past. Billy Page tried to make small talk with the Russian, who simply nodded and smiled politely.

Claremont pointed to a cluster of four-wheel-drive trucks parked on the narrow spit of land on the Hatteras side of the inlet. Gregory could not keep his eyes off her. Backlit by the early morning sun, blondish hair swirled around her face despite her repeated efforts to brush it aside with the stroke of a hand. They almost clipped a channel marker. Claremont leaned into Gregory to steady herself as the boat began to rise and fall with the swells coming through the inlet.

Gregory gently clasped her arm with one hand, keeping the other on the wheel. "Easy now, we're almost out of it," he said reassuringly.

An artificial island, consisting of dredge spoil, grew larger off the starboard side.

Gregory nodded at the looming pile of sand. "There—that's where we'll be fishing. I know where we can get some real nice flatties, right where it drops off to deeper water."

Gregory slowed the boat and cut the engines. They climbed down into the cockpit.

"How do we get started?" Claremont asked, holding the rod ready in one hand.

"I'll put a minnow on for you," Gregory said, reaching around her from behind. "When you feel it tug, drop the tip and reel in the slack, then pull back hard."

The baits went overboard. It wasn't long before Claremont let out a sharp yell. "I got one!"

Gregory jumped for the landing net while Claremont struggled to reel in the fish.

"Six pounds easy! That's a citation fish!" Gregory said excitedly, holding up a doormat sized flounder.

Claremont couldn't stop laughing. "That was great!" she exclaimed. "Let's get another one."

Once again, Gregory found the action. Billy Page grabbed a rod and soon had two nice fish in the box. Gregory joined in. He and the mate vied to bait Claremont's line. To their surprise she insisted on performing the task herself. Between hookups, all three argued exuberantly as to whose fish in the cooler were the biggest. Stanizlow, on the other hand, did not seem inclined to participate. While the others pulled in one flounder after another, he stood on the opposite side of the boat gazing toward Hatteras Inlet and the open waters which lay beyond.

The fish stopped biting with the tide change, and they had all they needed. Gregory took a round about route back to the marina. Claremont rejoined him on the bridge.

"Since you like flounder, how about coming over for lunch tomorrow. I could cook one for you," Gregory suggested confidently.

"I'd love to, but I have plans."

"Like what?"

"I met this archaeologist. He's going to show me his site."

"Echo," Gregory said, trying not to sound sour.

"You know him?"

" Yeah I know him. Seems to think he's pretty slick."

A slight chop had built. Gregory throttled up for the run in.

"Seems like an okay guy," she said, raising her voice over the increased engine noise. "You know he's taken a special interest in the death of your friend."

Gregory let it go until they were back at the dock.

Gregory hadn't told Claremont about the suspected cargo on board the U-boat. Up until a few minutes ago, he wanted to confide everything. Now he figured it might be best to keep a few things to himself, for the time being at least.

"So what's Echo's interest in the murder?" Gregory asked as they stepped off the boat.

"He helped Sheriff Winston work the scene where the body was found. He's going to fill me in when we meet tomorrow."

"I see," Gregory said dryly.

Stanizlow, then Claremont, shook hands with Gregory and Billy Page, thanking them both for the outing.

"I'll call you," Claremont said to Gregory.

They watched her walk across the gravel parking area.

"Man, what a babe!" Billy Page said as soon as the doors to the Chevrolet Caprice closed. "Tell you what though, I'll bet she's busted some serious balls in her time. I'll bet you money."

"Shut up!"

Billy Page hopped on his bicycle. "Stay away from her, Eric. The woman is trouble," he called out as he pedaled away.

Billy Page never noticed the gray Crown Victoria that pulled out of the side street and shadowed him home.

✠   ✠   ✠

Echo gave Claremont and Stanizlow the full tour of the excavation project, including the small laboratory where artifacts were washed and stored to await analysis. In all, they spent over an hour on the site. Claremont asked question after question. Stanizlow too, seemed to have been equally fascinated by Echo's interpretive presentation of Native American life along the North Carolina coast.

Afterward, they met for coffee at the Fish House Restaurant. The building stood on pilings next to a cut channel leading out to Pamlico Sound. It was mid-afternoon and the place was nearly empty. They sat down in a corner booth next to two picture widows. One looked out to the Sound; the other opened to the small harbor where several worn looking fishing vessels lay tied up. Rusty pieces of machinery and stacks of crab pots cluttered the bulkhead lined basin.

"When I was a kid, I always wanted to be an archaeologist," Claremont said, stirring her coffee.

"A lot of people say that," Echo replied. "But let me tell you, it's pretty hard work."

"But you do it avocationally."

"It's my life. It's what I love."

Claremont kept prying. "So you're loaded, huh? How'd you come by the money to do all this on your own?"

"I won the Lottery."

"Really! I never knew anyone who actually won. What's it like?"

"It's great."

She laughed out loud. "Stupid question!"

Claremont's expression firmed. "So what can you tell me about the Sinclair case?" she asked in a businesslike voice.

"Not much more than you probably already know. I assume you have the autopsy report."

Claremont nodded. "I have it right here."

"There seems little doubt we're looking at a professional hit. One thing I did notice, there seemed to be some duct tape residue on the wrists. I had Winston take a sample of it. You'll have to get with him when the lab results come back from Raleigh."

Stanizlow leaned across the table. "You sure know many things about police work, Mr. Echo," he spoke out in his heavily accented English.

"I used to do it."

Claremont's eyebrows lifted. "Really?"

"Worked part time with the Knoxville Medical Examiner's office when I was in school. Didn't have a job after I got my master's in physical anthropology. So I did some consulting work for the surrounding rural law enforcement agencies—routine forensics on a case by case basis."

"How unusual a career path," Claremont remarked.

"I'm an unusual person."

"I can see," Claremont said, tapping the table with the end of her pencil. "So what else do you make of the murder? Any other insights?"

"Tell you the truth, it's not like anything I've ever seen. Right now, I'm thinking he was killed on the spot with his hands taped, then the tape removed and the arms splayed out. Seems to me the body was meant to be found there, as opposed to simply having been dumped. I mean, why shoot him six times and cut his throat, then lay him out like they did. The killers wanted to send a message."

"Could be," Claremont said. She unfolded a newspaper clipping—a profile of Preston Sinclair and the planned Atlantis World project to raise the *U-491*. "A Mr. Gregory gave me this," she said handing the article across the table. "It gives some biographical information on the man—nothing we don't already know."

Echo took the clipping saying, "Eric Gregory, I presume. Likes to be called Captain. You know him?"

"We've met."

"Nice guy, pretty much. I hear he's got one hot temper, though."

Echo scanned the introduction to the piece.

"So Mr. Sinclair was an old hand at the salvage business," Claremont began. "Do you know anything about the associates he might have had? Someone he might have crossed, perhaps?"

"I didn't know him all that well. But I did hear he used to hang with some pretty shady characters down in Florida. Treasure hunters—more like criminals, actually. Apparently most of the Keys was their turf. If anyone made a good find, they'd best take these guys on as partners, otherwise something might... happen, so to say. All straight from the rumor mill, though. Don't quote me on it."

"Interesting," Claremont said. She looked over at her partner. "Well Stan, what do you say we call it a day and go back to the motel."

The Russian nodded.

"There's one obvious issue we haven't touched on," Echo added quickly, raising the newspaper clipping in one hand. "You don't suppose Sinclair's murder could have had anything to do with the German U-boat he found. He was talking it up all over the island just before he got killed."

"We're exploring every possibility," Claremont replied while getting up. "Thanks so much for showing us your excavation. I really enjoyed it."

Stanizlow extended his hand across the table. "Thank you, Mr. Echo. It was a pleasure," he said in his slow, deliberate speech.

✠   ✠   ✠

As soon as they left, Echo ordered a drink from the bar and remained seated, trying to recall if Claremont's eyes were dark green or an off shade of blue. After two more drinks, he was still unable to get her out of his mind. Echo couldn't quite put his finger on it. Though attractive, it wasn't like she had picture good looks. In fact, a number of things were just a little off kilter. He also sensed a physicality that went beyond her stature. Further, the woman had an almost chameleon-like quality—something about her seemed to change with every variance in lighting or vantage.

The more he thought of her, the more intriguing she became to him.

✠   ✠   ✠

Claremont hadn't noticed Gregory standing behind her at the supermarket checkout. She handed the clerk the bill, took the change and picked up her single bag of groceries.

"How was your date with the illustrious Professor Echo?"

Claremont spun around. "Eric! I didn't see you."

"I didn't think you had."

"It wasn't a date! It was business. He just showed us his site before we went over the Sinclair case."

"You need help with that?" he asked, taking the bag from her arms.

"Thanks. We're tired of eating out so I went and bought some groceries."

He followed her through the glass doors toward a red Saturn parked in the first space. "What happened to your big piece of pig iron?"

"This is Stan's rental. We drove down separately." She let out a short laugh. "For some reason, he likes his cars smaller."

Once by the car, Claremont turned to face him. "This Echo guy, the man's quite a character, to say the least."

"If you say so," Gregory said in a flat voice.

"I can't help but be envious. It must be great to win the lottery and not have to work."

"Echo didn't win any lottery!" Gregory scoffed. "I told you the man was full of it."

Claremont looked surprised. "No?"

Gregory placed the bag onto the back seat. "It's an open secret 'round here Clifton Echo is ex-CIA," he said, closing the door.

Claremont looked at him inquisitively.

"Spent the better part of the 1980s in Central America running guns and money to the Nicaraguan Contras."

Gregory leaned his forearm on the car roof. "I probably shouldn't be telling you this, but one day he pulled a deal of his own down there and disappeared."

"He took the government's money?" Claremont asked incredulously.

"Their money and their drugs."

"They didn't come after him?"

"Never said the guy was stupid. He must have known something 'cause a week later, the whole Iran-Contra thing hits the fan back in Washington. Having been in the thick of it, he's got so many top guys by the balls—pardon the expression—nobody dares touch him."

"How do you know all this?"

"Pretty much common knowledge. Old Echo, he got to drinkin' bourbon whiskey one night—ran his mouth to someone he wishes he hadn't."

Claremont didn't respond.

"Anyway, he's set for life. I'm sure the money's in a numbered account in the Caymans or the Bahamas or somewhere."

"Interesting," Claremont finally said. Getting into the car, she seemed absorbed in thought. "Thanks for your help," she then said briskly. "Got to go."

The Saturn sped away, leaving Gregory standing alone in the small parking lot.

Chapter 17

CLIFTON ECHO WHISTLED GINGERLY AS HE TOWELED HIMSELF DRY after a long and thorough shower. He shaved for the second time that day. It took almost fifteen minutes to trim and clean his fingernails, clip any errant hairs and generally make sure everything was in order. Cologne came next.

Late Saturday afternoon, he thought. She's probably sitting in the motel bored to death right this very minute. It's just a visit. I'm sure she'll be glad to see me.

He put a bottle of chardonnay into the refrigerator to chill before checking on his stock of red. It's just a visit to say hello, he cautioned himself. You never know, though—have to prepare for any possibility—cover all the bases. Maybe a little chit-chat, a casual suggestion for dinner. Maybe some vino to top the night at the Chateau d'Echo.

At precisely the same moment, Gregory stood in front of his living room mirror palming the creases out of his favorite floral pattern shirt. He too was freshly shaven and well scrubbed.

I should come clean with Ms. Claremont about what Preston saw in the U-boat, he told himself. Living in a motel. Saturday afternoon. Why not? Ivan's probably watching the hockey game on cable. She'll be happy to have someone to talk to.

✠ ✠ ✠

Echo pulled into the far end of the motel parking lot. Just as he was about to step out of the truck, he caught sight of Gregory standing on the far side of the street. Through the fading light, he saw Gregory slip back into his truck and sag behind the wheel. Echo turned to see Claremont and Stanizlow emerge from the motel breezeway. He was fairly certain they hadn't seen him. They stopped in front of her door. She leaned up against the Russian and slid her hand around his waist, whispering something in his ear as they stepped into the room.

✠   ✠   ✠

Echo and Gregory sat at opposite ends of the bar, neither willing to openly acknowledge the other's presence. Mary Margaret, the proprietor of the Mad Shrimper, stood behind the bar directly between them. Not an unattractive woman, she was a little on the thin side, with dark hair, freckled skin and sharp features accented by a lipstick smile.

Mary Margaret was normally quick with a hello or a light remark from behind the counter. Tonight, however, she looked bored and seemed about as cheery as her two early customers who sat slouching to either side.

"Sure, I'll have another one," Gregory said, without looking up.

"Clifton, what about you, sweetie?"

Echo failed to reply.

"What's up with y'all?!" she exclaimed. "You look like you been to a funeral or somethin'. Cheer up, fellas!"

Just then Billy Page strode through the door, cue case in hand. "Eric!" he said, placing the case on the floor between the two men at the bar. "Hey, nice shirt, buddy!"

Gregory mumbled something under his breath.

Billy Page turned to Echo, lifted his nose and sniffed twice. "Say, Echo, what is that you're wearing?"

Mary Margaret watched with bemused interest.

Billy Page was just getting started. He leaned over the bar toward Mary Margaret. "These guys, you see, they've been tripping over themselves chasing that FBI lady," he said, just loud enough for both Echo and Gregory to hear. "Now word at the store is they been spurned."

Mary Margaret perked up considerably.

Billy Page vigorously bobbed his head. "Stan's the man. Maggie's been telling everybody them two's been fixin' to be a number."

"The Russian guy?" she asked, surprised.

"That's right, just this afternoon he comes in the store and buys two bottles of wine and a candle—nothin' else." Billy Page could not help but laugh. "Hey, you gotta admit, the old goat's got it."

"I got to find me a bigger island," Echo groaned.

Mary Margaret glanced toward Gregory, who said nothing. "Billy, I think he's getting mad," she cautioned.

Billy Page could not resist. "Let me see here," he said crossing his hands in front of him and pointing to either side. "We have Double-O Echo versus Captain Romeo here—and now everyone is drinkin' all dog faced 'cause the commie geezer gets the babe! Man, who woulda thought it."

"Billy, I think you need to stop right there!" she repeated.

"All right, guys," Billy Page said, letting up. "Lemme buy y'all a beer. Come on."

"Go away," was all Echo had to say.

Gregory continued to pretend his mate wasn't even there. Mary Margaret just smiled and rolled her eyes.

✠   ✠   ✠

Once inside the motel room Claremont and Stanizlow began to help each other undress. As soon as he was fully unclothed, she forcefully pushed him backward, falling on the bed on top of him. She grabbed his wrists, pinning them above his head. Her tongue slid into his mouth for a long, probing kiss.

"Stan!" she breathed, pulling back. "You know you've been driving me crazy."

She again lowered her mouth onto his, then pushed herself up and began to massage his broad and surprisingly firm chest.

"Don't move," she ordered, getting up off the bed.

Stanizlow blinked an acknowledgment.

She stood to the right of the bed in front of the mirror, her back to him. The lights went out. A match flared and the flickering glow of candlelight filled the room. Her movements were languid and smooth, rife with anticipation but free of the slightest haste. She tilted her head and removed one earring, then the other, laying them on the low dresser on which the mirror stood.

She reached around and unsnapped her bra. In the reflection, he saw her breasts go free. Still facing away, she bent forward to step out of her panties. She turned and stood before him. The candle threw the outline of her form across the far wall and ceiling. His eyes followed the flare of her hips, moving down the full length of her long, well-toned legs.

Smiling, she climbed onto the bed and remained kneeling. Bracing herself, she lifted a leg to straddle him. She settled back, pushing her crotch against him. She lifted her hair back over her head with both hands. Her upper lip curled as her hands and fingers followed the curve of her own body. Her hands repeatedly moved down across her hips and back up to her breasts, pushing them together and rolling the hard nipples between her thumb and fingers.

She relaxed momentarily, straightened and arched backward, catching herself on outstretched palms. She lifted one leg and swung it around, deftly displaying the swollen groove of her sex.

Back on two knees, she bent forward and her hair splashed across his groin.

✠   ✠   ✠

Stanizlow lay flat on his back, breathing shallowly and seemingly unable to move. She lay alongside him, viscously lipping his bristly ear. Though she hadn't intended to finish him off, she enjoyed having done so.

This was hardly the first time she'd lain with a much older man. She found their knowing touch, together with an almost schoolboy enthusiasm, to be a powerfully exciting combination. And they were ever so thankful for the favor. Surely though, she could expect no more from him tonight.

"You certainly are in shape for someone who's in their sixties," she said playfully, while moving one hand across his chest. She reached up and ran her fingers across his spiky, snow-white hair.

"Thank you."

"You tan well, too. This wintertime sun just doesn't do much for me."

"So it would seem."

She threw herself across him abruptly saying, "You know what?"

"What?"

"I just remembered. When I was at the Academy, I used to have this fantasy about doing it with a KGB guy. I used to think about it most every night."

Stanizlow rolled onto his side. He'd not moved off his back since she'd first pushed him into the bed. "What would your instructors have said?"

She hardly noticed his hand moving down the length of her spine, his fingertips barely grazing.

"I think I would have washed out as a security risk if they'd known," she laughed. "Maybe not, though. I think they sort of liked me."

"I am sure they did."

She suddenly became acutely aware of his delicate caress. His fingers brushed her side, then moved in circles along the small of her back. Her eyes closed and a shudder rippled through her. In an inexplicable way, his touch was maddening. He massaged the nape of her neck, sending quivering jolts through her extremities. His fingertips moved down her spine, across her ribs, past the side of one breast, down an arm, and back again.

When she could stand it no longer, she reached over and was surprised to find him fully erect. He rolled onto his knees, parted her thighs and pushed her legs back. She tugged at his waist and her mouth opened in a breathless gasp.

✠   ✠   ✠

The Mad Shrimper slowly filled until it was near capacity. Echo stood up from the bar to take refuge in a corner booth. After some apparent reluctant hesitation, Gregory shuffled over to join him.

"Hey, this one's on me," Gregory said, placing two fresh bottles on the table.

"Thanks."

Gregory took a long pull on his beer, then asked, "Listen, can I talk to you about something?"

"Sure. This is about Sinclair, isn't it?"

"Yeah. I just want to know what you make of all this."

"Who knows," Echo said, lifting up his cap slightly. "I don't really know what to say—other than whoever did the killing probably wasn't new at it. It's got all the markings of a professional hit." He paused. "One thing strikes me though," he went on, "I can't help but feel the whole thing has something to do with the wreck he was talking so much about."

Gregory quickly looked about. "I know it does," he said, leaning across the table, his voice dropping to a hoarse whisper. "I want this to stay between me and you."

"Tell me."

Gregory poked his thumb at his chest. "I found the U-boat!" he hissed. "Not Preston! I marked it with the depth finder last summer. Then saw it from the surface. Told Preston about it. He dived on it. Twice, with my boy Billy Page."

Echo listened intently.

"But there's more to it than that. Preston got inside and took some video. I've seen it. Preston said there's cargo on board—he told me just before he was killed. He was drunk and I figured it was his usual BS. But Preston was right—submarines don't carry cargo—not unless it's something really special."

Echo suddenly felt uneasy. "So why are you telling me this?"

"Because I'm scared, that's why."

Echo said nothing.

Gregory leaned even closer. "Whatever this cargo is, it got Preston killed. I'm sure of it!"

Echo ran his hands across the sides of his head.

"That's why we got the FBI involved," Gregory declared confidently.

"Let's not forget the KGB," Echo added. He thought about his visit from Frank Bruford.

They sat in brief silence.

"And this Claremont," Gregory started, avoiding eye contact. "What do you make of her?" Gregory really didn't know why he'd brought it up—the question just seemed to have slipped out.

Echo took his time, then said, "I don't know. Something about her doesn't seem to add up. I just don't know what it is."

"I think I know what you mean."

"So did Sinclair ever say what he thought was on board the U-boat?" Echo asked. He lifted his beer.

"Nazi gold."

Echo set the bottle down without taking a drink. "What do *you* think is in there?"

"Trouble," Gregory replied, slumping back into the booth. "I wish to hell I'd never found the goddamn thing."

✠   ✠   ✠

Echo thought he'd drop by the motel to see Stanizlow. Not that he had any intention of going very far with Bruford's request for information, but ever since his ex-colleague's visit, followed by his meeting with Claremont, Echo's innate inquisitiveness was aroused. The murder of Preston Sinclair and its possible connection with the U-boat wreck only made matters more intriguing. If there was anything Echo liked more than a good mystery, it was being in the middle of one. Moreover, Echo hadn't ever had much contact with his former adversarial counterparts. So, if for no other reason than to satisfy curiosity, he wanted to get one-on-one with the ex-KGB man.

Stanizlow came to the motel room door and graciously accepted Echo's invitation to visit his home, but begged momentary pardon for he was in a consultation with Claremont. Through the closed door, Echo heard what sounded like an argument break out.

"No Stan, I don't mind you going over there. If that's what he wants, just go over there and be done with it!" Echo overheard Claremont say in a strained voice.

Stanizlow reemerged from the room and the two climbed into the truck. Saying nothing, Stanizlow looked perturbed.

"What was that all about?" Echo asked unabashedly.

"I don't know," Stanizlow replied with uncharacteristic openness. "First she says I can't talk to you on my own; says it would be against procedure. Then just says, okay, do it."

"Women," Echo shrugged, steering the truck through a curve in the road.

He turned off Highway 12 to follow a set of sandy tracks that led straight into what looked like an impregnable forest. Pine branches momentarily slapped across the windshield and the truck began to bounce down the rutted, deeply shaded drive.

They stopped and got out of the vehicle.

"Welcome to the Buxton Woods Manor," Echo declared, standing before the dilapidated trailer, tucked against the reedy swamp. "The verandah has a view of the water."

"Very nice."

"Do come on in, please," Echo said in a purposely formal voice, while making for the porch.

Stanizlow suddenly froze in his tracks. Echo's steps had become hesitant and Stanizlow instinctively picked up on and reacted to the other man's caution.

"What is the matter, Mr. Echo?"

"That's odd. The screen door—it's shut. I never close it all the way. I can't. The frame is warped."

The two men cautiously approached the trailer.

"Stay here and don't move," Echo hissed, motioning Stanizlow behind the large live oak.

Echo went back to the truck and pulled a nickel plated .38 from underneath the seat. He reached around for one of several half filled sandbags he carried in the bed. Echo dropped the bag next to Stanizlow and crept around the far side of the trailer, keeping his back nearly flush to the metal exterior. Clutching the weapon across his chest, he peered into the corner of each window.

He circled his way around to the front, keeping as low a profile as possible. When he got back to the oak, he crouched down and tucked the pistol under his belt.

"Stay down," he ordered.

Echo got up and took the sandbag in both hands. He began to swing it back and forth, gaining momentum each time. The bag went sailing in a graceful arc directly at the porch door. Echo ducked behind the thick trunk, pushing himself against Stanizlow and pressing his face to the scaly bark.

The bag hit the door with a soft thump. In virtually the same instant came a blinding flash and thunderous, crushing shock. The two men collapsed from behind the oak tree. Echo tried to stand up; his ears were ringing so hard he could not find the balance to do so. A blizzard of leaves swirled through the air and an acrid cloud of smoke and dust darkened the scene.

"Stan! Are you okay?!" Echo gasped, trying to fill his lungs.

The older man managed to find his feet and steady himself. "I think so, yes."

He was bleeding profusely from both nostrils.

Echo stood and surveyed the scene. "Holy Shit!" he let out.

The porch was gone. Much of the trailer was gone, save the frame. What was left lay crumpled to one side like a metal lunch box partially crushed by a truck. Small fires burned all around the wreckage. The stout trunk had spared them the direct force of the blast. Several smaller pine trees, however, lay prone, pointing away from the epicenter.

Off in the distance, the siren on the Frisco Volunteer Fire Station let loose its monotone wail.

Sheriff Winston was the first on the scene. "I heard about an explosion on the scanner," he said getting out of the patrol car. "Lord Almighty!" he exclaimed, as the extent of the destruction became clear. "What the hell happened here?!"

"Propane," Echo stammered.

Sheriff Winston peered around at the scattered debris.

Echo kicked at the sandy ground. "Damn it! I thought I smelled gas. I shoulda done something!"

"There've sure been some mighty strange happenin's 'round here," the sheriff said warily.

Winston strode to the cruiser and got on the radio. The first fire truck arrived a few minutes later. A teenage volunteer hurriedly uncoiled a thin hose from the drum and began to systematically douse the minor brush fires burning all around. Soon a second unit arrived and began to spray water on the smoldering wreckage of what once was Clifton Echo's modest home.

✠   ✠   ✠

Claremont gently dabbed peroxide on Echo's forehead. Stanizlow lay on the bed with a towel under his neck. His head was tilted back and he held a bloodied washcloth under his nose.

"Tell me again what happened," Claremont said, rubbing Echo's shoulders. "You knew the door was rigged?"

"Call it intuition. I just had a feeling something wasn't right."

"And?"

"I tossed a sand bag and jumped behind the tree. KA-BOOM! The shock was incredible. There's nothing left of the porch. The shell of the trailer is pushed to one side and crumpled like it's been stepped on."

Claremont frowned. She ran her fingers through his brown hair, then patted him firmly on the shoulder.

Echo forced a laugh. "Hey, at least the brush is down. I always wanted a better view of the pond."

"Any idea who might of done it?" she asked. "Who would want you dead?"

At first Echo did not speak. "You know, Sheriff Winston was right, there're some pretty strange things going on around here," he said, somewhat pensively.

Stanizlow righted himself and said, "Mr. Echo, you and I have more in common than you may realize."

"Yeah, like we both almost ended up equally dead," Echo replied sarcastically. "I can't really think of much else."

Stanizlow stood and poured himself a glass of water. "I am a guest in this country, courtesy of your government," he began. "On the other hand, it was not long ago I carried a price on my head.

Your government wanted me out of the way. I was very good at my job. Too good, perhaps. I made some of your people look foolish. To your old associates I was—how should I say—a thorn in their side." Stanizlow looked to Claremont, then back at Echo. "Believe me, they tried to get me," he continued, raising outstretched hands to either side. "But as you can see—they failed."

"And? So?" Echo demanded, sounding irritated.

"According to Agent Claremont here, you may not have exactly endeared yourself to your former colleagues, either. If there's anything I have learned about your friends in the trade, it is they will hold a grudge."

"Bruford!" Echo hissed.

Stanizlow nodded. "It's a New World Order, but the old ways die hard. He's still on the island. We have been watching him closely."

"He saw the opportunity to take out two birds with one stone. It was more than he could resist," Echo said, thinking out loud. He began to pace the narrow confines of the room.

"So it would seem."

Echo's mind raced. The Russian may have a point, he thought. On the other hand, how would Bruford have known they'd be together? He hadn't noticed a tail.

Suddenly, the notion of Bruford trying to kill him struck Echo as ludicrous. Something else must be going on, he thought. Blabbing about the U-boat got Preston Sinclair killed, that much I can be sure of. Eric Gregory tells me what Preston knew and the next thing, someone tries to blow me to bits. There has got to be a connection!

"Bullshit!" Echo spat out. "I know Bruford. He's a friggin worm! He wouldn't have the nerve to pull off something like this."

Stanizlow and Claremont looked blankly back at Echo.

Echo continued to pace, then stopped. "I think I know what this is all about," he said abruptly. "It's about the U-boat wreck—or what's in it." He pointed a finger at Claremont. "You're not here on any murder investigation! No one called in the FBI!"

Claremont remained expressionless.

"Preston Sinclair knew something was on the wreck, and it cost him his life," Echo stated emphatically. "Now I've been doing a little snooping of my own. You want to know what I think is in the U-boat? How does a big, fat load of gold bars sound?" Echo walked over to Stanizlow. "And what might your role be in all of this? I suppose your government thinks it has a claim to the stuff?"

Neither Claremont or Stanizlow had a response.

Echo grabbed his jacket off the bed. "I smell a rat here. Some sort of secret sweetheart deal in the making, perhaps? I'm fishing here and no one is talking. Well, let me tell you one thing, whatever you two have going, it's not gonna fly. The press is gonna have a field day with this."

Echo opened the door to the room. "I'm gonna need a place to stay so I'm going to the office to check in," he declared. "Now, I'm going to make you all an offer. Come clean with me by tomorrow with exactly what's going on, or I start making some calls to the media. Y'all think about it."

Chapter 18

GREGORY BURST INTO THE SHERIFF DEPARTMENT'S HEADQUARTERS. "Where's Winston!" he gasped.

The dispatcher pointed with a pencil to the office.

"I've seen 'em!" Gregory exclaimed, pushing open the door.

"Seen who?"

"The two men who keep following me. I know where they're staying. Let's go get 'em!"

"Mr. Gregory," Sheriff Winston said, rising up from behind his desk, "I'm not going to arrest somebody just because you think they followed your car."

Gregory was incredulous. "They're the ones who killed Preston!" he half yelled.

"We have no suspects in the case as of right now," Winston said firmly, adding, "I would also advise you to leave my office!"

Gregory glared stiffly at the sheriff before storming back out the door.

✠   ✠   ✠

Echo was standing in front of Claremont's motel room ready to make good on the previous night's ultimatum when Gregory's truck roared up. Gregory jumped out of the cab, shouldered his way past Echo and pounded on the door.

"I've seen 'em!" he exclaimed as soon as the door opened. "The two men who came into the store!"

"Where?" Claremont snapped.

"At the Sea Breeze Motel—in Hatteras—by the ferry landing."

Claremont reached for her FBI Smith & Wesson 10 MM and slammed home a clip. "Let's go," she ordered. "Both of you!"

"Where's Stan?" Echo asked, surprised at her demand.

"Not here. There's no time. Lets go!" She turned, reached into her suitcase and pulled out a second weapon, handing it to Echo. "Here, take this. You may need it."

"Thanks, I have my own," Echo replied dryly.

She gave him a quick shove in the direction of the truck.

Gregory's Ford pickup hit 85 miles an hour on the long straightaway leading into Hatteras village. Claremont sat squeezed in between Echo and Gregory.

"Can't you go any faster?" she barked. "We may already be too late."

"Jesus Christ, lady! I have it floored!" Gregory yelled back at her.

Echo stared straight ahead, a thin bead of perspiration trickling down his forehead.

Gregory turned in at the Sea Breeze office and inched past the row of doors.

"There. That's the room," Gregory said, pointing excitedly.

Claremont nudged Echo out of the cab. Gregory sprang out of the driver's side. "That's the room. I'm sure of it," he repeated.

Claremont clicked the safety on the automatic. Echo drew his .38. She approached the room, flanked by the two men. They stopped a few feet from the door.

Claremont turned to Gregory. "Break it down," she whispered firmly.

In an instant, Gregory was ready to blindly obey her order. He lowered himself into a three point stance with knuckles resting on the pavement. In a flash of the moment, Gregory was struck by what he was about to do. A macabre sense of *deja vu* washed over him. Feeling like he was watching himself on a movie screen, any sense of caution vanished as an overwhelming anger surged through his body. He flexed like a bull ready to charge.

Gregory lunged forward, throwing his 240-plus pounds against the door with all the strength he could muster. The cheap wooden laminate splintered like a bottle struck by a stone. Gregory's momentum carried him stumbling into the room, landing spread-eagled on the floor. The entire door jamb, ripped loose by the force of the impact, fell onto his back.

Claremont and Echo charged through with weapons leveled. Claremont went in high while Echo dropped behind the first bed.

"FBI! GET ON THE FLOOR! ON THE FLOOR!"

The room was empty. Claremont bolted for the bath, stepping on Gregory's hand and neck in the process. She kicked open the door and burst in with the automatic out front. Nothing.

Claremont began to curse like a sailor. "Goddammit!" she yelled, booting a plastic wastebasket into the far wall.

Echo holstered his gun and began to take stock of the surroundings. The air reeked of alcohol and stale tobacco smoke. Empty vodka bottles stood perched on the television set. He picked the remains of a cigarette out of an ashtray and held it up. "*Papirosa.*"

"What?" Claremont snapped.

Gregory moaned and tried to pull himself up off the floor.

Echo passed the crumbly, cardboard-filtered butt to Claremont. "*Papirosa,*" he repeated.

"What does that mean?"

"It means the Russians are here. No one would smoke these things unless they grew up with them. Even then you have to wonder."

Gregory heaved himself off the floor. Once standing, he cradled one arm with the other. "You didn't have to step on me!" he winced.

"The Russians?" Claremont asked.

Echo gave her a long look, then said, "I think it's time we had a talk with your friend Stan."

✠   ✠   ✠

Claremont called Stanizlow from her cellular phone on the way back to Buxton. He agreed to meet them at Gregory's house and was waiting when they arrived. Sheriff Winston pulled into the drive right behind them.

"We got company," Gregory said, spotting the cruiser in the rearview mirror.

They got out of the truck. Sheriff Winston walked briskly toward them.

"Lady," he said sharply, "just what the hell do you think you're doing?!"

"Checking out a tip."

"Where's your warrant?"

"This concerns an urgent matter of national security," Claremont said coldly. "If you have any questions, feel free to speak with my superiors in Washington. The numbers are on the letter I gave you."

Though Winston was visibly angered by Claremont's arrogant tone, his response was even and measured. "I don't know how you Federal Agents run your business up there in Washington, but we have laws here in North Carolina." He pointed a finger at Claremont. "One more stunt like that and I'm running you in, and I don't give a damn who you're working for!"

Claremont handed Winston her card. "Have them bill me for the door," she said acidly.

Sheriff Winston looked over at Gregory who stood sheepishly to one side, working his aching shoulder. "Gregory, do yourself a favor and don't get mixed up with these two." Winston walked back to the cruiser, "Y'all don't make me come back now," he called out before pulling open the door and getting in.

✠   ✠   ✠

Echo and Claremont settled in around Gregory's living room table, anticipating some explanation from Stanizlow as to why two Russians were lurking around the island. Gregory pulled up a chair and joined them. Echo produced a manila folder from his briefcase and laid it before him. Claremont too, was ready for some answers and was taken aback by Echo's heated barrage of questions aimed at her, rather than her partner.

"Who the hell are you and who do you work for?" he demanded.

"What do you mean?" Claremont replied, startled.

"Who are you? You're not FBI! You broke about five different regulations back there—not to mention the law."

"I don't play by the rules," Claremont said. She sounded defensive.

"Obviously," Echo stated sarcastically. He opened the folder and laid a thick stack of fax paper on the table. "Preston Sinclair was on to something," he said to Claremont. "And now you're going to tell me exactly what it was. I'm going to get to the very bottom of this, not the least of which is…" Echo stopped short, looking at Stanizlow, then back at Claremont, "…which is to find out *who fuckin' tried to kill me!*" Echo regained his composure. "I don't take too kindly to that sort of thing," he said unapologetically.

Gregory sat transfixed by Echo's performance. Claremont seemed uncomfortable. Stanizlow looked bored.

"Fact," Echo said. "There's a German U-boat half buried in the sand just off Diamond Shoals. No record exists of it being sunk and no one ever knew it was out there—not until Captain Gregory here stumbles across it with his depth finder. Preston Sinclair dives on it, gets inside, and sees it's carrying cargo. When the man starts running his mouth, he ends up dead. Now I notice a little something strange is going on—and I'm next on the hit parade. Answers people! I want answers!"

Echo shuffled the papers. "Since no one is talking, let's get back to this business about Nazi gold that got Sinclair so worked up," he said, rapping his knuckles on the table. "Seems during the war most Soviet reserves never fell into German hands. A little bit here and there perhaps. The bulk of the stuff was moved east of the Urals, well out of reach. Quite a bit of gold was smuggled out of Eastern Europe during the Nazi occupation. Mostly to Switzerland. Again, some was intercepted and shipped to Berlin." He flipped over a couple of pages. "It's not until near the end of the war things get hairy. Seems while the *Wehrmacht* was pulling back through Eastern Europe, Himmler's boys cleaned out the Romanian treasury. Ditto for Hungary and whatever might have been left in Czechoslovakia. But that's only part of it. With millions having been murdered in the camps, a good portion of the SS hoard was said to have been melted down wedding bands and dental work."

"Where are you getting your facts?" Claremont demanded.

"The CIA did a study in the fifties," Echo stated, waving the stack of papers in the air. "Seems none of this particular loot was ever accounted for. Now it could have been the Soviets got it, but the conclusion of the report was: One–it was stashed somewhere and still lay hidden, or Two–it was lost in transit, probably at sea. If it were still around, the estimated two to four tons of bullion that is, the idea was to get it before the Reds did. Nothing ever came of it and the project was dropped."

"How did you get this?" Claremont asked, pointing to the papers.

Echo returned them to the folder. "Through the Freedom of Information Act. It's been declassified for years. An old CIA buddy of mine faxed it to me this morning."

Gregory again felt like he was living a movie script.

Echo wasn't finished. "About this mysterious cargo," he continued, turning to Stanizlow, "both of you know damn well what's in there!" Echo pointed with his pen at Claremont. "What's your angle in all this? Have the Feds grab the gold and hand it to the Russians, perhaps? Who's to say the government has any claim to the stuff anyway?" He looked back at Stanizlow. "What's the plan? Use the gold as collateral for yet another credit line to shore up the basket case you Russians call an economy? Put subsidized meat and vodka in the government stores through the winter—up until the coming election at least? Let me see here," Echo went on caustically, "three quarters of a billion dollars, that ought to last about…"

Stanizlow cut him off in mid-sentence. "I have heard enough of this nonsense. I can assure you there is no gold on board the submarine."

Gregory squinted at the man sitting across the table, uncertain whether he should believe his ears. Sandra Claremont turned white as a sheet. The slow, deliberate speech and plodding accent were gone, replaced by sharply spoken textbook English.

Gregory bolted upright out of his chair. "How do you know?!"

Without hesitation Stanizlow calmly stated, "I was on the *U-491* when the boat went down."

A stunned silence filled the room, only to be shattered by Gregory's fist crashing full force onto the table. "You're *Kessel!*" he bellowed, his voice both incredulous and accusatory.

Echo sagged into his seat. Claremont's jaw dropped, teeth parting behind bloodless lips.

"Yes, I have been he. But again, I have been many people."

Chapter 19

GREGORY STOOD ACROSS FROM STANIZLOW, HIS FINGERS TIGHTLY gripping the end of the table. "You're him," he finally said. "You're the one who washed ashore in '45!"

Echo and Claremont exchanged bewildered looks.

"What are you talking about?" they both asked.

Gregory ignored them. "What happened? How did the U-boat go down?"

"We were hit from the air. That's all I know."

"What about the other survivors?"

"There were none."

Gregory made for the kitchen, returning with a bottle of bourbon and four glasses. "Let me get some ice," he said, placing the bottle in the center of the table.

"I'll have mine straight up," Claremont said hoarsely. "And make it a double."

"Clifton?"

"Yeah, me too."

Stanizlow politely declined.

Gregory poured the drinks. "So, since you were on the U-boat, perhaps you could tell us about this mysterious cargo?"

"There is no gold," Stanizlow stated flatly. "No treasure. Nothing of any monetary value."

Echo cut in. "If there's no treasure, what's the big deal. What were you carrying?"

"Something more valuable than you will find in any bank vault."

"And what might that be?"

"Information."

"How old are you?" Claremont interrupted.

Stanizlow gave her a thin smile. He seemed to relish the question. "I will be seventy-four next month."

Claremont looked away, her mouth curling into a narrow sneer. Gregory reached over and refilled her glass before topping off his own.

"The cargo! What's this cargo?" Echo demanded.

"Canisters of welded aircraft grade aluminum. Vacuum sealed and totally waterproof, I assure you."

"And?"

Stanizlow took a breath and wetted his lips before again speaking. "They contain, among other things, personnel records, files and dossiers, intelligence reports, minutes of meetings of Hitler's staff, Swiss banking transactions, Nazi party rolls—names, dates, addresses, photographs. The material was meticulously culled from the millions of documents generated by the Gestapo, the *Abwehr* and the intelligence arms of both the *Wehrmacht* and the SS. Also included are select files of the *Sicherheitsdienst*, the security service of the Nazi Party. In short, the cargo of the *U-491* consists of a detailed compendium of the internal workings of the Third Reich and its occupation of the European continent."

"And this stuff got Preston killed?" Gregory asked skeptically.

"Yes. In fact we are all in more danger than you could possibly imagine."

The room went silent, with everyone waiting for Stanizlow to continue. Echo reached for the bottle and helped himself.

Viktor Stanizlow wore the expression of a man given more responsibility than anyone would want to bear. He looked tired,

older than he had just a few minutes before. Sitting directly
beneath the ceiling lamp, the creases on his forehead seemed
deepened while bags had formed under his eyes. To those around
the table, he appeared to have aged years in a matter of minutes.

"This information, it is of immense interest to certain parties,"
he said, with deliberate emphasis on the last two words. "They will
stop at nothing to get it. Absolutely nothing."

"Who are these people?" Claremont interjected. "What do
they want?"

"The ruins of the Soviet Union lie teetering on chaos," Stanizlow droned, ignoring her questions. "Russia is humbled before
the world. Factories have no raw materials. Food stores are empty.
Pensioners can hardly feed themselves with the pittances they
receive in turn for having toiled a lifetime. Worse yet, organized
crime has permeated every level of society. People are tired of this
upheaval. They long for order and stability. I'm afraid times are
ripe for yet another revolution."

Gregory was becoming impatient. "Tell me what the hell this
has to do with who killed Preston!"

Stanizlow ignored the demand. "It would seem the Russian
government, those at the very top, are also bent on recovering the
cargo—if only to keep it from getting to the public. To say the
information sealed in those boxes is of a sensitive nature would...
would be quite the understatement." He clasped his hands and
rung them tightly. "Things, you see, are never quite as they seem.
The Great Patriotic War, as we used to call it, was indeed a heroic
struggle for the Soviet Union. On the other hand, the propagan-
dists would have one believe it was all black and white—good
versus evil—Mother Russia set against yet another horde of
invaders rolling across her precious earth. Nothing is ever quite
so simple. Some, you see, actually welcomed the advancing Nazi
armies—White Russians, old Czarists, ethnic minorities chafing
under Russian rule, not to mention peasants who survived Stalin's
ruthless drive to transform the countryside to fit his notion of the
communal ideal."

Stanizlow paused.

"So what are you saying?" Echo demanded.

Stanizlow glanced around the table. "Let's just say the Kremlin has a personal stake in what's on the U-boat."

"You can't mean there's a Nazi collaborator running the country?" Echo exclaimed. "The man's a little young for that."

Stanizlow gave a wry look. "No one can be guilty of their father's sins. Yet, given the already explosive political situation in the county, if the information on board the *U-491* gets into the wrong hands, the government will fall, even before the elections."

"And?"

"And the opposition, therefore, has enlisted some very powerful criminal forces to try and make it happen."

Echo leaned back in his chair. "So a couple of goons try and stop the wreck from being raised to give these people time to get the documents themselves."

Stanizlow nodded. "So it would seem."

"Let me see," Echo said, "are you saying the opposition enlisted the Russian Mafia in the election campaign?"

"They are the Mafia," Stanizlow stated as a matter of fact. "The National Salvation Front, as you in the West might know them, is a coalition of the opposition parties, all of which are underwritten by Mafia money. Further yet, the money flowing to these parties is controlled by a mere handful of people. They call themselves *Predpriyatie*—the Enterprise. Their ultimate goal is nothing short of a *coup d'état*. In the campaign, the National Salvation Front preaches a return to the security and stability of the old system. Privately, they articulate a vision of Russia where economic power is concentrated amongst a criminal elite, and all others know their place. In their Russia, the worker's most basic needs will be met, if only barely. All other resources will be relegated to the state—that being the military and the new oligarchy."

"This Enterprise you mean?"

"Yes."

"Being multi-millionaire mafiosi isn't enough for them," Echo surmised. "They want to run the country to boot."

Stanizlow was deadpan in his response. "This is true, but I am afraid it is to be more than a grab for power. The *Predpriyatie*, you see, are the spearhead of a powerful, clandestine movement. Their ideology is steeped in a xenophobic ultra-nationalism, while they drape themselves in the mantle of the Orthodox faith. Their government, should they succeed, will be absolute, openly militaristic and intensely anti-West. They will seek to restore what their shallow minds perceive to be the glory of Russia's imperial past."

Echo let out a low whistle. Claremont was speechless. *How the hell did I get mixed up in this?* Gregory thought.

Stanizlow wasn't finished. "If these forces come to power, as they well may, this new world order will come crashing down. It is not in my nature to be overly dramatic, but I need not remind anyone Russia still bristles with nuclear intercontinental ballistic missiles."

Claremont reached for her purse. "I've got to get on the line to Washington and…"

Stanizlow placed his hand over her forearm, pressing it gently against the table. "Do not bother. I already had a talk with your President, the very afternoon I arrived. Quite an engaging fellow, really. I think I like him. Your boss, the Security Advisor, also attended."

Claremont jerked her arm from beneath his touch.

"Can't we go in there or something—secure the stuff and be done with it?" Echo asked quickly.

"Believe me, we discussed all the options," Stanizlow replied, clinical as ever. "Your President feels the best course is inaction—that the material is safest where it lies, at least for now. I, myself, am not so sure. With so much small boat traffic in the area, I feel I must worry."

Echo was visibly agitated. "What's his problem? Why won't he just move on the sub?"

"The President feels because of the media coverage the U-boat received, retrieving the material without the public's knowledge may be problematic. Myself, I can't comprehend this American penchant for having to give away your government's secrets."

"Doesn't he understand what's at stake?"

"Your President has a full grasp of the situation. The decision on how and when to proceed is his alone," Stanizlow said firmly. His voice eased somewhat. "If the material is retrieved, in his mind the question arises of what to do with it. If word of its existence leaked, he would have a major scandal on his hands. To release it is out of the question. He also feels to have the Navy destroy it where it lies would be equally objectionable, on moral grounds—and could lead to even more trouble for his administration. So right now everything is on hold."

"What's your role?"

"As a representative of the Russian government, I am their man on the ground, so to speak. I came here, to the wreck site, to learn exactly what was happening in order to make recommendations. Ms. Claremont was assigned to me by your government as a personal liaison, to assist and facilitate in any way."

Claremont gritted her teeth, her angry stare remaining focused on the far wall.

Echo sat quietly before giving Stanizlow a faintly cutting look. "So what's your plan?"

"Plan?!" Stanizlow exclaimed. For the first time his voice carried a hint of emotion. "There is no plan," he said briskly. "I had a plan! I was going to tend my roses and my vegetable garden. A little hiking and gathering mushrooms in the forest. Enjoy the few years I have left in peace. I was given use of a summer cottage—a two-room hut actually, in which I could live out my retirement—in the Lake District outside Berlin, near the Wannsee. Just a simple roof over my head. It's all I wanted, or needed. That and to be left alone."

"And...?" Echo asked.

"And what is one to do when the President of Russia personally asks? How could I refuse? It started with a telegram. Then a limousine ride to Schonefeld. A special flight to Moscow followed by a private meeting inside the Kremlin. The next thing I know I am sitting in the White House addressing the President of the

United States. Then, of all places, I find myself right back on this little sand bar of an island... doing my best not to get killed."

"Why you?" Claremont demanded.

"I was recommended—to the President of Russia by a person he trusts—and there aren't many of those anymore. You see, the Russian Security Forces are, in part, aligned against him. Even some of his closest advisors have turned. Because of my previous involvement, he only became more convinced I was the man for the job. I did not want any part of this. But now that I am here, I fully intend to uphold his confidence."

Echo tried to focus. "The men who killed Sinclair, they were with this Enterprise, as you call it?"

"Probably."

"What do you suppose their next move will be?"

"I doubt very much they have any real plan either," Stanizlow replied without hesitation. "Their methods are crude, as you can well see. We can assume they were given orders to halt the salvage operation at any cost. Beyond that, who knows. Everyone, including myself, is waiting to see what happens next." Stanizlow looked about the table. "Time, I must say, is on our side. If they are to make a move, I think it will have to happen very soon."

Viktor Stanizlow lowered his gaze as if to suggest enough had been said. The other three persons at the table looked about. The wall clock read just after 10:00. Everyone seemed to have forgotten their drinks. Echo promptly reached for his glass and downed the remaining contents in one gulp. "Jesus, I need another one after that," he said, breaking the silence. He reached across the table for the bottle.

Gregory's eyes narrowed as he continued to study the man sitting across from him. "I think you still got explaining to do, Mister!" he declared, his voice fraught with suspicion.

Stanizlow turned to him. "Yes, Captain?"

"For one thing, just how did you go from a Nazi sub to being in the K-G-B? Or is that just another one of your bullshit lies?"

"It is no lie. In my service to the KGB, I rose to the rank of full colonel. My "everyday" career, so to speak, was that of a Stasi officer—East German State Security. I spent the better part of thirty years working out of East Berlin."

Claremont let out a low hiss.

Echo rolled his eyes. "KGB and Stasi?" he asked disparagingly.

Stanizlow gave a slight, hollow-sounding laugh. "Odd to think on, isn't it?"

"Yes, it is," Echo agreed. "Now just two more questions, if I may. How were you both KGB and Stasi? And, once and for all, are you Russian or are you German?"

"To be KGB, I took Soviet citizenship. In the Stasi, as a German in the employ of our Russian masters, I watched those who watched their own," Stanizlow said in a curiously self-deprecatory manner. "I functioned, among other things, as the eyes and ears of Moscow's long arm. I was but one of many planted in most every level of East German society."

Echo exhaled loudly.

Gregory wasn't yet satisfied. "And another thing," he said quickly. "It was the end of the war. What the hell was a U-boat doing off North Carolina with all those Nazi papers or whatever in the first place? Didn't y'all have more important places you shoulda been?"

"Yes, we did," Stanizlow replied plainly.

"Like where?"

"Argentina."

Echo reached up and locked his hands on top of his head. This is all so bizarre, but it's starting to make sense, he thought.

Stanizlow looked at Gregory and said, "Captain, I would like to have that drink if I may. Water, no ice, please."

Gregory got up and went the kitchen, returning with the requested mix.

Stanizlow took a long pull, exhaled and set the glass before him. "We have two Russians on the island, as you already know," he said nodding at Echo.

Claremont physically tensed ever so slightly.

"You must realize there are probably others," Stanizlow stated as a matter of fact. "Exactly who they are and where their allegiances lie, I cannot say for sure. But as we have seen, the danger is real."

Gregory swallowed hard, for Stanizlow's words merely validated a nagging fear building inside him for weeks. "So what about Argentina?" he asked dryly.

Stanizlow's face tightened and he appeared to retreat into thought. Only after the longest apparent contemplation did he begin to speak. "I have told you these things because, whether we like it or not, we find ourselves together in this," he said slowly. "So at this point I see no reason to withhold anything. Of what I am now about to speak, very few persons have any knowledge."

His hard-set expression eased as a thin, ironic smile passed his lips. "If it were not for the most random stroke of chance, history may well have been different."

Stanizlow again paused. Silence. The faucet in the kitchen hammered out a relentless, ticking drip.

"The mission was part of a larger plan—Dönitz' plan. Admiral Karl Dönitz, you might recall, was the head of the U-boat arm, then Naval Chief and ultimately the "Last Führer." He took over what was left of the Third Reich after Hitler committed suicide in his Berlin bunker."

Stanizlow took a short sip of his drink.

"With the end near, much of the Nazi elite withdrew behind a curtain of self-delusion. Hitler himself sank deeper into a fantasy world, his decline fueled by ever-increasing amounts of prescription drugs. Admiral Dönitz, on the other hand, had a plan. Early in the war, Dönitz believed in the inevitability of German victory. Then, following the invasion of the Soviet Union, he formulated a contingency plan in the event Hitler's mad gamble in the East failed. As things began to unravel, this plan, code named Tannhauser, was put into effect. The Admiral could not fathom yielding the Reich to the forces of Bolshevism. He was determined to fight on."

Echo and Claremont were on the edge of their seats.

"Students of such history may recall during the final winter, Dönitz organized a massive sea lift which moved ethnic German civilians out of the eastern lands away from the advancing Red Army. It was more than a humanitarian undertaking. Dönitz was counting on the dispossessed to form his core constituency. Using his position, and whatever was left of the U-boat arm, Dönitz was able to marshal considerable resources. The idea was to set up an underground Nazi government-in-exile in South America. Dönitz was convinced of his ultimate success for he was sustained by an unshakable conviction in the lasting power of *Das Volk*—the German people. His Tannhauser operation was to lay the foundations for a New Germany; a Germany who rejected the excesses of the Hitler era while remaining true to the original ideals of National Socialism. Following the inevitable victory over communism, he would make his triumphant return to the Fatherland. I doubt he ever fully gave up on his dream until shortly before his death. It has been but a few years now."

Stanizlow moved his glass aside. He cast a deliberate glance around the table before continuing.

"Now, in addition to those in the Kremlin, there are other very powerful persons, outside Russia, who also have an intense interest in this sunken submarine. The canisters on the *U-491* were loaded with all manner of information; political currency if you will." He paused for emphasis. "Much of the cargo consists of detailed and exhaustive accounts of Nazi collaboration throughout Europe. To a large extent, the documents were compiled as a listing of potential allies or assets—likely sympathizers and supporters in the coming struggle to liberate Europe from the grip of Soviet communism."

"It was never meant to…" Echo interrupted, stopping to search for the right words.

Stanizlow nodded knowingly. "It was never meant to be the stuff of geopolitical blackmail."

Stanizlow again looked around, methodically making eye contact with everyone at the table. "But today, there is at least one camp desperate to get at the U-boat cargo. At the same time, there are others who equally wish it never to see the light of day, for, sealed in those metal boxes, lie the unwanted records of an entire continent's nightmare."

Echo and Claremont exchanged wide-eyed glances. "I can't believe this," he muttered.

"Believe it," Stanizlow stated.

"Why Cape Hatteras?" Gregory interjected.

Stanizlow was again deadpan in his reply. "It was as far as we could go. We didn't have the fuel. We sailed from Danzig, on the Baltic. Everything was going to pieces around us. Most of the *Wehrmacht* had already left, but the shipment of diesel for the voyage had not arrived. We began to hear artillery in the distance. Every day, the Red Army was getting closer. Finally, a short train consisting of two tank cars pulled onto the docks. Hours later, the harbor was hit by Allied bombers."

"What happened?"

"The boat came through unscathed. The oil train went up in flames. After the raid, teams were sent ashore to scour the city and commandeer any fuel they could find. We picked over the deserted *Wehrmacht* camps, siphoning diesel from battle-damaged armor and other abandoned equipment, hauled it back in milk cans on horse-drawn wagons. Used it to top off what was already on board. There was no choice but to leave. The Soviets were already in the city by the time we pulled out. Through our people in Buenos Aires, last minute arrangements were made to rendezvous with a neutral freighter for the cargo to complete the trip."

"You needed a coastal landmark to make the meet and Cape Hatteras is about as obvious as it gets," Gregory said quickly.

Stanizlow nodded. "Indeed. We certainly could not have lingered near the convoy lanes. It would have been suicide. Cape Hatteras seemed perfect. And it almost worked. Almost."

Seemingly satisfied, Gregory leaned back into his seat.

"Gentlemen, and Madam," Stanizlow said. "There you have it. Make of it what you will. Now I would suggest we get some sleep so tomorrow we have fresh wits. I suspect we will need them."

"I agree," Echo said, adding, "I would also suggest we watch each others' backsides on the way out of here."

✠   ✠   ✠

Claremont and Stanizlow left Gregory's house and made their way to the dark gray Chevrolet Caprice parked in front. Stanizlow got in. Claremont circled around and yanked open the driver's door. She ducked in and slid her long legs under the wheel. The engine fired to life. Sand flew through the air as the big sedan's wheels spun violently. The car roared off, then screeched to a halt by the main road. She jammed the gearshift into park, flung her hair out of her face and glared at Stanizlow, who sat impassively beside her.

"Just because we have to work together doesn't mean we have to get along!" she spat.

Stanizlow was tired and longed for bed.

✠   ✠   ✠

Back at the house, Gregory locked the doors and bolted the windows. The exterior lights stayed on. He took his loaded shotgun out of the closet and placed it on the chest-of-drawers. Lying in bed, he thought of his daughter, and didn't even bother trying to sleep.

Chapter 20

December 9, 1993 05:00 hours
Naval Amphibious Base Little Creek, Virginia Beach, Virginia

SLOWLY AT FIRST, THE LONG, DROOPING ROTOR BLADES OF THE SH-60 Seahawk began to slice the damp and chilly pre-dawn air. The motion became ever faster with the rising whine of the turbines. The door slid shut and inside the chopper the thumping of the blades dropped to a muffled rumble. Up in the cockpit, the pilot methodically checked over the indicators and gauges, the glowing displays reflecting off his bubble-like visor.

Behind the pilot, Chief Michael Harper, leader of the UDT/SEAL squad, double checked his gear. The other men did the same. Everything was in order.

They had been called to base and briefed on the mission only the day before. Following the briefing, they were taken to special quarters and told to get some sleep.

Awakened at 0200 hours, they were given final instructions. The helo was to drop them over a World War II submarine wreck off the North Carolina coast. Using explosives, they were to blast access into the hull just forward of the deck gun. A tender ship with launches would be waiting over the site. After opening the hull, they were to extract twenty metal canisters to be picked up by the launches on the surface. If everything went according to plan, they could expect to be in the water less than an hour.

The assignment came as a surprise. Several of Harper's men were set to go on leave just the day before. As Navy SEALS, however, they were trained to go into action at a moment's notice, and this was what the situation called for.

The drop was timed for first light. Speed and stealth were paramount, as every aspect of the mission was to be kept from the public eye. Originally planned as a night operation, it was moved to just before sunup. After careful review, the swift currents and limited visibility likely to be encountered were deemed to make a night dive prohibitively difficult. The multitudes of sharks normally present around wreck waters at night was another risk factor that was considered in the mission planning.

Harper had total confidence in his men, for speed and stealth were the hallmarks of their trade. That and an unthinking, killing efficiency; "Death From Below" was the tiny unit's unofficial motto. As the elite of the elite, Harper and his men were relentlessly drilled in all the arts of clandestine warfare—infiltration, sabotage, assassination, and not least, every nuance of hand-to-hand combat.

During the briefing, Harper was struck by the seemingly odd nature of the mission. At first he wondered if it were not some drill. Still, for all he knew, this was to be an advanced exercise. It didn't matter. His job was to complete his assigned task as quickly and efficiently as possible. Any other thoughts were left in the briefing room. He knew his men had done the same.

The engine noise rose to a high pitched roar and they eased off the tarmac. Its navigation lights off, the Seahawk rose steadily into the night sky. The nose angled down slightly and the aircraft headed east toward the open Atlantic. Behind them, the hotels and streetlights of the Virginia Beach resort strip lit the horizon. Ahead lay only darkness.

✠   ✠   ✠

Harper looked around. The other men sat stone faced, contemplating the task ahead. As a veteran of special operations in the Gulf War, Harper was at least seven years older than the men under his command. After the Gulf deployment, his enlistment had been nearly up. He hadn't planned on staying until his CO recommended him for a leadership development program.

When Harper had first joined, he found the military gave his life a structure and focus he'd never thought was possible. On the other hand, he wasn't sure he made the right decision about re-enlisting. He'd been ready to move on. One thing was certain though. The path he'd chosen out of high school more than likely kept him out of prison, or an early grave. Michael Harper knew wherever his military career would ultimately lead him, it was going to be a long, long way from the housing projects and unforgiving streets of south Philadelphia.

✠   ✠   ✠

Dawn began to break as the helicopter cruised south, well off the barrier island shore. To the east, pale clouds were faintly silhouetted by the first light of day. Far below, the Atlantic waters remained cloaked in the lingering mantle of night.

Ten minutes later, they turned southwest and began to descend. The pilot lowered the aircraft further as the tender ship anchored over the wreck site came into view. A quick radio call confirmed everything was on schedule. The pilot eased them closer until the chopper hovered about thirty feet above the surface.

Harper slid open the doors. Seas were light with lazy four foot swells. Directly below, the rotor wash whipped the surface into a foaming frenzy. Harper tossed the ropes overboard. The pilot looked over his shoulder, signaling thumbs up with a gloved hand.

"*Go! Go!*" Harper yelled at the top of his lungs.

In quick succession, the divers slid down the ropes, landing in the middle of the concentric rings of frothing water. Harper was the last to go. With the divers out, the pilot lifted the aircraft up to await the radio call to return.

✠   ✠   ✠

After the hellish noise and commotion of the drop, the stillness of the cold, dark water seemed surreal. With a trail of bubbles
rising behind them, the squad worked their way down the buoy
line anchored to mark the wreck, fighting the current all the way.

The plan was to be executed like clockwork. Every man knew
his part and each carried equipment specific to his task: explosive
charges for blasting through the steel hull; a miniature hydraulic jack similar to the Jaws of Life used at auto accident scenes to
pry apart recalcitrant metal; extra air tanks to fill vinyl balloons
needed to lift the canisters to the launches on the surface.

Harper and his partner inched their way forward along the
deck to place the first set of charges. They would be set to go off
ten minutes after being armed. That would give them ample time
to reach the surface and board one of the launches. Afterward
they would go back down, equipped with electric winches and
other equipment to complete the job.

The two leading divers stopped and hung motionless over what
had been the forward hatchway area—the deck plating had been
neatly cut away and a gaping hole blasted through the pressure
hull. Harper recognized the effects of shaped charges—explosive
devices contoured to direct the force of the blast in a particular
direction. The charges had sawed through the steel as cleanly as
a jackhammer would cut asphalt. With just a foot or so between
them, Harper and his buddy stared disbelieving at the break, then
back at each other. Both recognized the work of a master.

Harper was the first one through, followed closely by the second man. The rest of the squad hovered alongside the break. Once
inside, the two divers methodically swept their flashlights through
the inky darkness. They negotiated a maze of pipes and machinery
that lay about the narrow passageway. Harper saw what he knew to
be a human femur in the middle of the gangway. Further ahead,
disarticulated vertebrae lay half buried in a fine layer of silt.

In the crypt like confines of the hull, both the divers felt like
intruders—living souls, uninvited and keenly out of place in this
realm of the dead. Against the perfect calm of the submarine's
interior, the rush of their regulators was deafening. Behind them,

exhaust bubbles fluttered upward to remain pinned against the ceiling like quivering globs of quicksilver.

They squeezed their way through several bulkhead doors frozen partially open until they reached the control room, directly under the conning tower. There a closed bulkhead blocked further progress.

Turning back, they made their way past the opening in the hull and forward to the bow torpedo room. Their flashlights meticulously probed every nook and corner of the forward compartments. They saw nothing. The canisters were gone.

☧   ☧   ☧

Admiral Jonathan Forsyth nervously paced his office overlooking the main piers of the Norfolk Naval Base. The window behind his desk offered a full view of the harbor. The USS *George Washington*, a *Nimitz* class carrier recently returned from patrol in the eastern Mediterranean, dominated the harbor skyline. He stood and watched the activity on the flight deck as supplies and equipment were off-loaded.

He walked stiffly to his desk and sat down to place the call he'd been wishing he didn't have to make.

"Hello, Sir, Admiral Forsyth here," he said as the other end picked up.

The National Security Advisor leaned back in his plush chair with his feet propped on the desk. "Jonathan, how the hell are you?" he said mildly, rolling a ball of paper between his hands. The wad went arcing though the air, landing in a wastepaper basket along the far wall. "Swish."

He pivoted in the chair, dropping his feet to the floor. "How'd it go this morning? Mission accomplished, eh?"

"There's a problem."

Admiral Forsyth heard the man's palm strike the desk. "What kind of problem?"

"The items to be recovered were not on board."

"Are you sure?"

"Absolutely certain. Seems someone beat us to the punch. The hull's been blasted open. The canisters have been removed. All of them."

Admiral Forsyth held the receiver away and shielded his ear from a barrage of expletives.

"Listen," the voice on the other end boomed, "he's going to want a personal briefing on this! Get your facts straight and get yourself in the air. There'll be a driver waiting at Andrews."

Click.

Chapter 21

WITH THE WEATHER FRONT BEARING DOWN, NIGHT WAS RAPIDLY falling over Hatteras village. Ragged clouds rolled in over the Sound, bringing with them a cold, steady rain.

One man stayed behind the wheel of the dark-colored sedan while the other walked briskly toward the pay phone out in front of the Burrus Red and White supermarket. It was almost full dark and the parking lot was empty. Making his way across the wet pavement, the man glanced around. Back in the car, the orange glow of a lit cigarette repeatedly flared, then lingered behind heavily tinted windows.

After spotting the two Russians, Claremont and Stanizlow shadowed them all afternoon. Echo and Gregory, meanwhile, set up a base of sorts in the shed behind Sinclair's empty house. Using his cellular, Stanizlow kept them continually informed as to their quarry's movements. Echo and Gregory jumped into the truck to meet him as soon as word from Stanizlow came over the phone.

Holding a coin up in one hand, the man at the pay phone hunched against the wind and rain. A small notebook came out of his pocket. Just as he picked up the receiver, a brilliant white flash filled his vision. The blinding light was accompanied by a crushing sensation that enveloped his entire body. In nearly the same instant, everything went black.

Even had the driver been paying attention, he would have been in no position to aid his fallen partner. The passenger door was yanked open and Claremont's 10 mm pressed to his temple. The driver's face was frozen in a distorted grimace with one cheek pushed against the side window by the jarring force of cold steel.

"Flinch and you're dead. Comprendski?" Claremont stated calmly.

The man didn't even try to blink. Behind them, the back door of the sedan opened and Gregory's hefty forearm slid around the man's throat, pressing it back in a chokehold. With the other hand, Gregory stuffed a chloroform-soaked rag over the mouth and nose. The driver struggled feebly before going limp.

The body thudded into the back of the pickup together with the sound of a breath being forcefully dislodged. Gregory threw the truck into reverse and backed to where the other man lay splayed out in front of the pay phone. Echo slipped the high powered stun gun under his jacket. He and Gregory lifted the man, by far the heavier of the two, up off the pavement. Grunting, they rolled him into the bed of the truck. Echo slapped on a set of handcuffs, locking the two unconscious men together. A section of moldy carpet went over top.

Claremont quickly looked around before jumping into the cab. The main road was deserted, asphalt glistening under the occasional streetlight. Across the street, the bays of the Hatteras Volunteer Fire Station were quiet and dark. She looked back as the truck pulled out of the lot. Through the brightly lit storefront, she saw the checkout person chatting idly with her lone customer. Start to finish the operation lasted no more than 45 seconds. No one had seen a thing.

✠   ✠   ✠

One man lay prone, manacled hand and foot to a steel pillar in the center of Preston Sinclair's cinder block work shed. Around him, the concrete floor was stained with oil and grease. Various tools and engine parts cluttered the small space. The larger man sat on a stool against the near wall, his cuffed wrists hoisted above his head by a length of chain locked around a ceiling joist. Still unconscious and with his head slumped down, he looked like a cartoon characterization of a lost soul languishing in a medieval dungeon.

"Is he okay?" Gregory asked, pointing to the seated man. "I mean, his hands are blue."

"He better be 'cause we need to have a little chat," Echo said firmly.

"Show time!" Claremont sang out, breaking open two capsules of amyl nitrate and shoving them under the man's nose.

Looking somewhat bemused, Stanizlow watched the proceedings while warming his hands over a small kerosene heater. The man on the stool groaned and blinked his eyes. He looked to be about 35. Physically the man was quite large with a stout, muscular build. It took every bit of strength Gregory and Echo could muster to heave him into the truck. His close cut hair and hard, chiseled features easily lent the impression of a professional soldier.

"Who are you?" Claremont demanded. "Who sent you? What are your orders?"

The man blinked groggily at his interrogator. His head ached as if it would explode. Through bleary eyes, he could make out the hazy image of a tall woman standing before him. Not being able to find the strength to speak, he just stared back at her.

"*Name!*" Claremont yelled at the top of her lungs, trying to take full advantage of the man's vulnerability in his half-conscious state.

Fully coming to and peering about the room, the prisoner looked scared and confused.

"Tell her nothing," a raspy voice called out in Russian from the floor behind them.

"*Shut up!*" Claremont screamed. She strode across the room and kicked the bound man full force in the mouth. Gregory cringed at the sound of the impact.

She returned her attention to the man sitting against the wall. "Who sent you?" she asked walking back toward him.

"*Ya ne...*"

"Don't give me this *Nyet* shit!" she shrieked directly in his face.

The man seemed genuinely frightened. Claremont backed away. Her face, which was contorted by rage, eased into an expression of steely resolve. She reached into her purse and pulled out her cellular phone.

Echo stood against the wall, his eyes following her every move. The stance, the intonation, the timing and delivery—it was all there. Man, this chick is good, he thought.

Gregory's sun scoured complexion had notably paled.

Behind them, the other Russian managed to rise to his feet. He stood against the metal column, holding himself up with his cuffed hands behind his back. Lean, but not standing overly tall, the man had pasty skin and cold, gray eyes. His small nose was pushed in and looked to have been broken several times in the past. It was obvious he'd been in charge and it was no coincidence Claremont chose to work on the subordinate.

The smaller man glared at Claremont, a thin stream of blood trickling out of the corner of his mouth. Seething, he imagined what it was going to be like to shackle the woman standing in the center of the room. Over and over he envisioned the exquisite retribution he would exact at the very first opportunity. Claremont leered contemptuously back at him.

"Preston Sinclair. Dead. Murdered," she said, turning to the seated prisoner and extending the antenna to the phone. "Oh, don't give me that look like you don't know what I'm talking about!" She moved closer. Her viper-like stare closed in on the man's bewildered eyes. "Never mind who you are, we already know. We also know you killed Preston Sinclair. Why you killed him is what we want to find out."

The man tried to speak. "*Ya ne...*"

She moved closer still. "I'm not the police, but they're just one call away. A warrant for your arrest was issued this morning," she lied, holding up the phone. "Murder One. You're looking at life in a Federal pen so you'd better know how to make fast friends."

Claremont took a half step back, deliberately looking the man up and down. "You think you're tough big boy," she sneered sarcastically, then leaned directly into his face. "Does fresh white meat mean anything to you?"

"Talk and you're dead," the smaller man repeated in Russian. Although slightly puffy and bloodied, his lips lay set in a narrow, sadistic grimace.

Gregory's eyes remained locked on the man standing against the pillar. In an instant, something snapped deep inside. The terrible image of Preston Sinclair's mutilated, partially decomposed body flashed through his mind. Gregory passed many an hour thinking of nothing but Preston's killer. Now the killer had a face, and it was grinning mockingly back at him. "*Shut the fuck up!*" he screamed.

Gregory's smashing blow hit the man squarely on the cheek. His face snapped sideways into the metal pillar, shattering the jaw. The man sagged onto his knees. Cuffed arms stretched tight at his back kept him from toppling flat on his face. His mouth gaped open as thick red drops fell steadily to the floor. Several broken teeth lay on the concrete amid a gathering puddle of blood.

Echo raised one eyebrow. Stanizlow's dispassionate expression hadn't changed.

Claremont wheeled around at the sound of the blow. "Now once again," she said turning back and addressing the other prisoner. "Why did you kill Preston Sinclair?"

The man's eyes were wide and frightened. Again he tried to speak.

"*Nyet* is *nyet* the answer I'm looking for!" she hissed, seemingly on the verge of another rage.

In one smooth motion she drew her automatic from under her jacket, racked the slide, leveled the weapon to the man's face and pulled the trigger. Within the confines of the shed, the 10 MM was deafening. The slug grazed the man's cheek before shearing away part of his ear and punching through the cinder block wall directly behind his head. The crater like hole was left ringed by a fine, bright red spray.

The man fell from the stool, howling in pain and fright. With knees bent, he hung by outstretched arms, the cuffs digging ever deeper into his flesh.

"*Ya ne govoru po-Angliski!*" he gasped.

Stanizlow took a step and a half forward. "He says, he doesn't speak much English."

Claremont holstered her weapon. "Oh."

A panicked, rapid-fire plea flew from the man's lips. "*Ne strelaite! Ne gubite!!*"—"Don't shoot! Don't kill me!" He managed to find his feet.

Stanizlow began to translate as the man found his voice. "Please don't kill me! Please! I have a wife and baby girl. I haven't seen them in a year. I'll tell you everything I know."

"*Yazykom ty trepesh, zatormozi!*"—"Slow down don't talk so fast!" Stanizlow commanded.

Hearing Stanizlow speak his native tongue, the man cast him a look as if to beg for deliverance from eternal damnation. Blood oozed down his neck, soaking one side of his shirt.

He cast a frightened glance toward Claremont, then looked back at Stanizlow, who continued to translate.

"I didn't kill anyone! I swear to it! My name is Sergei Zhukov. True, we were following the man—but we didn't kill him. Someone else did. I swear to Mother Mary!"

The Russian grimaced as he hunched one shoulder against his mangled ear, letting out a sharp groan at the touch of the wound.

"We had standing orders to observe what was going on," Stanizlow relayed, motioning for Zhukov to halt at the end of each sentence. "We were here to collect information. Standing orders. We were to observe only. We found out the submarine was going to be brought to the surface. We passed the information to our people in Moscow. Then we left. I swear to it."

Echo pointed to the bent figure leaning from the pillar and said, "Ask him who fuck face is over there."

Stanizlow queried him, translating the response: "That's Beklemishev. Igor Beklemishev. He's the boss."

Still speaking in Russian, Stanizlow let loose a barrage of questions, which were answered at an equally rapid pace. The others stood and watched the exchange, unable to comprehend a single word.

Stanizlow leaned over and appeared to whisper something into the man's remaining, good ear.

"You're dead, Zhukov! Dead!" the other man snarled, spitting blood through broken teeth.

Stanizlow stepped backward. "Cut them loose," he ordered.

"Says who?" Echo challenged.

"Cut—them—loose."

Echo glanced over to Claremont who lowered her eyes and nodded almost imperceptibly. He raised his weapon, as did Claremont. Echo reached into his pocket for the keys. Standing behind the smaller man, he braced the pistol against the neck. The man's hateful sneer receded as he felt the muzzle press against his second vertebrae.

Echo tossed Gregory the keys. "You heard the man. Cut 'em loose."

Gregory unshackled the two Russians who, once freed, remained motionless, apparently unsure of exactly what was going on. With a wave of her pistol, Claremont pointed them to the door. "Go on. Get outta here."

Keeping their backs to the wall, the two men cautiously stepped sideways. Echo and Claremont held their weapons trained on the bleeding figures as they turned past the open door and staggered off into the misting darkness.

✠   ✠   ✠

Claremont broke the extended silence, which pervaded the room after the two Russians were gone. "So you really think they didn't do it?" she asked, while hosing off the concrete floor of the shed. She directed the spray at a recessed drain in the center of the shed. A watery, crimson-colored pool swirled around the small grate.

"I know they did not," Stanizlow stated.

"How can you be so sure?"

"Zhukov is not lying. The man is *Spetsnaz*—Special Reconnaissance Forces of the old Soviet Army. I know the mold. I was an instructor for a few years at one of the training centers, outside Moscow."

Echo rolled his eyes. Just when I figured I'd heard it all, he thought.

"In fact," Stanizlow went on, "I think I have seen his face before. I just can't recall exactly where and when."

"Doesn't seem like such a tough guy to me," Echo chimed.

"When a man doesn't believe in what he's fighting for, he is easily broken," Stanizlow said wearily. "Or bought."

"What about the other guy?"

"Beklemishev, he's a common hoodlum," Stanizlow said. The contempt in his voice was hard to miss. "Straight from the St. Petersburg sewers."

"What about Zhukov? How does he fit?"

Stanizlow sighed before answering. "The Enterprise can afford all the hired guns they need, and the best. Times are hard and there are plenty of men who need work."

Claremont turned the water off and hung up the hose. "But he betrayed the Enterprise. Won't he be a marked man."

"Indeed he would be—if they found out. But they won't."

"What do you mean?"

"Yes, he betrayed the code of silence. He knows what that means—he has no choice but to come to us."

"What about the cockroach with the bad teeth?" Echo cut in.

Stanizlow gave a weak smile. "'Fuck face,' as you say, is soon to be out of the picture." He looked at his watch. "That is, if he isn't already. Zhukov is ours. He knows what he has to do. I slipped him back his knife. Nothing needed to be said."

Claremont exhaled loudly while locking her hands on the back of her neck.

"The sad thing," Stanizlow added, "is this Igor fellow is too stupid and vain to have any idea he is about to die."

"I sure hope you're right about this," Echo said.

Gregory remained seated between the tool strewn workbench and a pair of acetylene tanks. Looking perplexed and angry, he got up to speak. "If these guys didn't kill Preston, then who did? I mean, what do we do now?"

"I'm sorry your friend is dead, but we have more pressing concerns at the moment," Stanizlow said brusquely. He turned to Claremont. "It seems our friends think the cargo may already have been removed from the wreck. That's why they came back — to try and find out what might have happened."

"I'll call the office first thing in the morning," Claremont said. "Maybe something has changed. Bear with me, I need to think this through." She looked intently at Stanizlow. "So what's-his-name told you the cargo was taken from the wreck? By who? Where is it?!"

His mind racing, Echo broke in. "I think we mustn't lose sight of the fact Preston Sinclair's connection to the *U-491* is what probably got him killed — if we can find out who did him in, we might know what's going on here."

Claremont folded her arms, shooting Echo a hard-edged glance. "Didn't you say Sinclair hung around with some pretty shady characters down in Florida?" she asked. "Salvage people of some description."

"Pretty much," Gregory stated, before Echo could answer.

Claremont began to pace the room. "Maybe he got hooked back up with those guys — after all, he was convinced the wreck was full of gold." She turned to Gregory. "Eric, didn't you say Sinclair wanted to raise the sub, before he got the company involved?"

"Yeah, but Preston always had some grand scheme going."

"Just a hunch," Claremont went on, thinking aloud, "but let's say Sinclair realized he was out of his league trying to raise the wreck himself..."

"Right," Gregory agreed.

"So he swings a deal with the company in California, then realizes the wreck might actually have treasure on board. He's getting a base salary for his part, but that's it. What would he do? Who would he turn to?"

Echo said, "We need his phone records."

Claremont gave a sour look. "The bills are probably at the Post Office. Getting his mail would take some doing. Besides, it's Saturday night. We'd have to wait 'til Monday."

"Make a call to the Bureau and have them get the records," Echo offered.

"That'll be Tuesday—maybe."

Gregory bounced off the stool. "Preston was missing for the better part of a week before he was found," he said quickly. "He didn't have any family—least that I know of. No one probably stopped the mail for who knows how long. Maybe there's something sitting in his box right now we can use."

Echo and Claremont exchanged short glances. It couldn't be so easy, they thought.

In an instant, Gregory was across the room and out the door. The misting drizzle had not let up. The yard was completely dark and it took a few moments for his eyes to adjust. A strange feeling crept over Gregory as he made his way past Sinclair's house—to rifle his mail of all things. He came to the end of the drive and pulled open the box. Sure enough, it was crammed to capacity. Straining to see, he thumbed through the crumpled stack of bills, notices and assorted junk mail. Halfway through, he found it—November's phone bill. Pushed all the way to the back was the October bill.

Gregory burst back into the shed, grinning broadly and waving the envelopes over his head. He slapped them down on the table.

Claremont and Echo each reached for one and pulled it open. Gregory watched intently over their shoulders.

"A couple of calls to California," Echo said. "I think that's the company who was going to raise the sub.

"We already know all about them."

"Bingo!" Claremont called out. "Islamorada. One call—a couple more. Islamorada, that's in the Keys isn't it?"

Gregory was beaming. "We got a number and that's a hell of a good start."

Claremont slipped the phone bill into her bag saying, "I'll get this to the right people in DC first thing."

Echo turned to Gregory. "You're good, Captain. Are you sure you haven't done this kind of work before?"

"Positive," Gregory replied, while absently rubbing the bruised knuckles of his right hand.

Chapter 22

AFTER SEVERAL TRIES, CLAREMONT FINALLY GOT THROUGH TO WASHington. A message was left for her with the lone duty officer on Sunday morning. She powered up her laptop to run the encryption program. The phone communication would be secure from all but the most sophisticated electronic eavesdroppers—more than adequate for this sort of fare.

She hit the receive command and the printed message flashed across the display:

```
Navy reports the U-491 has been compromised.
Canisters no longer on board. Notify V. Stanizlow.
Unknown party involved. Moscow has been informed.
Report to schedule briefing.
```

Stanizlow took the news with the same deadpan expression he carried day in and day out. It was the same matte face he'd worn since she first met him at the arrival gate at Dulles. Boredom. Contempt. Contemplation. All three, or none, she could never be sure.

Initially, Claremont figured it was jet lag—except the face never changed. Now, in half seriousness, she wanted to ask him if he knew what a Vulcan was. But she didn't know how to approach him, or whether she even wanted to. Other than forced, mechanical communication concerning professional matters, they had not spoken since the bombshell he'd dropped that night at Gregory's house.

✠   ✠   ✠

Claremont was excruciatingly tired. The events of the previous night, not to mention the whole of the last week, left her exhausted. Too fatigued to rest, she passed the afternoon walking the beach. The day was cloudy and unusually warm. Despite a noble effort, the weak late autumn sun never quite broke through the low deck of clouds. Nabbing the two Russians the night before led nowhere. The accompanying letdown only added to her weariness.

She showered after returning to the room. On the way in, she had seen Stanizlow sitting in the breezeway, staring down the marshy canal that led to the Sound. She hadn't acknowledged him.

After drying off, she lay down on the freshly made bed to rest, only to fall instantly asleep.

It was dark when she awoke. Disoriented, she stepped out of the room for air. The clouds were gone. It was about a half hour after sundown and the stars were just beginning to emerge. A thin, powder blue band lingered on the western horizon. Strangely, it seemed even warmer than during the afternoon. Wearing only shorts and a T-shirt, she went back into the room and grabbed a sweatshirt before making her way down the breezeway.

To her surprise, Stanizlow was still in the chair, sitting rigid and motionless as if sculpted of stone. She hesitated, then kept walking.

"Hi," she said, stopping at his side.

He lifted his gaze and smiled briefly.

"Can I join you?"

"Of course."

She pulled up a chair. "Nice night, huh?"

Stanizlow looked off. For a moment, it seemed as if conversation might end right there. As they sat in awkward silence, a puff of wind stirred the pines lining the canal. The southeasterly breeze, straight off the Gulf Stream, was thick and warm. Though the sun had long since set, the air temperature was near 70 degrees.

Claremont reached over and touched his arm. Her fingers ran up under his short-sleeved shirt. "Can I ask you something, Stan?"

Stanizlow continued to gaze straight ahead. "Yes."

"You're actually German, but you worked for the Russians, yet Stanizlow is a Polish name. How's that?"

"It was not my name. I took the name because I liked it."

"Whose was it?" she asked before realizing how silly the question probably sounded.

"It was my maternal grandfather's Christian name. His family was originally from Poland."

She hadn't expected an answer. "What about your father? What was his name?"

"My family history is a complicated affair," he sighed. "I can explain if you wish." The offer sounded reluctant.

"Please do."

It was full dark. Across the road, the canal waters shimmered dimly under a waning quarter moon.

"My mother was born to the union of a Turkish diplomat and an Austrian seamstress. An unusual pairing, I should think," he said, still looking away.

Claremont shrugged and continued to study the side of his tightly set face.

"It was the time of the Austro-Hungarian Monarchy, before the turn of the century. The Austrians and the Turks had been adversaries for hundreds of years. Eventually the Ottomans and Austrians learned to get along. Both had found a common enemy in Czarist Russia."

Claremont could feel him steering off the subject. Her curiosity aroused, the last thing she wanted was a history lesson. She began to prod. "How'd your parents meet?"

"The Austrians and Turks may have learned to get along," he said ignoring her question, "but my grandparents never did. They fought all the time. It was a very unhappy home. Mother was an only child, yet her father, he treated her like a servant girl, perhaps worse. One day, she just left."

Stanizlow no longer seemed hesitant. Claremont sensed he actually wanted to talk. She guessed he probably hadn't spoken of his family for years. In actuality, it had been decades.

"You must understand," he said turning to her, then looking away, "it was different in those days. A woman couldn't just do what she wanted, no matter what the circumstances. That didn't stop my mother, though. She ran off. Ran as far from Vienna as she could—to the island of Rügen—on the Baltic Sea."

"What did she do there?"

His face eased slightly. "Within a short time, she was engaged to the son of one of the wealthiest landed families in all of Meckelenburg—the von Rostocks. You see, not only was my mother headstrong, but she was a very, very beautiful woman. Any man would have wanted her." He turned to Claremont and smiled. "My, how horrified the von Rostocks were," he said with a sparkle in his eyes. "The family was scandalized—a commoner mind you, from Austria, no less—a real Hilly Billy."

Claremont burst out laughing. Coming from him, the expression sounded hysterically funny.

"Anyway, they eloped to Berlin." He raised both hands. "And, two people loved each other, so—here I am."

Shaking her head, Claremont kept smiling back at him. He seemed so fresh and relaxed, she thought. So open. She'd never seen him like this. It was as if he'd suddenly become a totally different individual. It struck her perhaps she'd been allowed a glimpse of the real person, deep inside—the one who lay perpetually hidden behind the steadfast expression and unyielding blue-green stare. "Didn't you say you grew up in Moscow?"

The window slammed shut. Without so much as blinking, his entire body changed. Within a fraction of a second, he was as before.

"This is true," he said dully, after a full ten seconds passed. "Soon after getting married, my father began his studies at Leipzig University. Leipzig, that's where I was born. His father, you see, wanted to disown him—cut him off from the family name and fortune. Father's eldest aunt, the matriarch of the von Rostocks, would have none of it. She kept sending him money—enough to keep him in a student lifestyle." He paused as if to weigh his words. "They were tumultuous times, after the Great War," he finally said. "The university was a hotbed of politics. My father, he became a sworn communist."

"Why?"

"He hated capitalism. It was the war that turned him—three years in the trenches. Most every boyhood friend was killed, or mutilated. There were millions more. Some of those who did come home had been gassed—vibrant young men turned into wretched, wheezing shadows of their former selves. Then there were the living dead. Untouched by lead or shrapnel, they wandered the streets or lay in hospital wards—their minds lost to the horror. My father saw it all, and blamed the system for everything."

Claremont pulled her feet onto the chair. Wearing only shorts and the sweat shirt, she wrapped her arms around her bare legs, pressing them against her chest. She peered at him with the side of her face resting on one knee. "And?" she asked solemnly.

"And so my father took his young family to the new Soviet Union. There were others like him. From all over, they came to Moscow to devote their lives to building socialism."

He stopped speaking and resumed staring down the swampy canal. The wind picked up. They sat and took in its warm caress as the nearby pines rustled softly in the night. Down the way, a house was brightly festooned with Christmas lights. The bulging figure of a plastic Santa Claus stood illuminated in the front yard.

Deep down, Claremont didn't want to ask. She again reached over and ran her hand under his sleeve. One fingertip stopped at the faint knob of scar tissue. "What's that?" she whispered.

"That was a tattoo."

"You had it removed."

"Yes."

"It was your blood type, wasn't it?"

"Yes."

"You were SS."

"Yes."

His gaze set straight ahead, Stanizlow did not so much as blink. The breeze died. An eerie stillness enveloped them.

"I was so young," he began dully. "So very young. Mother sent me back to Germany to attend school. It was 1938. I really don't know why I joined the *Partei*. Maybe I was rebelling against my father and everything he stood for... I don't know... Maybe it was the wanting to be part of something—something new and exciting—the feeling of making something happen. Later, after the war started, I volunteered for the Waffen SS. I was assigned to Intelligence." He turned and looked at her. "The Army Group I was attached to spearheaded the invasion of Russia."

Claremont was speechless. She could hardly believe one person could do so many things, in different places, in different times.

"The Waffen SS worked like a finely-tuned machine," he droned. "Everyone knew their part. We were all like cogs in a wheel."

"What was your part?"

"I formulated estimates of enemy units' fighting strength based on casualty figures and intelligence reports. A desk job really, though we were constantly on the move."

Stanizlow paused. He visibly tensed. "Going in, our troops were told the Russians would be poor fighters; that they were barely subhuman and should be treated as such. Frontline men quickly learned otherwise. Falling back on home soil, the Red Army fought with a tenacity almost beyond belief. One time," he said, his speech gaining tempo, "we encountered a detachment of Russians holed up in grain elevators. They beat back an entire battalion for two days. Heavy artillery had to be brought in from a different sector. When we went through the rubble, we found no more than thirty some dead. They were the toughest fighters. The Russian who cried out when wounded seemed the exception rather than the rule."

He stopped and drew a deep breath.

"Then there were the *Einsatzgruppen*," he said, exhaling slowly. "The killing squads that swept in behind the advance; the mobile, primitive precursors to the death camps of the Final Solution. Fourth-rate troops, drawn from prisons and punishment battalions, thrown together with a few enlistees deemed too old or physically unfit for frontline duty."

He looked her directly in the eyes. "I once saw them in action."

Claremont felt her flesh go cold. An icy tingle crept down her spine.

"I have never been able to forget that day," he said turning away. "Hundreds of Ukrainian Jews and Gypsies, herded into an open field and made to dig their own mass graves. It was a hot August afternoon. Hour after hour the guns hammered away. Again and again bodies toppled into the pits. Some were still living—pinned between bloody corpses when the first spadefuls of earth went over them. The smell of blood and cordite lingered in the still summer air long after the pits were filled in."

The face hadn't changed.

Looking down, she saw his hands were balled into tightly clenched fists.

"The officers in the occupation forces, how I despised them. At first, some Soviet peoples saw us as liberators—only to be treated with contempt and cruelty. It was not long before partisans were active in those same areas."

Claremont had asked about his family; one thing led to another. Now she didn't know what to say. It didn't matter. Once started, Stanizlow was not about to stop. It was as if some trigger had been tripped deep within his psyche. She realized the monologue had become a calculated confession of the secrets he'd carried for half a century. His voice low but firm, the words flowed forth, steady and relentless as a mid-river current.

"One day I just crossed the Russian lines. I went over."

Claremont remained speechless.

"Late summer '43, south of Kursk, in what is now Ukraine, I crossed over—to the other side."

"How?" she choked.

Stanizlow hardly skipped a beat. "Things were going very badly. Even some of the better units were a patchwork of older veterans, raw recruits and men pressed from the occupied countries. Even support personnel had to fight. Myself, I was given command of an anti-partisan squad." His voice went on edge. "I was never trained as an infantry officer. I just did the best I could." He hesitated before continuing. "One day we were out on patrol. Lines were fluid in our sector. We were on an anti-partisan sweep. I went ahead to scout a tree line. Ordered the squad down. The area had been contested for weeks and I came up on a number of rotting Russian corpses scattered about the forest floor. It wasn't an impulse, I'd been thinking about it for weeks. I took some of the dead men's weapons—blew the magazines off in the general direction of my squad, fired my pistol in the other hand. My men, they were cooks and mechanics. Just as I suspected, they put their heads down and didn't even try to come to my aid. After a while, they probably just went back to base and reported me killed. I got up and walked in the opposite direction. The next day I came up on a Red Army position. It was no small feat to convince them not to shoot me on the spot. Thoroughly confused, they turned me over to the local NKVD commander, who decided to execute me himself."

Seemingly amused at the reminiscence, he smiled at Claremont, adding "I was wearing the field uniform of a Waffen SS officer and spoke perfect Muscovite Russian. It totally threw the fellow."

"Anyway, my father moved in some high circles and I started to drop a name or two. I convinced him he would be shot if the slightest thing happened to me. They brought me to division headquarters where it took two days to get through to the right people on the one field telephone they had. The next day, I was on a rickety old plane bound for Moscow."

Claremont's mind was reeling. "But you were on the U-boat! How on earth...?"

He ignored the interruption. "Once in Moscow, I was able to meet with some old friends of my father's—men in very high places."

"Why'd you do it? Was it the killings, the things you saw?"

"It was all of it. All of it and everything together. After the disaster at Stalingrad, I knew the war was lost. What I'd seen behind the lines only further convinced me the regime in Berlin was insane. It had to fall—through whatever means, and the sooner it did, the less Germany and its people would ultimately suffer. So I went over."

"And you thought you could make a difference," Claremont stated, totally exasperated.

"Yes."

"You told them everything you knew, then became a Soviet agent."

"You're catching on," Stanizlow said, flashing his thin smile. Just as suddenly, the smile was gone.

When he again spoke, his voice had totally changed. It was thick but taut, dry like a raspy whisper. "I was taken back to near where I crossed over and given a cover—four German POWs accompanied me. We were to have been trapped behind the lines after the last Red Army offensive. Their names, ranks, units, home towns, everything added up to support my story. When we neared the lines, I was sent on alone. I… I never should have looked back. Never. In my worst dreams I still see their faces. Boys, all from small towns in the south—so frightened… about to be forever swallowed by the vastness of the Ukraine." His voice wavered and almost broke. "I heard the four pistol cracks as I made my way to the forward German positions."

The silence was intolerable. A car, headlights glaring, drove past. The sound of tires on pavement faded and the night was totally still once more.

"The cover held. Later, I received transfer orders from Berlin. I was to be attached to the SD—the *Sicherheitsdienst* headquarters in Danzig. The orders seemingly came out of the blue, but they were part of a greater plan. I did not know until long after the war."

He paused.

"Know of what?" she asked.

"That the entire SS hierarchy had been penetrated by Soviet agents."

Claremont blinked at him in disbelief.

"Back in the very early thirties, someone in the Foreign Ministry foresaw the rise of a fascist, militaristic Germany. A plan was put in place. Young Germans living in the Soviet Union, men like my father, were recruited and thoroughly trained. They were provided new identities and sent back to Germany. There they joined the ranks of the Brown Shirts and later, the newly formed *Schutzstaffeln*—the Nazi Party guard units who would ultimately grow to be the giant SS organization. True sleepers, most attained relatively prominent positions in the Waffen SS, the SD and the German police. There weren't many, but all were highly effective. As far as I know, not one was ever exposed. Anyway, with the war drawing to a close, Stalin became increasingly obsessed with the notion Hitler might somehow escape his grasp. All assets were mobilized to keep tabs on the Nazi elite. My handler, he positioned me to infiltrate part of the Tannhauser Operation."

Stanizlow waved a hand through the air. "The rest you already know," he said, as if summing up a ball game score.

Claremont slowly shook her head. It all seemed too much to grasp. She tried to focus. "Then, after the war, you worked for the East Germans." Her face contorted. "How could you!" she said sharply. "After all that!" Her voice went further on edge—shrill almost. "Berlin! The Wall! The Border! The wire and the towers—that scar cutting across the countryside—separating towns and friends and families! How could you willingly have been a part of all that?!"

Stanizlow was genuinely surprised by her tone. For a brief moment, he was ready to snap back at her, but quickly steadied himself. "Most Germans," he began evenly, "most Germans blindly, enthusiastically even, followed the Nazis into the madness that was to be the Third Reich. A few didn't—men like my father. A few resisted; most of those ended up in the camps. You see, there was a small minority, the ones who survived that is, who felt themselves to have been liberated by the Soviets. We saw ourselves as the rightful heirs to a new Germany—a new Germany built from the ashes of the old; one based on the principles of socialism and equality."

"And you believed all that crap?"

"I did, yes. Or at least I wanted to. Think of what I had been through at the time."

They sat in silence.

Looking somewhat contrite, Claremont regretted the outburst. "What about your parents?" she asked, trying to change the subject. "Did you see them after the war?"

Stanizlow stared off. He glanced at his watch.

"Before the war, my father was killed on direct orders from Stalin," he stated without apparent emotion. "He and millions of others died at that man's hands. Died for nothing—for no reason other than believing in communism. Still, my father went to his death totally committed to the Cause."

Claremont didn't know what to say. "I'm sorry," she finally whispered.

He looked at her. "Mother was able to get me out of the country—back to Germany."

Behind the unyielding stare, she saw the terrible pain.

"No one told us about Father after he was taken away," His voice firmed. "But at the time, Mother knew she would never be allowed to leave. It was all she could do to get me out... She was so very strong. At the station... for me, leaving seemed the beginning of a grand adventure. I was but a lad. As the train pulled out, I waved and waved from the open window until she was gone. Standing alone on the platform, she must have known she'd never see me again."

"What happened?" Claremont asked, her words barely audible.

"Being German, she was sent to Siberia immediately after the invasion began. I only found out from friends many years after the war. Her health left her after my father's death. She didn't last the first winter."

Claremont reached for him. Slowly, she ran her fingers across his hand, stopped and held on. She found herself unable to let go. Reaching across, he put his other hand over hers. They sat in silence.

✠   ✠   ✠

Back in her room, they fell upon the bed in a desperate, clutching embrace. For what seemed hours they lay entwined, holding on so tightly as if to let go, even for an instant, would send them forever tumbling apart through the blackest abyss of utter nothingness.

They made love as the first gray light of dawn filtered through the curtained windows.

Chapter 23

IT WAS AS THOUGH THE NIGHT BEFORE NEVER HAPPENED. Standing by the bed, Claremont briskly pulled a brush through her hair. She packed her things during the short hour in which he'd slept. A last look in the mirror brought out the lipstick for a quick touchup.

Stanizlow rolled over under the sheets. "Where are you going?"

"I have to go to DC for a meeting. I'll be back in a couple of days," she said, dropping the cosmetic case into her handbag.

She strode across the room, picked up her suitcase and walked out the door without so much as saying good-bye. Stanizlow flopped back onto the pillow, wondering.

✠   ✠   ✠

The drive up the mainland was uneventful. It took just over two hours to reach the Virginia Tidewater. That was as far north as she was to go. After turning off I-64, Claremont pulled into the long term parking lot at the Norfolk International Airport. The shuttle bus brought her to the terminal. Paying with cash, she bought a one-way ticket at the US Air counter under an assumed name.

With almost 90 minutes before the flight, she took a seat in the departure area lounge and ordered coffee. She casually deflected several opening inquires from the adjacent patron, a salesman from Toronto, with polite, one and two word responses.

Sitting at the counter, her hair was neatly pinned under a wide-brimmed hat. Even though skies outside were overcast, she wore dark designer sunglasses. A jacketed dress and heels completed the outfit. As much as she stood out from the airport crowds of businessmen and homeward bound college students, the look seemed perfectly in place for a holiday flight destined for Miami.

☧   ☧   ☧

Claremont parked the rental car on a side street, well away from the Islamorada waterfront. She scouted the area the evening before after getting in from Miami. Islamorada wasn't a big place—just large enough to lose oneself amid the peak season throngs. This shouldn't be too difficult, she told herself. After making the rounds and familiarizing herself with the town, she drove to the outskirts and checked into an Econo Lodge for some much needed sleep.

☧   ☧   ☧

Thinking it was as good a place to start as any, Claremont paused in front of the Pink Flamingo Restaurant and Lounge. She pulled open the door and made her entrance. Heads turned as she seated herself at the center of the bar.

"Soda and lime, please," she said to the bartender as he came over.

"You got it."

Her previous outfit was replaced by a sheer blouse under a Bolero jacket and a close fitting navy skirt. She was also sporting elbow-length white gloves. One spike of her white heels was hooked around the bottom rung of the bar stool. With her legs crossed, the other foot rested casually in midair. Between the gloved fingers of her right hand rested a freshly lit Dunhill.

Few women could dress like a mannequin in a vintage clothing store and get away with it. Not only did Claremont pull it off, but she looked incredible doing it. With her hair tied back by an embossed silver barrette, she was nothing short of elegant.

The restaurant was half filled with the late lunch crowd. Patrons at the surrounding tables, both men and women, repeatedly glanced her way. Several of the staff found reason to walk past. She pretended not to notice, even though to be noticed was the point of the exercise.

An attractive woman, Claremont knew only too well the effect she had on men. There was more to it than her body and striking looks. Though aware of her unique sexual charisma, she could never fully shut it off—even if she needed to. She could, however, torque it up whenever she wanted, and at that moment, while seated at the bar, it was screaming out at the equivalent of 120 decibels.

The place began to clear and the bartender had a few minutes.

"You here on business or pleasure?" he asked, finding opportunity to wipe down the counter in front of her.

He was a somewhat short, rounded off figure of a man. From behind wire-rimmed glasses, inquisitive but friendly eyes looked straight back at her. His thinning hair lay combed straight back from a tanned and creased forehead.

Claremont quickly gauged him. He seemed sincere enough, and not the least bit intimidated by her. "Business, most definitely," she smiled.

"You in sales?" he guessed. He slid her a clean ashtray.

"Journalism. I'm a reporter."

"Really? Who do you work for?"

"No one. Well, myself actually. I'm down here doing a little freelancing."

"I wanted to be a reporter. Before I dropped out of school, that is. Hi, I'm Gary."

"I can see," Claremont replied, eyeing the name tag on his regulation dark blue polo shirt.

She reached into her purse and pulled out another cigarette. "I'm Virginia," she said blandly.

He leaned across the bar to give her a light.

"Thanks," Claremont said, making eye contact. "So, Gary, you lived here long?"

"Yeah, almost ten years now. It's kind of hard to leave, if you know what I mean. Why?"

"I'm looking for story material. Something on human interest. Maybe profile some local characters. Former drug pilots or," she paused, "treasure hunters, perhaps. I hear this is a good town for types like that."

"They're not allowed in here anymore," Gary stated flatly.

"Who?" Claremont asked, somewhat startled by the emphatic response.

"The James Gang. 'Least that's what we always called 'em. They fancy themselves treasure hunters all right. Truth is, most of them got rap sheets 'bout as long as this bar."

"Where do I find these folks?"

Gary pointed to the door. "At the Barbados Grill. Left around the corner and up the street three blocks. You can't miss it."

"What's the place like?"

"Lots of neon. Usually has a couple of hogs out front. Most people think of it as a biker bar. Got a great burger, though."

"Check your weapon at the door?"

"Not that bad," he laughed. "It's just a hangout for local roughnecks and the usual flunkies. If you want color, that would be the place."

"Sounds like my kind of joint," Claremont grinned.

"Tell you what, try going in there after 4:00 o'clock and ask for Shamus James. Or don't ask, for that matter. You'll meet him anyway."

Claremont gathered her bag and slid off the barstool. She placed a five dollar bill on the counter. "Thanks Gary," she said, turning to leave.

"Hey, no problem. Hope to see you around."

"Yeah."

✠   ✠   ✠

Sitting in the Barbados Grill, Claremont was actually a little disappointed. The way the bartender had talked about the place, she half-expected to walk into something akin to the Cantina scene in "Star Wars." On the inside, it looked much like any other establishment along the South Florida coast. In this particular case, the decor was heavily rattan, with split bamboo framing the windows and lining the molding. Ceiling fans swirled the air, which carried a passing hint of disinfectant.

The bartender was right about the neon, she thought. The aqua and pink was a little much. He'd also been right about the burger. It was delicious.

Claremont finished eating and was pulling her gloves back on when a tall, heavily built man barged through the swinging doors. He was wearing a white button-down shirt with the sleeves cut off just below the armpits.

"Hey, James," the waitress said without looking at him. "How ya doin', darlin'?"

Claremont immediately figured she had her mark. The man wore canvas deck shoes without socks. His shorts had seen better days. Unneeded sunglasses, together with a thin gold chain, hung around his neck. Although freshly shaven, he looked disheveled enough to have probably been up only a few hours. She glanced at the clock on the wall. It read 4:05.

The man leaned onto the bar and ordered a beer. A similar dressed patron standing next to him, a drinking buddy Claremont presumed, jabbed him with an elbow; both looked over at her. She raised one hand slightly and gave a short wave. After downing his beer, he ordered another, grabbed it off the counter and swaggered over to the corner booth in which she was sitting.

"Heard you was asking about me," he said, standing over her, his eyes lingering.

"Mr. James, I was hoping to buy you a drink."

"It's James, just James," he said, trying to sound cavalier. "Never do refuse a drink, 'specially from a pretty lady."

Claremont smiled back at him. He sat down. His broad face was lined and florid cheeks lightly pocked. A hefty chin with a pronounced cleft complimented his heavy-set features. He smelled of stale beer and aftershave. Although Claremont had only seen

Preston Sinclair in photographs, this James character reminded her very much of him. She was certain she had the right man.

"So why you wanna buy me a drink?" he asked, still eyeing her.

"I was hoping to get to know you. It must be obvious your reputation precedes you," she said demurely.

James leaned across the table. "You're not a lady dick, are ya? Because if you are, I'm telling you, I'm one-hundred-percent clean."

"Not to worry, I'm a reporter."

It fast became apparent to Claremont she was not dealing with the world's most sophisticated person. This should be easy, she thought—just as long as he's not gay. Man, sometimes you never can tell.

Remarking on the warmth in the room, she slipped out of the jacket. She flapped the open collar of the blouse, showing more skin and releasing her lightly laden scent. His response put her mind at ease; his eyes shifted and began to gloss slightly. "Can you tell me a little about yourself?" she asked. "What's it like being a treasure diver?"

"So why you want to know?"

Claremont slid a little further into the booth while looking James in the eyes. "I'm writing a piece on modern day fortune hunters. I came down here to research the subject—to meet people. You're the first person I've managed to get a hold of."

His libido fully engaged, she began to work his vanity. "I heard you were good. I mean really good."

"Aw, well, I dunno," he shrugged. "Actually, I have done a lot of divin'."

"Like what? Can you tell me a little about your work?"

James still seemed a little wary. "Salvage—it isn't all Spanish gold and pieces of eight, you know."

"Really? How do you mean?"

"I mean there are different types of wrecks you can work."

Hanging on his every word, she peered at him with softly-lidded eyes.

"Oh sure, everyone wants to find the *Atocha*," James said while beckoning the waitress. "Not that I haven't found any gold," he added. "Pulled up lots of it, actually. It's just that I wasn't the one getting rich off it. You know what I mean?"

She nodded sympathetically.

The waitress placed a round of beers on the table. James waited until she left before continuing. He again leaned toward Claremont. "If you really want, I'll tell you about one of my best hauls."

"Yeah?"

"It wasn't no galleon or nothin'. It was this Civil War transport we found. Hit a reef loaded with equipment and supplies to outfit a whole regiment. Buttons, buckles and things—it's amazing what people will pay for that kinda stuff."

"Oh, I know," she agreed.

James grinned mischievously. "We had to use explosives to break up the coral just to get at the good stuff," he said, quickly adding, "Don't print that part though."

Claremont gave an understanding laugh. Seemingly enraptured, she listened as he rattled on about every major wreck he'd worked and what he found. Two more beers landed on the table. His sea stories came next. Now and again Claremont would run her thumb and forefinger up and down the full length of the longneck bottle. James repeatedly failed at trying not to notice.

"Now I got a question for you," he proclaimed, pointing a meaty finger.

"Shoot."

"How'd you find out about me anyway?"

"Preston Sinclair," she said, watching his face for any sort of response. There was none.

"Oh, yeah, how's he doin'?" James simply asked.

Claremont continued to study him. "He's dead. I'm... I'm sorry, I thought you knew."

James frowned. "Well, I am sorry to hear that. Haven't seen the man in years. Used to work with him some. Kind of a strange guy." He promptly changed the subject. "How come you're wearing those gloves?"

Claremont pretended to be flustered. "The salt, then the sun; with my skin, I get a rash right away."

James didn't want to let it go. "But it's dark outside now."

"I broke out yesterday. You have to excuse me. I'm kind of sensitive about it, " she said, turning her head aside.

Another round of beers came to the table.

James took a long pull, set the bottle down and flashed a toothy grin. "I've never met no newspaper lady, 'specially one that can drink like you."

"Comes with the territory," Claremont replied. "If you can't hang, don't show up. That's what I say."

"I like that," James said, staring lustfully.

Claremont leaned close. Under the table, the tip of one heel worked its way around his ankle. "I've never met anyone quite like you either," she said in a dusky voice. "I'd really like to talk to you some more. Maybe in private." She gave him the look. "I need to go and freshen up a bit." She took a pen from her handbag and slid a napkin across the table. "Give me your number and I'll call you. Say in about an hour."

✠   ✠   ✠

Claremont left the bar and drove back across town to the motel. She slipped into the room and pulled out the napkin to compare the number with the call on Sinclair's telephone bill. They were one and the same.

Once at James's apartment, Claremont went straight to work. Sitting next to him on the couch, she continually had her hand on his arm or shoulder as he spoke.

"Are we still having an interview?" he laughed.

"You bet."

"Who do you write for anyway? Is this going to be in a magazine or somethin'?"

"I'm freelancing. I do what I want and sell my stuff. Right now I'm kind of just scraping by."

"Kind of like me…" His voice trailed off as he watched her absently adjust her bra through her blouse.

"Oh, excuse me," she said suddenly. "It's just you're so comfortable to be with, James. So anyway, tell me," she started.

James continued to stare.

"Have you ever worked in North Carolina? I'm really interested in the Outer Banks. That's where I got to know Preston. He spoke well of you." Her eyes glided down his hefty torso. Looking up, she smiled provocatively.

Claremont was a master at her art. Every move was pure entincement. Every nuance of body language seemed to extend an implicit invitation to revel with her in unbridled abandon—if only one told her what she wanted.

James was beside himself. "Listen, actually, I do got a scoop of sorts on North Carolina. Some friends of mine pulled a job up there. I'm gonna let you have first go at the story."

"Really? That would be great!"

"Promise me one thing, though."

"Sure."

"Don't tell no one where you got your information. Okay?"

"Of course," she smiled. "Good journalists always protect their sources."

"It don't make much nohow to me. I 'ready been paid. I just don't want anyone gettin' pissed off at me." He reached over and ran his hand along her thigh. "There're some pictures and stuff in the top drawer of the filing cabinet," he said pointing to the corner. "Let's just say you might find them interesting."

Claremont smiled approvingly.

James stood up, bringing her to her feet with him. "Don't hold back," he said, forcefully kissing her. "I know you want me. That's why you came over here." Grasping both her wrists, he kissed her again.

"Yes, James, yes," she sighed.

He guided her to the bedroom where they lost their clothes. James lay down on the bare sheets, leaving her standing next to the bed.

"You're not really gonna keep those gloves on are you?" he asked.

"I am."

James gave a sly grin. "In that case, would you mind maybe putting those back on," he said, pointing to the white heels lying on the floor beside her crumpled blouse.

"For you, James, sure."

She slipped on the heels, righted herself and walked slowly toward the bed. Grabbing her by one arm, he pulled her onto him, rolled over and took her.

✠   ✠   ✠

Claremont slid out of the bed, dressed and picked up her handbag. She went to the living room and pulled open the top file cabinet drawer. Some loose papers and several receipts lay on the bottom, covering a dozen or so photographs. She leafed through the pages, then scanned the snapshots. The material went straight into the bag.

Claremont returned to the bedroom with her handbag under one arm.

James lay on his back with his hands folded behind his head. "You're not gonna pull the ol' fuck and run are ya?" he chuckled. "I thought only guys did that."

"Think again," she said icily.

She placed the handbag on a chair in front of her. Keeping her back to him, she reached into the bag with both hands and twisted the silencer onto a .22 automatic.

James kept on grinning. "Man, you're somethin' else. You wanna go again?"

"Not hardly," she said, whirling around and popping three rounds straight through his forehead.

Chapter 24

THE PHONE RANG A SECOND TIME BEFORE STANIZLOW WOKE. He reached for the digital alarm clock on the night stand: 6:55 am.

"Yes?" he coughed into the receiver.

"Stan, it's me," Claremont's voice said on the other end. "Listen, I'm in DC. Something has come up. I'm on my way to the West Coast. You'll have to be on your own for a couple days."

"I think I can manage," he yawned. "No, nothing has changed around here."

"Hang tight and I'll see you soon. Bye."

Click.

Stanizlow fumbled to replace the receiver.

Over in the next bed, Sergei Zhukov rolled onto his side and gently placed the pillow over his bandaged ear. True to Stanizlow's prediction, Zhukov had, after disposing of the body of his former associate, returned with a proposition—protection for cooperation. Though Stanizlow freely agreed to shelter him in his room, he soon found the company to be an unwelcome distraction. On the other hand, he figured the man might yet be of some utility.

"Might as well go back to sleep," he said to Zhukov in Russian. "Things may have to wait a few days."

Zhukov grunted and closed his eyes.

Stanizlow sat upright in bed and clicked the TV remote. With the sound off, he flipped through the channels until he found the morning cartoons. For some reason, as ridiculous as it seemed, watching the flickering images helped him think.

They were right back to where they started, he lamented, and without any plan. Except now the canisters were missing. Where they were and who had them, there was no telling. He could only surmise Claremont came upon a lead and was following up on it. Hopefully she won't be too long, he thought.

Sitting upright in bed, Stanizlow had the feeling something was about to break. Exactly what was to happen he couldn't know. On the other hand, he always trusted his instincts, and was not about to stop doing so now.

✠   ✠   ✠

With the charter season all but over, things were relatively quiet around the marina. During the span of a week there was one calm day on which Gregory and Billy Page went out and did fairly well with yellowfin tuna. Prices were up and they managed to clear a couple of hundred dollars apiece.

Otherwise Gregory caught up on chores and minor maintenance to the *Hawkeye*. More often than not, while tooling with the boat, he found himself thinking of Claremont. At this juncture, Gregory could almost laugh about it. Fell for her like a ton of bricks, he thought. Must have looked ridiculous.

Gregory could not help but ponder what he found so incredibly stimulating about the woman. Looking back, he realized the time around her was nothing short of an adventure. It'd been a long time since he'd had that sort of excitement in his life. What Gregory would not bring himself to admit, however, was that he missed her.

✠   ✠   ✠

With the boat tied up, Gregory took to spending part of each afternoon having coffee at the small counter inside the Pelican Roost Texaco. The place was part convenience store, part bait and tackle shop, part local hangout. On rough weather days, time was easily passed talking fishing, bitching about the government or arguing football with the usual cast of characters.

Gregory had just walked out of the Pelican Roost and was about to get in his truck when three large sedans careened into the parking lot. The cars screeched to a halt alongside Gregory, totally blocking him in. Sheriff Winston's cruiser pulled up behind. Two men identifying themselves as Federal agents got out of the first car. Frank Bruford and another man rode in the second. Two more men, each in dark suits and wearing sunglasses, stood behind the open doors of the third vehicle. Although no weapons were displayed, the two agents behind the car doors were carrying enough firepower underneath their loose fitting jackets to cover most any situation.

"Mr. Gregory," the man standing next to Bruford said. "We're with the Federal Bureau of Investigation. We'd like to ask you a few questions."

Gregory tried to swallow the lump rising in his throat. "Sure."

"Follow us to the Sheriff's Department."

"Am I under arrest?" Gregory asked. God! They know about the other Russian! he thought.

"Not yet," another man said. "Now let's go."

Gregory maneuvered his pickup behind the first car, which turned to face the road. The other two sedans pulled around behind. Sheriff Winston brought up the rear. A gaggle of wide eyed faces watched through the store windows as the unlikely looking caravan pulled onto Route 12 and headed south into Hatteras village.

✠   ✠   ✠

The meeting room at the station felt cramped for the number of people seated at the small table. A deputy brought in an extra chair, after which the agent in charge invited him to leave.

When the door was closed, Bruford took the lead. "Mr. Gregory, do you know this person?" he asked, handing him a file photograph of Sandra Claremont.

"Yes, I do."

"What was your relationship with her?"

"I took her fishing, once. That's about it," Gregory answered defensively.

"Nothing more?"

"What's this about?"

The FBI agent who approached him at the Pelican Roost leaned forward in his chair. "Mr. Gregory, we're the ones asking the questions here!"

Bruford waved him off. "Sure, I'll tell you what this is about," he began. "Seems your lady friend is wanted for murder. She's on the run and we're gonna find her." A curious smile crept across his fleshy face. "I understand you've got some experience conducting murder investigations yourself, Mr. Gregory. Sheriff Winston here says you've been playing Columbo on the Preston Sinclair case." The smile vanished. "I'm sure you don't have many murders around here, but what was the big deal for you?"

"Preston was a friend!" Gregory said defiantly. "I wanted to see whoever killed him fry for it! I still do."

Bruford didn't back off. Gregory got the feeling Bruford was needling—trying to unbalance him. He wondered if they knew of his romantic feelings for Claremont. Bruford didn't leave him guessing long. He reached into his briefcase, pulled out a second photograph and dropped it on the table directly in front of Gregory. It was a slightly overexposed crime scene record of Shamus James, naked and very much dead. A tight cluster of three small bullet wounds was visible just above his brow. The dead man's hands were still folded behind his head, which rested on a blood encrusted pillow. Though its eyelids were closed, the corpse's mouth gaped as if expressing utter disbelief.

"This just came in from Florida," Bruford said dramatically. "Sandra Claremont was seen with the guy in an Islamorada club the night he was killed. Two witnesses identified her entering his apartment building. We have hair for DNA. A warrant has already been issued."

Bruford let Gregory study the photograph, then said, "Shamus James. Killed in bed—on his back—buck naked." The smile was back. "Looks the world like he came before he went."

A round of murmuring laughs filled the room. Gregory said nothing.

"Take a good look, Mr. Gregory," Bruford instructed, pausing for emphasis. "A .22 to the head, Mr. Gregory. Sounds familiar doesn't it?"

Gregory's face turned two shades darker than his normal tone of red. "You're not saying she killed Preston?!" he blurted.

"We're not ruling anything out at this moment," the FBI agent stated.

"When was the last time you saw her?" Bruford demanded.

"About a week ago. I went by the motel where she was staying. They… they said she would be gone a couple of days. That's all I know."

"That's everything you can tell us?"

"Yes."

"She didn't say anything about where she was going."

"No."

The agents looked at each other.

"In that case, you're free to leave."

At first, Gregory didn't comprehend. Just like that? he thought.

"You're free to go, Mr. Gregory," the agent repeated. "Now if you hear from her, I trust you'll let us know. Sandra Claremont is a fugitive. Any assistance you render her will make you a felon. Do we understand each other?"

Gregory nodded meekly. He rose out of his chair and stepped cautiously for the door.

"Good day, Mr. Gregory," Bruford called out after him.

Once Gregory exited, the FBI agent in charge turned to Bruford. "Just how did you peg her?"

"Pure dumb luck," Bruford replied smiling. "Someone from our office spotted her at the Miami airport and followed her south. Kept tailing her.

"How'd he know to follow her?"

"He didn't. To be delicate, I'll just say the interest in her was other than strictly professional. Seems one way or another he was going to get even."

"Let me guess," the agent said. "This guy was odd man out in the old love triangle?"

"More like a quadrangle," Bruford grinned.

"Looks like he got back at her."

"Did he ever," Bruford laughed, adding, "It was a clean hit on her part. We would've had no idea if he hadn't been on her. Hell, we thought she was here in North Carolina."

"So what's the connection with this James guy?" the FBI agent asked.

Bruford looked intently across the table. "That, my friend, is what we need to find out."

The door opened and a deputy entered the meeting room. "Telephone for Mr. Roundtree."

The FBI agent in charge got up and left the room. A short minute later he stormed back in, his face taut and jaw tightly set. "That was the Justice Department!" he said curtly.

"And?" Bruford inquired.

"We've been ordered to put the Claremont investigation on hold. As a special internal matter, they're assembling their own team."

✠   ✠   ✠

Confused and frightened, Gregory called Echo as soon as he got home from the Sheriff's Department, babbling something about Claremont having killed a man in Florida. Echo bolted over and began to question Gregory while doing his best to calm him.

"Now who was the guy doing the talking?" Echo asked.

"I don't know. No one ever gave any names. They were being kind of heavy with me."

"That's their job. So anyway, you said there was a kind of stocky guy—what did he look like?"

"Kind of fat, balding. Squints when he talks."

"Brown suit, synthetic fibers?"

"Yeah."

"Bruford!" Echo exclaimed. "It's got to be. I thought he was gone."

Echo leaned toward the window and caught sight of Stanizlow walking down the drive. He telephoned him as soon as he heard from Gregory. "They really think Claremont killed someone in Florida?" Echo reiterated, while drawing the curtains closed.

"They say she killed Preston," Gregory quaked. For a moment, he looked as if he were ready to break apart.

"They're trying to scare you," Echo said reassuringly.

"Well they're doing a goddamn good job of it!" Gregory wailed, rising to his feet. "Look, I got a daughter in college. I just bought the boat. I've worked my whole life to get where I am. I can't let something like this fuck it all up!"

Echo ignored the heated proclamations.

Gregory sat back down folding his hands on top of his head. "How'd I get myself into this shit?" he moaned.

Stanizlow's knock sounded on the door. Echo went to let him in. Stanizlow took a seat in a chair opposite Gregory.

"So who's this person that supposedly got killed?" Echo inquired.

"James something… I can't remember. They say they're sure she did it. They say they got witnesses!"

Echo glanced at Stanizlow. "Listen," he said, turning back to Gregory who sat slumped with his head in his hands, "Something doesn't add up here. Frank Bruford's not with the FBI. He's CIA. I used to work with him. This isn't a murder investigation."

Gregory lifted his head and looked at Echo. "So you don't think she killed Preston?"

"I very much doubt it."

"She did not," Stanizlow stated. "Preston Sinclair went missing… when?"

"The Saturday before Thanksgiving," Gregory replied. "The body was found on Wednesday morning."

"I was with her the whole week. In Washington. It was her assignment—to be with me."

Echo was emphatic. "That's why they haven't come for you," he said, looking over at Stanizlow, "or for me. Because they know we know they're full of shit." He turned to Gregory. "Don't sweat it buddy. They got nothing on you." Echo again looked to Stanizlow. "I also doubt very much they give a damn about this James fellow. They're going after the Captain here because they're trying to find Claremont. My guess is she knows something they don't."

"Yes, she undoubtedly found something out," Stanizlow said in agreement.

"Found out what?" Gregory asked, still holding his head in his hands.

"Like what happened to the U-boat cargo," Echo suggested firmly. He turned to Gregory. "Eric, did anyone say anything about where this murder supposedly took place?"

Gregory lifted his head. "Yeah," he let out slowly. "It was Islamorada. It came up when they were talking to me."

All three men looked at each other. Nothing further needed to be said.

✠ ✠ ✠

With his trailer home totally destroyed, Clifton Echo had salvaged what few of his belongings survived the blast and moved them into his new temporary residence at the motel, a few doors down from Stanizlow.

Relaxing in the room, Echo just propped his feet up and turned on the 6:00 o'clock news when the telephone rang. Startled, Echo hesitated before picking up. The voice on the other end identified himself only as a friend of a friend. He went on to say he desperately needed to talk to Echo in person. Recognizing genuine fear in the man's voice, Echo reluctantly obliged, agreeing to rendezvous in half an hour.

✠ ✠ ✠

After returning to the room, Echo realized he was dog tired. Even though it wasn't even 8:00 o'clock, fatigue was getting the better of him. He had spent the better part of two days closing down the archaeological site for the winter and was glad to be done with it. He also had not had a decent night's sleep since the attempt on his life. Figuring an early night might do him good, he pulled back the sheets. The television stayed on. Lying face down on the pillow, Echo heard a trailer for the next day's prime-time line-up:

"Live from New York on Great Mysteries: A German U-boat is discovered off the North Carolina coast."

His eyes shot open.

"Join us to witness expert divers remove water-tight containers from the wreck, one hundred feet below the surface. What secrets or treasures they hold, no one knows. Find out tomorrow when we open one—totally live before a studio audience. Nine o'clock eastern, eight central."

"*Holy fuckin' shit!*" Echo yelled, flinging himself out of bed. Seconds later he was pounding on the other motel room door. "Get dressed! We're going to New York!" he barked, as Stanizlow opened it.

"What are you talking about?!"

"I'll tell you later! Let's go!"

✠   ✠   ✠

The truck sped through the darkness. It was just after 10:00 as they approached the Virginia line. The road was deserted and Echo touched 90 miles an hour at times. Stanizlow was tired but opted against trying to sleep. He figured if he were going to die, he might as well be awake for his final seconds.

Approaching Washington, DC, Echo reverted to the speed limit. He continuously glanced at his watch as he drove.

✠   ✠   ✠

"So let me ask you," Echo spoke out, somewhere between Washington and Baltimore. He looked over at his passenger and gave an odd grin. "How's this Zhukov guy working out?"

"So far so good… I told him he must remain at the motel and out of sight while we are gone."

"Can you trust him?"

"We're going to have to."

Echo kept smiling and shook his head as he drove.

Daylight broke along I-95 somewhere north of Philadelphia.

✠   ✠   ✠

"So what kind of television program is this?" Stanizlow asked for the second time. The first time was as they were leaving Buxton.

"I told you already," Echo exclaimed, sounding irritated. "It's an entertainment show! What I want to know is how they got a hold of the boxes. We have to get to the studios before the Enterprise makes a move—assuming they know about the program." Glancing sideways across the wheel and trying to make light he asked, "You suppose them boys read TV Guide?"

Stanizlow simply shrugged and looked out the window at the northern Jersey landscape. To either side, tank farms and refineries stretched on under leaden skies. The twisting yellow flames leaping from the burn-off stacks stood in bright contrast to the dull gray horizon. The smell of petrochemicals seeped through the drafty pickup cab.

"What about your government, do they know?" Stanizlow inquired, still looking out over the seemingly endless industrial sprawl.

"You would think so, but maybe not. According to Claremont, this whole thing is really hush-hush. Only a handful of people know what's at stake. I guess it all hinges on how much they watch television. Jesus, what a thought!" he laughed. "You can bet the studio doesn't have a clue; that much I'm sure of."

"What is your plan?"

"First we need to figure exactly who knows what," Echo said, threading the truck through early rush hour traffic. "If the Feds know, they'll be all over the place, probably have the building sealed off. If the Enterprise is in on it, they shouldn't be hard to spot. I guess we'll find out when we get there."

Stanizlow gave a low grunt and closed his eyes.

✠   ✠   ✠

Even at this early hour, Manhattan was its usual chaotic collage of humanity. Though Echo had been living in the Carolinas for only a few years, he'd forgotten what this city was like. Traffic pulsed through the streets between cliff-like walls of steel and concrete. Car horns blared continually. Left and right, sidewalks carried an ever moving stream of people that collectively took on the appearance of single giant, strand-like life forms.

They had stopped at a fueling station in New Jersey, where, by calling information, Echo managed to obtain the studio address. Miraculously, they found a parking spot not very far away. It was 8:30 and the offices had just opened.

After a brief exchange, it was decided Echo would go in alone to scout things out. Stanizlow stayed in the truck.

Echo made his way through the large double glass doors and approached the receptionist's desk in the middle of the lobby. Unshaven and wearing clothes from the day before, he looked every bit like he'd spent the night driving.

"I'm here to see the man," he smiled confidently at the petite blonde woman who sat behind the desk. He had no idea who he was asking for. "Mr. Great Mysteries, the big Kahuna, need to talk to him first thing."

"Mr. Adilade is not scheduling any appointments this morning," the receptionist said politely.

"Oh, he'll want to see me," Echo stated emphatically. "You mind if I wait here until he gets in?"

She lowered her eyes, doing her best to ignore him.

Echo seated himself in a chair to one side of the receptionist's desk. Time and again the young woman nervously glanced his way, wondering what was keeping the night security guard who closed out his shift watching the lobby area.

The receptionist's head lifted. Echo looked up to see a short, slightly built man in a dark suit and tan trench coat stride through the double doors. Echo stood and stepped directly into the man's path. "Mr. Adilade?"

"Yes?"

"We need to talk. It's very important."

The man was hardly thirty. He was exceedingly groomed and sported an obvious salon tan. At a little over five feet six, with long-ish curly hair and a closely trimmed beard, he carried himself with the haughty, standoffish manner often seen in smaller men with large egos. "I'm sure," he snapped. "But it can't be half as important as what I need to do this morning."

"I think it is."

"I'm sorry, I'm busy. Now get out of my way," he said briskly, pushing Echo aside with his briefcase.

Echo followed him down the hall to the elevator. Adilade stepped through the open doors. He turned and pushed the floor button. Waiting stiffly, he eyed Echo in his shabby clothes with obvious disdain. Just as the doors began to slide closed, Echo lunged between them, blocking the startled producer in. Echo slapped his hand across the control panel. The doors shut. They began to move upward.

"You want me to call Security?" Adilade blurted. He sounded more frightened than angry.

"Do you want to die?" Echo growled. "Because if you don't, you'd better listen to what I have to say!"

Adilade paled but said nothing. They reached the floor.

Echo kept his hand on the Door Close button. "The show tonight—you have absolutely no idea what you've brought on, do you?!"

"I... I don't know what you're talking about," Adilade stammered.

"I didn't think so. I'll tell you what I'm talking about! You got the bear by the balls, Mister! And if you got one lick of sense, we're gonna go in your office and have a chat."

Adilade looked confused. "Okay, okay. We'll talk," he said meekly.

The doors opened and they stepped out of the elevator. Adilade kept facing Echo as he back peddled across the hallway toward his office. The producer reached behind his back and pushed open the door.

Though he did not so much as flinch, inwardly Echo convulsed at the scene before him. His bowels churned. The sight sickened but hardly surprised him.

Adilade backed into his office and turned around. "Mother of God!!" he gasped.

The entire office had been ransacked, with furniture turned upside-down and pictures pulled from the wall. The file cabinets and desk drawers were open, with their former contents scattered about. In the middle of the room lay the bodies of the two security guards and the night janitor. Each had their hands bound and had been shot through the head. The man at Adilade's feet had the top of his skull blown off. Bloody bits of scalp, cranium fragments and brain matter streaked the floor around what was left of his head. The others were no less gruesome.

Echo slammed the door behind him. "You think I'm shitting you?! Look around!"

The producer staggered sideways. Bracing himself on one corner of his desk, he doubled over and vomited into the wastebasket.

"I'll make this quick," Echo snapped. "Those aluminum boxes hold something certain persons want, and they're going to stop at nothing to get at them. I don't have to tell you these guys mean business. Now, you're going to tell me exactly where the boxes are and who you got them from."

Adilade looked up from the wastebasket. A trickle of saliva, together with traces of breakfast, clung to his chin. "Are you the police?" he croaked.

"I'm with the government. We don't have time for small talk. Now where're the boxes?!"

Adilade managed to straighten and say, "They're being filled. Across town at the prop studio."

"What?" Echo exclaimed. "Filled with what? What happened to the contents?"

Adilade again looked down at the bodies. He raised his hands and clutched at the thick locks on the side of his head. "There were none," he managed to utter. "A little brown goo maybe." He moved to shield his eyes from the floor. "The three we bought had leaked and were full of water. I have no idea what was supposed to have been in them... I'm having them packed for the show tonight."

"You mean you're faking the show?!"

"All our live specials are put on. Better results that way."

"*What?*" Echo roared, taking two steps forward and nearly losing his footing on a small blob of indescribable gore. "I watch your show!" he bellowed, standing directly between two corpses. "Goddamn you!"

Adilade fumbled through the top desk drawer. "Oh, God! I think I'm getting a migraine," he blubbered.

Echo regained his composure. "How many boxes are there?" he demanded.

"Three."

"Just three! All empty?!"

"Yes. That's all I know. I didn't do the buying." Adilade flipped on his computer. It alone was left untouched. "Look," he said desperately, reaching for the mouse, "I'll do everything to cooperate. I'll give you the whole file on the project. More I can't do."

Echo stepped over to the printer as it began to hum.

"It's warming up. It'll be a minute or two," Adilade said somberly. He again looked down at the human carnage sprawled across his office floor. "Who would do something like this?" he shuddered.

"Mr. Adilade, in your line of work, did you ever have to deal with the mob?"

Adilade's voice wavered in his reply. "Only once, thank God. When I was doing locations in Jersey. Had to ante up just to get our trucks in."

"Think of these people as the mob gone mad, only worse."

"They don't play by the old rules?"

Echo pulled the papers from the printer. "There are no rules, Mr. Adilade." He briefly thumbed through the printout. "Thanks for your help," Echo said while gingerly stepping around the bodies on his way to the door.

Adilade's hand trembled uncontrollably as he lifted the phone to dial 9-1-1.

✠   ✠   ✠

Despite Echo's worst apprehensions, his somewhat aged pickup carrying expired North Carolina plates and a worn looking passenger had not attracted the attention of New York's Finest while he'd been in the offices. "All done," he said, pulling open the door and springing into the cab.

Stanizlow looked up, rubbing his eyes. Just then, a half-dozen U.S. Government cars roared past.

"Must have found out about the show," Echo said, thinking aloud.

A few seconds later the whole city seemed to erupt in sirens as police cruisers with lights flashing screamed in from all directions.

"Let's get out of here!" Echo declared, pulling into traffic and turning down the cross street.

"Where are we going?" Stanizlow yawned.

"Back to Buxton."

Stanizlow folded his jacket against the cab window and rested his head on it. "Good," he said closing his eyes. "I like a man who does fast work."

Chapter 25

TIME PASSED SLOWLY ON THE LONG DRIVE BACK TO NORTH CARO-lina. To Echo's near maddening dismay, Stanizlow didn't appear to be the least bit interested in hearing about what happened in the studio offices, nor why they were heading straight back. So, for no other reason, Echo held his words.

It was not until early afternoon Stanizlow asked him what he learned. In response, Echo merely pushed the printout, still resting on the seat between them, toward Stanizlow. Saying nothing, Stanizlow spent a few minutes scanning the pages.

When he was finished, Stanizlow folded the papers onto his lap. "So the studio buys three empty boxes from an unidentified person in Florida. They were going to use them on a live television production in conjunction with a story on the *U-491*."

"Correct."

"Since these were empty, what do you suppose they were going to put in them?"

"Who cares. It doesn't matter," Echo replied tersely. "What we need to know is where the rest of them are."

"True," Stanizlow agreed. He began to muse aloud. "Shamus James — we assume the man had something to do with getting the boxes out of the wreck—dead. Then there is Preston Sinclair who brought the wreck to the world's attention to begin with—dead.

"Let's not forget the bomb under my trailer," Echo said caustically.

"Yes. Two more almost dead—almost, but not quite."

Echo smiled to himself, wondering if Stanizlow had any idea how funny he often sounded.

"What else did you find in the studio?" Stanizlow asked, after several miles of silence.

"Three more dead," Echo replied grimly.

Stanizlow let a deep sigh. "How?"

"The security guards and a janitor were killed in the producer's office last night. Large caliber to the head. It was pretty gross. The place was ransacked."

Stanizlow frowned. "The Enterprise must have gotten word about the show. Paid a visit to try and get directly at the material. What do you suppose they found out?"

"A whole lot of nothing, probably. At least we know where the three boxes came from, and that they were empty. Adilade kept all his records on his computer. These goons, whoever they were, didn't think to look in there—or couldn't.

"I see."

✠   ✠   ✠

Another hundred miles passed without much being said. They stopped and had pit cooked barbecue sandwiches in Fredericksburg, Virginia. It had long since gotten dark as they followed the taillights of a semi down a nearly deserted I-64 from Richmond past Williamsburg.

"Are you going to get a new trailer?" Stanizlow asked, breaking a long interlude.

Echo glanced over at him, thinking this may be the first time the man ever attempted to make small conversation. "Eventually, yes," he replied. "The trailer was not my main residence, though, so I think I'll just do without for a while."

"What is?"

"I own an old plantation in the South Carolina Low Country."

Stanizlow seemed interested. "A plantation, you say?"

"Yeah. Used to produce rice and indigo back in the nineteenth century. The property had been a working farm until a couple of years before it went on the block. It was in pretty rough shape when I bought it. I'm slowly fixing it up, though."

"Interesting."

"Yeah, it's all there, the main house, the barns and outbuildings, even a few of the old slave quarters, and the overseer's house."

"Being on Hatteras Island, how do you find time to work on your property?"

"I work on it all through the winter and spring, until it gets too hot. Usually May or June. I only excavate on Hatteras during the fall—usually until just before Christmas."

Stanizlow nodded. "I see."

"Actually," Echo said, "I have a small crew working on the property as we speak—a couple of local handyman-painter types. With time I want to completely redo the place—reconstruct the buildings that are down; restore some of the old machinery. Then I want to landscape it to what it would have been like during the early nineteenth century."

Stanizlow looked across at Echo, who kept speaking as he drove.

"Someday I'd like to turn it into a living history museum of sorts."

"A noble endeavor, Mr. Echo," Stanizlow said, nodding slowly. "I wish you success."

They rode on in silence.

✠   ✠   ✠

It was almost midnight before they cleared the Oregon Inlet bridge and settled in for the final leg down Hatteras Island. Passing the cluster of motels at the outskirts of Buxton, both men noted the cars driven by the FBI men who picked up Gregory were no longer there.

✠   ✠   ✠

Echo was up early the next morning. He went out for coffee and upon returning to the room, began to study the file given to him by the producer in New York. One thing was known for sure: Adilade arranged the purchase of three empty canisters for $8,000. Included in the deal was some underwater footage of the U-boat wreck and shots of the metal boxes being brought to the surface. Payment was received at a Miami bank. Although the name James did not appear anywhere on the documents, Echo felt certain the man was involved.

Echo put the papers aside and began to mull. His thoughts turned to his unlikely cohorts in whatever this mess was he'd somehow gotten himself into. Gregory had his own personal ax to grind, that much was obvious. Still couldn't really be sure what Claremont's deal was. Anyway, being on the run from a murder rap pretty much put her out of the picture. Stan. Stanizlow was in a league by himself, Echo thought. At that very moment, Echo became convinced there had to be something the man declined to share. He promptly resolved to find out just what that something might be.

Years ago, Echo had jettisoned a fast tracking career to spend his days poking around mosquito-ridden swamp margins studying the lives of people who lived there many hundreds, or even thousands of years before. Up until very recently, little else seemed of consequence. No more. Sitting at the table, Echo realized he'd been pulled so far into the bizarre vortex that surrounded the *U-491*, there was turning back. One way or another he was going to see things through.

Echo also had an intensely personal motivation. He'd already been witness to the scenes of four murders, and wasn't at all sure he'd seen the last of it. More than all that, however, Echo would not let go of the fact someone tried to kill him. He was bound and determined to see that person held accountable—even if it meant doing the son of a bitch himself. Most days, that very thought was never far from his mind.

✠   ✠   ✠

The day after returning from New York, Stanizlow checked into a new room, leaving Zhukov in his old one. That night, still fatigued from the marathon drive and thankful at the opportunity for some privacy and rest, Stanizlow drew the curtains tightly closed before retiring.

Shortly before dawn, the sound of a key being slipped into the door ripped him awake. Quickly, and without making a sound, Stanizlow rolled out of bed. He listened again. The key was being turned. The sound stopped, as if whoever was on the other side were testing the lock. Stanizlow crept across the room and leaned against the curtained window in a position to grab the intruder by the head and snap the neck with one sharp twist.

The door opened. Stanizlow lunged aside, grabbing a wrist and spinning the figure around. His other arm reached around in a chokehold. Instantly, he recognized the unmistakable feel and scent of Sandra Claremont's body. Not letting on, he pulled her through the doorway and flung her onto the bed.

"Fool! I could have killed you," he breathed, laying on top of her while keeping his palm across her mouth. He reached over with his left hand and flipped on the light. "What on earth brings you here?" he asked, lifting his hand from her face.

Claremont sat upright and straightened her hair. "This was my room," she said somewhat indignantly.

Stanizlow let out a short laugh. "So it was. Sergei is in my old room. I didn't think you were coming back."

"Where else was I to go?"

Stanizlow lifted himself off the bed and picked up her travel bag, which still lay in the doorway. He drew the door closed and placed the bag on the bed next to her.

With the lights on, he saw Claremont's hair was cut short and dyed red. A judicious application of bright makeup seemed to have totally changed her appearance. Together with hoop earrings, tight fitting jeans and an Angora jacket, the look screamed Truck Stop Trixie.

Stanizlow went to the toilet to relieve himself. "I heard you're wanted for murder," he said casually as he came back out of the bathroom. He stripped off his night shirt and stepped into his trousers.

"Oh, that," Claremont said, seemingly dismissing the whole affair with a wave of her hand. "I was down in Florida," she explained.

"Islamorada."

"You heard. See, I wanted to get some information out of this guy—butter him up a little—he pretty much tried to rape me. Stan, I know I shouldn't have done it... I'd just as soon forget about the whole thing."

"The FBI is in no mood to forget anything," Stanizlow replied sarcastically. "They've been all over the island. They tore apart the room and took all your things." He gave her a stern look. "What makes you think they're not going to catch up with you here?"

"Because, this is the last place they figure I'd show. But enough about that. Let me tell you what I found out."

Stanizlow sat down on the bed next to her.

"This character Sinclair called long distance," Claremont began, "Shamus James..."

"Now deceased."

"Yes, now deceased. Like we thought, he was in on the plan to get at the cargo. It was all Preston Sinclair's idea. I was right. Seems Sinclair became convinced the U-boat was carrying a fortune in Nazi loot. Since the wreck was going to be raised in the Spring, he figured he was about to be out the find of a lifetime. So, he hooks up with some old acquaintances to have a go at the supposed treasure before it's too late. It had to have been Sinclair who rigged the charges to blast open the hull—it was a professional job—first rate."

Stanizlow interrupted her. "You found this out in Florida?"

"Most of it, yeah, but I had a lunch date with this Atlantis World lawyer in California who handled the legal side of the operation to raise the sub. At first, it seemed like a routine matter—Sinclair had him convinced everything was on the up and up. Then, when his office started to do its homework, it turned out to raise the U-boat would have run them afoul of the law—some Federal preservation statutes or something. The company had put Sinclair on salary in exchange for what they thought were his legitimate salvage rights. They'd been had.

"Where did you find this guy?" Stanizlow asked.

"I just got his name from the company offices. Needless to say, the whole *U-491* project was dropped. And that was before the CEO got this real heavy visit from some DC suits—the day after the news release came out." Claremont let out a shallow laugh. "Imagine!" she added sarcastically. "Anyway, what happened was, seems somebody at Atlantis World got their wires crossed, because the news release was never supposed to have gone out. The lawyer, he didn't want to talk about that part at all!"

Stanizlow was getting impatient. "So what happened to the cargo?"

"Evidently, Sinclair and James got into the submarine and removed the boxes." She lowered her voice. "I saw photographs of them being brought to the surface. James had them."

"So what was this Shamus James' role after that?"

"Not much—except he kept a few empty boxes for himself. Sold them to some television studio."

Stanizlow explained to her about their trip to New York.

"This is starting to make sense," she said.

"And? Then?"

"Presumably, when James and whoever else realized what was really in those canisters, they just went back to Florida. The way I figure, what would they do with a bunch of paper—especially if the stuff incriminates them. I'm sure they left it on the island somewhere. They must have."

"We must find out where," Stanizlow said firmly. "Hopefully it did not end up in a landfill."

Claremont folded her hands together. Looking as if she were praying, her fingers interlocked so tightly the knuckles went white. "That's why I came back. I can help you… but I'm feeling the heat, Stan." She tilted her head aside and pleaded with her heavily mascaraed eyes. "I know I haven't been an angel—but I don't want to take a bum rap, either."

Stanizlow listened impassively.

"Help me Stan, and I'll help you. We're a team, remember." She reached for his hand. "Afterward, we'll get all that other business straightened out."

"You cannot stay here," Stanizlow said. He had already analyzed the situation and carefully weighed all options. "Captain Gregory gave me a key to Preston Sinclair's house. I'll make you an extra."

"That'll work!"

"Then we'll go over there and set you up. You should be safe there for a time. Before we went to New York, the island was full of FBI. They took Captain Gregory in for questioning. They were looking for you."

Claremont sighed. "No kidding," she said sarcastically.

"Most of them are gone now," Stanizlow said. "Somehow I don't think we have seen the last of them, though. I'll make the rounds and scout things out. Then we'll get to work."

"Thanks Stan. You won't regret this."

Chapter 26

DIMITRI YURCHENKO FELT EXCEPTIONALLY GOOD DRIVING DOWN the New Jersey Turnpike. America seemed to have a liberating effect on his spirit. New York City, in particular, made him feel very much alive. Nearly three decades had passed since Yurchenko, then a newly commissioned KGB officer, was attached to the Soviet mission at the United Nations. Without a doubt, memories of those years were some of his fondest.

After having cleared customs at JFK earlier in the afternoon, Yurchenko had spent the rest of the day visiting his old New York haunts. The next morning, he caught a Metroliner for Washington, where he was provided with an identity and a car for the trip south.

As a rising young star in the foreign counter-intelligence bureau, Yurchenko found himself in all the hot spots of the time—Cambodia in the early '70s, then Angola and Mozambique. It was in Afghanistan, however, where he forged his reputation as one of the most ruthless and efficient operatives the service had ever known. The bustling arms markets of Peshawar and the Pakistani border towns were his personal arena. Using his considerable talents, Yurchenko ran an operation to sow discord among the factious Afghan mujaheddin. Deceit, familial insults and murder were the tools of his clandestine campaign.

Despite many apparent successes, it was ultimately to be a futile effort. In the violent, tribal, free-for-all of the Hindu Kush, where U.S. Dollars and AK-47s were both the universal currency and force of law, a dozen more Yurchenkos could never have made much difference. Toward the end, he oversaw an operation in the capitol by which mujaheddin supporters in the city were identified and eliminated. The assignment earned him the well-deserved nickname "Butcher of Kabul."

Despite his fearsome reputation, Yurchenko was a somewhat affable-looking man with wavy brown hair, a ruddy complexion and slight jowls. His eyes were large and widely spaced while the corners of his mouth tapered upward under protuberant cheeks. In a way, Yurchenko's distinctive appearance lent him an anonymity that was often an asset. In public, most persons took him to be a street musician or traveling huckster of some variety.

Yurchenko smiled to himself as he drove on. As always, he loved the challenge of a new assignment. He was briefed on the news of the upcoming television show the day he arrived in Washington. At the time, Yurchenko volunteered to return to New York and personally handle the affair. The offer was declined and the local "office" took care of business. It turned out to have been the right action, for the studio operation turned up nothing of real value.

Yurchenko glanced at his watch, estimating within two hours he would reach his destination of Hatteras village. He was traveling with a false passport under the guise of a Belgian businessman out to combine his corporate travel with a few days to himself. He fit the part like a glove.

"Amateurs," Yurchenko muttered to himself, shaking his head. The two men the Enterprise originally assigned to the task failed to report. It was assumed they were apprehended, or possibly even gone over. The first order of business would be to find out what happened. If he could locate them, he would proceed with the interrogation, after which they would be liquidated. Then he would get to work—by himself. Yurchenko always preferred it that way. He relished not having to trust anyone.

✠   ✠   ✠

Maggie Tinsley's face lit up as Stanizlow walked into the Midgette Mart. "Mr. Stanizlow," she said, beaming, "it's so nice to see you again."

Stanizlow reached to tap the reservoir of gentlemanly charm that always served him well. "Likewise, Ms. Tinsley," he said smoothly.

"What can I do for you today?"

"A Coca-Cola, and today's newspaper, please."

She directed him to the coolers in the back and made a point to ring up her only other customer first.

"And what else?" she asked after the other man left.

"A little information, perhaps. I was looking for Mr. Roundtree—the FBI man. Have you seen him?"

"He's gone," Maggie stated. "You know, it was kind of exciting having all those people around."

Stanizlow smiled politely.

"Eric says you're going to find the people who killed Preston. Is that true?"

Stanizlow handed her the money for the drink and paper.

"I hope to, Ms. Tinsley. I hope to."

"I hope you do, too."

"Did all Mr. Roundtree's men leave?" he asked, taking his change.

"Nope. There're two left. At the Hatteras Motel." She broke into a sly grin. "They say they're not with the government, but everybody knows they are. You can spot 'em in any crowd. They got the car. They got a certain look about 'em too. Know what I mean?"

"I certainly do," Stanizlow smiled. "Thank you so much for your help. Good day."

"Anytime, Mr. Stanizlow," she called out after him.

✠   ✠   ✠

Stanizlow parked his car across from the motel lot, keeping an eye on the place in his rearview mirrors. It wasn't long before he spotted the dark blue Chrysler pull up. The driver got out carrying a pizza box. The woman was right, he thought—the man was as obvious as they come. Stanizlow committed the room number to memory before pulling out onto the main road and driving north.

Passing through Frisco, he stopped off at Bubba's Barbecue. Having taken quite a liking to that particular item of the regional cuisine, Stanizlow picked up a take-out order of two large sliced pork sandwich platters.

From behind a curtained window, Claremont watched Stanizlow's car creep up Sinclair's drive with the lights off. She opened the door to let him in and fell upon the take-out bag as if she had not seen food in a week. The massive sandwich was gone in about a minute and a half. "So, whaddidya find out?" she asked, dabbing barbecue sauce from her chin.

"Just like I thought. Most of them have gone," Stanizlow replied before taking another bite of his own sandwich. "We have two left in Hatteras. They should not be hard to keep track of."

"Good." Claremont began to work on her fries. "Tomorrow you can start looking," she said, talking and chewing at the same time. "I can tell you where to begin."

"That would be good," Stanizlow said cautiously. "But with you back on the island, I feel I need to lower my profile some."

"So?"

"So I'm leaving the car here for a while. Echo is giving me a ride to town."

Claremont shrugged. "Do what you think is best."

Upon bidding her good night, Stanizlow pulled the Saturn behind the house. He opened the double doors to Sinclair's shed and backed the vehicle in.

Standing in the doorway, Claremont watched him make his way down the drive toward the main road. She didn't shut the door until he was well out of sight.

✠   ✠   ✠

Preston Sinclair's house was without power and it had long since gotten dark. Claremont lit a candle in the hallway so no light could be seen through the windows and began to read the newspaper Stanizlow left her. Getting drowsy, she put down the paper, blew out the candle and slipped into the bedroom. In no time, she was fast asleep.

✠   ✠   ✠

With a frightful start, Claremont was instantly awake. The sound was unmistakable—someone was picking the front door lock. She did not hear a car pull up. Her mind raced. Maybe Stan was back, she thought. Instinctively, she knew it was not him. A second bolt of panic surged through her as she remembered she was without a weapon. Her service piece was left in the Buxton motel room when she flew to Miami; she had sealed the .22 in a trash bag and dropped it into a dumpster behind a Florida convenience store when she realized the authorities were on to her.

Yurchenko continued to work the lock. He'd been briefed on the killing of a Preston Sinclair and informed it was probably linked to the U-boat. He figured the dead man's house was as good a place as any to begin his investigation.

In short order, the lock was thrown free. There was no dead bolt. Claremont heard the door creak open. Perspiration dampened her body as the sound of footsteps drifted in from the living room. Go for the window! she thought, before remembering the storm shutters were bolted from the outside. She thought about charging the front door, but doubted she could make it. Frantic, she searched the room for a weapon—a knife, a baseball bat, a bottle even. There was nothing. She couldn't fight. She couldn't run. She had to hide.

The steps were closer. Claremont dropped to the floor and tried to suppress her rapid, almost convulsive breathing. There were perhaps eight inches of room between the bed frame and floor. If only she could squeeze under. She had to try. Ducking in head first, she pushed with her feet against the carpet. There was no way.

If it's them, I'm dead!

Claremont pictured how pathetic her end was going to be—shot on the floor—stuck halfway under a bed like a frightened dog. The thought angered her. She again kicked as hard as she could. Suddenly, a section of carpet tore away at her feet and her ankles scraped rough, unfinished boards.

"What the hell?" she breathed, lying perfectly still.

In the kitchen, cupboards and drawers were systematically being opened and closed.

With one writhing surge, Claremont managed to free herself from beneath the bed. On hands and knees in complete darkness, she patted down the rectangular area where the shag carpet was torn back.

Her hand found a cutout recess just large enough to form a grip. Not daring to hope, she slid in four fingers and pulled up. The hinged trap door opened to a pitch-black, mildew-smelling void. Working frantically, she pressed the section of carpet back over the wood and tried to tack it down with her bare hands. There was no time—the footsteps were coming down the hall.

She dropped into the opening to find sandy ground about four and a half feet below the floor joists. Praying the carpet would seat itself properly, she closed the trap door just as the bedroom knob turned.

Dimitri Yurchenko crept into the room with a small flashlight in one hand and his Beretta nine in the other. The thin beam traced the layout of the room. Holding the automatic sideways in front of him, he crouched down and shone the light under the bed. Cautiously, he rose, turned and made his way toward the corner closet. Claremont cringed in silent terror as a footstep landed on the trap door just inches above her head. One plank creaked and gave way slightly. She braced herself for the end.

To her amazement, the trap door stayed shut. The footsteps again passed overhead, and receded down the hall.

Yurchenko had not needed to check the date on the newspaper to know the house was being used. The barbecue sauce on the sandwich wrapper was fresh and the smell of paraffin filled the air. They must have left only minutes before, he thought. Vagrants squatting in a dead man's house? he wondered. He decided he would return the next day and lay in wait to see if anyone came back.

Claremont heard the front door quietly close. An engine started and a car drove off. Not daring to move, she crouched in the pitch-blackness for another twenty minutes. Finally, she reached into her pocket for her cigarette lighter. The wavering flame illuminated the sunken, enlarged crawl space, the sides of which were lined with creosote planks. Stacked before her were dozens of waxed cardboard seafood packing boxes resting on an impromptu floor of scrap plywood.

On hand and knees she crept to the nearest carton. Holding the lighter above her head, she pulled open the lid. In an instant, she knew: Preston Sinclair had stashed the contents of the canisters under his house. She alone found it. The cargo was hers.

✠   ✠   ✠

Claremont extinguished the lighter to let it cool. While kneeling on the moist sand, a wave of panic consumed her.

They'd known! The door was blocked! Trapped!

Panting uncontrollably, she fumbled to find the hatch. In her fright, it took a good thirty seconds to do so. When she rammed her shoulder against the wood, the door sprung open and she found herself standing upright with the bedroom floor at chest level. Moonlight cast patterns through the louvered shutters. In contrast to the space below, the room seemed light as day. She struggled to regain her breath.

Claremont chided herself for letting her imagination get the better of her. She climbed through the trap door, sat down on the bed and tried to chart her next move. Sleep never came.

✠   ✠   ✠

Sergei Zhukov spent much of the morning in the room with Stanizlow going over what they knew and discussing options. Somewhat to Stanizlow's relief, Zhukov stepped out to buy a pack of cigarettes, giving him a few moments to himself. Stanizlow generally operated singly and would have preferred Zhukov to keep his distance. On the other hand, he figured it might yet be best to keep a close eye on the man. Either way, with no new leads and things pretty much at a standstill, Stanizlow was feeling more than a little frustrated. He took advantage of the temporary solitude and tried to think matters over.

Just then a rapid knocking sounded on the door. As soon as he opened it, Zhukov slipped back through.

"We got company," Zhukov hissed in Russian while quickly closing the door behind him. "From the Enterprise!"

"Who?"

"Yurchenko! Surely you've heard of him?! He's formidable!"

Stanizlow didn't appear to be overly concerned. "Indeed. Quite the reputation. What do you suppose brings him to this little corner of the world?"

"Stupid question!" Zhukov exploded. "What do you think brings him here! The Enterprise sent him!" Zhukov reached for the knife in his boot. "He won't take me!"

"Calm down, Comrade," Stanizlow said. "Where did you see this fellow?"

"From the road—coming out of the store. Luckily he didn't see me. I'm sure of it."

"Tell me more."

Zhukov was near panic. "I'm telling you, Yurchenko's the best!" he spat. "Usually works alone. He's the last man I want hunting me." He looked directly at Stanizlow. "What are we to do?"

"We will think of something," Stanizlow said reassuringly. "In the mean time, I think you had best stay in the room."

✠   ✠   ✠

At first light, Claremont cautiously slipped out the back door and made her way across Sinclair's junk strewn yard. The military surplus ambulance parked against the fence immediately caught her attention, even though it looked not to have run in years. Set on a 4x4 Dodge Powerwagon chassis, the box end of the vehicle had been converted for refrigeration to haul seafood. The stenciled lettering of some long defunct fish house was still legible amid the streaks of rust and badly flaking paint.

Claremont took note that the tires had air and seemed to be in reasonably good condition. She approached the truck, wondering... just maybe. She pulled open the hood and saw the battery was brand new, as was one exhaust manifold. Belts and hoses were completely fresh. Leaning over and peering about the grimy engine compartment, she saw the alternator and starter shone with a factory new gleam. Claremont stood upright saying aloud, "Bless you, Preston Sinclair."

In no time she had the truck hot wired and running. After making sure everything was in order, she cut the engine, quietly forced the hood closed and slipped back into the house.

✠   ✠   ✠

Agent Roundtree sat sipping coffee in the Dare County Sheriff's Department. He was on his third afternoon cup. Sheriff Winston had been much relieved when the FBI entourage left the island; at the time, he thought he'd seen the last of them. Now, however, the small office was again taken over as a temporary command post. Sheriff Winston watched several of the G-Men, as he called them out of earshot, compare notes around a small table in the center of the room.

Agent Roundtree, the man in charge, did not look like the hard-nosed field agent he was. Standing moderately tall, he had a slim but muscular build. His straight black hair was always meticulously styled and fingernails professionally manicured. He was also rather fond of expensive shoes and silk ties to go with his regulation suit. Nonetheless, despite a somewhat preened appearance, his exploits were well known within the Bureau. These were, however, rarely spoken of and then only amongst trusted associates.

The agents at the table bantered back and forth while Winston and Roundtree began a discussion of their own. The door opened and the room fell quiet as Viktor Stanizlow entered.

"Well, if it isn't our Russian friend," Roundtree exclaimed, breaking the momentary silence.

"Good morning, Sheriff," Stanizlow said, nodding politely toward Winston. He extended a hand to Roundtree. "I don't believe we've met."

Roundtree clasped his hand. "True, we haven't met, but I know only too well who you are."

Stanizlow lifted an eyebrow. "I don't doubt that."

Initially, Roundtree's tone was cordial, but his words were hard and biting. "To be frank, Stanizlow, someone, somewhere, thinks your shit don't stink," he said smiling.

Sheriff Winston looked off at hearing the crude remark.

Roundtree didn't let up. "For some reason, word from the top is you can't be touched. Now if I had my way, I'd have you chained to a marshal and put on the next flight back to whatever sorry place you came from."

The other agents intently watched the exchange.

"Now that the pleasantries are aside, I was hoping we could talk," Stanizlow said evenly.

"And what might this be about?"

"I can do something for you."

"Mr. Stanizlow," Roundtree said, his voice dripping with sarcasm, "what can you do for us?"

Stanizlow carefully looked about the room, then said, "I will give you Claremont."

Chapter 27

YURCHENKO SPENT MOST OF THE AFTERNOON STAKING OUT PRESTON Sinclair's house, unaware that a woman remained hidden in the crawl space just a few feet beyond the foundation walls—crouched amidst the very items he was seeking. Claremont, now especially wary, noted his approach from behind a curtained window and quickly retreated through the trap door. During the afternoon, there was one tense moment for both when a Sheriff's Department car rolled down the drive. The deputy, however, hadn't bothered to get out and after surveying the front of the house from inside the cruiser, simply turned and drove off. Otherwise no one had come or gone.

Under cover of rapidly falling darkness, Yurchenko left his observation nest along the edge of the woods and made his way around to the backside of the house. A light rain began to fall. Standing in the yard, Yurchenko told himself he'd probably been wasting his time and there surely must be better leads he could follow.

Making his way across the back yard, he passed the massive pile of crushed aluminum cans. Something caught his attention. Amid all the cans protruded a portion of what appeared to be part of a cooking pot. He picked up a small tree branch that lay on the ground and poked at the pile. A minor avalanche of cans sloughed down to reveal the corner of a large aluminum container. Jabbing at the pile repeatedly brought to view one whole side of the canister. Gripping the stick with both hands, Yurchenko worked feverishly until two more of the crumpled metal canisters lay fully exposed.

"Dimitri," a voice called out behind him.

Yurchenko reached under his jacket, whirled around and trained his Beretta at Stanizlow who stood but ten paces away. He had moved out of the shadows to present himself while Yurchenko was noisily digging through the cans.

"Put away the gun," Stanizlow said. "You will see I am unarmed."

Yurchenko approached him with his weapon leveled. He circled behind Stanizlow and patted him down. When he was convinced that Stanizlow spoke the truth, Yurchenko holstered his weapon, leaving the safety off. "I was told you'd be on the island," he said.

Still hiding under the house, Claremont heard Yurchenko pass close by. Recognizing Stanizlow's voice as it called out to him, she lifted herself over the low plank wall and into the crawl space proper. Flat on her stomach, she squirmed toward a metal ventilation grate set in the foundation. Through the narrow slits she could make out the two darkened figures from a knee high vantage. She strained to hear what was being said.

Stanizlow saw Yurchenko's eyes briefly shift to the pile of scrap aluminum. "Empty," Stanizlow said, casting a deliberate glance at the crumpled canisters. "Every one of them. This Preston Sinclair, he seems to have had a penchant for hoarding aluminum. It appears he ran over the canisters with his truck to flatten them."

"Where are the contents?" Yurchenko demanded.

"That is exactly what I came to talk to you about."

"Talk to me then."

"I can lead you to where the material is stored. It depends whether you could make it worth my while."

It was full dark. The two men stood facing each other in the steadily increasing rain.

Under normal circumstances, Yurchenko would have elected to take matters into his own hands and extracted the desired information through means he generally found quite effective. But knowing who he was dealing with, he figured it would be best to negotiate, at least for now.

"I never thought you a man who could be bought," Yurchenko said inquisitively. "Word on you is you're arrow straight."

Stanizlow shrugged and said, "Times change, Dimitri."

"They certainly do," Yurchenko agreed.

"Times change and men change," Stanizlow said, maintaining eye contact. "Now I've been doing a lot of thinking lately. I devoted my life to my work. Everything. And for what? I don't even have a pension to speak of. In Germany, I live in poverty. Do you know how much a KGB colonel draws these days? Less than what kids make working after school at McDonalds in this stinking country!"

Yurchenko smiled. "My friend, why do you think I went private?"

Stanizlow took a step closer. "Nine o'clock tomorrow night at the Frisco fishing pier, in the parking lot. Meet me and let me know what you can do."

Yurchenko cast him a long, probing look. "Very well, tomorrow," he said, before backing into the drizzly gloom.

✠   ✠   ✠

Early the next morning, Stanizlow and Zhukov returned to the Sinclair house. Zhukov took up position well within the heavily overgrown tree line. Before leaving, Stanizlow assured Zhukov he would be back in no more than two hours. He left by way of a little used path, a game trail more than likely, that led through Buxton Woods toward the dunes.

While keeping an eye on the house through a small break in the nearly impervious vegetation, Zhukov looked about. Directly above was a solid canopy of twisted live oaks and windswept loblolly pines. To either side, large gaps were present where trees had been broken or pushed down by the recent hurricane. Below these breaks, patches of sunlight illuminated a dense understory of red cedar, bayberry and spiky stands of dwarf palmetto. Zhukov, born and raised in an industrial town on the Russian steppes, had seen a jungle only in photographs. Yet crouched amid the tangled growth, he doubted very much there existed anywhere on earth a more exotic looking forest than the one surrounding him.

Zhukov was about halfway through his watch when a man wearing blue jeans and a leather bomber jacket came walking briskly down the drive. The man repeatedly glanced over his shoulder as he made his way around the side of the house. Claremont met him at the back door.

Minutes later, Stanizlow reappeared behind Zhukov, carefully picking his way through the underbrush. Zhukov motioned Stanizlow down and waved him over. Laying prone, they watched Claremont and the newcomer emerge through the back door carrying heavily loaded cardboard boxes, which were placed in the back of the converted ambulance. Stanizlow and Zhukov looked at each other and nodded.

Claremont and the unidentified man nervously peered around each time they left the house with another load. After about half an hour, the task was complete. The two departed on foot by way of the front drive, but not before putting back the scrap lumber and junk items that were leaning against the ambulance doors.

✠   ✠   ✠

The tension inside the Sheriff's Department headquarters was not unlike a locker room before a big game. Kevlar body armor was fitted and strapped tight. Equipment and weapons were checked. Every face was set in a look of grim resolve.

Agent Roundtree stood and addressed his men. He spoke in a low but firm voice. "Okay, gentlemen, everyone knows their part. I want this to go flawlessly." Roundtree drew his service piece, pointing it at the ceiling about six inches in front of his face. The grip in his hand felt familiar and reassuring. He savored the fluid motion of interlocking metal as he pulled the slide. It snapped back with a sharp metallic clack. "All right," he said, holstering the weapon. "Let's go get the bitch."

☩   ☩   ☩

The car, its headlights off, appeared from behind the cluster of buildings fronting the main road. It pulled to a stop 50 feet from Roundtree, who stood motionless with his coat collar turned up and hat pulled low over his brow. He had viewed the occupant with night vision binoculars while the vehicle crept down the access drive toward him. From underneath the brim of his hat, Roundtree squinted at the figure sitting behind the steering wheel, back lit by a single street lamp. He was certain. This is it, he thought. His hand trembled slightly.

There was to be no need for any provocation. The scenario had already been fabricated and every detail thoroughly rehearsed.

Roundtree slowly raised, then dropped one hand. Two agents rose from behind parked cars and leveled Heckler & Koch MP5s. The first agent got off four, three-shot bursts straight through the windshield. Blasting away in sustained fire mode, the second shooter emptied his entire clip against the driver's door, bringing to bear a savage, flesh-shredding crossfire.

The ear splitting firing stopped and the last of the spent cartridges rattled onto the pavement. The combined impact of dozens of rounds ripped the door open. In quivering spasms, the riddled body toppled from the car.

Roundtree inched toward the open door with flashlight in hand. One agent kept his weapon trained while the other snapped in a fresh clip.

The first burst hit in the throat. A shoulder rested squarely on the asphalt, forcing the head aside at a sickening angle.

Bracing himself, Roundtree pointed the light at the body.

"*Who the fuck is that?!*"

Illuminated in the beam was Dimitri Yurchenko's lifeless face, the side of which lay pressed against the Frisco Pier parking lot. One eye had been shot through and the other bugged out grotesquely.

☩   ☩   ☩

Stanizlow and Zhukov watched the action from the rooftop deck of an empty rental cottage located a good distance away. They caught the twinkling muzzle flashes a full second before the gratifying, staccato reports reached them. Nonetheless, they were not so far away they couldn't hear Roundtree's anguished curses.

"Gone," Stanizlow dryly said, as soon as the last shots faded into the night.

Zhukov just grinned from ear to ear.

✠   ✠   ✠

"Do you think they'll come for you?" Zhukov asked, lying on the couch inside the cottage. The shades were drawn and it was completely dark in the room. After observing the killing, they had broken in to hide out for the night.

"Maybe, but not right away. It seems to me they will have some explaining to do first. Gunning down foreign nationals in cold blood is not exactly standard FBI procedure. My guess is they will await instructions from Washington before doing anything. We should be all right in the meantime."

"What about the damn crazy woman, and the boxes?"

"I think they are not going anywhere, at least not tonight. Go to sleep, my friend. Tomorrow we have a big day."

Zhukov took his advice and curled up on the couch. Stanizlow sat by the open window and listened to the muffled roar of the nearby surf.

✠   ✠   ✠

Dawn broke bright and clear. Stanizlow awoke sitting in the chair. He got up, stepped onto the porch and took in the vista of a deep blue and perfectly calm ocean. Stanizlow felt his confidence build with every breath of morning air. He made his way back inside and shook a befuddled and muttering Zhukov awake.

They helped themselves to some coffee in the kitchen, putting everything back in its place. Locking the door behind them, they made their way down the long stairs to ground level. To avoid being seen on the road, the two men crossed the dunes and covered the mile or so to Sinclair's house directly along the beach.

Zhukov again took his lookout position. Stanizlow crouched down beside him. It was not long before they saw Claremont emerge and hurry down the drive on foot. Stanizlow then let himself in and began to carefully search the house.

Peering into the bathroom, he saw Claremont's cellular phone sitting on the toilet tank. He reached for the unit and slipped it under his coat. Upon inspecting the bedroom, it didn't take Stanizlow long to note the seam in the carpet and find the trap door. He opened it and lowered himself through. As soon as his eyes adjusted to the semi-darkness, he saw the space was empty except for a mildew-ridden tarpaulin draping the far plank wall.

Crouching, Stanizlow made his way over and lifted the tarp back. Behind it were stacked many dozens of brick sized packets wrapped tightly in plastic. Stanizlow freed one of the packets, drew his penknife and cut away at the wrapper. He poked at the hard packed contents with the knife blade and let a handful crumble through his fingers onto the sand floor.

Something caught his attention as he let the tarp drop back—the sand adjacent to the walls was left undisturbed by the trampling evident throughout the center of the low space. In one small area along the wall, however, the ground surface looked slightly different—as if the sand had been churned and partially mounded at some point in time.

Stanizlow crawled over to the suspect-looking spot. His probing hand struck something hard at a depth of only a few inches. With several sweeps of his forearm, he cleared off a white, rectangular surface on which the word IGLOO was printed in raised letters.

He lifted the lid of the cooler. Inside were individual clumps of a yellow, waxy substance. The malleable material was pressed into roughly square forms. Stanizlow knew immediately what he found—a highly illicit but equally effective tool in what had been Preston Sinclair's legitimate trade—Semtex plastic explosive.

A small box of detonators, sealed in mason jars to protect them from moisture, rested next to the explosives. This is good, he thought, closing the lid. This is very good.

✠   ✠   ✠

Claremont came in through the front door to find Stanizlow standing in the middle of the living room, waiting for her. She gasped audibly. "Stan! Oh! You startled me... I wasn't expecting you!" She backed away, holding her hands behind her as if she were hiding something.

"I just thought I would drop by and see how you were getting along."

"Fine. Just fine, fine," she said, obviously forcing a quick smile. "I was going out but forgot my cell phone. You know how much I hate to be without it. Have you seen the thing?"

Stanizlow shook his head and asked, "Did you hear, there was a killing last night?"

"I thought I heard some firing. I wasn't sure. I was sleeping."

Stanizlow nodded.

"Things have just gotten so crazy around here," Claremont said, backing toward the door.

"Indeed they have."

"Listen Stan, I have to go out. Can we meet in, say, two hours?"

"I thought you were hiding out here."

"I'll be back."

"Be careful out there," he warned as she turned to leave. "Remember, you're a wanted woman. Roundtree and his men are back and I suspect they have quite an attitude this morning."

"Two hours," she called back to him.

✠   ✠   ✠

Stanizlow went to the bedroom and lowered himself into the crawl space. He lifted up the top of the cooler containing the plastic explosive. Using his penknife, he cut away two pieces the thickness of a slice of bread. He twisted open the jar with the detonators and placed several in his pocket before pulling himself through the trap door, closing it behind him. Stanizlow then let himself into Sinclair's shed and went to work.

Ever vigilant, Zhukov kept a keen eye about while Stanizlow was in the shed. He perked at the faint drone of an approaching aircraft. The twin-prop Beech King Air came in low over the water with engines throttled back. Zhukov could barely make out the propeller noise as the plane drifted in to the airstrip.

Zhukov slipped into the shed and informed Stanizlow that a plane touched down.

"Very well," Stanizlow said, without looking up. "It won't be long."

☩　　　☩　　　☩

Stanizlow and Zhukov had just closed and latched the back doors of the ambulance when they heard footsteps and two hushed voices approaching. Quickly, they fell back behind the thickets along the edge of the woods. From their hidden vantage point, they saw Claremont and a companion come around the corner of the house. Claremont hot-wired the ambulance and the man climbed in behind the wheel. The truck pulled around the side of the house and chugged up the drive.

Claremont stayed behind, having told the driver she would meet him at the airstrip in fifteen minutes.

She walked briskly to the work shed and pulled open the doors. Zhukov and Stanizlow watched her remove a small suitcase from the trunk of the Saturn and hurry off to the house.

"You were right again, Viktor," Zhukov whispered.

Stanizlow brought one finger to his lips. "Quiet. She will be right back out."

Claremont fumbled to get the key into the door lock. Once inside, she nervously glanced at her watch as she made her way down the hallway to the bedroom. She pulled up the section of carpet, recoiled and began to curse out loud. The trap door had been firmly secured with a locked hasp. She pulled at the padlock and pounded the boards with her fist. Lying hidden in the brush, both men heard the muffled banging and continual swearing escaping through the bedroom window.

Tools! The tools in the shed, she thought. Shit! There's no time! She stormed out of the house and made for the car.

Claremont threw the suitcase into the back seat. She jumped in and turned the key. The engine cranked but didn't start. She waited a few seconds and tried again. Nothing. She tried again and again. "Goddammit!" Claremont yelled, slapping her palm against the dash. Still cursing loudly, she leapt from the vehicle. She ripped open the hood to have a look, only to smash the cover down in a rage.

Half running, Claremont barged headlong into the woods in a desperate attempt to make a straight line to the airstrip. In doing so, she missed the head of the game trail by just a few yards. Flailing her way through the dense underbrush, she passed so close to the prone Zhukov she almost stepped on his hand.

When the thrashing steps passed from earshot, the two men stood up, brushing themselves free of sand and leaves.

"Do you think she'll get there?" Zhukov asked.

"Maybe. Maybe not."

"What made her stay?"

"Powder cocaine," Stanizlow stated. His left hand held the ignition coil wire to the Saturn. "Large amounts of it."

Stanizlow opened the engine compartment and replaced the part.

"Wait here until I come for you," he ordered, letting the hood drop closed.

Stanizlow fired the car up, pulled out of the drive and headed in the direction of the airstrip.

Chapter 28

THE GENERAL BILLY MITCHELL AIRPORT CONSISTED OF A SINGLE paved runway paralleling the backside of the dune line. Several single engine aircraft stood parked on the tarmac adjacent to the National Park Service road, their wings securely tied down and canopies covered in tarps. Otherwise, the airport was deserted, save for the King Air, its nervous pilot and single passenger, when the ambulance lumbered onto the taxiway.

Within twenty minutes, the cartons were loaded aboard and the truck moved out of sight behind the metal building that once served as the airport office.

Standing on the taxiway, the plane's engines droned loudly with the throttles well advanced. Both the pilot and passenger were ready and anxious to go.

The pilot ripped his head set off. "Where the hell is she?!" he shouted out.

"Just a few more minutes," the man in the bomber jacket implored.

A section of the airport entrance road was visible from the taxi-way about a quarter mile distant where it curved to pass over a high sandy ridge. The men in the aircraft peered anxiously through the windscreen for the approach of the car.

✠   ✠   ✠

Roundtree had a hunch. He wasn't even sure what brought it on but he thought he might as well check it out. He got into his car and drove north out of Hatteras village. Once in Frisco, he turned off Route 12 onto the airport access road.

A few moments later, at the same instant, both men in the waiting aircraft caught sight of what looked conspicuously like an unmarked police car crest the distant high ground and motor slowly down the access road in their direction.

The pilot was flying with forged papers and bogus numbers on his plane. He did not know what was in the cardboard cartons stacked ceiling high behind him—nor did he want to. In any case, the last thing he needed was a run in with the local law. "We're out of here!" he yelled, releasing the brakes and pushing the throttles.

The aircraft surged forward. As heavily laden as they were with the cargo, in addition to fuel for the long flight, the pilot was not about to attempt a downwind take off. He raced the plane toward the north end of the runway before putting the brakes to a test the likes of which they'd never seen.

✠   ✠   ✠

The Saturn sat parked on an empty *cul de sac* about half a mile south of the runway. Stanizlow stepped from the car. The roar of the plane's engines reverberated off the adjacent vacation cottages, all of which were closed up for the winter. The sound momentarily faded as the pilot slowed to turn the plane. Stanizlow made his way to the top of the low dunes.

"There's a better way, Stan," a voice called out from behind.

Stanizlow recognized it as Clifton Echo's, but didn't turn around.

"Finally got you figured, Stan. Been your shadow for two days now—don't do it!"

Stanizlow ignored him. They could hear the plane's engines throttle up to full power.

Echo had to shout to be heard. "It's history in there," he yelled at Stanizlow's backside.

The roar of the engines enveloped them. The vibrating din seemed to come from all sides at once as the aircraft lifted off the runway. It heaved into view just to their left.

"*History! Go to a library for history! Read a book for history!*" Stanizlow shouted at the top of his lungs.

The landing gear retracted as the plane passed overhead.

"*Read the newspapers for history,*" Stanizlow belted, still facing away, his voice taut with emotion. "*The Balkans—Bosnia—ETHNIC CLEANSING! I've seen what ethnic cleansing IS! Now it's in the news—it's on TELEVISION! And no one gives a... gives a GODDAMN!*"

The plane banked and kept climbing over open water.

"Stan, let the authorities handle it."

Stanizlow removed his own cellular phone out from under his coat. He calmly keyed in the number.

A millisecond after Claremont's phone beeped inside one of the cardboard cartons, the King Air began to disintegrate as the four ounces of Semtex to which the phone was wired literally blew the plane to pieces. For a fraction of a second the aircraft appeared to hang in mid-air with major sections spreading apart, after which spraying fuel ignited into a billowing fireball. A segment of fuselage with a crumpled portion of wing still attached fell from the mass of fire. It corkscrewed violently downward trailing a solid sheet of flame. The scattered wreckage hit the water a few hundred yards from the beach. One engine, propeller still spinning, sailed across the sky leaving a thin arcing trail of smoke. The fireball faded to a thick, black mushroom cloud as patches of burning fuel spread across the water. Bits of aluminum skin and other debris fluttered down, splashing around the flaming slick.

Stanizlow slipped the phone back in his coat and stood watching the pall of smoke hanging over the scene drift and begin to dissipate. He turned and came off the dune.

"You're one motherfucker," Echo said as Stanizlow walked past.

"I know," Stanizlow replied without looking up. He kept walking and ducked into the car.

✠   ✠   ✠

Roundtree watched the plane take off. He then spotted the abandoned ambulance and was about to run the license number when the sound of the explosion reached him. Seeing the fireball beyond the end of the runway, he jumped into the car and raced to the scene.

✠   ✠   ✠

Stanizlow returned to pick up Zhukov at Sinclair's house. Before getting back on the road, he pulled a New York Yankees baseball cap he'd bought from a particularly insistent Manhattan street vendor, low over his brow. He reached for the sunglasses in the glove box. Driving north, they passed several fire engines and rescue units speeding down the road in the opposite direction.

No words passed between them until they reached Buxton, at which point Stanizlow simply informed Zhukov his family was already out of Russia and arrangements had been made to resettle them in the States under Federal protection. He would only have to wait a day at the motel and an agent would arrive to escort him.

✠   ✠   ✠

Back at the motel, Stanizlow went to the sink and splashed water across his face. After drying off, he picked up the room phone and called the Sheriff's Department. Winston was on his way to the crash site when the dispatcher relayed him the tip. Stanizlow then dialed a White House number, leaving a one word, coded message.

Chapter 29

A TIDEWATER VIRGINIA TELEVISION STATION WAS THE FIRST OF THE media to arrive at the crash scene, having driven down early that morning to cover the FBI shooting in Frisco.

Several eyewitnesses were being interviewed beside a van with a satellite uplink mounted on the roof. Each person recounted how the aircraft exploded in mid-air before falling into the water. In the middle of an interview, the police frequency scanner picked up word of a major drug seizure underway in Hatteras village and the race was on to get three scoops in a single day.

✠   ✠   ✠

Preston Sinclair's house was cordoned off by the time the television crew, now accompanied by a small crowd of onlookers, reached the scene. A not so tight-lipped Sheriff's Department deputy confirmed in front of cameras that military type explosives were found along with cocaine. It was not long before the words "possible narco-terror" were being spoken and the story began to snowball. Crews from the major networks arrived by helicopter. The cluster of television reporters, desperate to make the 6:00 o'clock feed, jostled for position behind the police cordon to shout questions at the investigators trying to work the scene.

Things got so out of hand Sheriff Winston felt compelled to hold an impromptu news conference to restore some order.

"Yes, Ma'am," he said politely to a blonde television reporter, "cocaine has been found in significant quantities inside the house."

"I think it would be best not to comment on that at this time," he responded to a question about the plastic explosive.

Sheriff Winston was clearly enjoying himself. He diplomatically deflected a question as to how the local Sheriff's Department managed to pull off one of the largest drug busts in North Carolina history, right underneath a major FBI investigation. He did allow himself a quick smile at the inquiry, however. "Yes, in the back, there," he said pointing to the right.

Roundtree stood aside from the crowd, desperately trying to keep an even expression. "No comment," he snapped at anyone who tried to question him. He almost broke when he saw Stanizlow appear and begin to mill about. For a lingering moment, Roundtree imagined what it would be like to kill the man with his bare hands.

Gregory's truck rolled up. Visibly angry, he walked stiffly over to where Stanizlow was standing.

"Captain," Stanizlow nodded as Gregory came up to him.

"I don't know what you did back at Preston's house, but let me tell you!" Gregory said angrily. "Preston Sinclair was a lot of things, but he wasn't a dope runner!"

"Can we talk?" Stanizlow said quickly, reaching over and grasping Gregory's arm.

Having said his piece, Gregory eased up a bit. "Okay."

Stanizlow led him away from the now thinning crowd. "I'm sorry Preston Sinclair is dead," he began when they were out of earshot. "But he is. Murdered. And to be murdered is the most senseless of deaths." He kept looking directly at Gregory as he spoke. "Captain Gregory, you and but a few others know what this was all about—how much was at stake… I trust I still have your confidence?"

Gregory nodded, though reluctantly.

"How Preston Sinclair became mixed up in all this — the drugs — and who killed him and why, we may never know," Stanizlow said, pausing for emphasis. "Now true," he went on, "it is wrong to compromise a man's memory. But the way things now are, even as he lies in his grave, Preston Sinclair may well have helped preserve a better future — for millions. If that doesn't give meaning to an otherwise senseless death, what can?"

At first, Gregory did not respond. "It still ain't right," he finally said.

Stanizlow looked over his shoulder at the dwindling crowd, saying, "Captain, I just spoke with Mr. Echo on the phone. He's going to meet me at the Mad Shrimper. He said he has something to share concerning Preston Sinclair. Why don't you come along."

"Okay."

"Good. Let's go."

✠ ✠ ✠

The Mad Shrimper was abuzz. It was probably the most eventful day on the island in recent memory and all seemed to have their own opinion or theory on the matters.

Echo walked through the door and made his way to where Gregory and Stanizlow were sitting.

"So what's up?" Gregory asked as soon as Echo joined them.

"I can pretty much tell you what happened to Sinclair."

Gregory shifted onto the edge of his seat.

"I can't say where I got this from," Echo said. "The guy is about shitting his pants. That's why he came to me. I suppose he thought I could help him. Seems he got mixed up in the cocaine thing, though not inadvertently, as appears to have been the case with Preston."

"How's that?" Gregory asked sharply.

Echo looked about the table. "Preston Sinclair needed some help to have a go at this supposed gold before the U-boat was to be raised in the Spring. That's where Shamus James came into the picture. Together they found somebody to back them — some cash, a boat and equipment. The kicker is, they apparently didn't let on about the gold they thought was on board — the investors were only promised a load of Nazi artifacts and relics."

"Sounds like Preston," Gregory remarked.

"But listen," Echo said quickly, "what he didn't know, was he was hooked up with a big time Mexican drug ring. This Shamus James introduced Sinclair to some acquaintances down in Florida. These folks thought Sinclair's salvage plan was a really dumb venture — just what they needed to launder a few million narco-bucks."

Gregory frowned.

"That's not all," Echo went on. He again looked about to see whether anyone else might be listening. "Evidently the Mexicans saw the salvage operation as an ideal cover to run some of their cocaine in through North Carolina. Here. That's where my guy comes in."

"And? What happened?"

"The problem was, the people who wanted their laundry done thought they were investing in a legitimate enterprise — that being the whole idea. When they found out what Sinclair was doing was illegal, they flipped. Worse yet, at about the same time, they start feeling heat from the Feds down in Florida — coincidence probably. Anyway, they think they've been set up. They bug out of here and Sinclair finds himself stuck with a shipment of coke. He's scared and already in neck deep, so he stashes the stuff under his house. The Mexicans send a pro or two to clean up. Sinclair is killed and the shipment written off."

Gregory sat and contemplated Echo's explanation.

"From what I've heard," Echo added dryly, "these guys make the Medellin Cartel look like cub scouts. It doesn't take much to set 'em off."

Seemingly satisfied, Gregory gave a look as if a burden had been lifted from him.

But Echo wasn't yet finished. "Just one little problem I still have, though — none of this explains who bombed my trailer."

He turned to Stanizlow, who gave him a deadpan look. "You don't really suppose the CIA tried to take us both out?" Echo asked skeptically.

Stanizlow shrugged. "I think you would be in a better position to judge that than I."

Echo retreated into thought. "Maybe it was Bruford," he then said. "Man, I'd like to spend ten minutes in a locked room with the fat little fucker! I'd find out exactly what happened!"

A short silence ensued, with Echo staring angrily across the table at no one in particular.

"Clifton, I don't see why you have to stew over it," Gregory spoke out. "Hey, you're still here aren't you? Be glad and don't sweat it so hard." He cast a glance toward Stanizlow. "Unless you think they'll be back for you, that is."

"My guess is it's over with," Stanizlow said firmly.

"Good. So lemme buy y'all a drink," Gregory said in a loud voice. He held up three fingers for the bartender to see.

Mary Margaret nodded back at him.

"It's over," Gregory urged with sudden decisiveness. "Hey, at least as far as I'm concerned it is." He gave a shallow huff. "Lemme tell you, I'm glad, too. Jesus! If I'd known where all this would go, I'd never gone within five miles of that goddamn wreck!"

Mary Margaret placed the drinks on the table. "Here you go, fellas."

Gregory raised his glass. "Cheers."

Stanizlow followed suit.

"Cheers," Echo said without much conviction.

✠   ✠   ✠

From behind the bar, Mary Margaret watched the restaurant fill. It was the Saturday before Christmas and she figured it was going to be a good night. One by one the regulars showed.

Gregory got up and drifted over to talk with Billy Page, who was warming up on the pool table.

Stanizlow excused himself and ambled over to have a seat at the end of the bar. While hunched over his drink, Echo kept an eye on him from across the room. Stanizlow turned and was facing sideways. Sitting on the bar stool, he looked relaxed and at ease. Echo watched him exchange a few smiling remarks with Mary Margaret, wondering if the man gave any thought to the lives he'd taken that very afternoon. Outwardly there was no sign.

✠ ✠ ✠

Stanizlow awoke at dawn to spend a good part of the short December day walking the South Beach. He lingered for quite some time in the vicinity where Gregory told him he'd washed ashore, nearly one-half century ago. Try as he did, he could recall little of that fateful day. Later in the afternoon, he packed his few belongings in preparation for the long trip home, set to begin the next morning. He retired soon after it got dark.

✠ ✠ ✠

Not wanting to depart without a word, Stanizlow called Gregory and the two men wished each other well. He went and knocked on Echo's door.

Look, I wanted to talk about something before you left," Echo said, stepping through the threshold and walking with Stanizlow to the car. "There're some things about this Tannhauser thing I'm still not clear on."

"Very well, if you must know," Stanizlow said, lifting his suitcase into the trunk. The hatch stayed up.

"For one, there must have been more to it than reams of documents."

"Indeed there was," Stanizlow said, after the shortest hesitation. "As you remember, Admiral Dönitz' plan was to set up an underground National Socialist government-in-exile in Argentina. Dönitz, however, knew the Allies would never allow him any role in the resistance, or any future government. His plan was to run the show from behind the scenes. The documents were a key element of the plan. That's why they were sealed in those containers—to allow them to be hidden anywhere, even buried in the ground or put underwater, until the time they would be needed."

"Paper don't feed the bulldog."

"True, one would need more than paper. You would have needed people. The *U-491* was just one of three U-boats that sailed for South America."

Echo lifted both eyebrows.

"The second was the *U-977*, commanded by Heinz Schaeffer. It left Norway bound for Argentina during the last week of the war. The *U-977* carried the people. Posing as ordinary submariners, the crew consisted of highly trained operatives ready to devote their lives to Tannhauser. I am sure all were absolutely convinced of their ultimate success."

"Wait a minute!" Echo exclaimed, "I read about that voyage. Didn't they break a record of some sort?"

"Indeed. Using the newly developed Snorkel ventilation system, they cruised for 66 days without fully surfacing. The record stood until nuclear propulsion came about."

"And wasn't there speculation the U-boat took Hitler out of Europe?"

"Indeed there was. Later, Schaeffer was interrogated relentlessly by both the British and Americans. Whether they put any real credence into the Hitler theory, I don't know, but they made things fairly unpleasant for this Schaeffer fellow."

"So you say the captain was detained. What happened from there?"

Stanizlow backtracked in his reply. "As it turned out, Tannhauser could never have been put into effect, even if all three boats arrived safely. Somewhere, the plan must have been betrayed, for once the *U-977* put in at Mar del Plata, it was met by Argentinean Marines. The vessel was impounded and all aboard arrested and turned over to the Allies. Schaeffer and his men were taken to the United States and later Great Britain."

"What happened to them?"

"All were eventually repatriated."

"And the boat?"

"After a painstaking search, which turned up nothing, the *U-977* was turned over to the Americans. She was towed to Boston and eventually sunk off Massachusetts in a torpedo exercise."

"You said there was a third U-boat. What was it carrying?"

Stanizlow looked Echo directly in the eye. "That would have been the funding."

"Gold!"

Stanizlow momentarily lowered his eyelids in affirmation. "Two tons to be exact. Mostly in bar form."

"The Tannhauser Treasure!" Echo blurted. "So it exists!"

"Yes."

"What happened to it?"

Stanizlow shrugged. "No one knows." A twinkle flashed in his eyes. "But if I did," he added wryly, "do you suppose I'd tell you?"

"Come on," Echo urged, "what happened?"

"No one knows," Stanizlow reiterated. "It was the *U-1112*, one of the new Elektro boats—sailed just a week before we did. Veteran captain and crew. It left port and was never heard from again."

Echo stood and took in the notion.

"Most likely hit a mine and went down," Stanizlow said dryly. "After the war, Allied reports never mention a U-boat contact anywhere near its route."

"So it's still out there."

"Probably." The twinkle was back. "On the other hand, stories kept cropping up that a U-boat had been sighted in the Indian Ocean during July of 1945. Later, persistent rumors circulated that a submarine made its way up a river in Madagascar. Supposedly the commander scuttled the vessel below the falls—used the gold to establish his own fiefdom in the highlands beyond. It was thought the strain he'd endured on patrol finally drove him to madness. Nonetheless, the natives came to venerate him as their lord."

"And you're gonna tell me his name was Kurtz!"

"Kapitan Roland Kurtz. How'd you know?"

"Bull shit!" Echo erupted. "Don't think I haven't seen the movie!"

Stanizlow broke into a wide, uncharacteristic grin.

Echo conceded him his moment, then asked, "What did happen?"

"No one knows," Stanizlow again replied, looking over to see a gray Crown Victoria pull into the lot. "Like I said, probably hit a mine."

The car came to a stop just to their left. Echo tensed like a cat seeing a dog wander into its domain, for he recognized Frank Bruford sitting behind the wheel.

"Pipe down, Echo," Bruford said, stepping out of the car and walking toward them. "I know what you're thinking. There's something the both of you should see. Come on, let's go inside."

Echo warily followed Bruford into Stanizlow's motel room. Once inside, Bruford picked up the television remote and clicked the set to CNN. He glanced at his watch. "It's on a 20 minute loop. Shouldn't be much longer."

As soon as the commercial break passed, the anchorperson went straight into the headline story. The scene changed to a Telemundo feed of Sandra Claremont being interviewed in a Havana studio. Echo stared in disbelief at the television screen. Between two of the well rehearsed questions presented by the Cuban interviewer, Claremont ever so briefly turned her head at the camera. Her glance carried with it a look that was wry, a little triumphant perhaps—taunting even.

"White House staffer defects to Cuba. Quite ironic really," Bruford remarked smugly. "Direct access to the President!" he laughed. "You'd better believe they got their best spin people on this as we speak. I can't wait to hear what they come up with."

Echo remained speechless.

Bruford turned the television off saying, "I think we've heard enough, guys. Hey, don't feel bad, none of us knew—though some delicate questions were beginning to be whispered. Seems they have an a.k.a. Yolanda de la Rosa on their hands. Our people in Havana just informed us she's been known to be quite chummy with Castro himself." He again laughed out loud. "Can you imagine? Direct access to the President. Just think about it."

Still glaring at the darkened television screen, Echo's face turned a light shade of purple.

"Born Sarah Gwen Hargrove," Bruford went on. "Age 36. Heiress to a Northwest lumber fortune. Fell in with the radical fringe in San Francisco as a young runaway during the early '70s. Ended up attending Berkeley for a while. Then she just disappears. Resurfaces as Sandra Claremont at Columbia University. Doctorate in Political Science. Everything checked out when her original White House background was done. God only knows how."

Echo and Stanizlow accompanied Bruford back outside.

"A Cuban agent," Echo muttered shaking his head.

"Mole." Bruford stated as he walked. "In the White House. She was in so deep we haven't even begun to assess the full damage."

Stanizlow said nothing.

Echo remained dumbfounded. "I don't understand," he stammered. "Why would Castro want to get at what was on the U-boat?"

"Think about it!" Bruford said loudly, turning to face Echo. "Fidel Castro used to be a player on the world stage. Now he's a nobody. With his ego, he simply can't accept it."

"There has to be more," Echo insisted.

"I'm sure there was," Bruford replied. "Information is power. We all know that. And at this point, Castro needs all the power he can get—and money." He looked over at Stanizlow. "I understand the opposition in Russia had quite an interest in those papers. Perhaps Castro thought he could curry favor with his traditional benefactor once the new regime seized the reins in Moscow." Bruford looked off across the parking lot. "Hell, there was probably more to it than that. From what I've now heard, there was some real heavy duty shit in there—a veritable Who's Who in the world of Nazi collaborators, if you will. Nothing like a little blackmail to generate some positive cash flow." Bruford again laughed aloud. "I can just imagine the mileage old Fidel could have gotten out of the deal."

Echo's face darkened further.

"In any case," Bruford went on, "it mattered enough to him that he risked his most stellar asset on a very dicey operation. He lost. Her cover blew and she hightailed it south. Probably made it to the Keys and stole a boat to cover the Strait. We're checking on it down there right now."

Bruford gave a fiendish look. "Explains a lot of things, doesn't it, huh Echo?" he said tauntingly.

"It was her!" Echo hissed at Stanizlow, who avoided his violent glare. "First she didn't want you to go to the trailer, then... then she said... *the bitch!*"

Bruford looked to be thoroughly enjoying the moment. "Gentlemen," he said, "as much as I would like to stay and chat some more, I've got a windowdressing report to put together before I head back to DC."

Saying nothing, Echo leaned back against the Saturn, his arms folded tightly across his chest.

"Mr. Bruford," Stanizlow called out, before the man could get into his car.

"Yes?"

"One question, just a professional curiosity, if you don't mind."

Bruford moved to face Stanizlow. "Sure."

"You were working with Mr. Roundtree, then you left, and now you're back. Why?"

Bruford took a moment to answer. "When Claremont's cover came off and the full extent of the potential damage became known, the decision was made to liquidate," he stated as a cold matter of fact.

"That much I figured."

Bruford gave a thin smile. "I figured you figured that," he said, carefully avoiding eye contact. "But they wanted to keep the Agency out of it. Roundtree was to be in charge of the operation." Bruford shrugged his shoulders. "Hey, somebody's got to do the dirty work. Anyway, so Roundtree takes a call and proceeds to tell everyone we're all off the case. I leave and he gets down to work." Bruford let out a short, cutting laugh. "Well, tried to."

"I see," Stanizlow said. "Thank you very much."

Echo waited until Bruford pulled out of the lot before turning to Stanizlow. "You knew !" he snarled. "You knew, didn't you?!"

"I knew. Not at first, but yes, I knew."

"How?!"

"It has been my life's work to come to know such things," Stanizlow sighed, looking straight ahead.

Livid, Echo burst out shouting. "*She tried to kill me! Hell!* She tried to get the both of us! And you didn't do anything! *Why?*"

Stanizlow's expression hardened. Looking like a schoolmaster ready to reprimand an unruly pupil, he turned to face Echo. "Perhaps, Mr. Echo," he said evenly, "it was because she and I may have once had something in common."

Echo held his stare for a few seconds. "Yeah, like you're both freaks!" he let out, slumping back against the car. Echo suddenly threw his hands in the air. "Oh, forget it," he said. He looked back at Stanizlow and began to laugh. "Forget it," he repeated, shaking his head. "It's over."

"Over," Stanizlow agreed.

"To think I could have… maybe… I… Oh, never mind!"

Stanizlow reached to close the trunk lid.

"Listen Stan," Echo said, still shaking his head, "this brings me to what I actually wanted to talk to you about. Look… I think you're weirder than snake shit, okay? But I like you. I really do. Now I know you don't have much to go back to so I was wondering, well, I just finished the overseer's house on my property in South Carolina last summer. I could use someone in there. No rent, just do a little yard work and keep an eye on the place when I'm not there. Besides, I wouldn't mind having someone like you watching my own backside, if you know what I mean. What do you say?"

At first Stanizlow didn't reply. He let go of the trunk lid while seemingly considering the offer. "What is it like, this Low Country in South Carolina?" he asked.

"It's quiet there. Nothing much ever happens."

"I like that."

"And it's warm most of the year."

"I like that, too."

"Winters are very short. Fall and Spring are long. It's hot in the summer, but that's what air-conditioning's for."

"Thank you," Stanizlow said, sounding a bit contemplative, "but no." He slammed the trunk shut, adding more firmly, "I think I shall go back."

"I know, I know, back to your little cottage by the lake and your vegetables. If you ever change your mind, though, just give me a call."

Before Echo could reach over to shake his hand, he caught sight of Sheriff Winston approaching. Neither had noticed the cruiser pull in.

"Mr. Stanizlow, Mr. Echo," Winston said politely, touching the brim of his hat. "I saw you two standing here and wondered what was going on." He eyed the open car door.

"I am getting ready to leave," Stanizlow said.

"That's good," Winston stated. He glanced at Echo.

"Yeah, me, too. Tomorrow."

Sheriff Winston nodded approvingly. He reached down and adjusted his gun belt. "Y'all don't come back now," he said, before turning and walking back to the cruiser.

Stanizlow and Echo stood and watched him drive off. When the cruiser disappeared from sight, Echo extended his hand. Stanizlow took it firmly. "Anytime Stan," Echo said. "If you ever change your mind, just give me a call."

Chapter 30

STANIZLOW STEERED THE SATURN THROUGH THE MID-DAY TIDEWAter Virginia traffic. He glanced at his watch, wondering if he would make his flight—a quick connection from Norfolk to Washington, then on to Berlin via Frankfurt. Suddenly, almost without thinking and at the last possible moment, he veered onto the Route 13 exit and began to follow the small blue and white signs directing the way to the Chesapeake Bay Bridge-Tunnel.

Earlier, while studying the road map, Stanizlow noted the thin line spanning the mouth of the Chesapeake Bay. Never had he intended to go near it.

In leaving the freeway, Stanizlow acted on impulse. It was a rash and sudden change of plan—the sort of spontaneous action he generally preferred to avoid. Several times in the past, however, spontaneity saved his life. More than once, seemingly idle or random changes in plan spared him death. Stanizlow was anything but a religious man, but he believed in the course of fate. Somehow, he felt sure more than caution and savvy kept him alive to see his seventieth year. Driving on, he thought of the assassin's bullet that nicked his ear in a darkened Berlin alleyway. He recalled the time shrapnel cut open his SS field jacket without touching flesh.

Fate.

Fate, he thought, whatever that might be, was what first brought him to the narrow strip of land on the far side of the Chesapeake Bay.

And now it seemed fate was beckoning him there once more.

✝   ✝   ✝

Stanizlow paid the $10.00 toll and pulled through the gate. Before him lay twelve miles of two-lane highway, held up by spindly concrete legs. Solid ground fell away as he entered the narrow span that stretched into the slate gray horizon. The afternoon sky was darkening and the lights mounted over each side of the bridge were lit. Two by two, the bronze colored orbs passed through his peripheral vision while the vehicle bounced rhythmically over the deck sections.

Up ahead, low clouds moved across the choppy water. Terra firma faded in the rearview mirror.

His hands tightened on the wheel at the approach of the concrete chasm leading to the first of two long tunnels. The car nosed into the brightly lit, tile lined tube. He felt his ears pop as a duo of tractor-trailers blasted by, just off the left fender.

After passing through the second tunnel, it was with no small measure of relief he crested the high bridge over the North Channel and began the descent toward landfall on Fisherman's Island.

From the fleeting vantage of the high bridge, Stanizlow caught sight of the windswept dunes and empty marshlands that comprise the tip of the Virginia Eastern Shore. The muted colors and rippled textures reminded him of the Island of Rugen—of holiday with his mother and father—memories of childhood innocence, lost so long ago. In the dulling afternoon light, the Chesapeake could easily pass for the Baltic Sea late on a waning summer's eve.

Overland Route 13 was four lanes, and ran arrow straight through the level countryside. He passed the sign for Kiptopeke, proclaiming itself Virginia's newest State Park. He did not remember there being so many trees along the roadside. For a moment he became disoriented and began to question the wisdom of the excursion.

Rain began to fall. Again, he thought of turning back. Suddenly, up on the right, he thought he saw what he was looking for. He braked to a stop along the gravel shoulder. Stanizlow squinted past slapping windshield wipers at the farm, tucked in about 100 yards from the road.

A green tin roof capped the white frame house with distinctive gingerbread trim. A large porch adorned the front. He noted the outbuildings and the flanking oak trees, their massive crowns laid bare for the winter. He recognized the shed with the rust colored roof. There was no mistaking—it was the Schifflett farm.

Looking around, he saw the entrance to a dirt road a short distance ahead. After a moment's hesitation, Stanizlow pulled ahead and turned down the drive, following it to the end. A bitingly cold wind greeted him as he got out of the car. It was a damp, bone-chilling cold that cut straight through him; a cold more numbing than anything he'd ever faced in Siberia. His joints protested bitterly.

The precipitation had partially changed over. An abominable mixture of rain, sleet and wet flakes fell from leaden skies. Ice pellets stung his face and collected on his arms and shoulders.

A footpath extended on from the end of the track, disappearing into a darkened pine forest. He followed the path to the water. Somewhat to his disbelief, Stanizlow found himself on the sandy terrace overlooking the marshlands—the very same spot where he stood on that summer afternoon, almost half a century ago.

Traces of the dock were still there—two pilings jutting forlornly from the muck. He looked out over the stark, empty marshlands. Winter transformed the verdant scene he had always recalled so well. The grasses were brown and withered. Thin bands of ice clung to the creek banks along the high tide mark. He wrapped his arms tightly around himself.

The precipitation abated briefly, then began to fall even harder. Occasional fits of snow swirled around the lone figure, planted motionless by the water's edge. There was no reckoning how long he stood staring out across the muddy waters. Daylight was fading fast before he realized his hands and feet were numb.

It seemed a lifetime ago.

It had been.

Stanizlow turned and walked back into the pine forest, pockets of sleet crunching underfoot. He stopped in his tracks at the sight of the fork in the path. With the vegetation down, the small lot where the shanty had stood was discernible though the woods. Nothing remained. Through the gathering darkness, he could see nature had all but reclaimed the area. The gray, skeletal remains of a single apple tree were all that protruded from the tall grasses and scrub pine. He hastened up the path.

The battered Chevrolet pickup, its lights off, came barreling down the farm road just as Stanizlow reached the car. It skidded to a stop a few feet from the Saturn's bumper. A burly man in a tan jump suit and a blaze orange cap sprang from the truck. The cab door stayed open, the shotgun on the window rack within easy reach.

Stanizlow approached the man. "I am sorry to trespass on your land," he began, sounding genuinely apologetic. "I mean no harm."

The farmer's stance eased.

"I saw the trail here and wondered where it led. I hope I did not alarm you."

The farmer moved closer, studying Stanizlow's face. "That's okay," he finally said. "I don't mind people on the property. Bird watchers come down here all the time. They say it's a really good spot. Like folks to check by the house first, though."

The farmer continued to eye the man standing before him. Already uncomfortable with the encounter, Stanizlow became increasingly perturbed at the man's relentless gaze.

"It's just that kids come down here at night sometimes," the farmer went on, motioning to the woods. "Drink beer and smoke pot, or whatever it is they do; leave cans around and mess up the road with their four-wheel-drives."

"I'm very sorry to have bothered you," Stanizlow reiterated.

"It's no problem," the man said plainly. "Besides, I know who you are."

Stanizlow knees went weak. How?!

"I'm Eddy Schifflett," the farmer said, reaching for Stanizlow's cold, trembling hand.

Stanizlow hazily recalled the young boy who watched him work in the shed, the one who taunted him and threw the stone.

"I'd like you to come up to the house," Schifflett said abruptly. "There's something I think I should show you."

✠   ✠   ✠

Stanizlow followed the man through the back door and into the foyer, where the farmer peeled off his work suit and hung it on the wall. The inside of the house was tidy and modestly furnished. A well worn sofa sat to one side of the small living room.

For Stanizlow, it took a minute or two for the warmth of the fire that burned in the large cast iron stove to fully envelop him and drive the chill from his bones. Savory aromas of dinner cooking wafted from the kitchen.

"Can I offer you something?" Schifflett asked. "Some cider maybe? Emma can warm it for you."

Stanizlow politely declined.

"Please have a seat."

Stanizlow eased himself onto the sofa while Schifflett reached for a photo album that rested on a shelf above the television set. He opened the album and set it before Stanizlow.

The page was open to a photo of Carmen. A much older woman, she looked smaller than he remembered her, frailer. White hair was up in a bun. Her face was lined, but in a way that accented her well. As striking as ever, she beamed a prideful, radiant smile. Standing beside her, a full head taller than she, was a young man in the dress uniform of a United States Naval officer. The young officer was undeniably handsome, with chiseled features and taut skin the color of coffee with cream. Stanizlow immediately knew the man to be her flesh and blood—and his.

He stared at the photograph a full minute, his mind insensate.

"Mr. Kessel, they're both gone," Schifflett finally said.

"How?" he asked, seemingly emotionless.

"It's been almost 25 years now. Carmen died from cancer, of the women's sort. It was mercifully quick, though. Conrad...," he hesitated, "Conrad was killed in an A6 over North Vietnam."

A nearly unbearable silence ensued.

"Please tell me more," Stanizlow said hoarsely.

For the first time since their meeting, the seemingly unflappable, ruddy faced farmer looked uncomfortable. Twice, he shifted on the sofa. "Carmen, with the child and all, she couldn't really hang on down there on the water. After a while Dad had them move in with us... My mother, she died when I was a baby."

The farmer stopped short, taking a shallow breath before continuing to speak. "Anyway, Dad had to do it all, around the farm, around the house. Carmen looked after me when I was a kid. After she moved into the house, she became like family. Cooked supper and all. When Dad had his first stroke, he couldn't leave the house much, let alone run the farm. Carmen looked out for him too. I was fifteen and had to drop out of school."

"And Conrad?" Stanizlow asked. He could barely get himself to say the name.

"Growing up, we was almost like brothers," Schifflett said, his voice low but steady. "Later we sort of drifted apart. It was the early '60s—things were different. Conrad, he finished high school at seventeen and went on to Virginia Tech. Got in with a part-time football scholarship. He wanted to be an engineer. By the second year, the college was paying for everything."

Schifflett paused momentarily, the corners of his mouth turning downward. "Me, I never finished high school. It's not hard to figure who had the brains around here... Anyway, something happened his last year at college. Never did get the right of it. He dropped out and joined the Navy. Couple of years later he was flying jets—the latest models." The farmer's expression again tightened. "He seemed to be good at just about anything he did."

"To Carmen," Schifflett went on, "Conrad was everything. She was so very proud."

"How was he lost?" Stanizlow asked, breaking a short, aching silence.

"We didn't know for years. After Carmen died, he listed no next of kin. We didn't even get a telegram. One day this Navy guy comes knocking on the door. He explains he's not here on official business—just he'd been transferred to Norfolk, and being so close, he felt he had to get over. He was the squadron commander on the carrier. The man... I can't remember his name, he spoke really well of Conrad. Said he was the finest pilot he'd ever flown with. Proud to have served with him. Said he was as courageous a flyer as he'd ever known. He'd take that Intruder places you'd think a Huey couldn't go; tree-top level, 500 miles an hour, at night. Said his weapons officers loved to fly with him. He wasn't reckless or anything—just fearless, and always in control."

"What happened?" Stanizlow asked, the words barely passing his lips.

"Coming back from a high-level bombing run over the North... got nailed by one of the new SAMs. Nobody saw it coming. Direct hit. Scattered bits and pieces over half of Indochina."

Stanizlow sat stone faced, motionless except for the slightest trembling in his left hand.

"Dad saw you go down to the water, you know," the farmer finally stated. He could have called the MPs, but he didn't. Said he never knew why he didn't. He just didn't. And Dad didn't much like Germans. Least not after he got back from France. W-W-One. Said you was okay, though. And he just let you go on."

A woman's voice called from the kitchen. "Honey, Jake's being dropped off from practice. It's coming down again outside and I don't want him getting wet. Dinner will be ready when y'all get back."

Schifflett pulled the cellophane from the album page and peeled back the print. "Take this," he said. "I have others."

Stanizlow slipped the photograph into his breast pocket.

"Mr. Kessel, I wish you could stay a while," the farmer began.

"No, I should be going."

"Yeah, I reckon you should be."

✠   ✠   ✠

Stanizlow walked to the car through a cold steady rain. He started the engine, drove out to the main road and headed back in the direction of the Bridge Tunnel. He pressed on in a dream like trance. Headlights stabbed the misty darkness, the windshield wipers slapping back and forth.

It began slowly, increasing with ever building force. Like a massive, breaking wave, inexorably hurling toward a climax on a rocky shore, a churning surge of raw emotions welled from deep inside. Anger. Pain. Self-recrimination. Crushing loneliness.

The aged master spy began to shake uncontrollably. He could barely pull over to the side of the road before deep convulsive sobs wracked his body.

Slumped against the steering wheel, he grieved for the son he never knew. He cried for a life subjugated to the service of countries that no longer exist, fighting for ideals that no longer mattered. He wept for a life not spent with the only woman he ever might have loved.

In his mind, he saw the faces of the men he'd killed over the years—men who undoubtedly cared for nothing but themselves; good men who fought and died for what they believed was right. He wept for them all and tried to comprehend why his own end was so long in coming.

"I should have been dead in that goddamned U-boat," he groaned, sagging even lower behind the wheel.

Watching beads of rain trickle down the heavily fogged windshield, Stanizlow began to regain his composure. For the first time in many years, he wondered why his life ran the course it had; wondered just how he came to be who he was.

But again, he had been many people. As an expert in the trade, Stanizlow could all but transform himself into his cover. At times, it seemed, he *was* his cover.

With his forehead again resting against the steering wheel, Viktor Stanizlow realized he indeed had been all those people he pretended to be. His true identity, whatever that might once have been, bore no more validity than the many roles he so masterfully played. Caught up in the maelstrom of some of the worst the twentieth century had to offer, tenacity, fortune and the power of his intellect kept him alive. Though alive, somewhere along his clandestine passage he lost the one thing as dear as life—he lost his self.

At that moment, on a cold, dark and wet Virginia wayside, Viktor Stanizlow realized that, in the very twilight of his years, he truly did not know who he was. A consuming despair spread through the void of his soul.

Suddenly, and in a singular motion, he raised his eyes to meet the glare of an oncoming car's headlights, while reaching into his coat. The realization crystallized in his consciousness like a thunderclap. As he pulled the photograph from his breast pocket, he knew.

Clifton Echo's parting words kept running through his mind.

Konrad Kessel slipped the photograph back into his pocket. He started the car, pulled onto the road, crossed the Chesapeake Bay Bridge-Tunnel, took a left and headed south.